REAP

VIKING

75 years

Eric Rickstad

REAP

VIKING

VIKING
Published by the Penguin Group
Penguin Putnam Inc., 375 Hudson Street,
New York, New York 10014, U.S.A.
Penguin Books Ltd, 27 Wrights Lane, London W8 5TZ, England
Penguin Books Australia Ltd, Ringwood, Victoria, Australia
Penguin Books Canada Ltd, 10 Alcorn Avenue,
Toronto, Ontario, Canada M4V 3B2
Penguin Books (N.Z.) Ltd, 182–190 Wairau Road,
Auckland 10, New Zealand

Penguin Books Ltd, Registered Offices:
Harmondsworth, Middlesex, England

First published in 2000 by Viking Penguin,
a member of Penguin Putnam Inc.

1   3   5   7   9   10   8   6   4   2

PUBLISHERS NOTE
This is a work of fiction. Names, characters, places, and incidents
either are the product of the author's imagination or are used
fictitiously, and any resemblance to actual persons, living or dead,
business establishments, events, or locales is entirely coincidental.

LIBRARY OF CONGRESS CATALOGING-IN-PUBLICATION DATA
Rickstad, Eric.
Reap / Eric Rickstad.
p.   cm.
ISBN 0-670-88517-7
I. Title.
PS3568.I356R42   2000
813'.54—dc21   99–34919

This book is printed on acid-free paper.

Printed in the United States of America
Set in Janson
Designed by Kathryn Parise

For my Mother,
and my sisters, Susan, Judy,
and Beth

Jessup emerged from the hardwoods, stood at the edge of a cornfield, and peered down a row of corn, wanting to plow through the stalks, to be swallowed by them; he liked the way they dampened sound and hid him from the world. But he had his fishing rod and creel with him, hindrances, so he edged along the field instead, skirting its boundary. Trodding along he paused now and again to pick up a clod of earth and break it apart in search of worms.

On the other side of the field he wandered through the softwoods, along the banks of the Lamoille River.

Alone among the alders and poplars he turned over logs and kicked stones, scouring the damp, ever-rotting, ever-flourishing floodplain. This summer, since he'd turned sixteen, he'd found himself here often, roaming the riverbanks, searching. Each spring, since long before he was born, the river had swollen over its banks, as if to defy its boundaries, to prove its violence. With the retreat of the water, artifacts revealed themselves as bits of local history, pieces of lives lived on the river. Each spring the river unearthed more relics, long thought lost.

From where he pushed through a tangle of wild grapevine, he could hear the river, but he could not see it. A woodcock burst into hectic flight, startling him. He imagined, as he often did, what he might find along the riverbanks. What scrap of his father might have been left behind by the river? A belt buckle? A wedding band? The gold crown from a tooth? Material goods that had endured beyond bone and flesh. He imagined all the fishing expeditions he and his father might have undertaken; at home, in his room, he stowed dozens of old Outdoor *and* Fishing *magazines in a box. Countless nights he'd fallen asleep poring over the magazines, dreaming of excursions to the Allagash, to Canada, Labrador, New Brunswick, Alaska, even Argentina and New Zealand, where the world's most magnificent and dogged brown trout finned.*

On previous scavengings he'd found rusted teapots, bent license plates, baseball mitts, the inhumanly pink arms of babydolls, dentures, a lawn mower, countless toys and machinery concealed in these wooded burial grounds.

Always he wished Emily were with him.

Once, he'd found a pocketwatch, and had taken it home and washed it free of mud and silt, polished it, and secreted it away in a box with his bird nest collection. But after weeks of deliberation he'd decided his father wasn't the pocketwatch-carrying sort, so he'd brought it back and placed it precisely where he'd found it, in case someone else might be searching the riverbanks,

1 🌿

as he was, and the pocketwatch was the very piece of their lost life that they needed to find.

Fighting through grapevines he spotted a silver object sticking out of the earth. He broke free of the vines and ran toward it, his blood an ocean in his ears. But as he drew closer, he saw the object for what it was: the handle of an old refrigerator.

By afternoon he'd tramped into town. The day had grown remarkably cold for August, and a steady rain fell. Not a soul was about on a desolate Main Street. Outside the library he concealed his rod and creel behind a lilac bush and went inside.

Alone in the library's echoing entryway he stood staring at the faded black-and-white photos that hung from copperwire. He paid some attention to the older pictures, of young men in military uniforms, grouped in front of a war memorial cannon, and pictures of the town when it was no more than a few old storefronts along a wagon-rutted trail; horses in the photos. Horses. But what drew his attention most, what he'd come for, were the photos of the town taken during the flood, displayed throughout the library, and all over town. One of his favorite photos hung in the bathroom of the Bee Hive, warped and mildewed, its glass long ago fallen from its frame, still in pieces behind the rusty toilet.

He straightened a photo before him and moved on to the next. Cocking his head against a glare reflecting off the glass, he leaned in closer, studying the faces of those who fought to sandbag their homes against the rising waters, waters so high it seemed the moon must have fallen from the sky and caused the ocean to flood in from afar. He took a snapshot from his canvas wallet, a snapshot yellowed and brittle with age, pieced together with cellophane tape. He rubbed the photo and looked at the ghostly face in it, gazed at another photo on the wall, searching the faces of those in rowboats, rescuing the elderly from second-story windows, the faces of those that milled and gawked and cried, faces frozen in disbelief and desperation. He searched studiously, hopefully, but still he could not find his father's face.

PART I

From where he lay on his cot, Reg Cumber could hear the wind threshing the juniper and cedars along the shore of Unknown Pond, whistling, and he thought of Pap, those years ago when he would whistle, low and sweet, for the kids to gather around him on the front stoop. Hoisting himself upright, back to the wall, Reg buttoned his union suit, scratched his unshaven chin and rose in the dark still of the cabin. Lowering his head to accommodate the doorway, he shuffled into the kitchen.

From a shot glass atop the stove he took a wooden match and struck it on the counter, his breath smoking in the matchglow. He lit a burner; the gas caught and a ring of blue flame sputtered, steadied itself. From a tobacco tin he fished out a joint, crouched and lit it, cranked the faucet and leaned against the counter, smoking. The faucet vomited chunks of filth. Pipes moaned. When the water finally ran clear he filled a coffeepot, dumped the last of the grounds into it and sat it on the burner. Rubbing his hands together he stepped to the back door.

The door creaked as he pushed it open, and a rush of cold air stung his knees, bared through holes worn in his union suit.

Outside, the moon sat low and shone pale through gathering clouds, and the trees between the cabin and Unknown Pond stood dark and formless. He could hear the muted gaggle of unseen Canada geese rafted against the shoreline. The late-August snow had held off, for now, the worst of the cold front remaining just north, in Canada. The grass was white with frost, and looked as if it would shatter if he were to walk on it.

He flicked the roach out into the dark and breathed into his hands and leaned back to stare up at a starless sky.

The air smelled of ore. Of snow.

"Fuck," he said and stepped back inside, the door squeaking shut behind him.

Inside he poured a cup of coffee and turned off the burner, wincing at the stink of propane. The coffee seared his insides, but he drank it anyway. He rapped a fist on the counter, knuckles like beaten knots of wood, then opened a pie safe on the counter and looked at the pistol. A .45. Pap's. He picked it up and considered it in the room's growing light. He licked his thumb and rubbed at a stubborn smudge on the grip, then set the pistol on the table.

In the bedroom he dressed: duckcloth trousers from the back of a chair, a flannel shirt, a wool shirt over that. Workboots on, he went to the kitchen and drank down his coffee, now cooled, stuck the .45 into his pants. He grabbed an army fatigue jacket off a nail in the wall. Taking a cap from one of the jacket pockets, he tucked his hair back behind his ears, snapped the cap against his thigh, creased its bill and set it on his head with a tug. In the other pocket was a camouflage headnet. He didn't put it on. From under the sink he grabbed a rucksack, looked inside it, nodded. He opened the back door and crept outside, the door settling in its jamb without a sound, the cold air rushing at him once more.

The early-morning sky was low and gray. Beneath it, beneath the trees, Reg was a speck on the mountainside, a nothing in a mess of wild reckless blackberry cane that scratched and snagged like pike's teeth in his jacket and pants. He clambered up ravines in the graylight of dawn, pushed through slash and header debris, up and up, the rucksack cumbersome, its straps gnawing at his collarbone, sweat gliding down his back, chilling him. He stopped and rested against a larch, gasping, wriggling his toes. It was difficult to see very far: the mountains of August were not the mountains of April; in the spring the mountains were a landscape of scrawny wintered trees shot green with peeping buds; the summer woods were choked and fuming with leaves and vines and ferns. He preferred the woods during winter, the silence of them, the harsh landscape, carved by the glaciers so long ago, bared before him. He rooted in his jacket and brought out a cigaret pack, shook a butt loose and lit it. Inhaling deeply, he adjusted the .45 where it dug into his hip, then trudged on, head bent as if into a violent wind.

Fending off sapling branches, he came onto a vast clearing, logged years before, and tripped and fell. A tomato stake lay on the ground beside him, a section of chicken wire near it. Fiddlehead ferns closed about him like giant green ostrich feathers. He could hear the distant *thockthockthock* of a lone pileated woodpecker.

Standing, he saw the plants, just ahead, rising from the underbrush, a thick grove, mossgreen and reeking. Deer had made recent use of the downed fence, the frost stamped with their tracks and littered with shit. He took off his cap and put on the headnet. Stupid not to have worn the netting from the start. Stupid.

Two years ago, he and Lamar and Bump Duclos had been growing out in back of Bump's barn, and some son of a bitch had barked about it. Cops had pictures of Bump. The list was long as to who might have talked, but from the beginning Reg had thought it was the Lavalettes who'd run their mouths. Mack and Elis, likely.

Reg looked around the woods.

Bump had called him in a panic that afternoon, told him he suspected the cops had been out at his place, had been watching it. Said he was going to rip up the plants behind the barn, destroy the seedlings in the cellar. Reg had told him to calm down, he'd dig up the plants himself, transplant them up in Moose Bog, but no one was ripping them out of the ground and losing him all that money.

"What if they come back?" Bump had said, his voice low, as if he were trying to keep from being heard by people in a nearby room.

"Plead the fifth," Reg had said. "I'll take the plants, sell em, get yah the money if yah need a lawyer. But don't yah say a *fuckin* word if they come back."

He'd driven directly to Bump's farm. He hadn't noticed, until later, the cruiser parked behind the barn, and he'd found nothing remarkable about the front door being off its lower hinge when he'd let himself inside and walked down the hallway to the back of the house, to the kitchen, where Bump often sat in the evening waiting for one of his "*rare*" birds to show itself at the back feeder: a scarlet tanager, a Baltimore oriole. But when he'd stepped into the kitchen, instead of being greeted by Bump, he'd been greeted by a pistol barrel jammed under his chin; two men had wrenched his arms behind his back and forced him down flat on the kitchen floor, his face pushed into the grit of road salt and dirt.

"Fuck," he'd said, his face ground harder to the floor. "Fuck you." The taste of blood.

The troopers had cuffed him and yanked him to his knees, and he'd glanced into the living room to see Bump sitting on the edge of the couch, peering at him through the fingers of his unhandcuffed hands. He'd had a pitiful look on his face, as if he were trying to convey that he was sorry, that he'd had no choice. The fuck. There was *always* a choice. Reg had tried to stand, to get at Bump, but a trooper, the taller and older of the two, had wedged a baton between his arms and cranked it. The other trooper, who wore sunglasses and was short and broad and thick-necked, a real gun-happy sufferer of littleman's disease, had stood a few feet away, legs spread, a revolver leveled at Reg's face, its hammer back. The other trooper had rooted Reg's wallet out from his back pocket.

"Mr. Cumber," he'd said. It wasn't a question, it was an affirmation.

He'd wanted to know everything Reg knew about the plants behind the barn, the ones downstairs, about the guns in the house, a felony when involved with possession with intent.

Reg had denied knowing anything. He'd come to see his friend, that was it.

"You always walk right in?" the trooper had asked.

"Known em all my life."

"Not too well, apparently."

Reg had tried to stand again and had gotten a baton across his back for it.

"You know a *Lamar* Cumber?" the first trooper asked.

Reg hadn't said anything.

"He's your cousin, isn't he?"

"I don't know a fuckin thing."

"Apparently," Gun Happy had said, pushing his glasses onto the back of his head with two fingers as he stepped over to Reg. He put the gun to Reg's cheek. "How'd you get here?"

"Yah saw me pull up."

Gun Happy had shaken his head. "So, if we go out to that truck of yours and we look in that tool vault, we aren't going to find anything? Not so much as a pipe, a joint, not so much as *one fucking seed?*" Reg had thought about the bags of vermiculite, the baggies of seeds, the quarter-pound stash, his pipe and papers, his grow lights, all in the truck. "No," he'd said. "And when yah don't find nothin, I'm gonna sue yur fuckin ass. I come over to shoot the shit, and I get *this.*"

Gun Happy had straightened up and looked at the other trooper, who'd leaned back on the kitchen table and said: "Check it." Gun Happy had nodded and stalked off down the hall. The other trooper had walked over beside Reg and looked out the window: A scarlet tanager, a male, plumage bright as blood, had lighted outside on the feeder.

"We got you on tape," the trooper had said, so softly that, at first, Reg had thought he'd been talking to the bird. "The call your *friend* made. To get you over here. We taped it."

Reg had tried once again to get at Bump, but the trooper had proved too quick, and too vicious, with the baton.

Reg had found out later that the troopers had arrested Bump immediately. Said if he didn't cooperate, they'd seize the farm. He'd do five. Minimum. A felony. He'd *cooperated.* He'd given up Lamar and Reg, and the Lavalettes.

It showed you.

Reg had done fifteen months at Fairland. Lamar had, too.

Bump'd only done twenty days.

First couple weeks inside, Reg had planned how he would burn down Bump's barn and farmhouse when he got out. But he hadn't been allowed the chance. Claude Lavalette, Mack and Elis's brother, had cut a deal, walked away clean, which made Reg believe they'd been part of it all along, somehow. Claude had made it to daylight and come knocking for *Mr. Cooperation* the day of his release. But by the time he'd arrived at the farm, Bump had given a blow job to the barrel of a twelve gauge, and pulled the trigger.

That was the story, anyway.

Stupid fuck.

Reg rubbed his face, his bitten nails catching in the headnet. He stepped into the fenced area. The plants dwarfed him. Water dripped from drooping leaves to patter the ground. A mist eddied in his wake. Exhausted and hungry from the hike, he sat down, his back against a stump. Deer had been at the lowest leaves and buds, stripped some of the plants for the first few feet. Leaves and leaders lay scattered about, but most of the buds seemed to have withstood what the summer, and now this cold front, had brought. The plants were healthy, but needed a few more weeks. He stretched his legs out and sighed.

Pap had first brought him here, years ago, one of the few times Pap had been around for deer season. Pap had driven trucks. At first, dump trucks for Nullhegan County Lime and Granite, then his own, leased rig, hauling anything anywhere: Florida, California, Toronto. Pap's life on the road had taken most of his time, but it had allowed him to support a family and have a home, that in return had allowed him to be alone on the road without being lonely. He'd beat sense into Reg, taking the easy way out. You didn't fuck with Pap, he didn't fuck with you. It was a good way to be. A hard way to be. Reg had always known where he'd stood with Pap.

This wasn't the easy way out, humping up mountains every spring, carrying seventy-pound loads of manure and vermiculite and chicken wire, one after the other, in the dark, in the rain and mud; digging in the stubborn ground with a foxhole shovel, stringing fence; worrying all summer about the plants taking, about animals or thieves or game wardens discovering them, about too much rain, or too little. But, even with all that, it still beat having to answer to someone; and he didn't mind hard work, not if it paid. Pap had believed that hard work somehow brought a man integrity; Reg had never bought into it: There were too many men who worked hard who had a lot less integrity than those who hadn't held a steady job their whole life. Pap had had integrity, but it hadn't come from how hard he'd worked. You could watch his face when he spoke to another man, not knowing a damned thing about what kind of worker Pap was, and know that to be true. It had been in his eyes, bright and alert, concerned, his gaze steady; it had been in his good posture; it had come from within, and had been more about the way he chose *not* to live, than the way he did live: Pap hadn't drunk, to excess, or womanized, as far as Reg knew, and he'd never said anything about anyone that he wouldn't have said to their face, and even then bit his tongue more often than not; all traits Reg could admire, but could rarely claim.

Reg had held a job, of one sort or another, since he was fourteen. Stan had given him his first job, at the Bee Hive, washing dishes, the September Pap had died. Within a few weeks Stan had had him waiting tables; Reg had given it a go, but had ended up, by choice, back with the dirty dishes. He'd enjoyed being out back, alone, the radio on, able to take cigaret breaks, sneak beer from the walk-in, take a hit now and again from the whipped cream canisters' CO_2 cartridges. He'd been able to wear jeans and a T-shirt instead of those hellish black slacks, and the cotton button-up shirt that had looked like a blouse. And if he'd come into work pissed off or hung over or depressed, he'd been able to stay that way, he hadn't had to put on an ingratiating smile for anybody. He'd liked that no one hung over him or told him what to do; as long as the dishes were done, Stan had stayed clear, poking his head in once in a great while to see if he wanted a soda or fries, or to say "How goes the war?" or "Looking good, America."

As a waiter, Reg had felt everyone's eyes on him, expecting him to slip up. He hadn't liked the out-of-staters talking of the town's *quaintness* and asking what there was to *do* around here. He'd loathed having to pretend that some of the most demonic and homely urchins he'd ever encountered were cute and saintly children. He hadn't known how Barb and Ruth, the two waitresses, had handled it. How they'd sucked up to anyone who'd sat in their sections. It was different for them though. They had families. A family changed things.

Mornings, before the Bee Hive opened, Reg had stuffed napkins into holders and filled ketchup bottles with Ruth and Barb, listening to the two women carry on. They'd given him his first cigaret, a menthol 100, and with his first drag they'd traded witchly grins, and he'd understood that these were women who remembered being girls, and no matter the passing years, they'd never feel very far from those nights they'd spent parked at the end of the dark dead-end roads, in the back seats of their boyfriends' cars, their skirts hiked up and their knees pinned to their chests.

At seven A.M. when Stan flipped the Open sign in the front window and tourists and locals alike wandered in, Barb and Ruth had been Professional. A state of mind Reg could never muster for a job he disliked. Actresses, the both of them. Jesus. He admired them, but not a second passed that he wasn't glad their lives weren't, in any way, his.

Reg had worked for Roland Dupree, too, a mason who was a better drunk than a bricklayer, and who'd filled some small need in himself by calling people "Little Fuck Face" and "Little Puke;" Roland had been as likely to pick Reg up for work at noon as he had been to show up at seven in the morning. Whatever time he'd shown, he'd expected Reg to be waiting: "I own you from seven to five." He'd never offered a reason for being late, and had never paid Reg for the time Reg had sat around waiting. Once, when Roland hadn't shown up by one o'clock, Reg had taken his shotgun and gone bird hunting out behind the house. When he'd come back a couple of hours later, Roland had been waiting in his truck in the front yard.

"Where in Christ you been?" Roland had hollered from the truck as Reg set his shotgun and a brace of woodcock on the porch. "I been sitting here nearly an hour. I gotta depend on you. You don't want a job?"

"Yah dint show," Reg had said, his chest tightening.

"I'm here, ain't I?"

"It's three-thirty." Reg had pushed his fists into his thighs, angry at how he'd let Roland take advantage of him, angry that he'd had to learn of the likes of Roland the hard way, had learned a lot of things the hard way, with Pap gone. He'd glared at Roland, who was only in his thirties then, but might as well have been at the hard end of fifty years, with his bitterness and drunkenness and beat-up truck and pitiful life.

"I'm your goddamned boss," Roland had barked. "Your ass is mine from seven to—"

"Yur crazy," Reg had said, wanting to drag Roland out of his truck and kick him into the ground.

"Come again." Roland was trying to get out of the truck but seemed to be having difficulty.

"Yur crazy."

"I'm your goddamned boss." Roland was looking at the inside of the door, a puzzled look on his face, as if the door handle had disappeared.

"Bullshit." Reg had taken up his shotgun.

"You little prick." Roland had reached out the window to unlock the door from the outside, and Reg had run over and brought the butt of his shotgun down on Roland's fingers. Roland had howled: "*I'm* crazy?" But he'd made no move to get out; he'd sucked on his bloody hand, glowering, and backed out of the yard.

Reg had seen his share of hard work, for what it was worth, and he hadn't minded it. But if someone were to point him in the direction of easy, just once, he'd have gladly gone down that road. Name one person who wouldn't. Just one.

He shut his eyes; listened to his breathing.

He awoke to find the frost had melted and clung now to his skin and hung in the trees about him as a cool moist gauze. The woodpecker had fallen silent, or retreated to some deeper reach of woods. A cold drizzle fell.

He gained his feet, his back and shoulders curdling with a heated pain that ended in a shiver. He walked among the plants. One of the leaders looked as if it had been cut clean, with a knife. Some others looked cut, too. It was hard to tell. He considered the downed section of fence, wondering if someone had been fucking with the plants. The Lavalettes, he thought.

Mack and Elis had done six months at Fairland, less than half the time Reg had done; they'd thought Reg had run his mouth, as Bump had. He hadn't. It didn't matter. It wouldn't have mattered to him had it been the other way around. But one thing was certain: They'd better pray it wasn't them fucking with his plants.

He lit a cigaret and made his way from the plants. Ferns jigged in the rain. He took a foxhole shovel from the rucksack and unfolded it. He straightened the tomato stake, stretched the chicken wire taut and, with the shank of the shovel, pounded the stake until it sank deep into the rocky soil.

The woodpecker was hammering away again, closer:
thockthockthockthockthock

I am a bootlegger, Jessup thought as he skulked among the trees. He'd never been this far up Smuggler's Gap. It had been an exhilarating, prosperous expedition. He'd set out early, in the dark, the crickets' silence in his ears and the frost's cold seeping through the bottom of his canvas sneakers as he'd traipsed logging road and field, pausing periodically to take out his penlight and check the map he'd sketched in his notebook. Smuggler's Creek had proved worth the bushwhacking, his wicker creel gratifying with the weight of neck-broken native brookies.

He opened the top of the creel and peeked inside. Five brook trout lay glistening on a mat of wet ferns, eyes milked. His heart knocked to look at them, to think of each tug on the end of the line. Each set hook. There was nothing better.

Except Emily.

He closed the creel, opened it again, snuck another peek, let the lid fall.

A cold rain dappled his face; steam rose in tendrils from his hands.

Ambling out from the woods, mindful of his rod tip, he came onto a smidgen of steep muddied road. He halted at the sight of a vehicle, parked to the side in a way that allowed little room for any logging truck to ease past.

He snuck toward the vehicle, his creel snug and reassuring against his hip. He rubbed his hand over the wet fender, over the insignia.

"El Camino," he whispered.

Cupping his eyes, he pressed his face to the black-tinted window, noticing in the reflection his copper hair, a profusion of twists and snarls, like some old woman's pile of scrap yarn. He could just make out shadowed shapes on the floor and the fur-covered seat of the El Camino: wrenches and screwdrivers, old chains and rope, topographic maps, loose shotgun shells, a Styrofoam cup. From his back pocket he fetched a handkerchief and wiped the window where his nose had left a smudge.

Slipping back into the woods he scrambled down a logging road. He did not wonder who might be parked up this far or why. Already he was reliving the thrum of life that had run through the fishing line, down the cork handle and into his wrists.

And Emily's kiss.

It was afternoon when Reg finally found his way back to the road. He waited for a logging truck to pass, then stepped from the woods and threw his rucksack and headnet into the back of the Camino. About to open the door, he glimpsed something at his feet: a yellow scrap of paper; he looked up and down the road, into the woods. The slip seemed to glow in the mist. He rubbed his chin and touched a fingertip to the paper. Murmuring, he picked it up and crept his eyes across it, slowly, slowly. The rain came harder. Nearly snow, it spattered the paper. He folded the paper and stuffed it in his pocket. He surveyed the road around the Camino. Footprints. The rain had nearly washed them away, but he saw them now, footprints that were not his own, footprints minutes away from becoming ghosts.

"Son of a bitch," he said and knelt at the clearest tracks, which headed into the woods. His heart pushed against his rib cage. "Son of a bitch," he said and stood and kicked the El Camino's door. "Sonofa fuckin bitch."

Marigold Please sat staring out the trailer window, watching the rain and wet snow fall, waiting on Hess. Lately he'd taken to disappearing for days, like some wounded stray looking for a place to die, each disappearance longer than the last.

In her lap a mug of coffee warmed her fingers. She lifted it and took a quick taste, then another, wincing, her lips pursed with the expectation of being scalded. The coffee needed condensed milk.

Skidding the chair away from the cold window she tucked up close to the kitchen table. A table of soft pine, scarred and gouged, stained to resemble a finer cut of wood, same as the paneled walls. For four years she and Hess had eaten at this table, but now they tended to eat on the love seat in the living room, more and more often alone.

And where were the days when Hess would come through the door, jacket already half off, jeans unzipped? She'd not expected the sex to go on that way forever. Even at nineteen she'd known enough to realize it wouldn't, couldn't, not if they ever wanted to *accomplish* anything. And it hadn't; the frequency and intensity of it had leveled off, then lessened as they'd settled into routine. But Hess's lack of interest these past months had been so immediate and complete, and *lasting*, that she'd begun to question if it had more to do with her than with his accident. Perhaps what she'd taken before as a normal gradual decline in interest had not been that after all. She'd tried, for a spell, to comfort him, to please him; she'd worn the tight jeans and cutoffs he'd liked so much, walked around in a T-shirt without a bra, or nothing but one of his flannel shirts, her butt barely covered; but he'd not so much as glanced at her, and, after a while, wearing those things had made her feel ridiculous and cheap; her attempts to console him had failed, and her compassion had turned to insecurity and resentment, and now, loneliness; more than the sex, more than talking to each other, more than waking up beside him, more than *him*, she missed herself, the part of her that had been reserved for her husband, but was of no worth now that it was not welcomed or returned.

She picked a fresh pack of cigarets up from the table, fiddled with it, unwrapped the cellophane. She was quitting. Trying. Trying. Shifting in her chair she gazed at the oven, it's door open wide, insides splattered with grease and charred with burnt clumps like railroad coke. The coil glowed molten orange. For two days she'd sat here, huddled at the stove, half the kitchen pregnant with heat, half cold. She had no propane left from last spring and Roz Fuel only delivered out this far on Wednesdays. Unless you could afford an emergency call, an extra fifty dollars.

She rested a fingertip on the phone beside her on the wall. Her wool-socked feet toed the linoleum that curled up from the tin strip dividing the kitchen from the worn living room carpet. Lifting the phone's receiver from its cradle, she dialed and turned back to look out the window again. Outside, down where Skunk Hollow Road came out on Gamble Hill, a blue car labored to climb; its tires churned in the muck and slush and chunks of clay roostertailed high into the air. Maybe Hess was in the car. Had found a ride. No. No one got out, and she felt foolish for thinking such a thing.

The phone on the other end rang and rang and rang.

She was about to hang up when a winded voice huffed: "What? What is it?"

"It's me," she said; her voice came out as a whisper, startling her, and she realized she had not spoken with anyone in days. She kept an eye on the car.

"Oh. Hey, darlin," Reg said, distracted.

"You busy?" she said.

"Jus got in. I'm soaked. Fuckin snow."

"I can call back."

"I got a little time fore I head to Ma's."

"Ma's?"

"Gotta check up on the place. Coons get in and tear shit up. And I don't want no one fuckin round up there."

"Who'd do that?"

"No one *you* know."

She sighed.

"Hey," he said, his voice rising. "Gonna be round tomorrow? Got somethin I need yah to look at."

"Where am I going to go?" She slipped the pack of cigarets from the cellophane.

"Whadya want, anyway?" he asked.

"Nothing."

"Yah all right up there? Yah sound mopey, darlin."

"Sure. I'm OK. You didn't by any chance see Hess around town today, at the Bee Hive or anything?"

"I knew it. That fuckin husband of yurs. I'll fix his ass I see em."

She sighed. "You stick to fixing cars."

"All right. Darlin. *All right.* Whatever yah say. Listen, I gotta get a move on."

"Nice talking to you."

"Sure, darlin."

She hung up.

Outside, the car had stopped; tires spun in place.

If the car went into the trees, she could get Mildred cranked up. Mildred: a stake-bedded '64 pickup with a spiderwebbed windshield and a three-on-the-tree with only first and reverse of any use the linkage worn so smooth. It had been Hal's. She remembered the two winters when she and Hal had driven Mildred to the ski area roads, thirty, forty miles away, looking for cars to tow. Jay Peak. Cold

Hollow. Ivers Mountain. She'd been fourteen and fifteen, and Hal, twelve years older, had taken her along. He'd shown her the ropes, shown her how to make more money than she knew you could, taught her how to drive. She'd been frustrated at first, grinding gears and stalling the truck. But he'd encouraged her. Told her to be a trooper. She'd learned to love to drive those treacherous roads. Always, on the way back from Ivers Mountain, Hal would stop at Moose Lips Tavern and treat her to a clam roll and a banana split. When she'd turned sixteen, seven years ago, Hal had given her Mildred. He'd bought himself a new truck. New to him. "A little surprise," he'd said. Though it had been much more than that, they both knew.

Down on Gamble Hill the car jerked and slopped toward the roadside. Marigold rose, eager, expectant. She tugged up the collar of her burdock-infested barn jacket, whipped a scarf around her neck. The scarf stunk of hay and cigarets and its raw wool pricked her face and neck. She scratched at her nose and sneezed. She wrested on her boots, wrapped long yellow laces around the backs twice, three times, tied them, drew them tight. She could not find her gloves.

Outside, snowflakes licked her face and her breath plumed. The smell of woodsmoke drifted from the Isham farm, down at the bottom of Gamble Hill. She breathed in deeply through her nose and hugged herself, praying the cold front would soon break.

Below Mildred's engine block pools of transmission fluid and oil seeped into the fresh skim of blown snow; she'd have to have Reg take a look. She wiped snow from the windshield, exposing a faded green inspection sticker. Down below, the car whined, fishtailed and careened backward; its front tires cranked as it tried to back onto Skunk Hollow but instead slid into the ditch. She shook her head and a small laugh escaped her.

She kicked Mildred's door to get it to open, then stepped up and in. The vinyl seat was cold and stiff. The keys were in the ignition. She cranked the engine over and played with the choke. The truck stalled. She cranked it again and matted the gas pedal to the floor until the wet fuel line blew clean and the tailpipe blatted a sooty cloud of exhaust. She struggled to find first gear, then crept the truck down to Gamble Hill.

A couple, a man and a woman, stood by the car, glaring at it, kicking its tires, and circling it as if it were a wounded beast they'd felled but did not know how to finish off. They both wore shiny, purple and lime-green parkas, zipped tight to their chins.

Marigold got out of the truck.

The couple climbed out of the ditch to stand in the middle of the slushy road. They looked to be in their late thirties, at least. Their faces seemed unnaturally tanned, orangish and leathery. The woman, who was gangly, with a bladelike nose and dark bug eyes, moved to stand beside the pudgy man. She removed one of his heavy gray mittens and locked pinkies with him. The man scratched his forehead through a yellow knit cap that was pulled down to his black eyebrows. He had thin sideburns that ran the curve of his soft jawline to meet at his chin. He unzipped his parka halfway, exposing a black turtleneck and the bib of his snug snowpants. His zipper was littered with ski passes.

The car was foreign. Skis on the roof. Québec plates.

"Looks like we are stuck?" the man said, winking.

Montreal, Marigold thought.

The man shifted his feet and looked at the car where it idled quietly in the ditch. A wisp of white, almost clear exhaust trailed from its shiny tailpipe.

"I've seen worse," Marigold said. The car had slid backward into the ditch; all of its tires were off the road. Marigold wiped her nose with the back of her hand and sniffed.

The man unlocked pinkies with the woman and stepped carefully over to Marigold, his arms out for balance. The pom-pom on his yellow hat looked as if it might topple off, as if it were not attached to the hat, but only balanced precariously atop it. "I am Roberge," he said. Snowflakes lighted on his eyebrows and the tips of his eyelashes, then quickly melted. "How are you?"

"OK," Marigold said. "Least my truck's got all four tires on the road."

Roberge grinned and extended his bared hand to Marigold. It was pale and warm and smooth, but his grip was strong, his handshake firm. "That is Valerie," he said. The woman managed a curt nod and looked across the road, staring off at the great breadth of cornfields and trees, their wet leaves dark and somber in the snowy dusk. The

Ishams owned this land now. Marigold's family had owned and worked it for four generations, until Pepé had died, long before Marigold could remember, and Memé had been forced to sell it, acre by acre, until all that remained was Ma's old place out on Plank Road, and the land upon which the trailer sat.

Valerie wore skin-tight black leather gloves with fur cuffs. With the very tips of her fingers she snatched a lipstick out from her parka. She removed the cap, scrutinized the lipstick, then applied it to her pouty mouth. Hot pink. She smacked her lips lightly and put back the lipstick. Roberge tugged his mitten back on.

"I'm Marigold," Marigold said.

"Pleased," said Roberge.

"Pretty name," Valerie said, still staring soberly at the woods and farmland, her voice surprisingly deep and liquid. She stuck her hand back in her parka and brought out a pack of cigarets and a gold lighter. She stuck a cigaret in her mouth. It was a long thin brown cigaret. She lit it. When she finally exhaled the air smelled of spice. She took another drag and Marigold sucked in a small breath.

Roberge surrendered a big smile, revealing two gold-capped teeth. "You would not happen to have a rope or chain in your truck?"

"I might."

He glanced over at Valerie. "I will pay," he said.

Marigold nodded. "Twenty ought to do it."

Roberge pounded his mittens together; he looked over at Valerie again, but she had turned her back on them completely.

Though both Roberge and Valerie were a good ten years older than Marigold, they somehow seemed much younger. He seemed like a boy. And Valerie seemed like a girl, a petty girl on the edge of a tantrum.

Roberge would have his work cut out for him to get back in Madame's good graces, Marigold thought. She climbed into the bed of the truck and lifted a heavy rusted snarl of chain from among scraps of firewood and two flat tires, and dropped it over the side with a groan. She could feel cold imprints on her palms and fingers where she'd grabbed the chain. She flexed her fingers, appreciating the familiar sting, despite the actual cold that caused it.

"What can I do?" Roberge offered. He removed his mittens, tucked them under an arm and blew into his hands.

"Nothing." Marigold jumped down. Grabbing the chain, she scrambled under the front of the car, on her back. The ground was cold and sloppy and the slush came through the thin denim of her barn jacket. She looked up at the undercarriage and felt around for a place to secure the chain. A clump of slush broke free from the chassis and fell into her mouth and she spat and wiped her lips and cheeks with her sleeve; she hooked the chain behind the bumper and scurried back out. Standing, she yanked the chain, then wrapped the other end around Mildred's trailer hitch and got in the truck.

Valerie dropped her cigaret butt to the ground and tapped it out with the sharp toe of a white leather boot. She lit another cigaret.

Marigold rolled down her window and told Roberge to get in his car and put it in first.

"It's an automatic."

"Low one, then."

"Check."

"And *don't* horse the engine, just give her a little gas when you feel the car being pulled out. But not *too* little. We want to get the whole car out, not just the bumper."

"Check," he said, and gave her a thumbs up. He put on his mittens again.

Valerie looked on as Marigold pulled the truck forward. The chain uncoiled between the pickup and the car, rose from the ground, and snapped taut with a scattering of rust flakes. Marigold eased the truck forward, its tires barely turning as the car inched behind it. Now and again the clutch plate slipped and she lost first gear and some of the ground she'd gained. But slowly, steadily, the truck moved forward and the car climbed out of the ditch, back onto the road.

Marigold got out of the truck, undid the loose chain, and heaved it back into the bed. She rubbed her hands on her jeans, smirching them with streaks of mud and grease and rust.

"You better turn around, so you're facing downhill," she said. "But be careful this time."

"Checkmate," Roberge said.

Roberge turned the car around and faced it down Gamble Hill. He got out and stood beside Marigold. "Not a scratch on her," he said, admiring the car, his hands on his hips. He pushed his ski cap back off his eyebrows. His forehead was sweaty and blotched pink.

Valerie got into the passenger's side of the Volvo and fidgeted with the radio.

"Where you trying to get to?" Marigold asked Roberge.

"Jay Peak."

"What for?"

"To ski."

"*Ski.* They can't be open."

"They had a ad on the radio. They are open at this time earlier than any time in history. It is history."

"That's crazy."

He shrugged. "Valerie wished to ski in August. She has not ever skied in August."

"Well. You came too far south. By over twenty miles. If you . . . "

Valerie had run the driver's window down and was calling: "*Roberge.*"

"Pardon," Roberge said. He went to the car and leaned in the window. Valerie leaned toward him and said something in his ear.

He returned mittenless.

"Sorry," he said.

Marigold nodded. "If you want to get to Jay Peak, go back down to the stop sign, where the barn and the big white house are." She pointed down Gamble Hill, toward the Isham place.

She gave him the directions, and he thanked her and shook her hand. This time his handshake was weak. She could feel the folded bill in his palm and she took it without looking at it and slipped it into her jacket pocket.

Roberge looked around for a moment. "A nice place to live. Out here," he said.

"It is."

"You are probably used to it? The weather? All this land? All this prettiness?"

"It can catch you off guard, sometimes."

"I like that. That is good. That is a good way to draw it up."

Valerie looked over and hit the horn. It gave a tiny, apologetic beep.

"That was great of you," Roberge said.

He broke her gaze and went to the car. His fingers on the door handle, he stopped and turned. "You do not know anyone who might be interested in selling their land around here?"

She kicked slush from one of Mildred's mud flaps. "Just about anyone. If you catch them at the right time."

He shook his head. "Most people would kill to live here." He offered a small wave. "*Au revoir*," he said, and got in the car.

"*Au revoir.*"

Marigold stood in the road beside her truck, watching the car's flickering brake lights disappear down Gamble Hill.

The snow had turned again to rain.

She drove back up and parked Mildred and stood in the yard. She stared at the trailer. Hay bales, skirting it for insulation, sagged from the rain and wet snow. Summers ago, Hess had nailed siding to the trailer, built a false angled roof, trying, failing, to make it appear more like a small house. He'd cleared saplings with a brush hog in a vain attempt to grow a meager lawn in the hardscrabble. Marigold shook her head.

Inside, her scarf fell to the floor as she sat down in her chair. She patted a cigaret from the pack she'd opened earlier. She looked at a box of wooden matches that sat on the table. Looked away. She stuck the cigaret between her lips, not lighting it. She and Hal had made good money, those two winters. But soon he'd left and she'd allowed herself to be swept up by Hess. Married at nineteen. Hess. Hess. Hess. Where was he?

She closed her eyes, wishing Hal were home; a couple more weeks. It seemed a long time to wait. Hal was easier to talk to than Reg; not that she shared everything with him. But, unlike Reg, who got a thrill out of riling people, Hal didn't pry. He listened, without judgment or advice. Still, she'd never fully confided in either of her brothers. She supposed it was based on the unchangeable fact that they *were* her brothers; the feeling reminded her of the one she'd started to have toward Ma when she, Marigold, had lost her virginity at fourteen; until then she'd shared everything with Ma; afterward she'd become protective of her feelings, defensive against Ma's everyday questions, which had begun to feel more and more like invasions.

It would be good to talk with Hal, but what she really wanted was, simply, his presence. To have him home, where she could see him, so she could feel sure that at least one thing in her life hadn't changed. Gone bad. Keeping her eyes closed, she slipped the bill out from her pocket. She thought she'd give herself a little surprise. She smoothed it out before her on the table, took a deep breath, and opened her eyes.

A five.

Canadian.

And something else too: a card, a business card that had been tucked in the folded bill:

ROBERGE BELLEVUE

Courier d'Immeubles

IMMOBILIERS DE SOLEIL

2525 Rue de Sainte Catherine

Montréal, Québec

Télé 514 294 9987

"Asshole," Marigold said and let the card fall to the kitchen floor. She stared down at the five dollar bill, taking in the foreign, pinkish-blue watermarkings of the Canadian money. It had always seemed like play money, to her. She folded the bill in half. Looked at it. She folded it in half again, put it down with a sigh. She sucked on the cigaret, still in her mouth. Still unlit. She picked the bill up once more and folded it again, and again; she folded it into tinier and tinier squares, one fold over the other, pressing down hard on the edges to crease them tightly. To allow one more fold. As she did this, she began shaking, shaking so awfully that she could barely see her fingers as they worked the money, folding the bill until it could fold no smaller. Then she squeezed the bill in her fist and threw it to the floor, where it skidded beneath the dusty bottom of the oven.

If this weather kept up she'd have two more days of heating the

trailer with the oven, before Roz Fuel made their first run of the season. Later tonight she'd turn off the oven. It was too dangerous keeping it on at night, made her too nervous to sleep. She'd be OK if she
burrowed deep beneath her army blankets. She'd always been OK.
Always would be. Hess wasn't coming back tonight, she knew, but she
stared out the window anyway, working the cigaret back and forth in
her mouth. Her back was damp and cold. She shivered. She rubbed
her shoulders, picked up a match from the box and popped it on the
tabletop. She watched the flame burn down to her fingers, then shook
the match out and set it on the table, set the cigaret down, too. For a
moment she remained still, then she rose to fix herself another pot of
coffee, wondering at how young nineteen was, and how old twenty-
three could be.

Outside, on Gamble Hill, evening shadows leaked from the wood-
edscape of raindripping trees; farther away, between distant purpling
hills, the sky appeared as if it had been rubbed black with charcoal.

Reg set his beer down on the card table beside the pile of empties and
shifted the phone receiver from one ear to the other.

"Hullo," said a voice full of sleepgravel.

"Hal?" Reg said.

"Hold on a sec. Hold on. Jesus H."

Reg drank. Knocked his knuckles on the table.

"What?" Hal said.

"Sleepin?"

"*Was.*"

"Someone's been up there."

"Where?"

"Smugglers."

"How do you know?"

"Went up."

"What the fuck for?"

"It was cold. Shit. It's snowin right now."

"Snow ain't goingta last this time a year. You know that."

"Well. Someone's been fuckin with em. Tried to make it look like
deer."

"Probly was deer."

"Might've thought so. But when I come down off the mountain, I seen tracks round the Camino and a piece of paper somebody'd dropped."

"Paper?"

"Little yellow slip."

"Mighta blown outta a truck or something. You coulda dropped it."

"I'm not stupid. Lavalettes fuck with me . . . "

"You oughtta let that rest." He coughed. "You got the plants off Smugs then?"

"No."

"Jesus."

"Dint know, for sure, till I come down to the road. I was too beat to go back up. There's too much. That's the good news. They pretty much all took. Big bastards, too. I'm gonna need Lamar's help."

"That's what you need. Lamar's help."

"Goin up to Caratunk next coupla weeks, to help him take care of his plants. He can come down with me and we can get up to Smugs before anyone else gets back up there. Figure whoever fucked with em will wait right up till bird season before they go back up."

"Better figure right. Some a them're mine. Half."

Reg picked up the .45. "Oughtta see the plants out to Ma's place. Fuckin trees; and the buds. Sticky."

"You shoulda grown them out ta your own place."

"I got too many boaters and hunters out here. Creepin round."

"Creeping around."

"I do." Reg jabbed a match between his teeth and excavated a strand of jerked venison, examined it, and wiped it on his jeans. "Lamar was right, bout growin indoors. He says—"

"I don't wanta hear what that paranoid loon has to say. Look. I gotta go. Say hi to Trooper."

"Sure."

"She making out okay?"

"If she'd shoot that fuckin husband a hers, she'd feel a lot better."

"Check up on her."

Reg hung up.

A flock of Canada geese were feeding out on Unknown Pond. Reg looked at his shotgun in the corner, by the door. Back in high school he and Lamar had kept guns in their cars—twelve gauges, smooth blued barrels, hardwood stocks, good to grip, and .22 rifles, light compared to the shotguns, two of each between them on the front seat, muzzles to the floor. They would drive the back roads at night, through fields and woods, waiting for coons or skunks to cross in front of them. When they did, whoever was driving would lock the brakes and they'd jump out, guns in hand, flashlights ready, the car rumbling, its headlights on, doors flung open, its eight track blaring, so it looked and sounded like some alien spacecraft that had just put down in the middle of the road. In the woods, they'd chased the coons or skunks along scrubby fence lines, thickets and brambles scratching their faces, tearing their clothes. They'd listened for shuffling sounds in the dry leaves and undergrowth, trying to catch a glimpse of panicked eyes, filmy blue in the flashlights' rays.

Separating, they'd stalk through the woods, circling up ahead of the quarry. They never spoke in the woods. Never needed to. Lamar had clucked like a squirrel. Reg had whistled different bird calls. They'd always known where the other one was, and what to expect from him.

The skunks proved easy. They'd stop and turn to spray and Reg and Lamar would hold the flashlights on them and shoot them in the head and leave them where they'd died: Worthless. The raccoons they'd tree. It was hard to see a treed raccoon at night. They'd rustle the slightest bit up in the shadowy limbs, hold tight and still and ball themselves up. You could see them only by their glowing eyes. The ones that never looked down lived. The ones that did, got neat round holes in their skulls. Fifteen dollars for each whole raccoon, that's what Albino Racine's old man had paid. They hadn't even had to skin the raccoons. Just threw the carcasses on Albino's porch in fat stiff piles and took the cash. Some nights those carcasses had piled up pretty high and Reg and Lamar had stuffed their pockets with greasy, crumpled tens and twenties, flush with cash and friendship, and the prospect of how easy it all was.

Lamar was a loony bastard. Hal was right about that. Ever since Fairland, Lamar'd become a recluse. He'd moved into a cabin in

Caratunk, along the Canadian border, and grown sick with fear, worrying all the time about selling to the wrong boys, about having so much weed. He'd started packing pounds of the bud he'd grown indoors, into vacuum-sealed bags, then burying the bags in fifty-five gallon drums in the woods around his cabin. He kept a gas can and a box of wooden matches in each corner of the cabin, just in case anyone discovered him. Last time he'd called from the pay phone at the Caratunk General Store he'd ranted about unloading his weed to Reg, for nothing. "I don't want the shit around me no more," he'd said. He wanted Reg to have it, just between them. No one else. Not even Hal. That was all right with Reg. Still, Lamar carried things too far. Being wary was one thing: smart. Being paranoid was another: dangerous. And not just for Lamar. Reg had tried talking sense into him, but there seemed to be no helping him.

Down on the pond the geese had swum closer to the shore, but were still out of shotgun range. A few ducks were mixed in with them. Mallards and blacks. It would be a couple months yet before the whistlers and bufflehead came down from Canada. Reg had been hunting whistlers and bufflehead with Lamar, on Broken Leg Lake, the first time he'd had a run-in with a Lavalette, Jack, the old man. Reg'd been fourteen. It was November and both his and Lamar's mas had thought it would be a good idea for Reg to get out of the house. He'd hardly left the yard, hardly spoken, since Pap's death.

He and Lamar had trudged the two miles of railroad tracks to Broken Leg, lugging burlap sacs, heavy with the cork decoys Pap had hand-carved when he'd been their age.

At the lake they'd climbed down an embankment to the shore. A north wind had howled out of the darkness, down from Canada, blowing a snow that stung like bits of ice against their faces. The waves had crashed in the dark before them, the rocks slick and icy. Lamar had unwound the anchor cords from around each decoy, checked to make sure each anchor was secured, then handed two decoys at a time to Reg. In his hip boots, Reg had walked out into the choppy lake and thrown each decoy out into the water, standing on the tips of his toes when large swells threatened to spill over the tops of his boots. A few decoys had landed upside down, then righted themselves. Good, solid decoys.

With the last of the decoys set out, Reg had returned to shore. He remembered clearly, staring out at the dark water, just able to make out the small white patches on the cheeks of the closest decoys. Then he and Lamar had pushed into the cattails.

Earlier that fall, they'd built a blind out of wood pallets and canvas mailbags, spray painted flat army green. They'd wood-burned their names into a pineboard plaque, which they'd nailed to the outside of the blind.

In the blind they'd sat on overturned buckets frozen stuck to the pallet floor; they'd dug shells out of their pockets, took off their mittens, quickly loaded their shotguns, and blew on their hands.

With his shotgun loaded, Reg had stood up from his bucket and peered out. The tops of the reeds and cattails bent over double in the gale. He'd been able to make out half the decoys. Black forms bobbing and lilting on dark swells.

"Be careful. Keep down," Lamar had said, pouring each of them a cup of coffee from their Thermos.

Reg had sat back down.

"We're going to nail em," Lamar'd said.

"I hope."

"I can feel it."

A crashing had arisen from the reeds beside them. Then an explosion: A shotgun blast. So close their ears had rung and they'd fallen off their buckets, startled and disoriented, their coffees flying from their hands and scalding their lips. From the water's edge had come a bellowing. Another shotgun blast. Another. They'd both recoiled with each blast, then stood to see a man standing ankle deep out on the sandbar, among the decoys. Bearded, he'd worn a purple snowmobile suit and blue moonboots and a Russian fur hat. He wore mittens as big as baseball mitts and was grappling with shells, dropping them into the lake in his haste to reload. The shotgun was huge. A big ten gauge. Perhaps an eight. Illegal for decades. He'd finally loaded it and aimed it at the raft of decoys and fired. Once. Twice. Three times. Pieces of cork and wooden decoy heads had flown into the snowy air and landed in the dark chop to float as wreckage. Reg had stood immobile, struck dumb by the chunks of cork floating out into the broad water.

"Hey!" Lamar had screamed as he'd scrambled out of the blind.

He'd thrashed through the reeds, slipped and fallen and stood again and ran out into the water shouting: "Hey! Mister! What in hell do yuh think yur doing?" his shout muffled by the wind and snow and waves, as if he were calling from deep within a cave of snow.

The man had spun around. Gun raised, he'd fired a shot. Water sprayed in front of Lamar and he stopped his charge. "What do yuh think yur *doing?*" he'd shouted.

The man stood out on the sandbar glaring. With each irregular gust of wind the fur of his hat had matted and puffed.

"What in hell?" the man had hollered. "I thought them's real damned ducks. Who the fuck're yuh? This's my duck spot."

"*Mister*" Lamar had shouted and pointed back to the blind. "That's *our* blind! We got our names on it! We've hunted ducks here a long time!"

"*Long time,*" the man had bellowed. "I'm Jack *Lavalette.* My fuckin famly's been shootin up this pond since before yur old man could get his pecker up. Better find yerselfs nother place to hunt ducks."

"We were here first," Lamar had protested. "We got us legal rights to be here."

"*Legal.* Jesus fuckin Christ."

"You can't do this! It ain't right!"

Jack had leaned back as if to catch snowflakes on his tongue and whooped; "*Right? Right?*" He'd fired a shot up into the sky then spun away from them and fired. The shot had sounded so hollow and loud it seemed to have come from inside Reg's head. A bufflehead decoy blew apart. Lamar had splashed out toward Jack. But Jack had shoved the shotgun barrel into Lamar's chest and Lamar had fallen back and sat in the cold lake; soaked, he'd stood again, dripping and shaking near to convulsions.

"Goddamn you! Them're my cousin's decoys! They were his pap's!" He was blubbering now, bawling, spitting words forth as if he had a mouth full of mud. "He's dead and yur shootin up his decoys! Goddamn you!" He'd stamped his foot in the waves, water splashing all over and freezing to his coat's zipper. Reg had stood still as Lamar'd screamed: "You sonofabitch! Them're *our* decoys! You sonofabitch!"

"Only decoys I see's mine. Y'two boys got 'bout five seconds. . . . "

He'd counted as he fumbled to reload.

"One."

"Two."

"Three."

"Four. . . . "

Lamar and Reg had struggled up the bank, toward the railroad tracks, wincing with each shotgun blast that had come from behind them.

Finally, they'd gained the railroad tracks and paused and unloaded their shotguns and shouldered them. They'd hung their heads and their breath had come long and shallow, Reg's union suit sticking with sweat to his skin. They'd waited until they'd caught their breath then continued on.

As they'd plodded into the wind, Lamar had said, "Hell. I'm sorry, Reg. Hell."

Reg had shrugged and shifted his shotgun to his other shoulder; he'd stooped and picked up a loose railroad spike and thrown it up ahead where it landed with a clank. He'd hung his head and watched his boots on the crushed limestone, stuck a hand in his coat pocket and rattled the shells around. "Least you did somethin." He'd wiped his nose with his coat sleeve. "I jus stood there and took it."

"That don't matter."

"The fuck it don't."

"I'm sorry. About the decoys. About Pap. Hell." Lamar had patted him on the back.

"It's all right," Reg had said. But it hadn't been all right. Not at all.

Hess Please was awake, but had yet to flinch, to unstick a gummy eyelid. He lay with his head wrapped in his arms. His mouth tasted like an ashtray. A wiry spring poked out from the couch, into a sore rib. He scrunched up, curled in on himself like a porcupine protecting itself against the snapping jaws of hounds.

He rubbed a hand on his bare inner thigh, over his stomach, touching the memorized smoothness of torn and sewn flesh, a ropy keloid to remind him of a lousy foot misplaced on an unsure outcrop.

After those two long days of cold rain and wet snow, the sun was out as if clouds had never existed; he felt its warmth coming through the window, heating his lower calf.

Water pinged in the kitchen skink.

Something tapped his forehead, dead between his eyes, like a woodpecker mining for grubs. *Peckpeckpeck.* A fingernail. He grimaced and his eyelids fluttered, hesitant against the bright spill of morning. A shape, Clare, blocked out the light; his eyelids cooled.

He tried to swallow.

"I'm going to work. Fix the sink before you leave," she said.

"Mmm-hmm."

"You can't be here tonight. Max's coming over." A set of keys janlged.

"Where'm I supposed to go?" The words tumbling from his slow mouth.

"Go home."

"Mmm."

"Remember the sink. And Max. I'll see you."

"Mmm."

The front door closed, the boxy house shook; outside, a car door slammed, twice and the car gasped away. Silence. Save for the sound of water dripping in the kitchen sink.

Frame washed, chain oiled, spokes polished, the Huffy Santa Fe assaulted the dirt road beneath Jessup's pumping untiring legs. The derailleur clickclacked as he shifted to take on the last steep hill, a sweet ache and burn in his calves and thighs, each pebble sending vibrations to his fingers, his canvas pack flapping against his back, nearly spilling over with the crushed beer cans, bottles, and candy wrappers he'd collected all morning from the roadside grass.

At the top of Hardscrabble Hill he dismounted. The sun felt like a gift after the previous days' cold and snow. He picked up a cigaret wrapper and stuck it in his pocket. He'd acquired the habit of cleaning up litter from his mother. For a couple summers, when he was eight and nine, his mother had taken him fishing down to Bloomfield Reservoir. The fishing had been fast, but effortless and uneventful. Perch and panfish mostly, fish that hit anything you threw at them.

Other boys would slam the sunfish and rock bass to the ground or throw them in the bushes, where they flopped all afternoon.

Jessup would have rather been fishing a cold stream for trout. Lily pads and lukewarm water, and a bunch of other kids fishing from the tailgates of station wagons and pickup trucks was not his idea of fishing. He did not let on to what he thought of his mother's fishing destination, however: She was trying.

It had pleased her to watch him fish. She would take his picture with his catch, and although he'd been embarrassed as the other boys glanced over from baiting hooks, or minding bobbers, when he'd smiled for the camera, he'd smiled genuinely. Not because he was proud of the panfish that shivered and gasped on their stringer, but because of the smile on his mother's face.

Before they left the reservoir, his mother would inspect the fishing access, collect cans and bottles, food wrappers and Styrofoam worm containers and dispose of them in the garbage bag she'd brought, which Jessup held open as he walked behind her.

People would look, especially when she snuck in between a couple of teenagers, or a father and son, saying "excuse me," grinning and plucking a bottlecap from the ground at their feet. Mostly, they ignored her. She'd never scolded or preached. She'd simply made her rounds.

On the day that would be their last at the reservoir, she'd decided to rescue the dying fish from the bushes, and was heckled. The boys, discovering what she was up to, had grabbed the fish they'd been keeping in buckets and had begun throwing them into the woods. Jessup's mother had rushed around in the underbrush, emitting startled throaty sounds.

She'd managed to get hold of a couple of fish and had run from the trees with them clutched in her shirt and dumped them in the lake, a harried look on her face as even other parents shook their heads at her.

She kept at it, and the boys took to the woods themselves, surrounded her, and ran from fish to fish, stomping them and beating them with sticks. "Jessup!" she'd called out. But he hadn't helped. He'd dropped his rod and run down the dirt road, away from the access.

He'd been walking for some time, lame from his all-out sprint, when she'd pulled up alongside him. After a moment of pretending to ignore her, he'd climbed into the car and folded his arms across his chest, staring at her, fuming.

They'd sat, the car idling. Her cheeks were grimy and she'd been breathing hard through her nose. Her hair had spilled out from its bun. He'd broken the gaze first and looked in the back seat, where she'd lain his fishing rod.

"They were laughing," he'd said.

"I don't think those poor fish I saved cared much. Do you?"

"They're junk fish."

"*Junk* fish?"

"*Any*one can catch them. They're junk."

She'd looked down at her left hand and wriggled her fingers. He'd felt ashamed for saying something meant to hurt. But it was true: They were junk; any man would have known that.

"Well," she'd said, "I had no idea. Thanks for letting me know that some fish deserve such treatment. I wish you'd told me sooner. I wouldn't have wasted my time."

Jessup shook his head and patted his bike's seat. "Good girl," he crooned. He turned and looked back down upon the river valley and the town of Ivers. At its center, the church steeple, its green-slated roof sheening in the sun like the scales of a beast, spired above the crowns of maple and oak, above the red and weathered snatches of brick and clapboard. From where he stood, the Lamoille River looked like a vein of melted silver that had seeped up from a fissured earth, coiling between the post office and Rosie's Hardware, the Bee Hive and the Ivers Town Library, wending among cornfields and woods, and beneath the Sawmill covered bridge. Main Street and Limekiln Road, the two roads that descended from the hills to intersect at the only stop sign in town, looked like ancient scars fixed into the landscape.

Jessup imagined the town submerged under water. Waters so deep and muddy that only the cross atop the church steeple stuck out above the waterline. He pushed off down the hill, away from town, the road falling steeply beneath him, the bike gaining speed. When the road forked he took Gamble Hill for a short ways, then pulled the bike over and hid it in the woods, behind a stone wall.

In the overgrown sugarbush he lurked, then broke into a loping gate over Hock Knoll and down the other side; he leapt from rock to rock among the summerpuddled bed of Cobb Creek, then out of the cool rocks and water. At the crest the sun shattered through treetops, scattering light, leaving the woods to tremble. He leaned against a failing yellow birch, its papery bark peeling in great sheaths. He pulled down a branch tip, bit off a bud and sucked its wintergreen. He looked down through the birches and beeches that broke to fields gone to seed, the flashes of white and green and red, like misplaced puzzle pieces. The forsaken house and condemned barns of the Barker farm.

He hadn't been here since the Fourth of July. With Emily.

He bounded down the rocky grade, backpack flapping.

Outside the trailer the late-morning sun felt like a splash of cool water on Marigold's face.

"What color do you think? For the trailer?" She spoke around a mouthed clothespin, removed it, and let it pinch the threadbare polka-dot panties to the rope that sagged between two birches. "Hess? Where are you?" Her voice died in the hills.

Upside-down flannel shirts flapped and settled with an irregular wind, cuffs whisking the ankle-high grasses. She swam among black acid-washed jeans, towels and shirts, gray bras with safety-pinned straps. Hess was gone, no longer sitting in the grass, where he had been. "What?" He was in the bedroom window, his face dark and checked with shadows behind an insect-spackled screen. "I'm right here."

"You going to go help me choose the color paint?"

He smooshed his cheek against the screen, but didn't look at Marigold. "Ain't up to it."

"Come on outside at least. It's gorgeous out here. Come on out and sit with me." She stepped over to the window. Pollen made her tonsils itch, eyes burn. She clicked the back of her throat.

"I was just out there, y'had to be messing with the laundry," Hess said.

"Well, I'm not now. I'm enjoying it outside."

"And I'm joyin it inside."

"Grab a soda and come on out. Talk."

"Not thirsty."

"I am."

"Are yah?"

"We can go for a walk. Or go fishing."

"Fishin?"

"Or whatever."

He peered out the screen. She could just make out his eyes.

"I want to rest," he said.

"How can you rest any more than you have already? It's not natural. Besides, you can rest out in the sun."

"Perfeckly natural. Sun makes me sick, makes me want to puke."

"Well. Maybe later, when it goes down and cools off, we can have a barbecue."

"We don't have fluid. Or charcoal, stupid."

His face was gone from the window.

"Well," she said to the empty screen, her face hot, eyes blinking. She bent and laced her shoe, scratched her milky knees and shins where nettles had swept against them; she stood, light-headed. Her hands trembling, she strung up the last of the clothes.

From behind the trailer, up on Hock Knoll, going over to the Barker place, came a racket in the trees and leaves. She paused and listened. Something running, tramping. Then, nothing.

Deer. Probably.

The dirt lane cut through the swale grass to end at the collapsing hay barn; Jessup stood looking across the road, opposite the once-grand house.

He considered it his own house: found, like a shipwreck.

He listened, head cocked, but heard nothing but the scrape of wind in leaves, and, from far away on Avers Gore, the persistent howl of a chain saw.

He looked at the house, its white paint chalky and maligned with bird shit and black pine sap. Mud daubers droned from between the slats of decrepit green shutters, their back legs dangling, as if their parchment wings were unable to keep aloft the whole of their awkward bodies. He watched their lazy flight, fascinated and determined to discover their destination. Their pattern. But the wasps seemed to sense his eye and winged themselves in fleeing spirals, away, high and airborne, as if suddenly wanting nothing of the afflicted estate.

The porch's green lattice lay in the thick ripe grasses and weeds; the once-white dental trim had yellowed and alligatored with age. Jessup jumped up on the broad floor of the wraparound porch. Beneath his sneakers brittle deck paint crunched like crisp insect skeletons. He bent at the knees, testing the boards, nodded his approval, then rapped his knuckles on a pillar. *Thock*. "You have carpenter ants," he whispered. "You ought to get an exterminator out here." He sat on the rail and locked his feet between the intricate spindles. Arms spread winglike, he leaned backward. He enjoyed the sound of his own voice and wanted to scream, Emily! But he didn't dare shout, for fear someone might hear. He whispered the word, her name, over and over, a seamless murmur. Then he stood and ran along the edge of the porch, fingers rattling against the spindles.

At the side of the house he vaulted over the rail and stood at a bulkhead. He hauled up on its handles and the doors surrendered a tremendous metallic yawn, revealing a dank, lightless root cellar at the bottom of wooden steps defeated by time. He slunk down, mindful not to scrape his bare back on the low entrance.

In the darkness, he paused; the sweat on his face cooled. He lapped the air, breathed in the fetor of rotted potatoes. In the corner lay collapsed boards and moldering mud bricks that had once been canning shelves. He moved effortlessly in the darkness; daylight sifted in behind him from the bulkhead. He felt his way to the cramped, steep stairs and mounted them.

At the top he pushed open a door and stepped into a kitchen, desolate and smelling of onions and starch; its red floor, dull and scuffed with the traffic of generations, was tacky beneath his sneakers; dried husks of potted plants hung in the window above a steel sink; mouse droppings littered the countertops.

"Hello," he shouted between cupped hands, his voice resounding and returning to him from the unpeopled house. "Hello, I'm here to buy some wool. Where are all the sheep? Bring forth your sheep, I say. Bring forth the lamb and ewe!" In the faded newspaper clippings and black-and-white stills he'd found in the attic, he'd pieced together a scant early history of the Barker place; it had been a sheep farm that had prospered through the forties before over-investing in dairy and dwindling slowly into bankruptcy. He'd found newspapers and family memoirs in old trunks, deserted in place, like most everything else, as if the declining family had suddenly abandoned the house and farm one afternoon and wandered off to die of mass shame and futility in their barren fields.

He raked his fingers across the butcher-block island, a dark grime curling and packing beneath his nails. The open cupboards were lined with cups and saucers, plates and bowls and glasses that seemed to be awaiting the family's return.

He opened the refrigerator door. Dark. An algaed jar of dill pickles, a bottle of evaporating ginger ale, the warm plastic aroma of long-trapped air. "You really ought to open some windows in this place," he barked on his way into the parlor. His exclamations weren't for amusement alone; some small part of him required he yell out, some tiny black speck in the back of his mind feared walking in on someone unexpectedly, surprising someone doing something private, inexplicable or horrendous. In his magazines he'd read how seasoned outdoorsmen, when in grizzly country, wore bells, or called out loud when coming around a blind corner on the trail, to warn the bears of their presence. To walk up on a bear was dangerous, but to catch someone doing something they didn't want to be caught doing . . . well, humans were capable of much more damage than a bear: humans possessed imaginations.

No one was in the parlor, surprised or otherwise, when he entered. The parlor's hardwood floor and wood casings were dust-coated, but shone here and there where the sunlight poured through southern windows. A fieldstone fireplace occupied half the far wall and the room was faint with the odor of ash. Sooty wallpaper peeled at its corners. Across from the fireplace sat a couch, its stuffing gutted and strewn by rats and squirrels, the springs and wood frame exposed.

In the far corner, beneath the windows, an old upright piano stood, filmed with dust as thick as any woodshop's, its ivory keys concealed beneath their cover.

Jessup walked over and sat down on the piano bench, its cushion sighing.

He rubbed his palms beside him on the bench, where Emily had sat.

He'd been leaving Rosie's Hardware after charging a pack of hooks and splitshot, when he'd seen her; she'd stood across Main Street, in front of Harv's Barber and Tobacco, glowing in the sun, shining; a burnished bronzed statue of a nymph. She'd bent to pet Lucy, Harv's beagle who forever slept outside the shop. Jessup had watched Emily from across the street, gazing at the crescent of pale skin that revealed itself where her cutoffs met the tops of her plump tanned thighs. As she'd petted Lucy, she'd nibbled on the ends of her bobbed pumpkin-colored hair.

All afternoon Jessup had trailed her from his side of the street, staring into storefront windows to catch glimpses of her image. A spy.

For two weeks he'd biked to town in hopes that he'd find her; on those days he had, he'd followed her, his confidence growing with each pursuit, until he'd found it in himself to cross to her side of the street. He'd been shadowing her one afternoon when she'd halted her sassy stride and turned about-face; he'd run right into her.

She'd smelled of raspberries and chocolate; her round-rimmed tortoise-shell glasses had sat slightly crooked on her freckled nose. She'd wagged a finger, her big red-red lips seemed to move more slowly than her words: "You're spying on me."

Before he could lie, Jessup had said, "Yes. I am. I'm a spy. Of sorts."

"A slow trade, around here."

He'd brought her here, to the Barker place.

"Could we build a fire?" she'd said.

"I don't want anyone to see smoke."

She'd lifted the piano cover, tapped a key. Another. She'd poised her fingers above the ivories, then brought them down, fingers like jointless frolicking creatures. Oh she could *play*. *Oh*. But she'd stopped after a quick little spurt.

"'Coming around the Mountain.' Can you play that one? Or how about 'My Bonnie Lies over the Ocean'?"

She'd wrinkled her nose. "I don't know songs like that. Besides, it's out of tune. The change in temperature and humidity stretches the piano wire."

He'd shrugged. "I can't tell." He knew nothing of music, except that it pleased him.

She'd sucked in the corners of her mouth the slightest and had begun to play. On and on she'd played, wildly, the notes dancing off the cobwebbed chandelier and the pressed-tin ceiling, off each other. When she'd stopped, slightly winded, she'd turned and faced him. "Your eyes are like the insides of pomegranates," she'd said. Then she leaned and kissed him.

His face had burned with this, his first real kiss. He'd traded a peck or two, on the cheek, in junior high, with Samantha Hunt. She'd pecked and he'd pecked, out in the school parking lot behind the school bus, while a Little League game had played itself out on the town baseball field. But those hadn't been real kisses.

Emily's kiss had been so soft, so full and surprising, Jessup hadn't been able to bring himself to kiss her back.

He'd hoped she'd kiss him again, but she hadn't.

The rest of the summer had been a string of tormenting moments of his desiring to lean in, to kiss. He did not know what had kept him from kissing her. How many days had they lain beside each other in fields of goldenrod, or on smooth riverbank boulders, their bodies flooding with sun, without him trying?

On walks and hikes they'd often touched each other, banged hips together every time they'd discovered another food or song or book they both loved; they'd jabbed each other in the ribs when they were the butt of the other's jokes. The way they'd touched on their long walks and hikes, when he'd identified birds or animal tracks for her, had been casual, their motion and laughter a distraction from the touching itself, making him less nervous. But, when they became still, when she'd lain down beside him, so close he'd been able to smell the sweat on her freckled skin, or hear the thin whistling as she breathed through her nose, he'd lost all ability to know where to rest his gaze, what to do with his clumsy hands; it was all he could bear even to glance at her, to speak one coherent word. Each time she'd stretched out beside him, her thumbs hooked in the belt loops of her cutoff corduroys, her shirt riding up to expose her tanned, downy-tufted stomach, it had taken him every effort to dare inch his fingers closer to hers; he'd eased his fingers a half inch closer each day, his eyes shut, a lightness in his chest, a fluttering, until, one day, finally, his pinkie had brushed her hand and she'd taken his hand without a word into her own and flattened it to her warm stomach. So simple, to kiss.

The week before Emily had left, Jessup had shopped around for a piece of jewelry, deciding, finally, on a choker with a clear quartz pendant. He'd given it to her the afternoon before she'd left. She'd slipped it around her neck and had had him clasp it, his fingers trembling as they grazed the baby-soft V of hair that stuck lightly to her neck with sweat. The pendant had sat delicately in the hollow of her throat, glinting with sunlight.

"It's just right," she'd said and hugged him. "Just right."

That night he'd been awakened by a ticking sound; Emily had snuck out from her father's cabin and walked the two miles to Jessup's house to toss pebbles at his window. He'd come outside and they'd gone for a long walk, ending up here. They'd sat on the porch swing, which had creaked under their weight and nearly broken free of the chains from which it hung. He'd confided in her about his father, the way in which he'd died, just weeks before Jessup was born. He'd told her how he sometimes thought of his father as selfless, a man who'd done what was required of him at a crucial moment; other times he felt his father was selfish, thoughtless for not having cared enough about his own life, his own family, before doing what he'd done. "I don't know if he was brave or a coward," Jessup had said, pushing off with his feet to rock the swing.

"Sounds like both."

He'd stood and sat across from her on the porch rail. "Both?"

She'd rubbed her pendant between a thumb and forefinger. "I mean, who isn't? You could scramble your brain trying to make him one or the other, good or bad. Probably he didn't think at all. Probably he just acted."

Jessup had thought about this. Likely his father hadn't had time to think, *had* simply acted. Who wouldn't have? But, certainly, his father wouldn't have done what he'd done if he'd *known* the outcome.

The more he'd considered what Emily had said, the more embarrassed Jessup had become. Emily had the enviable ability to see the whole picture, to take a step back and weigh everything; she didn't hold to absolutes. He'd felt foolish, too, realizing he'd told her about his father with the hope that she'd settle his indecision for him.

He hadn't spoken to anyone about his father since he was six, when his mother had first explained to him what had happened, and told him not to mention it again, to her, or anyone: It brought her too much pain, and a town, like a person, couldn't heal if constantly reminded of its tragic past. He'd talked to Emily because she wasn't from Ivers, and wouldn't care if he dragged up the town's history. And he'd told her because he'd *wanted* to. Some tidal force seemed to be tugging at him, pulling the words from him, words he hadn't known he'd needed to speak, words stored inside him for her alone to hear. And, sometimes, more and more often since he'd turned sixteen, he'd felt it wrong for his mother to hold so much inside of herself, to bear the past without speaking of it; and he'd felt it was wrong of her to insist he do the same, live his life the way she chose to live hers. He was only just beginning to recognize that each life was its own and needed to be lived accordingly, if it wasn't to be wasted.

He plinked a piano key. Its note high and acute, fading. He dragged his fingers across the keys. He'd smiled when she'd kissed him, then he'd snapped his mouth shut, worried about his teeth. He hated them. The two upper front ones overlapped each other and the eyeteeth were stunted fangs; the bottom front row was a confusion of crisscrossing enamel chips. Cursed teeth. Grotesque teeth. But clean. The whitest around. Alabaster. He brushed ten times a day. Flossed half that. A tube of paste and a brush in his pants' pocket, always. He bought his own toothpaste. Expensive, at a tube a week. Toothbrushes, two a month. He ate apples after every meal, drank a gallon of milk a day.

Emily had left after the Fourth of July weekend.

They'd written every day. At first. Postcards and letters. She would enclose sea grass and shells, and sand dollars meticulously wrapped in tissue paper. He would send maple leaves and pieces of riversmoothed blueglass. A lock of hair. A feather.

He hunted through his pack, finding her latest letter, which was nearly falling apart along its creases. He unfolded it and smoothed it out before himself on the floor. Her cursive handwriting was precise and controlled, with a playful openness.

Jessup,
  Hey.
  How are you?
  Could I miss someone any more?
  Bad bad bad bad bad news! My father took on two new clients, so we won't be coming up for the last of August. Maybe Labor Day? But I can't count on it. . . . He'll have to go up sometime, so I'll ask about going with him when he does. I can't ask right now. He's being a dink these days!
  ANYWAY, maybe I could drive up there myself before summer's over. My Bug is still running. No thanks to you, (kidding), so I could come see you, if you wanted. It's an idea. If not maybe you could come down, somehow? Sleep on the beach?
                                            Emily

He held the letter to his cheek then put it back. He imagined the ocean as he'd seen it in books and photographs, and Emily's postcards. How would it be, kissing her in the sand dunes, the ocean smashing behind them? He took out a notepad and pencil and laid down on his stomach, the sun soothing on his neck. He began to write. His hand frantic.

Dear Em,
  Hello.
  You wouldn't believe *the trout I caught. A* Big Mama. *But overall the fishing's turned crappy since that NOR'ESTER. All the rain and SNOW. Prince Paper! Criminals! Farmers too! The streams get silty and limey after every storm. People think farmers are so great, but they ruin the streams more than anyone. How is a brook trout supposed to live?*
  I tried to start the Vega, it just clicks when I turn the key. Had my mom jump-start it, but . . . it died. Nothing. Have you been busy? Is your dad coming up soon? How about Labor Day? Only five days away! I was thinking . . . I can hitchhike down there, or

*ride my bike. I'm in shape . . . the Huffy's a good bike. You can
teach me how to clam.*

Write soon?

Jessup

P.S. Baa Baaaaaaa. . . .

He stared at the letter, the fifth one he'd written in two weeks.
He had not heard from her in all that time.

Reg lay on his back underneath Marigold's truck, his legs sticking out
into thistles and downy milkweed, the air rife with the smell of manure and drying mud and clay. But for the cool damp ground, there
was no sign of the snow that had fallen the day before. He wiped his
nose, leaving sweaty black smears on the back of his hand. Marigold's
feet fidgeted in the grass.

"How's it look under there? Can you fix it?" she said.

"I'll need some parts. Water pump, for one. And a oil pan." He
tapped the oil pan with a ratchet. "She ain't gonna run like new."

"I just need something to get around in."

"Where's Hess? He oughtta be helpin with this."

"He's off somewhere."

"He's always off somewheres."

"He doesn't know much about engines anyway."

"He don't know much bout much."

"Reg."

"He don't."

"He's recovering."

"Recoverin."

She sighed. "When can you get the parts?"

"Don't know why yah put up with his p'thetic shit."

"It's too nice out to talk about Hess."

"Jus don't unerstand em's all. When's the last time yah saw em?"

Marigold picked at a piece of rust on the truck fender.

"It's good to get it all out, darlin. Like poison."

"He was here, earlier. But he left."

"What're yah gonna do?"

"I don't know. He'll come around. I don't know." She locked her fingers behind her neck and closed her eyes. "I can't wait till Hal comes home." She opened her eyes. "When can you get the parts?"

"I'll get over to Skinny's sometime in the next week, fore I go up to Caratunk."

"I'd think you'd stay away from up there. From Lamar."

"No worries darlin."

"Don't *darlin* me."

"Don't mother me."

"I'd just think you wouldn't want to get messed up with him, or any of that, again; I'd think—"

"That's yur problem. Yah think too much. I jus need a chunk of change; ain't gonna get it workin for asshole Bishop, throws me scraps like I'm some dog."

She shook her head. Here *she* was, prying. The urge to meddle was *so* strong sometimes, she thought, aware of how much she shared with Reg the trait she most despised in him. It was laughable. Pathetic, but laughable. "I was thinking I'd start towing people. This winter. Maybe haul some firewood."

"Uh-huh."

"I might check on some of those openings over at that Mitel plant in Montgomery, too."

"Computers. Jesus. World's goin to shit. Cars runnin on chips. One little thing goes wrong and the whole car goes down. Can't work on it yurself. It's so yah havta bring it into the shop."

"I'd think you'd want to learn about new cars, have to, to race. I'm thinking of taking computer classes."

"Waste a money, darlin."

"I've got to do something with myself."

"Who don't?" He stuck his hand out from beneath the truck, palm outstretched. "Hand me a three-quarter-inch socket, top drawer. I jus wouldn't wanna work for a place like the one up to Montgomery."

Marigold dug around in the toolbox, among an assortment of oily sockets, lifting each one to check the size. She placed one in Reg's hand. He took it and a rhythmic racheting began, accompanied by the sound of humming. She listened as Reg hummed a nameless tune, a wandering melody that pitched and swelled, silence for spells, and then he'd pick it up again, a somber, delicate strain of notes. It had been a couple years since Marigold had heard him hum, since the week leading up to his time in Fairland. It had been longer still since she'd heard him sing. As a boy, the locals had always told him to go to Nashville. Be a country singer. "Your voice is lonesome as any," they'd pronounce. But Reg wasn't going to Nashville. After a while he no longer sang around anyone anymore, and hummed only to calm himself when he was preoccupied or nervous. Angry.

"There's nothin here for nobody less they wanna work for someone else the rest their miserable lives," he said, his voice raised over the rachet.

"That's how it is. Anywhere. For anyone. You have to work for someone. You're working for Bishop's."

"Not for long."

The ratchet slipped and he raked the back of his knuckles, sucked on his fist.

"Well," she said, "I don't mind working for someone else, as long as I get paid decent and treated decent. I wouldn't mind good benefits, either."

He scraped the starter post with a pocketknife. "Bennies. Jesus. Work in Montgomery and yah'll be workin for goddamned outta staters. Don't settle. Get somethin yah wanna do."

"You make a lot of sense. You know that? Tell me not to settle. Wait for the right job. Who's ever head of such a thing? *Right job.* Then you climb all over Hess. Talk stupid about kicking his ass. I ought to kick your ass." She kicked his calf.

"Don't make me get up," he said, rubbing his leg. "Besides. That's difrent. Hess's a man. Of sorts."

"It's not different." She plucked a long blade of grass and rubbed it to green pulp in her palm.

"It is," he said. "He's a husband. Yah shouldn't havta work. I'd like to break his goddamned neck."

"That's nice talk. Besides, I like having my own money. I used to love towing. Working at the Lucky Spot."

"And they let yah go because of the new Short-Stop. Outta staters, darlin. The enemy. The En-uh-mee."

"I'll take whatever I can, from whoever owns it. I'm easier to please than you."

"That's yur problem."

"Tell you what. You quit bitching and fix Mildred, and I'll set my mind to thinking about what I want to do with my life, fixing all my problems, how's that?"

The ratchet stopped and he scrambled out from under Mildred to lay on his back in the weeds. He blinked and picked rust flakes from his eyelashes and looked up at Marigold. "All right. Darlin. Okay. This truck's gonna need belts, too. I'll cover em. But my labor's gonna run yah a few beers and lunch. Maybe yah could bring over a girlfriend. Some little aching slut?"

She kicked him in the ribs.

He grabbed her ankle and pulled and she sat down hard in the grass, kicking at him as he grabbed her tighter. She pounded at his wrists. But he held fast and shoved her back with his other hand so she sprawled out on her back. Her jeans split at the crotch. He got up on top of her and straddled her chest, pinned her hands to the ground, his breath ragged. She shook her head back and forth, tried to buck him off, but he tickled under her arms and on her belly where her shirt rode up. Pinched her.

"You're *hurting* me, Reg. Get off me. *Stop* it."

He kept at it.

She managed to free a hand and swing at him, knocking off his cap; she grabbed a handful of hair and pulled.

He rolled off, howling and holding his stomach. He pulled his cap on.

She stood. "What's the matter with you?" She kicked his knee.

"Ow," he said. But he made no move.

She looked down on him. "Funny," she said, spreading her legs and bending to look at the rip in the crotch of her jeans. "Ripped. Goddamn it. It's not as if I have ten pairs."

"I'm sorry. Hell I'll buy yah a new pair."

"Just fix my car. I'll give you beer and lunch. You get your own sluts."

"All right. Darlin. All right. Yah just make sure that husband a yurs is round, so` he can learn somethin. Hand me my beer, at least."

"I'll try."

"See yah do. We'll get that truck runnin."

"Thanks."

He looked up from his back. The sun was brilliant behind her; she, just a twig of a silhouette. "Have him slap some paint on this place fore it gets too cold, too."

"I know. I know." She smiled weakly and reached a hand out to help him up. "Maybe you could show me what to do, anyway? I don't know what kind of paint to use, or anything."

"Sure. Course," he said, accepting her hand and standing in the sunshine. "Sorry bout them jeans," he said. "Really."

She shrugged.

They sat beside each other on a stack of cinder blocks that served as the trailer's front steps.

He brushed at his overalls and pulled out the scrap of yellow paper from his bib pocket. He handed it to her.

"What's this?" she said.

"I don't know. Read it."

The piece of paper had been folded several times. "It's pretty smudged," she said.

"There's something written there." He poked a finger at the slip of paper as she unfolded it.

"Hold your horses. Let's see . . . "

"Well? What's it say?"

"Jessup," Anna said: Anna Defalque, changed back from Anna Burke. She stood inside, behind the screen door. Freshly changed out of a skirt and blouse and into her sweats, she felt relaxed, but could feel the long day of inventory at Jensen Woolen Mill as heavy bags under her eyes. She'd stacked and bobby-pinned her silver hair on top of her head so only a few strands hung in her face, which, lately, she'd become all too aware, was losing its fight with gravity. She leaned against the doorframe, crossing her arms, watching her boy flip hot dogs and burgers on the hibachi balanced atop the porch rail. He drank from a half-gallon carton of milk and shook his head. "Wow," he garbled. Milk dribbled down his chin, his bare chest. "*Save* me from the cold."

"Jessup," she said.

He bit a hot dog.

"Use a fork."

He swallowed it in two bites. "Are hot dogs supposed to have crunchies in them? I almost broke a tooth. Toenail, maybe?"

"You got a postcard today."

"What? Where?"

"I'll get it." She took it from the hallway bench behind her.

He chugged the rest of the milk, breathless, then crushed the container.

She stepped out onto the porch and handed the postcard to him. From the cedar swamp behind the house the late afternoon brought a rash of mosquitoes, but the hamburgers' greasy smoke warded them off; they clustered in clouds, a few feet away.

He took the postcard and bit his lower lip. The picture was of a lighthouse perched atop a seaside cliff, seagulls drafting above the ocean. He flipped it over.

She looked over his shoulder:

Jessup,

Sorry I haven't written. Your letters were great. I'm trying to figure out a way to get up there. I'm working now, at Dino's, a pizza joint (can you believe that!) down by the pier. The one where that old guy hanged himself! ANYWAY. So it is hard to get away. My parents want me to "be responsible," "for once." I wanted to get up there for Labor Day weekend, at least, but it's not going to happen. My parents are "so busy."

Hopefully I can come up with my dad over Columbus weekend, when he goes up to winterize it. I want to see you sooner though. OF COURSE! Maybe a Greyhound! (My Bug is dead again. Is this the end?) Did you get the Vega running? You could get down here. How's "our house"?

Emily

"Columbus Day?" he muttered.

He read the postcard a few more times, staring, as if more words might materialize.

This girl, Anna thought, Jessup was spooney for her, and Anna worried how she might react when she discovered that Jessup's personality was not affected for her pleasure, but was genuine, ingrained and perhaps as unmalleable as his father's had been. Jessup had a charm and naiveté that made Anna proud, but also infuriated her, caused her to wonder about his immaturity, his seeming inability to take anything seriously. She worried too about how he would use his affable charm, once he discovered his possession of it.

Hot dogs swelled and burst. Anna forked them onto paper plates. She spatulaed the burgers into their buns.

"Is everything all right?" she asked.

He nodded.

She sat down in an Adirondack chair, setting her plate on its arm.

Jessup placed the postcard on the porch rail and set a stone on it, brought his plate over to the chair beside her. Underneath the deck crickets rubbed their legs together. He sat in silence as the evening grew darker. He nibbled on his hamburger, then set it down with a sigh.

Anna dragged her chair closer to his and put her fingers in his hair. "You look for a job today?"

He shook his head. "I was thinking about it. I thought," he touched a finger to his lips, "'Maybe *Rosie's.*'" Then I took a spill on my bike, and it came to me suddenly, this voice." He cupped his hands to the sides of his mouth, his voice plunging as he spoke in a slow hollow incantation, *"Your time is short. Hardware is not your line!! Hardware is not your calling!"* He picked seeds from his hamburger bun.

"I'm going to make up some business cards," he said, slapping his thighs. "Handyman type. Put em in stores. I can learn to fix things. I'm no good now, but I could work on that. I got dad's old tools."

"What old tools?" Anna crossed her legs.

"I found some in the shed."

"I thought I'd gotten rid of all that. Long ago."

"I can put them to use," Jessup said. "I can paint and repair. Be outside. I'll give you my first card, how's that?"

Every little fleabag store around had countless faded dog-eared cards tacked on bulletin boards or tucked under the checkout counter's Plexiglas. Painting. Yard work. Roofing. Construction. Driveway-sealing. Friendly attitude. FREE ESTIMATES. *There* was a selling point. She scratched at a mosquito bite welling on her neck. "Jess," she said. "I'm not pushing, but this isn't a summer vacation. You could learn a lot about home repair at Rosie's. That Edsel seems to know a lot."

"I only need enough money to get the Vega going."

She shook her head mournfully.

"Have *faith*, Mother. *Faith.*"

"Don't mock me, Jessup. You have to be serious. Think ahead." She waved a hand to fend off mosquitoes.

"I am. I'm off by October," he testified, spatula brandished. "When she comes up, I'm hitting the trail with her." The evening air swelled as the day's heat was forced into pockets by the cold of the on-coming night. "I've never been anywhere. I want to go to West Virginia and work in a coal mine. Deep in the black belly of the earth. I want to go to Montana. Wyoming. Big Sky. Feel the dust of the range on my face, in my throat. I want to go to Louisiana. The bayou. Practice voodoo. Kill chickens. Eat crawdads. Don't worry. I'll write." His eyes grew dark.

If he thought his teeth were a curse, his eyes were a blessing, Anna thought. Darker than hers, violet-black geodes; they were naive, preoccupied eyes. Startling. His eyes and good-heartedness had always made it hard for Anna to get angry with him.

Anna harbored no regrets in remaining single after Caldwell had left her with her daughter, Gwenn, and Jessup, still three weeks from being born. For a while, Anna had weighed her pride and sanity against the financial security that a thimbleful of local men might have afforded her; her pride had won, and she'd never bore the weight of bitterness or despondency she might readily have accepted in the lonely wake of lost hope. She'd gone on to Camden State College and been glad for it, though, more and more often lately, she felt regret at having lied to Jessup about his father. She'd told him the story once, making him promise not to repeat it, concocting some reason she now forgot, but that had been enough, at the time, for him to believe. She regretted, too, swearing Gwenn to secrecy; Gwenn had been nine at the time and had known the truth. In those few years following Caldwell's desertion, Anna had given, if not more love, certainly more concern and care toward Gwenn. She'd protected her daughter as well as possible from careening toward a lonesome future with dogs and sloths. Not that Anna hadn't taken on a few men, herself. Here and there. In confidence. She had. Though she'd always felt as if she'd betrayed herself in some vague way. The last of the men, a boy really, whom she'd happened upon at a pig roast three years ago, who'd been charming and attentive, at first, who'd perhaps given her a bit of hope, had proven, in the end, to be as idiotic and reckless as he had been young and hard; he'd broken her car windshield with a bat when she'd called it off.

In her warnings to Gwenn, Anna had not realized that she'd tainted her daughter against all men, painted the entire species as shiftless, so her daughter, instead of being wary and insightful, instead of holding out for a good man, had settled time and again for the foul and slovenly, unaware of any other kind. Good men *did* exist, fine men, Anna knew. But she did not want to love any of them. To be *intimate*. Love was a choice, of the mind more than of the heart, the heart weak and forever so desperate to indenture itself; it was a struggle she had no room for, to accept a stranger into her life; for that's whom even the best could hope to love, a stranger, with all their inevitable failings.

With her attention given to her daughter, she'd blindly allowed her sweet boy to grow up a castaway. She'd had the idea that a son could adjust more naturally than a daughter; there was less that might harm a boy, alter him. It had been luck alone that Jess had come out as well as he had. He was like a weed that had miraculously bloomed as lovely and precious a flower as any cultivated plant. As a child he'd played alone, amused himself without concern or need of friends, his behavior peculiar and furious as he dug holes in the yard or tried to revive dead baby birds that had fallen from their nests. Perhaps in all the energy Anna had spent trying to keep the world at arm's length from Gwenn, she'd neglected her boy. She worried that his childhood independence might lead to resentment or loneliness, or that his naiveté might be taken advantage of, now that he had to adjust to the world she'd worked so desperately to keep from her daughter. He was all she had.

Jessup looked at a mosquito that had lighted on his arm.

"You should have a shirt on." Anna rose from her chair, a hand on his shoulder.

"A mosquito's got to eat," he said.

She shook her head and took her empty plate into the house.

Inside Rosie's Hardware, Reg stood before shelves of spray paint.

He picked up a can of black and shook it, the ball bearing growing sluggish; he looked about the small, disorganized store and sprayed the back of a piece of sandpaper: FUCK. Paint bled onto the floor. Nodding, Reg placed the can back and ambled past the house paint, past plumbing fixtures that occupied dusty shelves like lesser artifacts, discovered and discarded.

In the far corner of the store fanbelts hung from hooks in elongated figure eights. The store smelled of rubber and oil. Reg tugged his cap over his brow, creased its bill. Above him a fluorescent light flickered and burned out, leaving him in shadows. He moved down the aisle.

Jumper cables. Gasket epoxy. Antifreeze. Radiator sealant.

He stared at the fanbelts. Took one down. He flipped a toothpick end over end with his tongue.

"Hey."

A voice and a clasping hand on his shoulder startled him and he jerked around, toothpick snapping and falling to the floor, the fanbelt squeezed in a tight, fist ready.

"Didn't mean to scare you," Edsel said. A gallon of paint hung by it's handle in his delicate curled fingertips.

"Well yah fuckin did. Sneakin up on me." Reg planted an open palm flat on Edsel's chest and pushed by him. He worked his tongue at the phantom toothpick. "Got a belt that would work on Marigold's pickup?"

"We don't stock belts that would fit anything that old."

Reg set the belt down on a stack of car batteries.

Edsel hung the fanbelt back on its hook. He opened the lid of a machine caked with dried paint drippings, clamped the can in it and shut its lid. The machine shuddered. "So what are you up to these days?" Edsel was ripe with the smell of cologne and sweat, the faint odor of . . . baby powder?

"Gotta get some spray paint for the Camino's fenders."

"You came to the right place. The road salt's the devil's work. Can you believe that snow yesterday? Snow in August. I've seen it all now."

"Have yah?"

Edsel shrugged. "You need sandpaper, too. I bet."

"Got plenty."

"You'll find it in aisle number four. By the spray paint."

"What'd I say? I seen it over there. Heard from yur old man?"

"Just last night. I guess they're going to stick it out in Orlando."

"That right? Shackin up, huh?"

"Your ma says to say hi." He cocked his delicate wrist. "Hi," he said.

Reg worked his tongue along the inside of his lower lip.

"I don't know how they can stand it," Edsel said.

"Got sick of livin in the same fuckin place all their lives. The god-damned cold."

"It's over a hundred degrees down there," Edsel said. "*Hum*id. It doesn't get any better until November, either. I went down there once, when I was a boy. Disney World. Sweated my narrow butt off."

Reg couldn't recall Edsel ever having a narrow butt.

Edsel went on: "Me. I'll take the cold over the heat any day. What I say is, You can always put on more clothes, turn up the heat, to keep warm. But you can only strip down until you're naked. And if you're still too hot . . . well."

"I'd rather not hear bout yah strippin naked," Reg said.

Edsel removed his glasses and wrestled with the monofilament that secured the lenses. He pinched a lens in the corner of his red smock, rubbed it between his thumb and index finger. He rested the glasses back on a pug nose forested with blackheads.

"Got air-conditionin don't they?" Reg said.

"*Every*where. People run their air-conditioned cars to air-conditioned stores and back to their air-conditioned house. Good way to catch cold. I had a runny nose the whole darn time I was there. It's not for me."

Edsel retrieved the paintcan from the stilled machine. "What kind of paint were you interested in?" he said. "I've got a wide variety of finishes, for all kinds of different jobs. You'll want something for metal, of course. Automotive. Let's go see what we have for auto body. We don't have a selection as great as I'd like. But I'm working on upping a lot of the inventory. It's not enough just to have it on the shelves. You need to have some out back, too. For the unlikely customer." He moseyed away, the paintcan swinging like a favorite lunchpail.

Reg walked behind him, in the wake of his stench.

Edsel straightened up the rows of spray paint, by color. "Let's see. We have flat, semigloss, gloss, hi-gloss, eggshell, oil, latex, enamel, acrylic, alkyd." He pointed at each respective paint product. "You'll want black, of course. I'd keep that cool El Camino black. How's your Galaxie running? Getting it all ready for the Autumn One Hundred?"

The Autumn 100 was the biggest race of the year, held annually on the third weekend of September. Reg had won three out of the last four, missing the one two years ago, when he was at Fairland.

"Carburetor's fucked," Reg said.

"That's a shame."

"I'll be up to Caratunk anyhow. Fishin."

"Well. There's always next year."

"Be down to Carolina next year."

"Carolina?"

"NASCAR."

"You're going to be a mechanic for NASCAR?"

"Gonna drive."

"Drive?"

"That's the plan." Reg cracked his knuckles. "Can't be chasin my own tail on lousy dirt tracks all my life. Charlotte. Waynesboro. Darlington. Those're the places to test my luck, my skill. If yah wanna make it, yah gotta set yur mind to it, the old man used to say."

"I always liked your father," Edsel said. "That will be quite a challenge, racing. Must be pretty hard to get into; a lot of sacrifices, I'd think. Hardship."

Reg thought of Pap lying on the downstairs couch. He thought of himself, the pillow in his hand. "Hardship and me get long all right," he said.

"Won't be the same without you tearing it up at the Barre Fifty next summer."

Reg grunted. He grabbed three spray cans of flat black.

"Darn it," Edsel moaned. He examined a piece of sandpaper, shook and lowered his head as if looking down at his old dog that had just been hit by a truck. "Vandals." He showed Reg the graffitied piece of paper. "Who does a thing like that? Destroys something? For kicks?"

"Pity."

"I can't sell it now. Here, you might as well take it."

Reg looked at the warped piece of 80 grit.

"No charge," Edsel said.

Reg took it.

They walked to the front of the store, to the register.

"You want me to put that on an account?" Edsel said.

"Account?"

Edsel disappeared behind the counter, shot back up again with a slip of paper clutched in his hand, as if performing some magic trick. "Here, just sign your name. You have thirty days. No limit. I'm running this show now, and want to gain a greater client base by showing a recip'ocated trust." He set the slip on the counter. He shook a ball-point pen, handed it to Reg. Reg held it awkwardly. Stared at the slip.

Edsel tapped his finger at the bottom of the slip. "Right there. On the X."

Reg squinted and scribbled next to the X.

Edsel brought out a calculator and began to punch keys.

From his wallet, Reg took out the yellow slip he'd found by the Camino.

"Found this," he said.

Edsel looked up from the calculator and took the scrap of paper; he turned it over in his hand.

"Whose is it?" Reg said.

Edsel made a clicking sound at the back of his teeth. "Can't say."

"Yah can't tell?"

"I can't say. Customer confidentiality. It's one of a few folks. I've only had five patrons, *six*, counting you, sign up for the unlimited credit plan."

Reg grimaced, repulsed by the thought of how close he and Edsel were to becoming family, even if only by law. "Who're the five customers?"

"I can't say. Policy."

"Jesus."

"Why do you care, anyway?"

"Got a feelin it's a friend's."

"I didn't know you had friends."

Reg picked up a rubber ball from a counter display, bounced it once, squeezed it. "Someone I told not to fish my spot without me, anyway. Found it fishing and thought, if it was his, I could trap'm in a lie, wring his neck." He winked.

Edsel shook his head. "Mr. Detective. Well, it wasn't a friend's."

"Tell me."

"No can do."

Reg rubbed the .45 through his jacket and shirt. If it were anyone besides Edsel, Reg would have gone behind the register and taken the goddamned credit clips himself. But Edsel would announce to the next fifty customers how Reg had attacked and robbed him.

"You going to Broken Leg Lake after the One Hundred?" Edsel asked.

"Dint plan on it."

"I'll be due for some drinking by then. A little carousing. Work hard. Play hard. Right? You ought to go." Edsel glanced at the slip of paper. "The Lavalettes will probably be there, though."

"And?"

". . . Nothing. They aren't your favorite people, that's all."

"Ain't no one's favorite people." Reg thought maybe Edsel was hinting at the slip being theirs; the Lavalettes. Edsel would never reveal the name on the slip, directly, especially if it was Elis's or Mack's. Couldn't blame him. The Lavalettes drew no lines.

Reg pointed at a shelf of ammo behind the counter. "Gimme a box a them forty-five rounds."

"At your service." Edsel reached behind him on a shelf of ammo boxes and stacks of fishing and hunting licenses. He tossed a box on the counter. He picked at a scab on his elbow. "What do you have for a weapon?"

"Got this." Reg lifted up his camouflage jacket and shirt. He drew the .45 out from his pants and set it on the counter. Edsel peered around the quiet, customerless store.

"Forty-five. Army issue. Was the old man's," Reg said.

The bluing was worn to steel on the hammer and trigger guard. Edsel shook his head and whistled. "That is a fine piece."

Reg picked the .45 up and sighted down the barrel at Edsel.

Edsel ducked and wove as if being buzzed by a bee. "That thing loaded?" he said.

"Don't use it to pound nails." Reg shoved the pistol back in his pants and pulled his shirt and coat over it. He grabbed a handful of jerked beef from a glass jar and stuffed it in his shirt pocket.

"How many do you have there?" Edsel said. He had the pen in his mouth, blue ink smudged his fingers and lips.

"How's that?"

"The jerky." Edsel pointed at Reg's pocket with the pen.

"Don't know, a few. Five or six. Five." Reg picked up the box of shells; his jagged fingernails scarred the smooth waxed cardboard. He looked at the box in his hand. "Say there ain't any limit on this credit?"

Edsel hesitated. "No," he said.

"Might's well make it two boxes a shells."

After dark, Jessup lay on the living room floor with an old *Field and Stream*, while Anna sat on the couch, her legs drawn beneath her, she in just a cotton slip as she worried over a crossword in the glow of a brass lamp, scribbling and erasing, scribbling and erasing.

She sighed and squirmed, rubbed her feet absently, then looked up as if someone had spoken and said, smirking, "Why don't you fix your tired old ma some iced tea?"

Jessup glanced up from his reading, stood and strolled into the kitchen.

He returned from the kitchen with a tray of sugar cookies and two glasses dark with tea. He moved aside his magazines and set the tray down on the coffee table.

"Here." He handed her a glass.

"Thanks." She drank half of it, then set it down, sweat gracing her upper lip.

He sat at the other end of the couch, chugged his tea and thumbed through his magazine. He munched on the cookies, crumbs collecting on his T-shirt.

Anna sipped her tea, then held the sweaty glass to her forehead and stretched out her legs so her bare feet rested in Jessup's lap.

"Mind?" she said.

He took one foot in his hand and pressed his thumbs into the bottom of it, massaged.

"That's nice," she cooed.

With his free hand he sloshed ice in the bottom of his glass. He tipped the glass, crunched ice cubes. He continued to rub his mother's feet. She closed her eyes. She sang: "My Bonnie lies over the ocean, my Bonnie lies over the sea. . . . "

After a while she stopped singing and said, "Gwenn used to rub my feet. You do it like your father. Forceful, but you take the ache away. Gwenn tickled too much."

He smiled and plied her feet, rubbed and pressed until steady breaths expelled from his mother's open mouth; her bosom rose and fell. Her nose twitched.

He removed her feet from his lap and slipped from the couch and slowly, quietly, ascended the stairs to his room. In the attic he crouched beneath the steep-pitched roof, the heat ferocious, sweat creeping over his skin, and moved to the center of the room where he was able to stand. Above him hung a caged lightbulb.

He undressed.

Beneath him was Gwenn's old bedroom. Her twin bed still covered with a quilt, its edges sharp and precisely tucked. Two tiny windows allowed a view of the shed and the cedar swamp. On the bureau stood, unmolested, photos of forgotten high school friends.

For weeks, during the winter Jessup had been seven, Gwenn's sobs

59

had seeped up through the floorboard joinings like the weeping of a lonesome ghost, tormented by its murderous end. He'd never spoken to Gwenn about it: So many years older than himself, she'd always seemed more an aunt, a kind aunt, than a sister, and besides, the sound of her moaning had lulled him to sleep.

One night, when her crying had not risen to him, and the house was silent save the faraway clamor of the basement furnace, he'd grown concerned. He'd listened for her sobs. Lain on the floor, ear pressed to the pineboards. After several minutes of silence, a fear, which seemed both ludicrous and perfectly rational, snuck over him: She'd hurt herself. He'd crept downstairs stealthily, afraid to disrupt the quiet.

In the hallway outside her room he'd paced, wanting to burst through her door, knowing he'd need to break it down, knowing somehow it would be locked, perhaps her bureau and desk blockading it from the other side. He'd wanted to rush in and rescue her from whatever was to blame for her silence. But he hadn't. He'd hid outside her door, glaring at it, listening. He'd edged closer, knelt at the blade of light escaping from under the door. But he'd seen nothing but the legs of her bed, a slipper. He'd stood still, cheek to the door, and listened to the door itself, life in the grain of the wood. He'd been about to pound on the door, to shout "Is everything all right?" when she'd coughed. And the house was again alive with noise. The wind whining in the chimney. His mother snoring in the next room. The toilet, its handle stuck again, trickling endlessly. And Gwenn coughing, and sniffing. Clearing her throat. Scratching her calf. Drinking her nightly warm milk. He'd sworn he'd heard her writing, the tip of a ballpoint pen digging into the page of a spiral notebook journal.

Soon after, she'd departed for New York City with her boyfriend, Carlton, and it had been Jessup who could not sleep for his own sobbing. He'd missed the sound of her stirring beneath his room. The murmur of her radio playing late-night talk radio out of Canada.

Gwenn had written over the years, from Pennsylvania, Michigan, North Carolina, Florida. The last letter had been postmarked Amarillo, Texas; she'd written that Carlton had left her and good riddance, and Leonard, Jessup's nephew, had finally, nearly, outgrown his homeliness, though he sure could use some braces. *P.S. Don't* ever *get involved with nobody unless you love 'em.*

Jessup stepped across the attic among a ruin of books, careful of nails that jabbed through the plywood roof. He stood beneath the lightbulb; pulled its chain. The room fell dark. He pulled the chain again, illuminating the room. He pulled on the chain repeatedly, the light strobing, his motions reduced to something cartoonish and exaggerated. Now I'm here. Now I'm not. Here. Not. Here. Not. Like Gwenn. Like Emily. Like my father. He yanked the cord until it broke and the room fell dark, except for a soft flood of moonlight at the far gable window.

He lay on his mattress on the floor, and fumbled around in a cardboard box he kept beside it. He located the candles and placed them on a sheet of old tinfoil agglutinated with years of melted wax. He found a wooden match and lit the candles. The room trembled in candlelight and shadows writhed on ceiling and floor.

Jessup took out Emily's letters, unbound them, and read them all, over and over again, memorizing them. It seemed as if he'd never see her again. As if he'd only imagined her. He bound the letters together and placed them back in the box.

He picked up the nearest book that lay on the floor and opened it to the middle.

19 September—All last night she slept fitfully, being always afraid to sleep, and something weaker when she woke from it. . . .

Hands jammed deep in his fatigue pockets, Hess walked a back road beneath a moonless sky of stars. Mud glopped about the soles of his gum boots, dark and leaden. He was not drunk, but wove like it, his eyes closed, a severe hitch in his step. He opened his eyes to find himself nearly in the trees.

He hunched his shoulders up, vulturelike, against the cold night. In his chest a heaviness, the size of a balled fist, sat like stone. He thought of it as his old self, compressed down to a dense core. At night this heaviness woke him, spoke to him as if to warn him of coming tragedy. But he turned an apathetic ear, as if it were the voice of an old dead love calling in the middle of the night, liquored and brimming with pathetic sentimentality. Twenty, thirty, forty, nights now, he'd awakened to the voice and roamed the roads. Each night he ranged farther and farther, up Gamble Hill, or down, to discover another untraveled dirt road. On one occasion he'd walked a logging road through Prince Paper land. But this had deeply saddened him, and he'd run wildly back down to Snake Mountain Road.

He'd worked for Prince Paper. Cleared the Canadian Co-op-Power lines that cut through Prince land, constructed dams in the Moose Bog quadrant; the Feds, these days, paying Prince to create wetlands. With a DC-10 he'd dozed cut tops and wastewood into brooks, flooded hundreds, thousands of acres. He'd operated a skidder, slogging stripped sixty-footers out from the clearcut to the header, where they were craned onto Macks and hauled to Haven's Mill in Montgomery, or across the Connecticut to Granite Falls, New Hampshire. Timber had been in him as God was in other men. Each morning he had risen in the dark, the day awakening languidly, silently, with him, as he rode with Albino, the foreman, and the crew up into Buells Gore or Ivers Mountain or Woodpecker Ridge. He'd loved to breathe in deeply the lumberyard's sour wet redolence of pulp in the early morning sawdust haze; he'd loved to work the forest, bereft of natural sound and order as the men slaved their dozers and skidders, horsed their Husqvarnas and Stihls, as those before them had whipped and prodded mules and oxen and drafts, worked their crosscuts and bow saws. He'd loved the sweet and acrid stench of chainsaw exhaust as it ribboned through the stands of trees and among the men like a silky blue thread of mist tying each of them to the other. He'd loved how, come Friday, his voice would be ragged from a week of shouting warnings and instructions above the engines' din, over the screech and moan and crack of massive trees that crashed through the branches of the unfelled, thundering a shock tremor through the ground so it quaked the soles of his boots and shuddered through his bones.

During lunch, after the catastrophic noise, the silence and calm was magnificent. Whitetail deer, normally wary, had learned that the silence meant treetops and buds could be found on the ground. Within minutes the deer would appear, stealing through the woods, unable to resist the tempting browse, even as, a few feet away, the men sat on stumps and gas cans and saws, ate lunches from paper sacks, admiring the deer and bullshitting about hunts gone by and their chances for the upcoming bow and rifle seasons.

Each day had left him as bruised and lame as a drunkard's dog. In the evenings he'd ridden with Albino off the mountain, back to the lumberyard, so tired his head would bounce off the window as the truck bucked down the skidder roads.

At home, he took a cold beer from the refrigerator, stripped to his underwear, and stretched out on the love seat, Marigold beside him, swabbing his face and chest with a wet washcloth, then sending him off to a hot shower. When he'd come back out, refreshed and clean, he'd felt as if he could crush the world; the slow ache in his muscles a reward as he'd wolfed down his supper as if it were his last.

But now . . . now . . .

He'd been working out in front of the trailer, clearing brush to burn. The weekend-warrior chainsaw he'd used, light and easily handled. And then. Somehow. The stones wet? a root? he'd slipped. He'd removed the safety bar from the saw, just the week before. Otherwise it would have shut off. For a moment he'd thought he'd regained his balance. But he hadn't and his legs had gone out from under him and he'd seen the chainsaw blade flash in the sun as he went down in the brush. Out of surprise, not pain, he'd howled. He recalled resting serenely on his back, listening to his deep hollow breaths and staring up into the sun, his hands lingering on his stomach and groin for a long time before he'd become aware that his jeans were sopped with something sticky and warm. Even then he'd lain there until, in a detached moment, as if he were asleep but aware of someone trying to shake him awake, it had dawned on him that he might be injured, that he'd been lying on his back in the secondgrowth below his trailer, a trailer, a life, he'd seemed, suddenly, to detest. He'd decided it would be best to stand. But when he'd tried his body had gone limp, his bones had turned liquid, and he'd looked down to see his intestines slip out; he'd tried desperately to catch them in his arms, to heap himself back into himself. But the pain. Sudden and fierce. Bewildering.

He'd been left spooked by machinery. Saws. His lifeblood. Scared to death of death. Even more of life.

After several weeks he'd gone back to work; but all that morning in the woods he'd obsessed over his injury, and when he'd lain his hands on the Stihl, he'd panicked and dropped the saw. He'd felt weak and sick, and had spent the rest of the day meandering among the men, forced to sit down often to collect himself. He'd not returned. He rarely went to town these days. His father and grandfather, both dead, had been loggers, and the embarrassment of running into any of the men had become torturous.

He wondered how he would ever get back to what he was before. If it were possible. If that was what he even wanted. Perhaps he'd been injured for some reason he had yet to understand. Some greater cause. He told himself if this were the case, perhaps he could live with it.

An owl lifted from a splintered larch limb, coasted silently above the road, predator's eyes searching remnants of a stone wall for careless mice.

Hess rubbed the inside of his right thigh through the hole in his pocket lining. His gait lame, eyes closed, he worried that, at any moment, the scar might split and his intestines unravel, his stomach and liver and heart spill in a reeking heap onto the ground before him.

The owl, on a felled larch stump, ripped at the mouse with its hard beak and swallowed.

PART II

"Where are you?" Marigold said, pacing as she switched the phone to her other ear. "Already? I'll be right there. Don't go anywhere." She hung up. "Hal's home."

Hess didn't budge from where he lay on the love seat.

"He got in last night. With Lucian," she said, thinking how during the cold and snow of two weeks ago, it had seemed as if time had stalled, would never pass.

She opened the refrigerator. A jar of mayonnaise, a can of spaghetti sauce. A quart of milk. Little else. She closed the door.

Hess buried his head under a pillow.

"You want to go with me?" She walked into the living room. "Lucian dropped him off at the Bee Hive, on his way to set up at the fairgrounds. I'm going to bring him to Ma's." When no reply came, she walked down the hall, fingernails tapping the walls.

She whistled. She sang.

The bedroom smelled of sweaty, sexless, sleepless summer nights.

She looked at herself in the cracked mirror atop her bureau, which was crammed into the corner, her image asymmetrical. Her skin was tan, but her nose had burned and peeled many times, and was pink and freckled. The tan was reddish on her cheekbones and pale along her hairline. She teased her hands through her hair. The humidity frizzed her curls in a way she'd never been able to manage. She hadn't had her hair cut all summer; it was past her shoulders; she'd need to get it cut to go on job interviews. The weight she'd lost startled her. Her fingers bonier than she'd ever remembered.

She selected a white sleeveless blouse from a box and held it up before her. It was wrinkled and had a grease spot on the pocket, but it was the best she could do. She grabbed a pair of black jeans, red panties and socks, then shed her T-shirt and cutoffs, her bra, smelled her underarms. Jeans and blouse in hand, she skipped to the bathroom and shut the door.

She splashed her face with water, hot first, then cold. She brushed her teeth and gargled, plucked her eyebrows, ran a stick of lipstick across her lips, kissed a square of toilet paper and tossed it in the toilet. Dressed, she put on a pair of cowboy boots, and went out to the living room. "Last chance," she said and kicked the couch. "Suit yourself."

Jessup stood in the parlor of the Barker place, stretching a white cotton glove onto his hand, then swept a finger along the piano keys. *I am the butler,* he thought, *I did it.* He performed a clumsy pirouette and tore the glove off, flung it, as if he were some beloved matador tossing trifles to his adoring crowd. He bowed, clunked his sneakers together. He took a bandana from his jeans and tied it over his head; piratelike. He kicked his sneakers off into the fireplace.

"Let's get to work," he hollered. "Let's not let the little lady down." Though he'd not heard from Emily since before Labor Day, he'd held out hope that she'd be coming on Columbus Day, as she'd last written.

In the kitchen he set his pack on the island and unzipped it; steel wool pads, sponges, and rags fell to the floor along with cleaning products and tin candle holders. He picked up the supplies and aligned them beside his pack on the butcher's block. He took out the rest of the items: candlesticks, linseed oil, a small pillow, plastic flowers and a plastic vase.

And something else, too. A single condom, which he'd wrapped in a square of tinfoil. He'd bought a dozen at Govey's Drugstore, put a ten dollar bill down on the counter and hurried away. All week he'd practiced. After struggling with the first few condoms, he'd decided it helped if he was excited. Though he couldn't seem to stay that way when he tried to put them on. They felt like seal skin and smelled of surgical gloves. He had the one left.

From the corner he took a metal bucket downstairs and came up through the bulkhead, into a day buzzing with sunshine and insects. Mindful of his bare feet among loose nails and slate shingles, shed by the house, he bushwhacked through burdock and milkweed to the backyard. Finding a spigot he filled the bucket.

Inside again, he squeezed a glob of liquid soap into the bucket and stirred the water with his hand. Bucket foaming, he padded out of the kitchen to the entryway.

Daylight crept across the floor.

He went to his knees, sponging, bucket at his side. All afternoon, as the sunlight arched through each southern window and pooled on the floor, he knelt and swabbed and rinsed, hauled buckets of filthy water to dump over the porch rail, filled it up again at the spigot, the burdocks finally claiming his scarf. Perched precariously on the piano bench, he whisked cobwebs from the chandelier, then set about dusting the mantlepiece, the hearth, windowsills, mopboards, and doors, raising a maelstrom of dust and flotsam that slowly settled to the floor. He swept it all out the door with a push broom, then surveyed his work, sweating and smiling.

He hauled couch cushions out onto the porch and beat them with a broom. He beat the pillows until his arms were too tired to lift the broom. He licked his chapped lips. He dunked a rag in the bucket, pressed the cold cloth to his face and forehead. "There," he said and strode back inside to collect his rod and creel, pausing at the doorway and imagining how surprised Emily would be to see how clean their house was.

Reg sat at the wheel of a doorless windowless '78 Cutlass Supreme in the back part of Skinny's Salvage Yard, where untold derelict late models, in every state of disrepair and disintegration, rested among the gnarled ghosts of crab apple trees and wild grapevines.

The Oldsmobile's hood was open and Skinny was under it, nothing but his ass showing.

"Giver a try," Skinny barked. He slapped the fender and stepped back from under the hood, hands on his bare hips, just above his sagging blue work trouse. "G'on," he ordered. "Crank the motherfucker up."

Reg turned the key and raced the engine. It screeched like a suffering animal.

Skinny waved his hands frantically. "Cut it. Kill it."

Reg did.

"Fuckin whorebag." Skinny slammed the hood. He jerked his T-shirt down from where it hung on the Cutlass's antennae. The antennae warbled. Skinny, who *was* skinny, except for his gut, pulled the shirt over his head and stretched it over his stomach. It rode back up.

Reg got out of the car. "Need a carb for the Galaxie," he said.

"Got one carb like that, but it's probly worsen the one that's in yur's already. Probly ain goin find nothin less yuh g'nup to Montreal. Yuh ain't given up on that racin shit yet?"

Reg looked out over scores of wrecked cars and trucks, a number of which might have been his. "I figure I'll give NASCAR a run."

"Go south and yuh'll be dealin with niggers everywheres, an assholes callin yuh Yankee all time."

"No one says Yankee anymore."

"Dont say nigger neither. Fuck they're still yammerinbout the war. God's fuckin truth." He raised his right hand. "My sis lived down to Carolina a few years. They got confederit flags flyin like it were yesterday. Yuh'll havta put up with Yawl this and Yawl that. Noshit."

"Listen," Reg said. "I need a water pump, too. For Marigold's old pickup."

"That, I probly got, if I search longnough." He leaned on the fender of a gutted Firebird.

Reg kicked one of its tires. "These rims fit my Camino?"

"Them's Pontiac rims, idjit. Might be able to use a Malibu's. Havta check. But I ain't fuckin round out here no more t'day. Smoke?" He rooted in his pockets and produced a brass bowl and a baggie. He broke a bud apart in his palm, picked seeds, flipped them into his mouth and chewed. He packed the bowl, rolled the baggie up, licked it, and stuffed it in his pocket. He took a hit and handed the pipe to Reg.

Reg wiped the stem and smoked. He held the pipe out and looked at it, squinting.

"Somethin wrong?" Skinny said. He took the pipe.

"Where'd yah get weed like this?"

Skinny tamped the pipe out on his leg and slipped it back in his pocket. "Elis," he said. "Its kind. Good clean high in front the skull; don't put you in a fuckin fog. Elis's got himself a green thumb. Mack, too."

"Early," Reg said.

"How's that?"

"Said it's kinda early."

"Think them two's growin outta their new place, that old A-frame offa Avers Gore. Growin inside. Yuh got any this year?"

"Will. Soon. More than yah ever saw."

"I seen plenty." Skinny swam his hands down the front of his pants and arranged himself. "Plenty."

Jessup fished, the Lamoille slapping and curling at his knees. The wind bore a metallic scent, and he looked up to see, along a spine of distant ridges, rain falling from stormclouds in dark misty bands. But the rain wouldn't reach here. Here, the sun shone. He waded against the current and cast, his line lofting in a graceful arch, to settle lightly on the surface. The current swept it downstream.

He reeled in, sighing at the sight of the lime-encrusted banks opposite him. Yearlong, chunks of farm pasture broke loose from the banks to tumble into the stream. From the honeycombed banks, swallows swooped low across the river, perched briefly, nervously, on the lips of their nesting holes, then glided back, bellies skimming the river's surface. Jessup forded back to the near side.

On shore a tiny fire snapped, flames nearly invisible in the daylight.

He squatted at the river's edge, fire to his back, and dumped two brookies and one rainbow from his creel onto the stony beach. Nothing to brag about. *Trout.* Where *were* they all in this secret pocket? Scarce, the natives anyway. These days hatchery trucks journeyed to the most remote corners of the state, dumped into streams and ponds tasteless, softfleshed fish that had been raised in cement runways and fed liver pellets. Junk fish. "Too many fishermen, these days," the town said. "That's why there aren't any good fish." *No.* Look at all that *lime. Phosphorous.*

He gripped a brook trout in his palm and slipped his knife from a hip pocket, unlocked the blade and drew it cleanly through the fish's glowing white belly. He severed its head, the entrails coming with it, trailing like fleshy ribbon as he tossed it all up on the bank. He did likewise with the next, then ran the knife through the rainbow's belly, keeping its head intact. He washed his hands in the river. The dried husk of a stone-fly nymph clung stubbornly to a rock, as if refusing to admit the body it had held was not returning. The September water was warm yet, and teamed with black-nosed dace, creek chubs, and other flashing schools of minnows. Cool nights would soon lower the temperature. Get the trout active again. His rod and creel rested on the bank, the worms in his coffee can putrid in the sun, the trout put down for the day.

He lay back in the grass.

His one good friend from junior high, Todd Perry, had been his only fishing companion since those days at the reservoir. He and Todd had fished every chance they'd had, brought their rods to school, so as not to waste time going home for them at the end of the day. Todd was from Maine, originally, "last untainted state east of the Mississippi," Todd's father had pronounced. Todd's father was a retired air force pilot, who had never followed through on his promise to get hold of a sea plane and fly them into Canada.

It was Todd who'd said you called a fishing "pole" a "rod." More manly, Jessup had agreed. It was Todd who had told Jessup how trout grew more active when the barometer dropped. But it was Jessup who had taught Todd that sometimes tributaries held larger brookies than the big water.

Todd had talked about girls in the same brash manner his father had talked about women. Not having anything to add to this particular topic, Jessup would fall silent.

He and Todd hadn't *always* fished. They'd experimented with fire, too, burning anything from their houses they thought wouldn't be missed. One dawn they'd stolen the stack of the Sunday *Ivev's Daily* from the steps of Govey's Department Store.

They'd smuggled the wirebound stack out to a field along the Lamoille, soaked it with charcoal fluid. They'd been careful to start the blaze near the river, taken buckets to fill with water. But a wind had picked up and lifted burning sheaths of paper out into the dry hayfield. He and Todd had tried to stamp out the tiny fires. But the flames had spread quickly and they'd decided saving their own skin was more important and had run the mile back to Todd's house. It was still very early when they'd snuck in. Only after the town's volunteer fire trucks had sped past the house, sirens crying, had Todd's parents and two younger brothers stirred from their bedrooms.

Jessup and Todd had feared for weeks that a state trooper would come to their houses, force confessions from them. They'd vowed secrecy, vowed to go down together. But they'd never been caught.

The October of Jessup's first year of high school, Todd's father had been offered a commercial pilot's job, and Todd and his family had moved away to Colorado. Jessup had never heard from Todd again; Todd would've liked Emily.

Jessup looked up at feathers of clouds streaking across a blue sky. Far far away a jet sparkled, a chip of glass. He stared down a finger at the plane. "Pow," he said. A grasshopper flung itself from the bent grasses and landed on his arm, stroked its antennae.

Emily. Emily emily.

The Camino idled in the middle of Avers Gore Road, the late-morning sun magnified brutally through the windshield. Reg stared out at the A-frame. No vehicles were in the yard. No kids. No dogs. Beneath a balcony, a dirtbike and a snowmachine sat parked under a torn sheet of clear plastic.

Reg checked the rearview. Adjusted it. Nothing but empty road.

He flipped his cigaret into the grass, finished his forty and threw the bottle on the passenger's floor. He cranked up his window; acid rose in his throat. No one had answered the phone when he'd called from the Bee Hive earlier. He tapped the steering wheel. He twisted his class ring around his finger. Putting the Camino in gear, he drove down the road and parked. He took the .45 from the glove box and stepped out.

With his army jacket and headnet on, he grabbed an empty duffel from the Camino's bed and entered the woods.

A catbird hopped from branch to branch.

Reg lumbered toward the house, hunched over, feeling like a con just gone over the fence. A truck rattled by on the road and he pressed himself flat against a tree, holding his breath. When the truck continued on, he continued on. At the edge of the backyard he paused. A rusted charcoal grill stood on a cracked concrete slab under a window with a catclawed screen. Grass burst thick and lush where septic water seeped.

He was about to sneak to the window to catch a better look inside, when he heard low voices. He turned and saw, at the far corner of the lawn, against the woods, a girl. She was lying on a towel, on a massive rock, soaking up the sun. She was naked, a whale of a girl, her flesh reddened from the sun. Beside her sat a radio: the voices he'd heard. Next to the radio sat what looked like a box of cereal and a bottle of cola. The girl wore sunglasses and lay perfectly still; Reg couldn't tell if she was awake, or not. He stepped closer to the edge of the woods. Standing behind a dead elm, he looked at the house; the window was no more than twenty feet away. A few quick steps and he could be inside.

He looked back at the girl. She looked familiar, but he couldn't place her.

Her sloppy tits fell off to either side. He wondered who she was. What she was doing here. She couldn't have been more than nineteen. Where in the house were Elis and Mack growing? The basement? The attic? A closet? A false room? He looked at the girl. Her breasts were gargantuan. He felt himself harden against the pistol. He hadn't had a woman since just before going inside. He and Lamar had gone at the girl together. They'd picked her up at the Rusty Bucket. She'd been playing pool and doing shots, a college chick, plastered and coked up, who'd decided to get back at her boyfriend by slumming it. Reg couldn't remember her name. Or what she looked like. But he remembered how eager she'd been to fuck. Until she'd sobered some. Bastards, she'd cried, gathering her torn clothes from the motel room floor. *You FuckingBastards.*

The girl shifted on her towel; her bush sprawled down her inner thighs.

What would she do if she caught him in the house? What *could* she do?

What would he do?

He took another step.

Her hand flew up, slapping her stomach.

He stiffened.

She reached a hand between her legs, and cupped herself.

Reg rubbed himself; he looked at the window, then at the girl. She sat up and drank from the cola bottle; she propped her sunglasses on her head and looked around.

Reg slipped back into the woods, aching.

Jessup stood roadside, thumb thrust out, *a fugitive of justice on an unknown road.* Those who picked him up had best beware, his mug was on the post office wall.

The Santa Fe had given up on him. The chain had broken. He'd made an effort to fix it, but you couldn't fix a broken chain: A broken chain was a ruined chain.

He wiped both hands on his jeans. He'd hidden his bicycle in the corn, back where things had gone so wrong. His rod and creel were back there, too. The one fat rainbow trout already beginning to splotch with the milkiness of decomposing flesh.

A nice fish. Fought hard.

Reg drove the El Camino fast through S curves that dipped and crested alongside the Lamoille River. On the most severe of left curves he took the Camino across the faded double-yellow line and into the left inside lane, cranking the steering wheel until he had to fight its wanting to center itself, everything to the left, accelerating all the way through, resisting centrifugal force, and then giving slightly to it coming out of the turn.

He smoked a joint, reached for the beer between his legs and took a long pull. In the trees now, a blur of maples and beech, five feet around and tall as silos; their branches, laden with leaves the size of a man's hand, twisted and stretched across the road toward each other, blocking out the sun, the leaves rust-tinged. In the shade, his skin pricked with the temperature drop. Down an embankment, through a rush of thickets, the Lamoille flowed; quick glints of sun flashed as though countless silver dollars lay scattered just beneath its surface. He thought about the weed that was his for the taking at the A-frame. He thought of the weed Lamar was going to dump on him. He raised his beer out the window. "Yah *crazy* bastard," he howled.

Out of a last turn, mounting over a steep blind rise, the Camino's body lifting from the frame, he felt weightless as he shifted up to fourth, dumped the clutch and trounced the accelerator. The Camino catapulted from the trees and into a wash of sunlight. A blue September sky. Nothing ahead but straightaway for two miles to test the top-end speed, the faded asphalt marred with wide black snakes left by dragging Camaroes, Malibus, and other V8s manned by drunk boys in the hours before dawn. This far out, no local authority, only state troopers, not straying too far from the interstate, and not staying.

He jammed the lighter into the dash, lit another joint.

Tar turned to dirt as trees gave way to cornfields; the corn, this September day, green and tall as it would ever get. The fields grew wider and wider, the Lamoille tucked out of sight along a line of alders that grew beside its banks.

Right hand resting at twelve o'clock on the steering wheel, left arm out the window, hand rubbing the door, petting it. Eighty-five miles an hour toward more trees and shade and curves, Reg bowed his head, heeding the engine. The temperature gauge vibrated. Seemed to be a ticking sound; it was hard to be sure. Might have been a stone in a tire, the fan belt. But, no. No. Tick. Tick tick. Slight and inconsistent. Goddamned loose lifters. The engine was running hot, too. Otherwise the engine thrummed along, a low hum, like the one in his head from the beer, the dope, and the September sun pouring through the windshield, warming his face.

He tugged his hair back over his ears and reached to the passenger's floor for his cap. With the cap just out of reach of his fingers he leaned over farther; the Camino swerved, the wheels shuddered and Reg, fixing his eyes back on the road, saw that he was heading straight for a hitchhiker.

"Jesus Christ," he said, stomping on the brake pedal.

Jessup stood listening to the rustle of the corn's whiskery leaves, thinking they sounded like rats rummaging in newspaper, when a black vehicle rocketed out of the woods. Bearing down on him it swerved and rode the shoulder kicking up dust and stones. For a moment Jessup believed the vehicle would drive back onto the road and avoid him. But it continued to barrel violently along the shoulder, and was upon him.

He jumped, tucked and rolled down the embankment to land in the corn. Red clay smeared his forearms and shins. The air smelled of burning brakes. He stood slowly, afraid, waiting for a flash of sudden pain, a flow of blood. He brushed his jeans. His bare chest and stomach were scratched; he picked road grit from his palm; he seemed okay, a bit dizzy, but okay. He took a step and grinned. His heart beat strongly. He was not angry at the driver. Rattled. Yes. And curious.

At the top of the bank the black vehicle idled, its chrome bumper flashing in the sun.

He scrambled up the bank to the driver's window. "Close one," he said, standing, his hands loose at his sides. The guy tapped the door with a pinkie ring. A cigaret hung from his lower lip. He wouldn't turn full around to look at Jessup. He adjusted the sideview mirror, licked his thumb and rubbed at pieces of insects that stuck to the glass, leaving black, smudged fingerprint whorls. It seemed the guy was eyeing something in the mirror; Jessup looked back down the road. No vehicle in sight. Alone out on the long flat strip of earth between the corn.

"Never seen yah," the driver said.

"I thought I was going to get run down."

"Never seen yah." The driver adjusted the mirror; face like a freshly uprooted turnip. Dirty and narrow. Unshaven. His eyes lay hidden behind mirrored sunglasses. "Was reachin for my cap on the floor and . . . never mind. Yah wanna ride? Still. I mean after me nearly runnin yah down, I don't know I'd jus hop in with me. Yah caught me on a good day."

Jessup nodded. "El Camino," he whispered. Black; *just* the color he would have, if he ever owned such a vehicle.

"How's that?" Turnip said.

"El Camino."

"Wanna ride, or not?"

Jessup nodded.

"Get in."

Jessup made to hop in the El Camino's bed. There was a wheelchair back there and some firewood.

"No. Up front. Here. With me." Turnip patted the seat and reached to unlock the door. "Had a dog jump out the back once."

Jessup nodded and got in, his feet struggling to find a home among saws and levels, shirts and bottles and cans. The cab smelled like—sour milk, and something else, too . . . skunk.

"Never mind all that crap. I'm Reg." Turnip offered Jessup the cigaret. Jessup declined with a wave of his hand. It wasn't tobacco. Turnip had yeasty breath, and a deodorizer with a picture of a nude woman on it did nothing to mask the cab's stench; the nude woman's arms were folded across her bare breasts, so Jessup couldn't quite see her nipples.

Turnip stuck the cigaret out to him again. His hand was trembling. "Sure?" he said.

Jessup looked out his window.

Maybe he should have walked.

"More for me," Turnip said. He smoked, hitching raspy breaths into his lungs. "Christ," he said, his voice high as he held in the smoke. "That one's in there, that one is over the *fence*." He blew the smoke out. "How bout a beer then? Grab me one, at yur feet, there. Then we can get this show on the road." Jessup grabbed two gritty cans and handed one to Turnip.

Turnip gunned the engine and the Camino tore up chunks of sod and they fishtailed back onto the road. Turnip palmed the wheel, bringing the Camino under control as he accelerated.

Jessup looked at the can; he peeled back the tab. Foam erupted from the teardrop opening, dissipated, and streamed down into his crotch. He wiped at the seat, shrugged and took a sip. It was all he could do not to spit it all over the windshield. Hot. Flat. It didn't taste like he thought it would. He forced a swallow, worried it might come back up.

Turnip drank unchecked, wiped suds from his rutabaga chin. "Listen to that. Yah hear that? Fuck."

Jessup tilted his head and squinted.

"Sounds like shit don't it?" Turnip said.

Jessup didn't hear anything.

"That tickin. Loose lifter. Rebuilt the whole damn engine and carburetor in April. Carburetors'll be the death a me." He stomped on the gas and the El Camino lurched forward, accelerating at what seemed a dangerous clip. The wind shrieked through cranked-down windows and whistled in through what looked like a homemade sunroof. Barn chaff, cigaret wrappers and straw papers swirled in the cab before being sucked out the window.

Jessup couldn't see the speedometer.

"Hear it? Hear it now?" Turnip asked, twisting his body and hunching over the wheel, ear nearly pressed to the windshield.

Jessup shook his head.

"Tick. Tick. Tickety fuckin tick. Like that. Mother of God. Lifters sound like fuckin baseball cards in bicycle spokes."

"I don't know much about cars," Jessup offered.

"Don't got to know anythin bout it to hear it. Yah can't hear that?"

Jessup leaned forward, put his ear to the dash and listened. He sat back and shook his head. He didn't have the ear for it.

"Some mechanic y'are," Turnip said.

Farms, with their dusty barnyards, mountains of split firewood, sugar houses and machinery, new and in disrepair, passed by like carnival sideshows. Toiling men and women, playing children, and dogs stretched out in the shade of trees, as if they might die there, all looked up at the black bomb as it sped by and beeped. Turnip waved and grinned like the crazed winner of the Daytona 500 making victory laps. Beep. Wave. Beep beep beep wave wave wave. BEEEEEEEEEEEEEEEP.

Folks waved back hesitantly, seeming uneager to acknowledge such a reckless driver. An endangerment.

"Whadya doin out here anyway?" Turnip asked. "Yah one them transients or somethin?"

"No. I live just outside of Ivers. On the Dansbury line, out on Turkey Lane?"

"Long walk, Turkey Lane."

"My bike broke down."

"Dint see no bike. I'm on th'other side a Ivers, but can go out yur way. What happened to yur bike?"

"Chain got ruined. I stashed it in the corn."

"Be a bitch gettin it out. How'd the hell'd yah get it down in there?"

"Just pushed her."

"Them chain drives are crap. Yah oughtta get a shaft drive. Five up, one down, at your toe, fifty in first in about four seconds. Unless yah're strickly off-roadin it. Then I guess a chain's all right. What yah ride? Piece of Jap crap?"

"A Huffy. A Huffy Santa Fe. A ten-speed."

"Oh. A *bike* bike. A pedalin bike. Well. Sonofabitch. What yah doin ridin around on one of them ass bruisers? What're yah, eighteen?"

Jessup nodded, lying. He feigned a sip of beer, then hung the can out the window and poured half of it out. He rested his arm gingerly on the hot doorframe.

"Gotta good eye at guessin age," Turnip said. "Hal. My brother. He's got the gift. Runs a booth on the fair circuit. Jus finished the one in Albany. Travels from California to Florida and up to Maine. South in the winter. North in the summer. Been out west this year. The Rockies. Kill to see them Rockies. Might be movin out there, someday, when I retire from racin."

Racing, Jessup thought.

"I only see that bastard Hal when he does the Ivers's County Fair." He polished off his beer and chunked the can out the window. "That's his life, guessin folks' weight and age. Two things they most lie about. After how much money they make."

Every year at the fair, Jessup passed these booths; fat men, slack-jawed and stubbled-cheeked, who barked and spat into saliva-soaked microphones. The crackling speaker shrieked: "Guess your weight!

Guess your age! Right here. Only two dollars! Right here!" An accusatory finger pointing: "What you got to *lose?*"

Jessup looked out the window. On the far side of a piece of corn, above the Lamoille, a pair of wood ducks wheeled and jacked into the alders.

"Ladies do it, hoping Hal'll underguess," Turnip continued. "It's a big compl'ment, to be seen as younger or slimmer than yah are. Makes all that junk they put on their faces, and them crazy diets, seem worth the money. But, boy, if he overguesses. He's a goddamned fraud. It's on the up and up." The cigaret jiggled in Turnip's mouth, and Jessup wondered if he was all right to drive. Turnip went on: "He used to practice on the family. We used to have family comin out the ass round here. Cousins comin out the woodwork. Everyone's scattered now. Shame. It don't feel the same. Like home. Hand me another, there? Grab that last one for yurself, yah sure do drink slow. We used to have reunions every summer. Barbecues, really, since we were in pissin distance of each other. Hal'd guess everyone's weight. The aunts were the hardest, got fatter and fatter, though some lost weight so fast yah swore they was stickin fingers down their throats. Hal set up a stand once. Under our dying elm tree."

Dutch elm disease. The summer Gwenn left, the elms in Jessup's yard had lost their leaves. The following summer, branches fell like broken arms and fingers, and soon the morning air was filled with the hammering of woodpeckers driving bills into punk wood. After that the trees had to be cut down: a danger in storms.

"If yah ain't gonna drink that other beer . . ." Turnip snapped his fingers and pointed at the beer.

Jessup, hesitant, reached down for one and pulled its tab, handed it to Turnip. Turnip's fingers, rough and dry, rubbed against his own. Turnip threw his empty beer can out the window, took a long drink.

"You shouldn't do that," Jessup said.

"How's that?" Turnip pressed his beer can to his bottom lip.

"Throw things out the window."

Turnip considered him; the Camino drifted across the road, into the oncoming lane, toward the corn on the other side. He took a sip of beer. "Someone'll pick it up, return it for the money."

He looked back at the road and, unfazed by the fact that they were seconds from crashing, steered the Camino back onto their side.

"Hal had this stand set up in the yard," he continued. "When he was a kid. Like a lemonade stand. Had this sign, 'Guess yur weight and age within two pounds and two years—one dollar.' So he's always had a bent toward that kinda work. He's got it good. Makes money doing what he loves. His own boss. Sees the sights. So yur eighteen. How come yah ain't got no car?"

"It doesn't run."

"What's wrong with it?"

"I don't know." Jessup spilled the rest of his beer out the window.

"What is it?"

"A Vega."

"Mmm-hmmm. Year?"

"I'm not too clear on that."

"Uh, huh. Well, yah oughtta get it fixed. Guy needs wheels. A place to mess round with girls. Yah gotta be mobile. Like now. I've gotta deliver my brother's ass from evil. That's his chair in back there." He ran a finger around the rim of the beer can. "Hal," he said. "Funny story. How he got crippled. Couple years back. He's sittin on the porch one night. Ma's porch. Came back for a visit after bein gone out west. He's sippin a beer, unwindin, and outta the swamp and into Ma's garden steps this deer. Big buck. Big rack. Hal's got his rifle right there, next to em. Like he always has when he's kickin back on the porch, in the evenin. So he can shoot coons. Well, he eases the rifle up. Slow and steady, takin his time. And he takes a shot and jacks another round in and fires and the buck drops right there in the corn, and Hal, he jumps up from the rockin chair to run out there in the garden. But his legs had fallen asleep on him, see, and in his big rush, his upper-body movin, but his lower body asleep, his legs collapse under him and he falls off the front steps and lands wrong. That's what the doctors said. Hal asked, 'How can this be?' And they said 'Yah landed wrong. We're sorry. Yah jus landed wrong.' Hal's kept on truckin, though. Pumps iron. His arms are huge now. Huge. Course his legs are nothin."

"That's crazy. That's awful," Jessup said.

"It's normal."

R   E   A   P

Cows stood in a field, shorn from grazing, save where dark clumps grew among clods of manure. Late-growth dandelions dotted the fields with their yellow heads. "HEY LAY-DEES! HEY THERE LAYYY-DEEEEES!" Turnip called, waving at the heifers. His voice shrill, he laid on the horn. "HEY GIRLS! HEY LADIES!" He finished his beer and tossed it on the floor at Jessup's feet. Jessup grabbed the last one and handed it to him.

"So. Hal calls me this mornin. Wakes me up. He's at Ma's place. Says, 'I need my old chair back.' I keep his old manual one in the shed out there at my place on Unknown Pond. Hal likes to cast for spawnin brookies, long the shore. Easier for him to get round in the manual one. He calls and says, 'My motor's on the fritz. And it don't work without it.' 'What,' I say, because he paid a fortune for the goddamned thing. Few fuckin grand. Well, insurance did. Ma's house insurance. I say, 'Yah mean yah can't jus wheel round with yur arms?' and he says he can't. I say, 'That's somethin. That's really somethin. Pay as much for it as yah would a snow machine and it don't run worth a damn without its batteries.' Is that somethin. Or what?"

"It's something," Jessup said.

"That's what I told em. 'Three thousand bucks for a wheelchair that don't work manually. That's somethin. 'Well,' he said, 'Never mind all that. Jus get out here.' He don't know where Ma put his crutches, not that they do em much good. He's settin in the middle of the livin room, waitin. Had to crawl cross the floor to get to the phone. Lucky I kept the phone hooked up."

Turnip jerked the wheel and raced the Camino down a one-lane road. Grass and saplings swashed the undercarriage.

"I got to put this joint up. It's got me all pie-eyed. Sure yah don't want some now?"

"I'm sure," Jessup said.

Driveway gravel crunched beneath the Camino's tires. Turnip killed the engine and planted a palm on the horn. "We're here," he said, twirling his collection of keys. "Come on."

He hopped out, tall in his boots.

Jessup stepped out and shivered in the shade of a ravine, which rose behind the house, eclipsing the sun's warmth and casting the yard into deep shadow. Here, in the yard, and the surrounding woods, the green of maple and oak leaves were bloodied with autumn.

A sound, a voice, words lost in the walls, came from within the house.

Turnip stood at the tailgate, yanking on the latch. He took off his sunglasses and tucked them in his shirt pocket. He turned his cap backward, and pulled on the tailgate's handle; his black seaweedy hair looked like a woman's cheap wig. The tailgate would not unlatch.

Jessup hauled himself into the Camino's bed; rust flakes snowed from the rear fender wells. He grabbed the old wheelchair, brushing off pine needles and twigs, and handed it down to Turnip with a huff.

"Remind me to fix that tailgate," Turnip said.

Jessup nodded, leapt out of the back. The air smelled of rock and moss and wet earth. Blue jays shrieked and mocked, unseen but for a blur of misfit blue and the spring of cedar boughs, their attack on the chickadees' suet thwarted by the Camino's arrival. Chickadees flitted from ground to branch to suet to porch rail. Wee chirps and warbles like a nest of baby mice.

"Jesus *H*," Turnip shouted, chickadees disbanding into the trees. "If yah don't like my beer, dont fuckin *waste* it. *Shit*." He hefted the chair up the porch steps, careful to step over the third stair, split and rotted from water that had dripped from the cracked raingutter. Moss plagued the cedar-shingled roof.

Nearly the whole length of the El Camino's passenger side was smeared with beer. Jessup's face grew hot. "I'll hitchhike the rest of the way." He got on his knees and spat on the El Camino, rubbed his palms in circles on the door.

"No. Jus don't waste beer. Don't pour it out all over my fuckin Camino. Come on, meet Hal."

Jessup licked his palms and rubbed.

"Stop it, fore I hurt yah," Turnip said. "Hal's been stranded long enough."

Jessup walked up the steps, the third one flexing beneath him, telling himself he'd make a point of washing the Camino for Turnip, in return for the ride.

A plywood ramp lay propped beside the stairs, on the edge of the porch. Following Turnip, Jessup stepped through a dark doorway, into a dismal unlit house. He blinked in the darkness. In front of him climbed a steep set of stairs, its balustrade ending at a decapitated newel. The afternoon sunlight diffused feebly through a leaded window, as if through murky pond water, a gloom settled among broken railing spindles. A strong scent of skunk came from a room out of sight, at the end of the narrow corridor.

"My *hero*. My brother, get in here and get me in a fucking chair that *works*." The voice like the shriek of an outdoor spigot wrenched open after a bitter winter. A voice destined for a dime-store microphone. Jessup clawed at his scalp, tore bits of burdock from his hair.

"I'm in *here*," screeched the water spigot.

"I know where yah're. And I'm gonna leave yur ass if yah don't quit yur fuckin cryin."

Turnip unfolded the manual chair and set it on a hardwood floor marred with black streaks that looked like puck marks on hockey-rink boards. He pushed the chair down the hall, its tires squeaking.

Aged black-and-white portraits of military men dangled from wires against walls shedding wallpaper. The wan pupils of the subjects pleaded for remembrance. Jessup slowed to regard each one. No photos of the flood. No men who stared back at him with his own eyes, smiled his own horrific smile. He trailed his fingers along the wainscot. The odor of skunk was so loud he prepared for an attack of them, grasping his toothbrush.

The living room was vast. The ceiling vaulted and propped by beams of dark ancient timber. Chunks of firewood, charred to carbon, rested in a cavernous stone fireplace above which hung a moose mount. Deer heads were mounted on the other walls; some possessed magnificent, thick-tined racks, others were spike-horns, or so old their heads were shaped more like a dog's than a deer's, their dusty glass eyes without life. In the middle of the room, a sculpted slab of a man from the torso up, the ruin of a man from the waist down, sat erect in his broken wheelchair. A scrap of muscle T-shirt clung to his massive hairy chest. His face was mottled red and sweaty, as if he'd just stepped out of a hot shower. His palms beat on the chair's armrests. Eyes, the color of cooked porkchops, looked Jessup over, weighing him.

"Yur chair, sir," Turnip bowed, wheeling the good chair around so it faced the dead one.

"Christ almighty, this thing. Get me out."

"Good to see yah, too."

Jessup looked at an etching of a steamboat being hauled behind two locomotive engines, along a railroad bed: *The Ticonderoga. Last Steamship to Commandeer Lake Champlain.*

"Who's this?" Wheelchair said, and nodded at Jessup.

"Hitchhiker."

"He got a name?"

"Jessup," Jessup said.

"What's he doing here?"

"He's on his way to Turkey Lane."

"And?"

"And I almost ran em down, least I can do is get em home; sides, the Camino's lifters are loose and I need to take a spin, listen to the engine. I'm goin up to Caratunk bright and early and I don't wanna have her runnin rough."

"Help this moron," Wheelchair said. "Get me out of this contraption."

"Jus get on the other side of it, and grab him under the arms," Turnip said.

"I'll do most the work," Wheelchair said.

Wheelchair released his slack legs from the metal wings and they fell to the side, lifeless.

"Okay, on three, lift me up, and turn me, so I can sit in the good one."

"Ready?" Turnip said. "One . . . two . . . three."

Wheelchair did most of the work.

"Freedom," he said, manipulating the wheels with his palms so the chair spun and tipped backward, small front wheels spinning. "Now maybe I can get something done today. Marigold's sposed to be coming back. Two minutes after she left the thing gives out on me."

"Why dint yah have Lucian help yah? That's what yah pay em for."

"He's working the fair." He set the chair back down from its wheelie and considered Turnip.

"I gotta get goin," Turnip said. "But I need to talk t'yah later."

Wheelchair glanced at Jessup. Then looked back to Turnip. "About?"

"Skinny gave me a lead."

"Lovely."

"Gave me a few ideas I checked up on."

"You better check your ass, see if that's where your head is." He didn't seem to be joking. He seemed angry.

"Look. I gotta go," Turnip said. "We'll talk."

"My hero." Wheelchair saluted him.

Turnip jerked a thumb at Jessup.

Outside, the blue jays protested.

Jessup wiped at the beer along the Camino's fender, then got in and shut the door.

Turnip got in and lit a cigaret.

He started up the Camino and began to back out, but hit the brakes.

"Jesus H," he said.

Jessup turned around to see a stake-bedded pickup a few feet away.

"Nearly rammed her ass," Turnip muttered. "Girl can't fuckin drive."

A woman, thin, but not tall, got out and walked over to the El Camino. Despite her slightness, she had hips.

"Hey," she said, leaning into Turnip's window. When she turned her head, the sun caught her kinky hair, highlighted varying shades of bronze and blonde and red. Her eyes were alert, and gray and shiny as splitshot.

"Hey, nothin. I fuckin near smashed into yah. What're yah doin?"

"Hal called me for backup. In case you got lost." She had cheek-bones that appeared and disappeared as she spoke.

"*Lost.*"

"In case that engine of yours blew up."

"Fuck him."

"Who's this?"

"Jessup," said Turnip.

"You must be hard up," she said to Jessup.

"My bike broke down."

"Why didn't you get Mr. Mechanic here to fix it?"

"Hmmm?" Jessup said.

"Nothing. Why isn't it in the back? His bike?"

"I don't know," Turnip said. "Guess we shoulda got it. Was it far from where I almost run yah down?"

"No."

"Why dint yah say nothin?" Turnip asked.

Jessup shrugged. "You were nice enough to give me a ride."

"Shit."

"Where'd you pick him up?" Marigold said.

"Back on the flats, past the Isham farm," Turnip said.

"Fishing?" she asked.

"Huh?" Jessup said.

"Were you fishing? That's a good stretch."

Jessup nodded.

"Anything?"

"Small brookies," he said, not mentioning the rainbow. Hand in his pocket, he flicked the bristles of his toothbrush. New stiff bristles.

"Listen," she said. "I'm headed back home. I'll be back out here to work the fair in an hour or two. If you want, I'll give you a lift. Get your bike. I got a load a firewood you can help me unload where it needs unloading."

Jessup looked at Turnip.

"Works for me," Turnip said.

"Let's go then," she said. "We should get your bike before dark." Her eyes scanned the darkening trees.

"Okay. All right." *Flick.*

Jessup eased out of the Camino. "Thanks."

Turnip nodded.

"Don't forget to fix the tailgate," Jessup said.

"Already forgot," Turnip said. "This weed short-circuits me."

The house was in shadows, and, downstairs, in part of the house Jessup had not been in, a window leaked an eerie pale blue.

"Listen," Turnip said. "Yah wanna go to the fair, for nothin, talk to her. Now get that fuckin junk outta my way."

They jumped up into the rumbling truck.

Her slim hand slipped into his. Fingers soft as sumac twigs. "I'm Marigold," she said.

"Like the flower," he said, not smiling, but staring at her.

She stared back.

"Like that," she said.

A cigaret hung from her lips, but she didn't light it.

"I got matches. I don't think they got wet, fishing," Jessup said. He lifted his butt off the seat to dig in his pockets; he pulled out lint and nickels and pennies, chewing gum, packages of hooks, loose splitshot; careful not to reveal his toothbrush and paste, he managed to extract a pack of matches. He struck one; it fizzled and stunk the cab up with burning sulfur.

"I don't smoke." She smiled. "Just keep them in my mouth to curb the urge."

"That's smart." He scratched at a mosquito bite at the back of his neck.

"You sure go a long ways to fish. For just having a bike."

"I like fishing."

"I gathered."

"That stretch is good. Water's still kind of low. And warm. They still aren't biting all that great."

"I don't bother with down there till late in the month, or October."

"You *fish?*"

"Sure, I fish. Probably fished that section longer than you been around. How old are you anyway?"

"Sixteen."

"How come you aren't in school or working?"

"I'm done with school. I tested out. And I can't find anything that pays worth working for. I don't need much money. I do need to get *some*. I got a friend coming to visit."

"What do you know how to do that's worth paying for?"

"I can do things."

"Like what? What can you do?"

"Well. I've been painting my mom's shed."

"Painting huh?"

"Sure. Painting. I paint. Fix things. No cars. But other things. I was going to make some cards up. You put em at stores and stuff. In the windows, sometimes at the counter or on a bulletin board. You know, people come in, they see a nice new card. I give free estimates."

"That's good."

She walked her fingers through her hair, then tried to dial in a radio station, but the radio only crackled.

"You want, sometime I'll take you to some ponds I know of. In October. For big native brookies," she said.

"I know places. Up past Lewis Pond, all that Prince Paper land, you go back in—"

"Everyone knows those places," she said. "I mean *secret* places. And *big* brookies. Brookies you size by the *pound*, not the inch."

"Who knows about those places up on Prince land?"

"Who doesn't?"

"How? It's so far in."

"Excited boys like you. That's how. Running your traps. I'll take you north of there."

"North? That's all posted land."

"So? It's just signs. Who's anyone to say I can't fish a stream?" Jessup had never thought of it that way. Flower slapped his thigh and a cord of heat unwound from his guts and spread to his groin as if he'd wet himself after holding it for a long time.

"Best time of year for brookies is in October, when they're spawning. Only time of year you can get them to strike when they're not hungry."

"I love their spawning colors," he said, sitting up. She *knew* her trout. "How their white bellies glow and the male's jaws hook so fierce, their bloodstreaked fins. They're the most beautiful creature. Don't you think?"

She nodded. "Tell you what. Last day of the season's always the best. It's on Halloween this year. The latest day it could be. We'll go. You come by, and I'll take you to a beaver pond that will stop your breath. You pack the lunch."

"I could make sandwiches. Bring sodas."

"You do that."

"If you mean it."

"I do. There's only two things a person has: their thoughts, and their word. My Pap used to say that."

The truck meandered along the washboard road, just more than idling, its engine whining, the stink of antifreeze and burned oil drafting in through the open vents. They passed in front of a particle board shack, spray painted black and stuck back among a snag of fallen, decaying elms; it looked like a big chicken coop backed up to an outhouse. Jessup could scarcely see the jungly yard for all the trucks and runny-eyed, ewe-necked horses milling about. A three-legged mutt ran out from beneath a jalopy, hobbled and jerked along-side the truck, its jaw bleeding strings of saliva; Jessup watched in the sideview as the mongrel yelped and snarled and snapped at the truck's tires. It kept with them for a spell, but tired finally, and fell off to the side of the road to roll over in the dirt, writhing, rubbing and scratching, screwing itself up like it was gun shot; then it rose from its cloud of dust and pissed on a rusted milk can, into which a mailbox post was jammed.

The truck trudged around the corner and out of the trees, the road running between the corn now. Up ahead an enormous quavering sun melted at the end of the dirt road, smearing itself into the earth, the sky left bloody.

"Look at that," Jessup said.

"Hmm?"

"The sky. The sun. It looks so big, setting. Close. Like if you sped up we could drive right into it."

"Good luck in this truck."

"When I'm on my bike and see the sun like that, sometimes it feels like, if I pedaled as fast and hard as I could, I would get closer to it. Reach it. Dumb, I guess."

"It's nice. Hang onto that way of thinking."

June bugs and fireflies winged from the cornfields to tick against the windshield, their spattered, neon green innards sparkling. Flower turned on the headlights.

"This is a good truck. It's not a junk, like Turnip said." Jessup slapped the seat.

"Turnip?"

"Your brother, he kind of looks like a turnip."

She glanced out the side of the window. "I see," she said. "He's grubby as one. He's right, though, about the truck. It is a junk."

"Sits up nice and high."

"Most do."

"Rides good. Good color, too. Kinda camouflagey, just in case."

"In case?"

"Of trouble."

"You plan on getting into trouble?"

"No. It can sneak up on you though. Like with my bike breaking down."

"Where'd you stash it anyway?"

"Up at the big dead tree, in the middle of the corn up here."

"You get a flat tire?"

"No. My chain came off and got all snaggled. I think it's broke."

"Maybe I can look at it."

"It's pretty broke, I think."

"Well, I'll look at it. Then you can help me drop this wood off the Handsons. I need to go home and eat before I go to work at the fair. I'm running late. You want to go to the fair?"

He played with the window crank. "I guess, sure. I have to call home first."

"We'll see you call."

"All right."

"You hungry? You want to eat with me?"

He was.

He did.

Hess awoke, suddenly, on the couch; a nightmare clung to him, then fell away.

The sun angled through the window. He could smell himself, his stink from weeks of infirmity. He sat up on the edge of the couch, sweating. His hair matted and greasy. Slowly, he became aware of the trill of birds outside the window. Straightening his shirt collar, he stepped to the door and gazed out; a flock of starlings sat along the telephone line, arguing. He stepped out onto the cinderblock steps. The sun was hot on his face. The birds quieted, then took into hurried flight. He went back inside.

In the bathroom he undressed and stepped into the shower. He recoiled from the hot water, then gradually grew accustomed to it and began to scrub himself. A filthy gray residue polluted the water that spiraled down the drain. His hands roamed over his groin. He scoured and scoured. Leaning back against the stall he bowed his head in his hands, feeling like a warrior come home from battle. He hucked up phlegm. The water ran cold and he got out.

Back in the living room, sniffing around a pile of dirty clothes, he threw on the least filthy of his jeans and T-shirts.

Outside, the sun tapped his eyelids. He touched his face, wishing he'd shaved. He walked down to Gamble Hill and stood in the middle of the dirt road, looking up and down the hill, hands on his hips. The sun grew soothing. He took a step, a tiny breath of dust puffing about his boot. He picked up a stick and twirled it, used it as a cane. The air smelled of pine and cedar.

Coming to the one-lane bridge that spanned Cobb Brook, he sat down, and dangled his legs over the edge. The brook ran clear, spilled through the alders and poplar, trickled around rocks, pooling below them, then continued on under the bridge and into the pines. The pebbled bed rippled below the surface; he could feel the coolness of the creek on his face. Brook trout darted from shadow to shadow, shadows themselves. He dropped pebbles into the current, wishing now that he'd gone with Marigold. It might have done him some good. He'd always liked Hal. They hadn't spent a lot of time together, but those few times when Hal had traveled through town, early on, before his own accident, they'd managed to get in some bow-hunting, or collect honey from the beehives Hal had maintained in back of his Ma's place. Hess had enjoyed his company. Hal was easygoing. Grounded. Reg, on the other hand, was a dreamer, always scheming, a lost cause for these parts.

A Bronco rumbled down the road, squalls of dust chasing behind it as it gained the bridge. Albino Racine sat behind the wheel. In high school, Racine's hair had gone white, thus his nickname. He'd married Louise Berdall, a quiet girl with an endearing simple homeliness and tremendous breasts that had caused plenty of boys to wake up to sticky sheets.

Hess got to his feet, gritting his teeth.

Albino cranked down his window and stuck an elbow out of the truck. A rosary dangled from the rearview, swayed slowly back and forth, its crystal crucifix catching the sun. Rifles gleamed in their gunrack.

"Hey Hess." Albino drank from a bottled cola. "You're a sight. What're you doing out here?"

"Albino." Hess stepped closer and shook Albino's hand, his own hand feeling weak. Racine's red chamois shirt smelled of pulp.

"How've you been?" said Albino.

"Comin along."

"When're you coming back? Louise says I'm a grump since you left. Intolerable. Says I ought to harass you into coming back. Says you tempered me. I told her, 'The Lord tempers me.' Still, I'd like to see you back in the land of the living. Seen a moose up to the notch. Crazy with brain worm. You coming back soon?"

"I don't know." Hess cupped his hands around his eyes to cut the glare of the sun.

"That's what I tell her. 'I'm not going to bug the man. A man doesn't like to be bugged. He'll come back when he's ready.'"

Hess nodded.

"You need a lift?"

"Nah."

"Sure?"

Hess waved a hand. "I'm halfways there," he said.

"Suit yourself. You take care, now." Albino slapped the side of his truck and drove off with a wave. The truck disappeared between a stand of saplings.

Hess tramped on.

After a while he came out between Handsons' Fields, an impressive sweep of kelly corn that rolled away on both sides of the road to points beyond sight. A stiff wind threshed the crop and Hess could hear the whisk of leaves as the corn leaned beneath the wind, swelled and settled, swayed and changed directions at once, like a flock of blackbirds. The sun was poised low and red and intense over distant ridges baring great swaths of clearcut forest.

Hess's eyes burned and he felt tired; his pace slowed. He held a palm to his forehead to staunch the flow of sweat. He'd forgotten his stick back at the bridge, but possessed no desire to return for it. The sun bore down on him with a consuming, bodily heat, the desolate country road seeming now to stretch away to nothingness.

As he came upon the end of his mother's driveway, he stopped to look up at her house; Max was in the yard, sitting at the picnic table, husking corn; beside him stood a brick barbecue, the air above it wavering with heat. The smell of burning charcoal filled the air. Max stopped husking to drink a beer. He looked up and spotted Hess.

"Clare," he said, his voice loud. "Clare, get out here."

Hess had hoped to find his mother alone, for once. As he turned away from the house, he could feel Max's gaze on his vaudevillian movements, hear his voice behind him: "Never mind. It's all right."

At the Handson place the boy had unloaded most of the firewood from the back of Mildred, while Marigold had spoken with Nat. The boy did not take a break; in earnest, he'd grabbed chunk after chunk of wood and heaved it onto the growing pile. He would be sore tomorrow.

Marigold pulled Mildred into her yard; the lawn had become long. The mower had died weeks ago and Hess had not bothered to look at it, let alone fix it. "Hey," she said. "Can you do me a favor, can you run down and grab me my mail? I forgot to check the box."

"Sure," he said. He climbed out of the truck and slammed its door and was halfway to the road by the time the hinges on the trailer's front door squeaked.

Inside, the trailer was dim, the shades drawn, the air still and humid. Marigold hurried about, picking up stacks of magazines from the floor and coffee table, shoving them beneath the love seat; she dumped Hess's spittoon cups into the sink, picked up his heaps of clothes in the living room and heaved them into the hall closet. She ran to the bathroom and sprayed a potpourri aerosol throughout the trailer. It did little to put down the stink of cigarets and soiled clothes and spore.

She pulled back a shade and looked out the window to see the boy bustling up the drive and across the sea of grass and briars that was her lawn. He stopped at the door and knocked, lightly.

She played with her hair. "Come in," she said, as she opened the door.

The boy scuffed his sneakers on the top cinder block, stepped in. He looked about the trailer while Marigold searched the kitchen for a couple of clean glasses. The sink and counter were a disaster of filthy dishes. "Be right with you," she said. He didn't reply. He was at the end of the hallway, peering into her bedroom. Keeping an eye on the hallway, she hid the grimiest of dishes in the oven. She searched the rest of the cupboards for a clean glass, for something to cook. She shouldn't have asked him back for dinner when she had so little food, and was in such a hurry. She shouldn't have asked him back at all. Most days, lately, she ate in town at the Bee Hive or the Railroad Car, bought pre-made sandwiches at the Lucky Spot; sometimes she forgot to eat at all. The past two weeks, hauling firewood and checking want ads and driving all day to fill out applications, she would arrive home and realize she had let a day slip by without having eaten. It had paid off though; she had an interview, with a manager, scheduled at Mitel in three days. He'd liked her application and had called her personally, to say so.

The cupboards held spices, a lone cereal box, two dented cans of soup and three packages of macaroni and cheese. She used to bake fresh bread and chocolate steamed pudding. Steam green beans and peas and broccoli. She and Hess had grown a little garden at one time, early on. She opened the refrigerator, winced at the glare of the bulb. She looked at the bare shelves; an embarrassment: a head of lettuce rusted with soggy blackened edges; a quart of milk with less than a glass left in it; a couple of ears of corn wrapped in plastic; spaghetti sauce. She hung her head and covered her eyes with a palm, then shut the door quietly and leaned against it. Her arms loose at her sides, she stared at her surroundings, her home, the black grit packed in the seams of the linoleum, the cobwebs stuck to the window sash and the ceiling corners. The boy appeared from the bathroom and zipped his fly. Marigold turned away, wiping her flushed cheeks dry with the back of her hand.

When she turned back around, sniffing, the boy was gazing at a snow dome that sat atop the TV. He tipped the dome upside down, shook it, and held it in his palm, close to his face. He pondered the imitation snow that stormed on the plastic town. His head tilted as the snow swirled. When the snow settled, he jiggled the dome again, agitating the snow into a miniature squall. "These are the best," he said, and rubbed the felt bottom against his browned cheek and set it back down.

"I like this place," he said. "Cozy."

"Cozy. Thanks," she said, over her shoulder, the sink filling with water. He was polite and respectful, in an effortless manner. Cute.

"Smells nice, too. Flowery."

"Hey." She turned around again. "Why don't you open that door and let some fresh air in here, put the shades up? This place is a morgue."

He opened the door and pulled the shades. He cranked the windows open, the afternoon air cool and fresh and the wind billowing the frayed curtains.

She stood at the edge of the kitchen. "Best I can do is macaroni and cheese." He looked at her. She'd never seen such eyes.

"I'm a big fan of macaroni and cheese," he said. She considered his bare flat chest, so tanned. His eyelashes and brows were bleached to near invisible. He fidgeted, his hands in the back pockets of jeans that hung low on his narrow hip bones.

"It'll take a few minutes. We can eat in here, at the table. Sit. Sit."

He sat and rubbed his bare arms.

"We ought to get a shirt on you," she said.

He nodded. "My mom won't let me sit at the table without a shirt on."

She went down the hall and took one of Hess's shirts, checked flannel, from off the back of a chair; she sniffed it and walked back out with it. "Here," she said, and handed it to him. "It's not the best."

The shirt was big on him and he rolled the cuffs up on themselves, three, four times.

She sat across from him, listening to the water boil on the stove. When the macaroni and cheese was done, she served him.

He didn't look at her while he ate. Head bent, he scooped at his bowl, blowing on the elbows of pasta, chewed, wiped his mouth, scooped. He ate without speaking, except to say please and thank you when she offered a second and third bowl, another glass of water. Finishing, he looked up at her, then looked at the table and tore pieces from his napkin. "Thanks," he said. "That hit the spot after all that hard labor." He pushed his sleeves up even more and flexed his arm and felt his slight bicep. He rolled his sleeves down again, blushing.

"My specialty," she said.

"Excuse me," he said and got up and strolled down the hall to the bathroom. She could hear running water, and then, she thought, it sounded as if he were gargling, *brushing* his teeth.

When he appeared again, she excused herself and went to the bathroom. She flicked her toothbrush's bristles under her thumb. They were dry and the toothpaste was where it always sat, untouched.

In the living room, she looked out the front window. The evening had begun to stain the hills with its blackness. She was turning to go to the kitchen when she spotted a figure limping up Gamble Hill. "Shit," she muttered.

The boy had cleared the table and was running hot water in the sink, about to tackle the dishes.

"Don't bother with those. I'll get them later," she said. "I have to get a move on. It's late."

"I don't mind," he said.

"I have to get out of here." She grabbed a denim jacket from a nail in the wall. "Come on."

Outside the boy stood in the tall grass.

"Where's that road go?" He pointed up Skunk Hollow.

"That? Nowhere." Marigold hopped into Mildred.

"It can't go *no*where." A moth swam about his calves.

"An old farm. The Barker place. *Get in.*"

Hess was covering ground and would be at the bottom of Skunk Hollow soon.

The boy climbed in, pulling the door shut. "I've been up there. I go up there all the time. Did you know them? The Barkers?"

"Not really." The truck protested but started, and Marigold backed it out of the yard and headed down the hill. "They've been gone a good fifteen years."

"Sheep farmers."

"No. The family before them was."

"You wouldn't believe all the stuff up there." He looked out the back of the cab, toward the farm.

"I wouldn't mess around too much up there. You're likely to fall through the floor."

"It isn't that bad."

At the bottom of Skunk, Marigold yielded for a tractor hauling a hay wagon that seemed about to sway over onto its side. When the tractor passed, she pulled out onto Gamble, glancing in the rearview. He was only a couple hundred feet away, fetching and waving, shouting, his voice thin and strained. He limped a few feet then stopped and stood in the middle of the road, waving both arms over his head as if directing landing planes. As the truck gained the hill he grew smaller and smaller in the rearview, finally disappearing altogether as the truck made the next bend.

"I go the back way. The woods," the boy said. "To get to the Barker place. Figured whoever lived up this road might be watching out. Make sure no one went up there."

"You figured wrong," she snapped.

"I guess," he said.

"Well," she said, trying to return lightness to her voice. "I guess the trailer being on the same road has stopped folks from going up there, destroying and looting the place. Plus the stuff that happened up there. I'm still surprised it hasn't been burned down. You can use the road," she said. "Now that you know I'm not going to shoot you." She winked.

"Think I'll keep to the woods. I like the woods."

"Me too."

"We live in the right place."

"I would say so."

"Who was that guy?"

"What guy?"

"In the road. Waving."

"Nobody," she said, turning onto another road. "Nobody."

Headlights lit the front porch, and raccoons, rummaging in the trash cans, swaggered for the woods, chicken scraps hanging from between their teeth. With the engine cut and headlights off, Reg stepped out of the Camino. A brisk night air drew in and settled in the dark hills.

From the house's downstairs windows, slices of bright light severed out from the edges of drawn shades.

Inside, Reg heard Hal's voice from down the hall, in the kitchen: "That you?"

"No, it's Johnny fuckin Appleseed."

"Well come on in, Johnny. We can use your agriculture expertness."

The thunk of his boots preceded him down the hall. He thrust himself around the corner into the doorway of the kitchen, whipped his hands up from his sides as if drawing pistols. "You're dead."

Hal's chair was pulled up tight against the edge of the table. Before him were heaped hundreds of marijuana buds, green and tacky with resin and coated with red hairs and sugary crystals. Hal picked a bud from the pile and, with a barber's deftness, trimmed it of its leaves and dropped it into a paper grocery bag beside him on the floor. He picked another bud and repeated the process. "Gotta hand it to Lamar, about growing inside. Thank the crazy bastard for me."

Reg winked and opened the refrigerator. He grabbed a bottle of beer and popped its cap with a key. He sat down. "Goin up to meet him tomorrow afternoon. He was sposed to call me from the general store up there. But never did."

"Big surprise."

Reg shrugged. "This year's gonna be a fuckin bumper crop."

"Sure." Hal snipped another bud.

"We got all this here. We got the stuff up on Smuggler's."

"If it's still there."

"It'll be there."

"You gotta learn ta cut your losses."

"Gonna go up there first thing, when I get back from Caratunk. Couple days, we'll have all that, too."

"You hope."

"I know. And I got more ideas."

"*Ideas.*"

"From Skinny, runnin his mouth. Inside stuff. What I wanted to tell yah about."

"Don't go fuckin around in no one's *house.*"

Reg peeled at the label on his beer bottle. Winked.

Hal set his scissors down on the table: "I'm serious."

"*You'd* do it." Reg chugged his beer. "If yah could."

Hal picked the scissors back up. "I gave up that shit before I ever got fucked up. I had enough close calls. If I hadn't been in the woods that time at Moose Bog. If I'da been trapped in a house instead, those bastards woulda cut my fuckin balls off."

This from the brother who used to go to Norris Nursery each spring and wait until someone who didn't look like the gardening type bought manure and vermiculite, grow lights, chicken wire, and then followed them home. In the summer he'd return to the house and check the surrounding woods; if he found any plants he'd return in the fall, have Reg drop him off at night so he could raid a shed or barn or garage of drying plants.

Reg looked at Hal, ashed his cigaret in his palm, rubbed his hand on his jeans. "I'm careful," he said.

"Careful don't mean shit. Luck runs things. Fate. Whatever you wanta call it. No regard to you'r me."

"Could say that bout crossin the road. Good plannin *makes* yur luck. I wouldn't go into somethin blind. Without mappin it out."

"All I'm saying—"

"I *know* what yur sayin. Yah did things yur way. I'm doin em mine."

"There's a big difference going inta someone's house. Their *home.*"

"Not as far as I see it." He finished his beer and took another and leaned against the refrigerator.

"It doesn't matter how *you* see it," Hal said.

"If yah hadn't gotten hurt, yah'd've ended up in someone's house, eventually."

"Don't make this about me."

Reg scratched his beard. "Fuck it," he said. Hal wasn't going to buy what he was saying, see it for the opportunity that it was: Hal'd become jealous and self-righteous the past couple years.

"What're them desert states like?" Reg said, changing the subject.

"They're hot," Hal said. "They're deserts."

Reg put his cigaret out on the woodstove. "And?"

"They have a lot more color than you'd guess. They're not all brown and dried up. A lot of flowers. A lot of weird birds and animals. Lizards and armadillos and roadrunners and shit. Buttes and mesas, layers of red and orange rock. You look out over the canyons and you disappear. And the Rockies . . ."

"I'd like to see them Rockies."

"They're something. *Impressive.* I missed the green though. No place greener than here."

Reg sniffed the air. "This place stinks like a goddamned skunk from outside."

"That ain't good. Bringing that kid here wasn't too bright, either."

"He was in a jam."

"He runs his mouth . . ."

"Kid's straight as a stiff dick." Reg peeled the label from his beer. "He spilt beer all over the Camino cus he dint wanna *drink* it."

Hal whistled. "Still," he said.

The sound of toppling trash cans came from the porch, and they both turned quickly toward the window. Reg drew the .45.

"Coons," Hal said. "Kept me up all last night. Forgot what a racket they make."

Reg relaxed. "I'll shoot the fuckers."

"That's what we need. Noise. Whatta you doing with that thing anyway?"

"It's the old man's."

"I know whose it is. Whatta you doing with it?"

"Just in case."

"You go around like you're in a goddamned western." Hal held up a bud and pointed at a pipe that sat on the corner of the table. "Smoke?"

"Dry nough?"

"It'll light."

"Fire one up."

Hal lit the pipe, the bowl glowed orange. He held the pipe out to Reg, shutting his eyes and leaning back in the chair as he blew out a stream of smoke.

Reg tamped his thumb over the bowl and drew. He doubled over and coughed, the smoke coming back up in a tremendous cloud. His eyes watered and he pounded his chest with a fist. "That one's in *there*," he wheezed. "That's one's over the fence." Gaining his balance, he stood upright, grinning. "Jesus. Stuff'll cripple yah."

"The *Crippler*," Hal said.

Suddenly the room was lit brilliantly. Reg dropped the pipe. "What?" he whispered; the pistol found its way into his hand again; the safety off.

"Get down," Hal hissed, and hunkered in his chair. "*Down.*"

Reg sunk to the floor.

Hal wheeled the chair out of line of the window, peeked out the side of the curtain.

Reg crawled along the floor to the chair.

The light in the yard went out.

Marigold pulled into Ma's. She needed to get to the fairgrounds, in a hurry, the sky dark already.

The kid got out and grabbed the Huffy from the back of the pickup.

"Thanks," he said. "For the bike. And the food."

"You earned your keep. You'll be sore tomorrow."

"I already am. A little."

Reg ran out onto the porch.

"Goddamn it. What in fuck're yah doing?" He stomped over to the truck window.

"Dropping him off." She jerked her head at Jessup, who knelt at the bike, looking over the chain.

"Droppin him off?" Reg leaned in the window, rested a palm on the roof. His eyes were bloodshot and rheumy.

"I'm late," she said. "It took longer than I thought."

"What did?"

"The firewood. Eating. Now *this*. I gotta *go*."

"Got any cigarets?"

"No." She revved the engine. "I quit."

"What in hell am I sposed to do with him?"

"Bring him home. Bring him out to the fair later. I don't know."

Reg looked over his shoulder at the house. "Hal . . ."

"He'll live. Look. I gotta go."

"Get goin, then."

"I will if you let go of the truck."

He slapped the roof of the truck and backed away. "Drive careful. It's gettin foggy."

Marigold put Mildred in gear and then leaned out the window. "Listen," she said, calling Reg back over. "Don't get that kid high. He's a good kid."

"I was, too, once," he said.

Dark, and the bug zapper outside Clare's place crackled and spat purple sparks and the fried corpses of fireflies and June bugs, then subsided again into its low electric hum. Clare and Max sat at the picnic table, plastered to each other, opposite a sullen Hess, whose thumbnail scrawled designs into the tabletop. Moonlight glistened on the yard's freshly cut grass.

Earlier, when he'd seen Max in the yard, Hess had gone back to the trailer hoping to find Marigold, to tell her he wished he'd gone with her to Hal's, only to find her pulling out with some damned kid riding shotgun. He'd bought a sixpack at the Lucky Spot and drank it all as he'd hauled his ass back here, not knowing where else to go.

"You ought to go home," Clare said.

Max nodded, sipped from his can of beer. He pinched the silver stud in his earlobe. Clare took a sip of his beer.

"I don't know," Hess said.

"I do," Max said, his voice phlegmy.

Hess gazed over Max's shoulder and into a light that seemed to gush from the window behind him, blurring the edges of both Max and Clare in an enshrouding glow.

"The person you need to talk to is your wife. I don't . . . look," Max said and turned the slightest to Clare. She rubbed his bare back.

"It's not like we don't want you here. You know," she said, rising. She took Max's lighter and walked over and lit the citronella candles that bordered the lawn. The white flames lengthened and wavered in the breeze. Done, she sat back down with a sigh. She rested her chin in her palm and dragged on her cigaret, neatened her slacks. The aroma of citronella drifted in the chilly air.

"Being out here. It's not doing you any good," Max said. "We can't help what's wrong. You ask for advice . . ."

"A good sign." Clare lit a cigaret, picked stray strands of corn silk from Max's beard.

Max finished his beer and dipped his hand into the cooler next to him on the ground. He grabbed another beer and cracked it open, took a taste and placed the can on the table. "I know what accidents can do," he said. "At least you can still get around. You didn't get disfigured or anything. I mean. Our advice, *any* advice, isn't worth shit if you don't at least consider it. You got to get yourself out of this slump. Get back into your life."

"Which is?" Hess asked, still gazing into the lit window. His eyes felt like blown glass. The two dark figures before him, less distinguishable, dissolving. Their voices remote, as if calling across the calm broad waters of a lake.

"Well," the voice said, "whatever you had before. A job, for one. A job goes a long way toward making a person feel whole. You could go back to Prince. Claude would take you on, start you slow at first. Part-time. I could talk to him."

"I don't need *you talking* to my old boss." He rubbed his arms, the early September night cold, summerless. The light from the window shone as if it were the light of the holy ghost. It was all he could see now, the light, its blinding bewitching glare. He focused on it as if he were staring into the bulb from inches away, close enough to hear the heated tick of its filament. He spoke slowly. "I don't need no fucking handouts. I don't want to be loading any lumber the rest of my life, anyhow. I never liked any of that crap."

"Where would you work?"

"I don't know," he said to the light. "I don't ask *you* where you're gonna work."

"I don't keep coming to you for help."

"I need something that pays."

"With Marigold working, you can get by with something a little less than what Prince paid," Clare offered.

Hess blinked and the blinding light from the window lost focus and his mother's frame regained the foreground, stark and real. Her badly died auburn hair leaked at the edges and bled into her scalp. Her face was as brown and wrinkled as a peach pit.

"She ain't exactly working," Hess said. "When'd y'talk with her?" He ran his tongue inside the abscessed pockets of his lower lip.

"I saw her in town, day before yesterday. Going to get a truckload of firewood."

"That beater truck ain't gonna last her. And when I get work, she can bet she won't be running wild. There's plenty to do up to the trailer."

"That's what she was saying." Max finished his cigaret and was working on another beer. He lifted himself up to pull a sweatshirt out from underneath him. He put it on. "She'd just come from Rosie's. Bought a case of paint."

"I'm gonna do that. She don't need to be humiliating me more than I already am. Hauling wood and goin all over fuck."

"Well," Max said.

Fireflies winked about them.

Hess pointed at Max. "Don't *you* fuckin *well* me. *Don't.* Don't sit here and fuck with me and pretend like *you* didn't sit around drunk and mean for a year after losin your pissant job as school janitor."

Max knocked his knuckles on the table. "*You listen.* You come here. We accept you. Give you a place to get a grip on yourself. Give you advice and keep our traps shut when we don't think advice would do no good. And you don't so much as lift a finger. I get home from work and you're still lying on the couch like a dead man. Eat my food. Come and go like a goddamned teenager. So don't *you* confront *me.* Hear? I'll beat your ass right into the *motherfuckin* ground."

"*You* think."

Max rose, his jaw working. "You got one night left here. Tonight.

I don't need Clare worrying again if you wandered home all right. But don't come back tomorrow. Go to your wife. Go anywhere. But don't come back here."

Clare leaned across the table and pulled Hess's shirt collar up around his neck. Then she got up and blew out each candle and unplugged the bug zapper. The two of them, she and Max, hands around each other's waists as if to prop each other up, walked up the steps and disappeared inside.

A short time later the light in the window went out and Hess was left to himself in the dark. He didn't know what to do, where to go.

"Cock sucker," he spat.

He grabbed a can of beer from the cooler and threw it at the house; it hit the gutter and fell on the lawn. He tipped the cooler over, dumping out water and ice and loose cans of beer. He picked up another can and threw it; it hit the screen door. The can spun and spewed foam from its split side. A light lit the bedroom window. Max hollered. *Fuck* him. Hess threw two more cans at the light. The second one smashed through the window with a hail of glass. He could hear Max screaming. The living room light went on.

When Max came to the door, Hess had already floundered halfway down the hill, and was entering the woods, laughing so hard it hurt.

"What's he *doing* in there?" Jessup asked Turnip. They sat in the living room of the old house, Jessup slouched in a ripped leather recliner and Turnip stretched out on the couch. Jessup picked at a piece of duct tape on the chair's arm. When he and Turnip had first come in, Wheelchair had shouted from the kitchen for them to stay out in the goddamned living room, he'd be out when he was done.

"Cleanin up. Countin his chickens." Turnip winked.

"Smells like he's skinning skunks."

"That too." Turnip sat up on the couch and brought out a marijuana cigaret from his shirt pocket and lit it. He leaned back and inhaled as if drawing his last breath. His face broke into a smirk. He left the cigaret in his mouth and spanned his arms over the back of the couch, smoking without using his fingers. He looked at Jessup from under sloe eyelids, pinched the joint in offering. "Some," he wheezed.

Jessup shook his head.

"A beer *then*," Turnip shouted. He tapped the cigaret out on the floor. "*Yes, a beer.*"

Jessup protested, but Turnip was already standing, slapping his legs, as if to assure himself of their existence. He rubbed his face and pulled up on the band of his underwear, then left the room. Jessup could hear him banging down the hallway, hear the up and down of voices in the kitchen.

Turnip returned with a beer bottle in each hand. He handed one to Jessup. Jessup shook his head.

"Humor me." Turnip shoved the beer at him, spilling some of it. Jessup took it.

Turnip slumped back down on the couch.

"This beer's cold," Turnip said, too loudly, as if misjudging the distance between himself and Jessup. He held the bottle up to the ceiling light. Jessup had to admit that, after a long hot day, the cold bottle felt good in his hand. He pressed it to his forehead.

"Beer's better cold," Turnip said. "Can't blame yah for pourin out that pisswarm crap. Giver a taste now." He eyed his beer then took a long drink and smacked his lips. "Ah, honey," he said.

Jessup drank. The beer was so cold he couldn't taste it until after he swallowed. It was bitter, but not bad. He took another sip.

"Not too bad, huh?" Turnip said.

Jessup sipped. "It's pretty good. Cold." He smiled. "Not bad."

Turnip winked. "I ain't as dumb as I look." He raised the bottle as if to toast, but remained silent.

Jessup grew to appreciate the beer's bite, but began to feel bloated, and light-headed. He finished the beer and tried to recline the arm-chair; it fell back in one movement and he dropped the bottle, feeling sleepy, his face numb.

Turnip made two more trips, to and from the kitchen, for fresh beers. Jessup finished them, the third seeming to have no taste at all. He could hardly feel the coldness of the bottle in his hand.

Wheelchair appeared and Turnip shouted: "Let's *hit* the *road.*"

With the wheelchair loaded in the back of the Camino, and Wheel-chair himself hoisted up and buckled in the passenger side, Jessup sat, crammed between the two brothers. The Camino slew out of the yard.

"To the fair, goddamit," Turnip howled. He grabbed a tin from the dash; fumbling to open it, he handed it to Jessup. "Open that," he said.

Jessup thumbed the lid open, revealing three rolled cigarets.

"Get that goin, will yah?"

Jessup stared at the cigarets. He touched one with his fingertip, hesitantly, as if it might sting him. Pinching it between his finger and thumb, as he'd seen Turnip do, he lifted it carefully, then set it in his palm.

"Here, let me see that," Wheelchair said. Jessup held it out to him, and accidentally dropped it in his lap. "I got it," Wheelchair said, waving him off. He lit the joint, held the smoke, then blew it toward the cab roof. He handed the joint to Jessup. Jessup took it, wanting to be able to pinch it as Wheelchair had, nearly dropping it again. He stared at it. "Smells good," he said.

"We don't grow shit," Turnip said. Wheelchair cut his eyes at him.

"Don't waste that," Turnip said. "Here. Give it here." He took it, smoking casually, as if it were a regular cigaret. "So. Yah like the fair?" Turnip jabbed an elbow into Jessup's side.

"Me?"

"Yeah, *you*."

"Sure. I like the fair. Quite a lot."

"Hear that Hal? Quite a lot." He passed the joint under Jessup's nose to Wheelchair. Wheelchair put it in his mouth.

Jessup had never thought of marijuana as a plant. It was a drug. A narcotic. He remembered Friday night dances and how the Leblanc and Ritchie brothers, and their girls and hangers-on like Johnnie Mero and Bobbie Odonovan, would hang out at the far end of the school parking lot, sit in the beds of their pickups or lean on their cars, cocky as the Canadian border patrol, thumbs hooked in belt loops, manure-reeking jeans stuffed into the tops of unlaced workboots, shirts untucked and unbuttoned to show off the latest concert T-shirts brought back from Montreal. The girls groped their boys, laughed, drank liquor from soda cans, squatted and peed, danced with each other and smoked, cigarets and marijuana. He'd hated them. But, maybe he'd been jealous, too, of their smugness, their assured, natural confidence with girls, every one of whom he'd had a crush on at one time or another. He'd never existed to them, never been part of the world they'd created for themselves.

The Leblancs had treated marijuana as something dangerous and criminal. Wheelchair and Turnip smoked it as if it were tobacco, except for passing it back and forth, which Jessup didn't understand. They were so casual about it, as if they'd smoke it in front of anyone, even a cop. When Wheelchair offered it to Jessup with a "Want some?" it was as if he were offering a glass of water. It did seem ridiculous, now, all those laws, all over a plant.

"You grow this?" Jessup said. He looked at the joint, remembering film strips from health class. One marijuana joint equaled a pack of cigarets. Marijuana, *cannabis*, made you tired, lazy, paranoid and forgetful. Not as dangerous as cocaine. LSD. PCP. Drugs that made you jump from buildings, drown babies in boiling pots of grease. *Your own baby.* The filmstrips had never mentioned anything about enjoyment. But Turnip had a dreamy look about him, a grin the breadth of which Jessup had never seen. He looked serene and satisfied, in possession of secret knowledge.

Wheelchair passed the cigaret stub across the cab.

Smoke curled.

Jessup took the joint clumsily. Its smoke smelled fruity. He held the cigaret to his mouth; the smoke burned his eyes; he held the cigaret away. He finished his beer and set it on the floor and put the joint in his mouth again; he winced against the smoke, but this time he drew in. He clamped his eyes against the sting of smoke. The El Camino sped down the dark road; tree branches scraped its sides. The marijuana seemed to have no effect on him. He sighed, exhaling, and took another hit. His lips felt pasty. He took another drag. The back of his skull seemed to be prying free and drifting away, allowing in a weightless icy air to touch his brain. Someone's sewed my eyes shut, he said, or thought he did. He could not seem to open his eyes. Glued shut. But he did not need to open them. He could live with being blind. He took another hit and coughed; dry, heaving coughs that made his tonsils feel as if they'd torn free from his throat; he couldn't seem to force the smoke out of his lungs, to exhale; he felt as if he were drowning. He leaned forward, locking his head between his knees, then shot upright again, opening his eyes. The road and trees were quick vivid paint-brush strokes; someone was patting his back; his breath was returning to his lungs. A hand plucked the joint away. He rubbed his wet cold face. Wrung his hands in his lap, their slow movement curious, marvelous, separate from himself. One of his hands reached for the radio, clicked it on, turned up the volume. Music filled him. Penetrated him and flowed back out of his pores. His other hand slapped Wheel-chair's dead legs. "Damn," he said and took the joint again as it passed before him.

At the front gate of the county fairgrounds, Wheelchair nodded to the ticket booth operator and led Jessup and Turnip into the fairgrounds, no charge. "First class," Turnip whispered into Jessup's ear. As they walked, Turnip continued to lean in and whisper secretly to Jessup, as if every-thing he said was of monumental importance . . . "She's a looker . . . We'll hit the beer tent . . . Is that asshole starin at us?" Jessup won-dered if he were hearing things, imagining them, because every time he turned his head to look at Turnip to give him a knowing grin . . . Turnip was looking straight ahead, as if he'd never spoken at all, a smug look on his face. Jessup would blink and the smug look would vanish from Turnip's face, and Jessup would look ahead to find they were farther along. Deeper and deeper into the dark belly of the fairgrounds they journeyed. Around him the crowd bustled, children cackled and trilled, and a scratched record hissed a beckoning chant: "Come! You won't be-lieve your eyes! Freaks! Now! The *Mutilator*! Drives railroad spikes into his ear! Come! And see!" The reek of manure and wet goats came from the 4–H tents; the grounds burst alive with horrendous color and mon-strous sound. Wheelchair seemed to know everyone. And everyone seemed to know, and like, *adore* him. Their fondness of him enviable. It seemed everyone was nodding, winking, saluting. *Everyone*. From dark

shadows of the tents and from the steps of carny trailers they jeered at
Wheelchair: "Get off yur ass for once and work," grabbed their crotches
and said: "How much does this weigh?" Jessup and Turnip rode the
rides: THE GREEN COBRA! THE WHEEL OF DOOM! THE
HOUSE OF DEATH!! Ride after ride, Jessup's organs churned and
sloshed; his brain shook; he gorged on free fried bread dough slathered
with maple syrup and powdered with confectioners sugar; he ate knock-
wurst, french fries, onion rings, candy apples, cotton candy, all for free.
"*Gratis,*" Turnip whispered. "*Graaa tees.*" Jessup found himself in "The
Beer Tent" where they drank *on the house,* everyone nodding and foist-
ing Styrofoam cups into his hands and slapping his back and grabbing
their crotches and shouting at Wheelchair, who magically appeared and
disappeared: "How much does *this* weigh?" Beer after beer, Jessup
drank. Turnip emerged at his side from a crowd, sawdust in his hair and
coating the front of his shirt. "Here," he whispered, and slipped a joint
in Jessup's shirt pocket.

The Ferris wheel turned and turned, as though it might never stop.
But stop it did, at its zenith, the chair rocking in the wind as Turnip
stood up in his seat and yelled and pounded his chest and swore at the
motherfuckin stars and goddamned black sky. Jessup peered over the
edge; the world below was dark, save for the hectic confusion of flashing, strobing lights, green and yellow and orange. Rivers of people
parted around tents and animal cages to converge again in front of
THE GREEN COBRA! THE VIKING SHIP! THE TWISTER!

"Is this somethin, or what?" shouted Turnip, leaning over the
safety bar. "Lookit all them fuckin ants millin bout down there."

"Why do they always have to be ants?" Jessup muttered; his voice
seemed to speak before his thoughts were formed.

"How's that?" Turnip crushed his empty beer can and threw it out
into the darkness.

Jessup waited to hear it strike something, but no sound reached
him. "*Ants,*" he wailed. "Why do they always have to be ants? Why
can't they be termites, or fleas or something? It's always ants. *Ants
ants ants.*"

He looked down again, holding onto the safety bar. They *did* look

like ants, he thought, hearing himself laugh, unable to stop, to catch
his breath. He seemed at the top of the world, up here, higher than
anyone else. He stood up. Stood right on the Ferris wheel seat, above
the safety bar, the chair swaying, his arms out to his side, the wind
tickling his eyelashes.

"Careful," Turnip said. But his voice was a squeak. Jessup tilted his
head back. The chair teetered; he planted his feet wider. The ground
was miles and miles below. It reeled as he looked away from it at the
sky, at constellations that were no more than a gigantic connect-the-
dots that he was on the verge of solving.

He reached into his shirt pocket to retrieve his joint and the chair
lurched backward; he pitched forward, the weightlessness he'd felt
before relenting to gravity; the safety bar struck his thighs and he felt
himself going over, the chair seeming to want to buck him now, rid itself of its disrespectful passenger. As he felt himself going over, he
felt, too, something choking him, grabbing his throat, and his body
was whipped backward with the rocking of the chair and he sat down
hard on the seat, pain shooting up his tailbone. Gasping, he grabbed
at his throat.

Turnip was reclining in the corner of the chair, his cap pulled
down low. He was drinking another beer that he'd taken from his
jacket pocket.

"Lucky I'm quick," he said.

The Ferris wheel began to turn.

Turnip brought his hands from behind his head and clapped them
together. "Whats say we get off this fuckin thing and check us out a
freak show."

The emaciated man, THE MUTILATOR!, perched at the back of
the carnival tent on a hay bale, tugged and stretched a triangular flap
of fleshy skin from his neck. He stabbed steel spikes into his elastic
skin, slid them into his flesh; he jabbed needles into his arms and
cheeks, piercing, skewering. Jessup looked away, head drooping, a
seed-burdened sunflower; he considered the strewn hay, the dirt beneath his sneakered feet. He lolled his head back. High high *high*
above, the tent roof, splotched and mildewed, was held aloft in the

center by a wooden pole like a ship's mast; the green canvas heaved and flapped, a gym rope hung from the pole, a steel ring at the end, *clack clackclack.* Sweat broke on his shoulder blades, cold as drops of water from the tip of a melting icicle. His eyes slid back to the thin man with the tatoos, the self-torturer, THE MUTILATOR!, hoping he might be finished. But no. A honed knitting needle punctured his Adam's apple. No blood, but no skullduggery. The pathetic crowd, corralled into the tent, gasped and gawked. A midget appeared from a hole in the ground, from beneath the straw, to stand on an apple crate, his overalls rolled up, so the knees were cuffs. His Styrofoam boater crooked atop his bloated Neanderthal head. "He will now drive a ten-inch spike into his nose!" *He can't.* Vomit boiled in Jessup's stomach, bubbled and burned its way up his throat, eating. *I am not here I am gone* For what, for what? A few scrunched-up dollars? THE MUTI-LATOR! grinned, beamed, his gums the color of liver, a ballpeen hammer in his fist. His eyes like rotted holes. The midget gripped two spikes in his paws, clanked them together. He leaned back and let forth a sound as if he were being strangled, bearing nubs of teeth; he rose on the tips of his pointy black elf boots, guided the spike an inch or two into the nose of THE MUTILATOR! *Clink clink. Jumpin Jimmy Christmas* Jessup's toes curled, blisters tearing. Faces squeezed about him, inches away, hypnotized moons. The tent's stench of dung and sweat and stale beer, moldy hay, cheap cologne and perfume seemed to press against his cold sweaty skin. The night chilled. Black gnats swarmed before him, tiny dancing black dots. Thousands, so close he could hear the hum of collected wings as they hovered in a cloud before him, his field of vision blurred by black specks, funneling, *bzzz bzzzzzz.* His tongue felt like waterlogged cardboard. The dwarf swung the hammer. *Clink clink—*

Battered sneakers. Leather workboots. Loafers. Corned, cracked bare feet an inch from his nose, his mouth, so close he could lick the grime. Voices now, like the gaggle of distant geese. His face felt like beeswax, pressed to the earth. His hands sparkled with numbness as they flopped at the ends of his arms, slapping at an invisible spider that skittered across his eyes.

A girl with a sooty face and a red sucker jammed in her mouth leaned down and poked him. "Look at his teeth, mama! His *teeth!*"

No.

"Hey," a face in his, breath mints and cigaret smoke.

A light slap left a warm handprint on his cheek. He tried to focus his eyes. Tried. He turned his head; hay stuck to his face; in front of his eyes, spokes, thin rubber tires. He looked up from his back. Wheelchair. And his brother. Jessup remembered being at the house, Flower dropping him off, the drive here, harrowing, fast, a roller-coaster ride in the black of trees, beer and pot and more beer. He remembered THE TWISTER! Thought of all the cotton candy and onion rings and junk food digesting in his stomach acid, and all of it rose in him and he vomited it back up in a sour stream that splashed onto surrounding feet that quickly disassembled, and ran away in fleeing pairs.

The fair.

Wheelchair leaned over the arm of his chair. Turnip crouched beside him, cradling Jessup's papier-mâché head. Arms snaked underneath him. He stood, wobbling, bent over. "Sit on the arm of my chair." He did. Turnip patted his face with a bandanna, swabbed his mouth and chin.

"Breathe deep."

He tried. In and out, in and out in and out.

Turnip took one of his arms and draped it over his shoulder and hauled him out of the tent.

Outside, Turnip laid him on his back in a pile of straw. Opening his eyes he found himself sobbing.

Never again. Never again.

Above him, as if part of the black sky, or some galaxy, the green and yellow lights along the octopus arms of THE GREEN COBRA! blinked and blurred as the ride cranked backward. He turned his head away only to see the murals of THE LIZARD MAN AND HIS SON! THE GIRL WHO WAS HATCHED FROM AN EGG! and THE PETRIFIED MAN! that hung outside THE HOUSE OF DEATH! The murals' once-bright paints had long ago bled and faded; or had they *ever* looked new? Perhaps they were *made* to look aged to evoke some sense of legacy, an inexplicable, inescapable legacy of freaks having always been among us. He shivered and turned away. From the corner of his eye, he saw, in the distance, towering above the writhing GREEN COBRA!, the bow of a Viking ship; it appeared in a sweeping, storeys-high arch, then fell away again. Appeared again:

sweeeeeep

sweeeeeep

sweeeeeep

He was behind a fried dough truck, the one where Flower worked. Turnip lifted him up from the straw and aided him slowly over to sit on a milk crate between two tractor trailers. Darker here. But the lights followed him, pounded at his head, pierced his eyes. Diesel vapors burned his sinuses. He slouched with his elbows on his knees, head in his hands; his face like lard. His teeth clattered. He hugged himself.

Turnip squatted beside him. Put a hand on his shoulder. "Yur fine," he said. His voice lost in the grinding metal grate of braking rides. Turnip walked away. Vanished.

Jessup slumped and waited for the ground to stop undulating.

i am shipwrecked, marooned

What was he doing here?

Something touched his cheek. Cool, relieving. He opened his eyes as a hand wiped at his forehead with a wet cloth, tenderly. Another hand held a soda.

"Here. Drink this."

Flower.

She handed him the soda and knelt, placing her hands on her knees. She looked up into his face. He looked everywhere but her eyes. Her apron was smeared with mustard and syrup and chocolate sauce, her cheeks streaked with confectioner's sugar, as if she were a child who had been in her mother's face powder. Her hair, pulled back behind her ears, revealed a rash of tiny pimples at her temples. She had symmetrical pockmarks above each eyebrow. Her black jeans hugged her thighs and crotch.

Jessup chugged, the cold soda blasting his skull, but quenching his thirst. He began to recognize his surroundings.

i am a butterfly larvae, sticking my head out of my cocoon

She placed a hand on each of his shoulders.

"You gonna be okay?" Her fingers, light and graceful, rubbed his collarbone and shoulder blades. It felt good.

"Yeah," he said.

"You got the whitest teeth. They glow like limestone dust in this dark."

His mouth snapped shut; a tooth clinked on the soda can.

"Don't do that," she said, shifting her weight.

"What?"

"Close your mouth like that." She cupped his chin in her palm and tilted his head back so he faced her.

"Let me see your smile," she whispered.

i am an iceberg

"Come on."

His lips quivered.

"Come on."

He allowed a weak smile.

"Forget it," she said. "Shit." She released his chin with a slight pull, rising.

"Wait."

She stopped rising. Her backbone cracked, her body balanced perfectly in a half crouch.

"Well." She rested on her knees again.

He smiled.

She smiled. "My Pap used to haul loads of limestone to the other side of the state back when they were building the highway," she said. "Used to get limestone dust all over his clothes and hands and face. In his beard. I used to call him my beloved ghost. Can I have a sip of that soda?"

He handed the soda can to her.

She gulped what was left. "One night, when I was six, I hadn't seen him in weeks, he was always on the road, I heard something outside my window. Like an animal, whining. It was real late. Everyone was sleeping. I looked out and saw this figure, glowing. I was scared, to say the least. I thought it was a ghost. I was too scared to move or scream. But excited, too. A ghost, right there in my yard, and no one awake to see. Then it moved. Stood up. It was him. Pap. The lime shone in the moonlight. In his hair, on his face and hands and legs, all over. Like a baker gets flour all over himself. He stood in the yard, next to his dump truck. I hadn't seen it at first. The truck. I don't know how. Maybe because he never drove it up there. Always parked it down to Isham's farm. Well, the truck was loaded with a mountain of glowing crushed stone. He was weeping into his hands. Just sobbing and sobbing and sobbing. I couldn't move. But I started sobbing, too. Just tears running down my face. I wanted to run out and ask him what was the matter. What was wrong. I had never seen him cry. I wanted to tell him how, no matter what it was, everything would be all right. But I couldn't seem to move. I watched and watched until I guess I fell asleep. In the morning I woke to birds chirping and no truck out there, and when I told ma, she said he hadn't been home. He was out on the road. I'd insisted, but she told me I had been seeing things. I'd had a dream, a nightmare. Six weeks later he paid a visit to the doctor. Six weeks after that . . ."

She spoke the last half of her story to the ground, then rose, pressing his face into her apron. She lifted his chin with a single finger, leaned down and kissed him.

Cinnamon and maple syrup.

He kissed her back, awkwardly, firmly. Felt, briefly, her tongue.

She pulled away, letting her hands linger on his shoulders; her fingers played with the nape of his neck; a warm shiver ran through him. She stared at him, locked her fingers behind his neck, drew him close and kissed him again. He shuddered and she grabbed his wrists and unlocked his arms from around her waist, her butt, and stood, smoothing her apron. "They're beautiful, your teeth," she said. "You should be proud."

He struggled for a word.

"Thanks," he managed, wanting to say more, unsure what that might be. But she was already walking back to the fried bread dough truck.

It was 3:32 A.M. when Anna heard her boy come home. Heard the vehicle first, some fool driver revving the engine as if it were midday in a high school parking lot. She spied from behind the drawn corner of her bedroom curtain, settling her glasses on her nose. She could not see the vehicle: the terrible brightness of headlights lit the streaming rain silver. The slam of a car door and Jessup's silhouette appeared, leaning over the side of the vehicle, hefting his bike up and propping it against a tree, and then him, blown in the gusting wind, like a scrap of paper, toward the front of the house. The creak of the front door. The roaring din of wind and rain. The metallic *click* of the lock. The black vehicle charged away as violently as it had come, slinging mud and grass. She knew these types. They were like the last man, *boy*, she'd been with. The idiot who'd taken the bat to her windshield. The idiot who'd bragged to her about all his gobs of money and marijuana plants. The one she'd turned in. The one who'd shot himself out behind his barn. Bump. That was his name. And that's what he'd been. A bump in her life.

She had not heard from Jessup all day, all night. He had not come home from fishing. No call. No note. A first.

On the stairs, his cobbling footfalls sounded as if a cow were climbing to his room. She waited until he was in the attic before she came out to heat a cup of milk on the stove. She would talk to him tomorrow. On the stairs lay his shirt and a sock, a squashed tube of toothpaste, it insides leaking out and smeared on a step like the entrails of a small animal.

Jessup lay on his back on his mattress. I am Casanova, he thought. His room was as dark as the cedar swamp behind the house. His boxspring squeaked with each restless movement. On the tin roof the pattering rain sounded like the clicking claws of squirrels, then drummed heavily as the wind gusted water from overhanging branches. Jessup extended his arms above him, breathing in steady controlled measure to keep the room from spinning, to keep from throwing up again. *I am a zombie.*

He kept his arms raised until they grew numb. They fell heavily to his side. He wondered if he'd broken an arm. He wouldn't know for a moment, until the numbness retreated, and feeling returned. What had Wheelchair felt, lying there, in his yard? Had he been sorry he had shot the buck out in his mother's corn patch? How long had he lain sprawled there, waiting for the tingling to come back to his legs, believing it would? Had he cried? Screamed? Passed out? Cursed?

Wet himself? Had he regretted every bad thing he'd ever done? Had he thought that somehow things had come full circle? Jessup wondered if all actions were balanced out by reactions. If people were, in the end, rewarded for good and punished for bad. Or if it was all random. He guessed he'd never know. But he knew this: Wheelchair was lucky to have a brother like Turnip. Someone to look after him. Someone strong and brazen, with a sense of adventure.

Eventually, the rain stopped.

Jessup wriggled his fingers as they came back to the living. Neither arm was broken. "Thank you," he whispered into the darkness, not knowing to whom, or for what, exactly, he was thankful, but thankful nonetheless.

His lungs and throat felt like scorched bones, the inside of his skull clogged with sludge. He reached up again and raked his fingers over the splintered plywood; a nail dug into his fingertip. He brought the finger to his lips and tasted the blood. I am Dracul, clawing at my coffin lid. Let me out let me out. I am the king of my domain. I am in exile.

He rose and shuffled to the gable window and looked down from his perch at the kingdom.

It was his kingdom.

He was the king.

The queen has kissed him.

"They are beautiful. You should be proud."

He did not know what to make of the kiss. His stomach cramped with the thought of Emily. I am Benedict Arnold. He felt, for the first time, that somehow he was his own enemy: unrecognizable and untrustworthy. His legs shook. Emily would *never* betray him, or kiss someone else. Especially an older man, someone as old as the queen. He could not take air. He felt like calling Emily. Confessing. Pleading for forgiveness, begging not to let this change anything. Before he knew what was happening he was punching himself in the eye. Red and silver dots glittered and he fell down, his jaw snapping shut. But. Still. The kiss; it could not be forgotten. Taken back. He'd returned her kiss. No thought. He felt nothing for her, in his heart, he assured himself. But when she'd kissed him he'd wanted more,

wanted to engorge her. He'd felt afire. He'd felt no fear in kissing
back. He did not understand; all summer he'd longed for Emily, been
rapt in every word she'd spoken; her throaty, warbling voice was music; he'd studied each fold of her sleepy eyelids, watched how, when
she was surprised or happy, they stretched taut over her large eyes,
each slow blink revealing delicate blue capillaries; he thought, how,
when she ran ahead of him in the fields, her left foot would kick out
to the side in its awkward manner. How had he not kissed Emily
back? Yet kissed the queen? And *liked* it.

Chilled feet finally woke Marigold. She pressed her palms into the
depression in the mattress beside her. Still warm. She yanked her
hand away. Sitting up, she drew her knees and quilt to her chin. She
kneaded her cold toes, then rose, found a pair of red long johns
among the pile on the floor and pulled them on over her panties.

That boy. He was so shy. So kind. As much as Hess had once
thrilled her and made her feel good about herself in other ways, he'd
never been overly gentle, or modest.

She scuffed down the trailer hallway in her wool socks and long
underwear. Hess sat on the cinder blocks at their front step. She
opened the door. "Want some coffee, breakfast?" she asked. He was
smoking a cigaret. He did not turn around. She could see the flaking
pink crown of his scalp through a wisp of black hair. His hair used to
be so thick. It had attracted her to him right off that day before
Christmas. Her tire had gone flat in the parking lot of Govey's Drugstore. She'd come out of Govey's with a pair of elegant black leather
gloves for Ma. They hadn't been the best gloves; the ones she'd liked
most had cost more than she'd saved with her towing money. But
even if she'd had the money, she really couldn't have justified spend-
ing it all on a pair of gloves of no practical purpose beyond driving.

Hess had strode over, blowing into his hands, rubbing them together. "Can I change that flat?" His dark eyes. His black hair flying
in his face, which he kept sweeping back, trying to make her out from
behind it.

The trunk of her car would not unlatch. It had been frozen, and even a deicer that Hess had run over to buy at Rosie's had not worked. They'd gone into the Bee Hive, drank coffee for two hours, and forgotten all about the flat tire.

Hess turned to look at her. "What's to eat?"

"Toast. Coffee."

"Who was that boy?"

"What boy?"

"Don't give me '*what boy.*' Yesterday, when I come home. Y'were pullin out. Tried wavin you down."

"I didn't see you."

"Didn't say y'did. I said I seen a boy. Who was he?"

"Nobody."

"Nobody?"

"Just some kid who helped me with the firewood I delivered. No-body."

"Since when y'pick nobodies up along the road?" He scowled, reached up and wrenched her wrist. Her skin pinched against the bone.

She tried to yank her wrist away, but he viced it harder.

"I asked y'a question."

She glared down at him. This disheveled man, his lower lip pouting as he squeezed her arm until she wanted to scream from the pain, was no one she knew, or wanted to know. He peered up at her. He blinked, his eyelids plagued with skin tags that she suddenly had the urge to bite off. His dull eyes watered. His boots poked into the grass.

"Since my husband hasn't been around to help me with anything for months," she said. Then: "You better let go of my arm. Unless you plan on going all the way."

His eyes narrowed. He released his grip. She rubbed her wrist, holding it gently in her other hand.

"I guess I ain't hungry," he said and turned from her and snubbed his cigaret on his pant cuff.

She stood behind him, the door wide open, letting in the cold.

"Y'better not bring that fuckin boy back to my place again. I'm not so stupid I'll put up with that shit in my home."

"*Your* home," she said and stepped back inside, closing the door quietly behind her.

She'd just finished vacuuming and dusting, bagging up all the dog-eared magazines and junk mail, washed and dried and put the last of the dishes away, when he entered the kitchen. She was wiping down the counter; he pressed up behind her, pressed her hips to the counter, his hands wrapping around her waist and pulling her backside against him. What was he doing? He reached a hand down and plied her ass cheeks apart to wedge his hardness against her, grinding. She dropped the towel and sucked in her breath. "I'm sorry about all that," he hissed. His breath stank of cigarets; he bit at her neck; warm saliva bubbled on her earlobe. She'd waited so long for his attention, hoping he might come around. But this, it sickened her. Frightened her. She could feel sweat collecting between her breasts. He crammed a cold hand down the back of her long johns, between her cheeks, searching, probing, fingering; the other hand pinched a nipple, twisted it so she straightened with pain. She tried to move his hand away but he pinned her so her hands were trapped at her side.

"Just a second," she said, and pushed back against him, gently, moaning. She reached back and rubbed his crotch. When he unzipped his pants she reached into the drawer behind her back and drew out a knife and spun around on him.

"Hey," he said groping for her.

She poked at his stomach and his shirt slit open on the knife's point. "Get out," she said, trying to keep her voice calm, assured. He reached for the knife and she swung it, opening the back of his hand. He jerked away, clutched his hand and looked at her, his eyes unable to light on any particular part of her face. A sheet of blood seeped from his cut hand and dripped off his fingertips.

"Take *one* step," she whispered.

"Listen," he said.

She grasped the knife with both hands. The end of the handle pressed against her breastbone.

He stared at her. Glanced at the knife. He pointed a finger at her face. "Bring that little fuck around again, y're the one's gonna get stuck. Both a you. Crazy cunt."

She gripped the knife tighter.

He backed away, carefully, and went outside. She stood at the door.

"Do what you do best," she said, her voice rising, wanting to betray her, to reveal the panic and disgust and fear she had of him. "Get out of here and go somewhere, *any*where."

He backpedaled down the dirt drive to the road, shouting something she could not make out.

Long after he was out of sight at the bottom of Gamble Hill, Marigold remained leaning against the doorway, her eyes closed and her blood knocking behind her eyes.

PART III

Outside the Caratunk General Store, Reg leaned on the Camino, smoking a cigaret.

The land here had not been logged in decades, and the fir and spruce stood taller, more true than in Ivers, their green boughs so dark they appeared black in all but the brightest sunlight. The rivers and streams ran colder and faster, and it seemed to Reg that the farther north he came, the farther into the past, an uncivilized world, he traveled. This was forest. Aged, its indifference menacing and seductive. Wilderness like this made his desire to race cars seem childish, and he suddenly felt an urge to make his way farther north, into greater woods, up into Canada or Alaska. To escape. Never return.

A black lab, its muzzle grizzled and frothed with saliva, lay stretched on its sunken side in the dirt lot, front paws tucked into its chest. Its tail swished and its cataract eyes blinked lazily at deer flies. Reg squatted beside it and scratched its ears, feeling scabs and callused pink scars. "Hey fella. Where's that sonofabitch Lamar?" He patted the lab's head; the dog blew through its nose and whined when Reg stopped scratching; it rolled around on its bony back, its legs spread and its slimy pecker slipping out.

Reg afforded the dog one last good scratch on the head, then entered the store.

A cowbell clacked and sunspots pulsed and faded in Reg's vision as the store emerged from a gloom.

A kid in dirty jeans, a blue chamois shirt, and a white apron strayed up and down an ill-stocked aisle. From a Styrofoam cup he sprinkled green sawdust on the warped wood floor, to keep down the dust. The sawdust smelled of pine, and Reg remembered sprinkling the same stuff at Sarah's Sawmill Tavern, where he'd washed dishes, for a spell, when he was twenty-two.

The boy swept, the stiffstrawed broom awkward in his hand.

"Where's Franklin?" Reg said.

The boy leaned the broom against a shelf of dented soup cans. He opened the lone cooler along the back wall and straightened out soda bottles, consolidating loose singles into cardboard sixpacks. Reg stepped down the aisle and stood behind the boy who was crouched and had his head crammed between two racks as he tried to grab a loose soda can from the back of the cooler.

"Where's Franklin?" Reg asked, his breath fogging the glass door.

The boy knocked a sixpack of soda cans to the floor; two of them broke free and spun over to a card table where a hot dog steamer and a crockpot of bubbling chili sat:

55 cents 2/4 A BUCK

The boy turned to face Reg, looking as startled and confused behind the glass door as a bird trapped inside a room of windows. He had the eyelids of a tortoise; each slow blink unnerving, as if at any moment he might weep, or fall asleep.

"Relax," Reg said and smiled as the boy snuck out from behind the door and scrambled on his hands and knees to retrieve the two cans from under the table. He stood, inspecting the cans. His smock had come untied and hung loosely from the thin strap around his neck.

"Can I help you?" he uttered.

"If yah can't I'm gonna kill yah," Reg said and took a handful of redhots from a jar beside the hot dog steamer and shoveled them into his mouth, his fingertips blood red. "Where's yur boss at? Franklin. He still run this place? Where's he at on a weekend? A funeral or somethin?"

"Mr. Mongton?" The boy gripped a can in each hand as if he had in mind using them as weapons. "He's not at a funeral."

"Where in hell is he? He ought to be helpin yah with this shit. Don't yah think? It's his store ain't it? I'll talk to him about givin yah a raise."

"Downstairs. He's downstairs. We've been having trouble with the fuse box."

"Point me in the direction of the stairs and I'll be on my way. Little as I know Franklin, I know he could probly use a hand jus holdin a flashlight." He slapped the boy on the back as he stepped nearer to him.

The boy ran a hand over a buzz cut that looked like a skim of mold covering his skull. He stared and shuffled and said, "I'll go and get em." With sudden animation, he disappeared behind a shelf of jarred lamb tongues and sardine and smoked oyster tins. He took the soda cans with him.

Reg went and stood in the doorway and looked out at the Camino. The last two hours of the trip the engine had run rough. He'd had to stop at one point and take off the distributor, dry and clean it; it had a hairline crack and needed to be replaced, as did the rotor. In the keen sunlight the El Camino wasn't the great beauty it appeared to be in the shade, or from a distance. The front fenders and wheel wells were scrap sheet metal pop-riveted in place and painted black with the spray paint from Rosie's. The sun danced on chrome bumpers and trim, but the black paint, dull and flat, reflected nothing. Rust pocks were already scattered along the doors and lower body, blossoming through the paint, like sphagnum moss on a boulder. His backyard paint job had not come out well.

Years ago, he and Lamar had driven the roads out to Buell's Gore and Montgomery Falls, searching for used cars, junks abandoned in the front yards of falling-down houses, their tires flat, windows soaped, $100 OR B.O., Oldsmobile Cutlass Supremes with rotted floorboards, Impalas with spider-webbed windshields, GTOs, and 442s, big dilapidated cars with mag wheels and monstrous appetites for leaded gasoline. They'd fixed them up. Lamar had always been the body man. Reg the mechanic. Lamar hated how the plugs were jammed in where he couldn't easily slip a socket onto them. He'd tear the skin off his knuckles trying to work a bolt out of a tight spot and kick his tools all over the driveway. He'd broken a foot once, doing

129

that. They'd always wanted to fix up two cars and race them across the country, to the Pacific. California. Baja. Down to Mexico, to see the donkey shows. They'd left Ivers once. But they'd only made it as far as western New York before Reg's Camaro had thrown a rod, and they'd had to pool their cash, sell Lamar's Impala and ride a Greyhound home.

Winter had been the best time to drive the roads, at night, after the plows pushed the snow to the sides in roof-high piles, the roads icy black and greasy under the slightest turn of the wheel, narrow and choked tight with snow. He and Lamar had driven like maniacs. Stomped on the pedal and tore through the trees until the snow piles were a white blur and the road was a conveyer belt, flying at high speed beneath them. Those old cars handled sloppy, fishtailed and slammed the banks of snow, smashing in fenders. They'd get stuck in the deeper parts, where the wind had blown the snow into drifts across the road. They drove automatics in the winter, automatics on the column, and they'd drop that lever from R to L2 and back, the accelerator buried to the floor. Back and forth until the car rocked in place, the engine racing and hot and whining. They'd slam the gears, tires spinning and churning, their studs biting into and spitting snow and ice in fantastic rooster tails, the interior stinking of burning rubber and grinding gears and boiling antifreeze. The dash a panel of red warning lights. But those engines, those 327s, 351s and 454s never quit, and the tires would chomp down into the frozen dirt beneath the snow and lurch them forward and through, and they'd tear off, deeper into the trees, knowing they could go as fast as they dared, the snow banks keeping them from flying into the woods.

They never thought about what would happen if a car came from the other way on a dirt road only wide enough for them. How, by the time they saw its headlights sweeping through and making the treetops real again, they would never be able to save themselves, or the others.

Reg pushed open the screen door. A wind had blown up and dust cycloned along the barren dirt road. Next door sat a squat, yellow brick house. Colonial. Its windows small and rectangular as cupboard doors; the front door was set into an alcove, as if the longdead builder had known of the wind that now blew and the damage it might exact. Pieces of roof slate lay about in the stunted brown grass, among Big Wheels and armless dolls, fallen-over pink flamingos, tricycles and rusting milkcans. The dog now lay in the road. The store and the house were the only buildings for miles. The cedars and spruce swayed and thunderheads gathered from the north, soon to block out the sun.

Reg turned at the sound of footfalls, his .45 poking him. Franklin, a few hairs less on his head since last Reg laid eyes on him, strutted down the aisle; the boy stood back by the cooler, watching.

"Help yuh?" Franklin said.

"I'm supposed to meet Lamar up here an hour ago, but I ain't seen no sign of him. I was wonderin maybe he hadn't left word."

Franklin shook his head and stared at Reg. "You look different with that hippie hair and sunglasses. Didn't recognize you at first. How're you?"

"Not too bad. Yurself?"

"Can't complain. Haven't seen em at all, lately."

"Son of a bitch."

"Doesn't mean much."

Franklin took two pretzel sticks from a jar by the register, offering one to Reg.

Reg took it and sucked on it.

"Where's he at up there, exactly?" Franklin said.

"North a Beaver Meadows."

"No phone then?" Franklin said, grinning.

"Hardly. Was sposed to call me from the pay phone here. I don't know if I should wait or set out for his place."

"Never make it in that car." Franklin looked past Reg, through the screen door to the Camino.

"Can only drive so far anyway, fore yah gotta hoof it. He's back in there a ways." Reg hoped he could remember the confusing logging roads. The few times he'd come up, he'd been stoned, and he'd left the Camino at the store; Lamar had driven his Willys in till they'd had to walk.

The boy swished the broom in place.

"I best shove off," Reg said.

"Guess maybe," Franklin said, and crunched another pretzel. "Supposed to be getting a storm."

Under a sky dark and roiling thunderously, Reg drove a one-lane dirt road, beginning to wonder if he hadn't made a wrong turn at the fork back when he'd first set out. As he drove the road grew treesuffocated, diminished finally to two ruts that eked a crooked and confounding way through the trees, a passage corrupt with frost heaves and hollows, fallen limbs and upcreeping springs.

Eventually he came upon a logging road that branched off to the right. He remembered Lamar pulling off onto a logging road, but had no way of knowing if this was the one. The road was blocked by a fallen tree a little ways up. The Camino wouldn't make it too much farther anyhow, and this was a good place to turn around in later. He pulled in, and heard the crunch of metal and breaking glass. "Fuck," he said and shut off the engine and stepped out of the Camino. A fallen limb had shattered a headlight. He touched the starred glass, burring his finger on shards; he sucked at the blood. "Fuck," he said. The woods were cool and the wind had grown stronger. Reg bent backward, kneaded his lower back with his fists. The wind lulled, as if catching its breath, then strengthened again. He put on his denim jacket, turned up the collar and threw the duffel bag over his shoulder. Hungry, he swore at himself for not having bought food at the store, some jerky, at least. He began walking down the overgrown logging road.

After a while, as one logging road branched off to another, and another, and his winded breaths had fallen in time with his steps, he began to feel the first spit of cold rain on his cheek. Some ways back he'd passed the head of a logging road that had been blocked by a state forest gate; he'd thought the gate had looked familiar; it was hard to tell: all of them were painted the same municipal yellow. He craved a cigaret, having forgotten his on the dash. And in the glove compartment, forgotten too, a flashlight. The afternoon had grown darker, it seemed. It was a tricky time. One moment the world grew lighter with each blink of the eye. The next, darker. It was hard to know how late it was. Reg stopped to gain his breath. It was raining harder now; up ahead he saw a seam, a broken vein that ran through quaking ferns, upsetting their natural harmony. It might have been the trail to the cabin. He looked up the logging trail unsure where he had to turn off, if he was even on the right road. He took a deep breath and set off through the ferns. Black gnats clustered about his head, bore into the tender flesh behind his ears, and flew into his nose and eyes and mouth. He swung at them, spat them out as if he'd bitten into bad meat. Goddamned didn't he despise the woods and never want to set foot in them again? Didn't he want to get as far away from this shit as he could?

The terrain gradually flattened, becoming a level land of boreal forest, the earth a brickish, acidic loam. Rusted pine needles cushioned his steps.

Soundlessly, he plodded on, hemmed in by tree limbs that cracked and snapped in the relentless wind, trunks that cried and moaned as they ground against one another. It was pouring now; the cold rain beat on him, soaked through him. He stopped and took out a T-shirt and a wool flannel shirt, and put them on. They warmed him some, but soon he was drenched again, and shivering. His hair stuck to his face.

The gnats long retreated, he quickened his pace.

Blundering through the mist, he saw what looked like a structure. He stretched the corners of his eyes with his fingers. It was hard to make anything out in the rain. He approached what he thought was the cabin, thinking of food and sleep and how he was going to tear Lamar a new asshole. But it wasn't the cabin; it was the first of a series of dark unfamiliar ledges, spoiled with lichen and moss. Tree branches hung low here and he was forced to stoop and scramble his way under the protection of limb and rock, his hands slick with mineral and fungi as he slipped and grappled for branches. Under the overhang, he struggled into a snug grotto that receded far into the ledge. He wormed in as far as he could and removed the duffel, trying to keep it clear of the water that ran down the rocks. He stripped with some difficulty, down to his underwear. His legs were pale, and patches of his black hair were worn away on his shins and thighs. He picked at scabs, at his blackened toenails. Coming this far was a mistake. He felt it. If Lamar hadn't promised him the weed, and he didn't need his help on Smuggler's, Reg would have turned around at the store and headed home. Turned around now. Soaking wet, muddy and cold and hungry, this far out in nowhere, searching for the cabin without any luck made him feel tired and old, desperate. He would be thirty in a few weeks and very little of what he'd imagined for himself when he was younger had panned out. He was no different than Roland Dupree. He felt sick with despair.

He took a bandanna from his duffel and dried himself as well as he could, pulled on the shirt and jeans he'd packed. They were damp. He lay down on his side, hugging his legs to his chest, exhausted and outraged at his stupidity. He longed for a cigaret. He'd not gone this long without one since he was fourteen. Since Pap had taken sick. No one had smoked around Pap during that time. Out of respect. Fear. Reg remembered the old U. S. road map he'd kept tacked to his bedroom wall. When Pap was on the road, Reg had drawn, with a green marker, the possible routes Pap might travel, towns where he might spend the night. He'd mapped out the miles Pap would have to travel before he'd return home.

When he was off the road, Pap had spent his time at home. Going bald, he'd kept his skull shaved, but had grown a beard the color and sheen of magnet shavings, neat and trimmed but forever smelling of coffee, diesel fuel and ten-cent cigars.

"The stories I could tell," he'd say. But he never told them. Those rare summer evenings when he was home, he sat on the front stoop, drinking a beer or a soda, an arm around Ma's waist while Reg and Hal and Marigold had sat on the tree that had lain rotting on the lawn. They'd scratch each other's bare backs as the crickets grew noisy, the birds quiet and still in the dusky woods. "What you kids been up to? Been good?" Pap would ask, swishing his cigar from one side of his mouth to the other.

"They been good," Ma'd say.

"Course. Course they have."

Reg opened his eyes. The rain had ceased and the afternoon, if still wet and cold, had grown lighter. Huddled under the outcrop, he collected himself and put on his pack, then set out again, imagining the cabin must be close.

He walked and walked, growing more and more hungry and tired, until he finally gave up searching and started to look for a spring or stream that he could follow down to a road.

Above the conifers, the sun began to part the clouds. As Reg bent to lace a boot he caught a glint of reflecting sunlight through the trees. He turned. The cabin. He could just make it out. How long had he been circling it, yards away? Laces forgotten, he stood, grimacing at a kink in his lower back, ready to lay into Lamar.

He worked his way toward the cabin. There was no yard; the forest grew up to its plywood door. Something snagged on Reg's pantleg and he looked down to find barbed wire stretched taut between the trees, surrounding the camp. Six strands from ankle to chest. He worked his pantleg free and lowered his duffel bag over the fence. Unable to slip between the strands, he climbed carefully over them at the closest tree. The wires squeaked. The air was calm and quiet. Pine needles soft underfoot. He left the bag and walked to the side of the cabin. Next to the door a dormant gasoline generator sat on cinder blocks. Metal wind chines reflected the sun in pieces. He tapped them and they gave a light tinkling sound. Porcupines, drawn by the salty glue, had gnawed all along the cabin's plywood skirting.

He rapped on the door. And again. He called out, "Lamar."

He drew the .45 from his jeans.

He called again, rapping louder.

As he eased open the door it snagged on something and he was forced to squeeze his way in. Entering, the humidity of the cabin smothered him and he gagged at a sour stench, cupping a hand over his nose and mouth. The cabin swarmed, trembled with dumb slow flies, their purpleback bodies shimmering as they crawled all over the body that lay at Reg's feet. Another body lay in the doorway to the back room. Dozens of flies ticked against the cabin windows. Something cracked beneath Reg's weight, a hand, and he stumbled back, his boots sliding on the slippery floor. His eyes watered and the pistol fell as he pinwheeled out the door and lurched into the trees where he fell to the ground and retched. The stink of the cabin seemed to stick to his skin and clothes.

He looked back at the cabin, wiping his mouth with the back of his hand; what the fuck? He hadn't been able to tell who it was in there. He'd been in fights with pool cues and ax handles, but he'd never seen such a mess. A vision of corpses, hundreds of them, putrefying in a jungle, came to him. When he'd been in Fairland, there'd been a massacre. Some nutty religion gone bad. They'd drunk poison. On the rec TV he'd seen footage of the FBI, politicians, reporters, walking among the dead, handkerchiefs to their mouths and noses. The prison had buzzed about it, inmates and guards strangely bound by the horror. He couldn't remember the name of the country. He wondered how things got so far out of control.

He rose to his knees, slowly, a dread creeping like the flu through his muscles, beneath it, anger. A heat in his stomach, a buzzing in his head that he couldn't temper. The Lavalettes.

Reg looked around the woods. He'd glimpsed a plant in the back room. If there was anyone else, they'd be close by, and likely be back. The wind chimes swayed in a breeze. If he left now he could claim he hadn't come here from the general store. Say he'd headed back for Ivers. So far he'd played no part. It was possible neither of the bodies was Lamar, that Lamar had escaped, or hadn't been around at the time. The place had stunk of rot, likely from the cabin being closed up so tight; the bodies couldn't have been there long: the floor was too slick. He had to move. Go inside, or leave. The plant he'd seen was huge. The barbed-wire fence squeaked, and Reg spun, reaching for the .45. It wasn't on him. It was in the cabin.

The fence squeaked again, behind him. The trees were dark, shadowy. Anyone could be hiding among them. He heard a rattle of branches. A red squirrel ran along the top wire of the fence and disappeared into a tree.

Standing, Reg took a handkerchief from his back pocket and tied it behind his neck so it covered his nose and mouth. Circling the cabin, he checked the ground for footprints, for—he didn't know what, exactly. He thought about searching for the buried fifty-five gallon drums, but the way Lamar did things Reg would never find them without a metal detector and a backhoe.

At the front of the cabin he looked around. An ax leaned against the barbed-wire fence; he hefted it, its handle smooth, and walked to a window and looked inside the cabin. Flies bounced off the glass. He raised the ax and swung it, shattering the window. Flies lifted in murmuring confusion from the cabin, most falling to the ground to spin on their backs.

He smashed every window, the ax lifted higher and swung harder each time. He came to the front of the cabin again and stood looking at the door. He wiped the ax handle with his handkerchief, then let the ax fall and went inside.

The corpse at his feet lay facedown; flies lifted and settled, crawled over each other to get at the gray mess inside the broken skull.

The other body lay facedown, too, disturbed little by the flies, a shotgun beside it on the floor.

Reg picked up his .45 from the floor and wiped it on his pants. Another pistol lay at the feet of the body before him. A .38 or .357. Its wood grip was cracked. He didn't touch it. Stepping over the corpse, he went to the other body and toed its ribs. It gave a gassy wheeze. He checked the shotgun, one shell, and propped it against the wall and straddled the body. He grabbed it by the shoulders and turned it over, brushing at flies. Lamar's face was bruised and swollen, as if he'd been beaten with a baseball bat. His chin and the front half of his lower jaw were gone, his tongue shredded; his forehead was encrusted with dried blood.

Reg tried to swallow. He swept Lamar's hair from his eyes.

Lamar's eyes blinked and his hand squeezed Reg's wrist.

Reg fell back, his hand sliding on the floor. "Fuck," he said and yanked his hand from the floor and wiped it on the wall. "Fuck *me*."

Flies droned.

Reg knelt beside Lamar.

"Jesus," he said.

Lamar's bloated upper lip spasmed. He attempted to lift his head, but it fell back to the floor. His chest wheezed. Reg wiped his hands on his jeans, put his arms under Lamar and lifted him so he was propped against the doorway to the back room. "Goddamn," he said. With Lamar propped up, Reg saw that he'd been shot in the stomach, at least once. And in the chest; a bright foamy blood seeped through his shirt: a lung shot, Reg knew, from deer hunting. Though Lamar's jaw was useless, its wound wasn't fatal. Unlike the others. Lamar stank like a wet dog. Of shit and piss. The area on the floor where he'd lain was sludgy with a greenish brown waste that smelled of swamp. Reg shook his head and slumped to the floor.

"Motherfuckers," he said.

He stretched his legs out before him and rested his head in his hands.

He looked at Lamar, then around the cabin.

A fuckin mess. But nothing compared to what he was capable of doing.

A pack of cigarets was stuffed in Lamar's shirt pocket. Reg took it and lit one. Lamar writhed, suddenly, then calmed. Reg stared at him and smoked. Lamar's eyes closed; his chest rose and fell, unsteadily. No time to get help, even if it was a choice.

Lamar moaned.

Reg shook his head. "I was all set to kick yur ass," he said. He took one of Lamar's hands, the hand that was missing two fingers. Years ago, when they were twelve, he and Lamar had stolen a johnboat from a summer camp on Broken Leg Lake. Armed with single-shot .22s, they'd poled to the back waters, where cattails grew taller than corn. They'd been on the hunt for Big Mosshead, a snapping turtle said to weigh two hundred pounds and possess the girth of a tractor tire. Said to have caused the disappearance of three children. As they'd pushed deeper into the bog, among lily pads and reeds, and muskrat huts that rose from the stagnant waters like the humps of submerged creatures, suddenly, from beneath the johnboat, two gargantuan snappers had erupted from the muck, locked in a death fight, a boiling fury of mud and claw and jaw and shell. The clack and snap of their beaked jaws sounding like bones breaking. Waves had upset the johnboat, and skeins of blood had spread out from the embattled turtles. Neither snapper was Big Mosshead, but true progeny. In their surprise, Lamar and Reg had lost their footing and nearly fallen in as they'd scrabbled for their rifles. Standing again, spraddle-legged, they'd fired, the crack of their .22s sounding like harmless handclaps. The turtles had warred on, closer, slamming against the johnboat, submerging beneath it, smashing against its bottom, to emerge again on the other side. Reg and Lamar had fumbled for more shells in the pockets of their cutoff jeans. Loaded and fired—*crackcrack*—loaded and fired, again and again—*crackcrack*—*crack*. Sweating and swearing and screaming at the creatures, they'd fired repeatedly until the stirred waters had calmed, and one turtle had sunk from sight in the muddied water, a trail of silver bubbles percolating where it had been. The second turtle had remained surfaced, its head submerged in the water. Blood had cauliflowered from its wounds, but Lamar and Reg had shot it again, anyway. Twice. The two of them had stood still, ankle-deep in the cold water that splashed over the sides of the boat, pale faces speckled with blood and mud, shiny with sweat. They'd gawked at the creature, its body ensnarled in weeds, the rocky plate of its shell slimed black, and splotched with algae. Its shell was scarred with bone-white divots from the bullets. The small waves, made by its twisting tail, slapped the boat. Lamar had stooped and reached over the gunwale, looking back over his shoulder at Reg, who had stood erect, shoulders squared, .22 trained on the snapper. Reg had nodded at Lamar, and with both hands, grabbed hold of the massive leathered tail and tugged. "Hell," he'd huffed, turning to look over his shoulder again, "Sonofabitch's heavy as a sack a wet cement." The turtle had turned then, its repulsive head thrusting out from the foam of mud and blood, its neck stretched beyond all reason, the inside of its beak pink and tender-looking and stringy with slime as it opened its maw wide and hissed, then lunged for whatever had hold of its tail. Lamar had recoiled and fallen in the bottom of the boat, and the turtle had vanished beneath the surface with a suddenness that had made Reg doubt it had ever existed. Lamar had stood again, grinning crazily, eyes blinking fast. "Hell," he'd stammered. His wet bangs in his eyes. "Sonofabitch was *alive*. Believe that? I thought it *had* me. Thought I was goin back right in the drink. If that sucker had got me, I hope ya woulda . . . What? What're ya lookin at?"

Reg looked at Lamar's nubbed fingers, the pink scar tissue.

"Fuck," he said.

He lay down and rested his head on Lamar's stomach, his chest heaving, his cheeks hot; he lay until his body quieted, then he sat up and looked behind him at the back room.

It was choked with plants.

Each plant grew in its own bucket, beneath a ceiling of grow lights, dark now, with the generator dead. In the room he walked among the plants, stroking their leaves as he counted. Twenty-eight. He scooped soil. Still damp. He picked a few buds. Tacky. Seedless. He smelled them. "Who said money don't grow on trees?" he whispered. His stomach growled. He hadn't eaten since early morning. "Got anythin to eat in this place?" he said.

In the kitchen area he found a box of crackers and a jug of water.

"Yah got the greenest goddamned thumb. Know that?" he said as he knelt beside Lamar. He tucked the few buds he'd picked into his shirt pocket. He swept Lamar's hair from his face. "Lavelettes won't get away with this."

Lamar's eyes opened and he shook his head violently; Reg tried to calm him, stroked his blood-matted hair. Lamar calmed. "Yah got Pap's eyes. Same's Marigold," Reg murmured. He recalled Pap lying on the sofa, remembered creeping downstairs from his bedroom that Sunday afternoon. Everyone had been gone but himself and Pap; he'd tiptoed across the living room floor and stood above Pap, who'd lain motionless, soundless, as he had for what seemed an eternity, save for awakening in the night with dreadful moans, calling out for his mother, who had died years ago. Pap's body had collapsed in on itself, the rot on the inside, deep in his marrow, his brain. His face seemed to have no muscle, possess no skull; seemed only to consist of bloodless skin, slack and attempting to maintain the illusion of life still beneath it. Pap hadn't opened his eyes for days. And he did not open them then, as Reg had pressed the pillow down, reminding himself that he was doing it for his father, but knowing he wasn't, entirely; it was for himself, too. He could not stand to look at what little remained of his father, or suffer one more day the stench of the stranger on the couch, so strong it seemed almost visible in the the shade-drawn room.

It had been the first time Reg had done something he'd thought would make things better, and learned afterward how wrong he'd been. He'd plotted what he'd done, for a week, enacted it in his mind. Not with malice or cunning, but with the idea that to have it done would bring relief, an end to the morbid, draining silence into which the family had descended. At night, when he'd thought his way through the plan, he'd told himself that *only* if his father awoke, opened his eyes, would he not follow through. He'd kept his word. But relief had not come. Instead, after Pap's body had finally fallen still, there'd remained only an appalling crush of regret and insufferable guilt. He'd fallen on Pap, Pap's skin still warm as Reg pulled his frailness to him, pressing him against his chest as tightly as he dared, until Pap's body had grown cold.

Reg rested Lamar's head in his lap. He lit a cigaret and smoked, crushed flies under his thumb.

Lamar's eyes closed.

"Relax," Reg said. "Rest." A gas can sat in the corner by Lamar's cot. Another sat by the door. Through the wall of plants in the back room, he could see a third can in the corner. "Dint get to em in time, I see," Reg said, and laughed. But his heart wasn't in it. For a second he thought he might burn the place down. Destroy any trace of his presence. But the smoke would be seen, no matter how far in he was. He lit another cigaret, then poured water onto the handkerchief and wiped Lamar's forehead. He dripped water onto what remained of his cousin's tongue. "We sure know how to find trouble. Don't we? Always needin somethin to get the blood pumpin. I'm cuttin out. In the spring. Sooner, *now*. Gonna race for NASCAR. Believe that?"

Psst psst psst. A bird, a cedar waxwing perched on a windowsill, a red berry in its beak. Lamar wheezed. Blood leaked from the corners of his eyes.

Reg stood. His bones felt fused at the joints; the afternoon had grown late, darkness was closing. He had a vision of being torn apart by Big Mosshead. The cedar waxwing regarded him with suspicion, then lifted with a peep and was gone. A piece of down floated to the cabin floor and stuck to it.

"I can't stay here," Reg said. He felt cold. His eye sockets felt cracked, too small for his tired eyes. The room was filling with shadows. A breeze blew through the broken windows, but the smell of blood and shit remained.

Lamar's eyelids fluttered. Reg felt his cousin's wrist, the pulse shallow as a baby bird's.

He had to get out before someone walked in.

In no time he'd picked the buds and stuffed them into a plastic garbage bag. Four or five pounds, at least. Dried. He triple-bagged them, to keep down the scent. Fingertips black with resin, he ransacked the cabin, finding a cache of bills in a cereal box. $1,750. Tens and twenties and fifties, wrinkled and wadded up and wrapped with rubber bands. He stuffed the garbage bag into his duffel, the wad of money into his jeans.

At the door, he looked out into the woods.

He thought of the weed buried around the cabin. But dusk had come and he would have to move swiftly to make it back before night fell completely.

He rolled the first body over, its skin making a sucking noise as it peeled from the floor; he pushed it on its side and kicked it and it fell on its back. There was no face left. A twelve gauge would do that. The corpse wore gray corduroys, a black-and-green checked shirt. Gum boots. Reg roamed in the jeans' pockets for a wallet. He looked around the floor. Nothing. He dragged the corpse by the boots, a little more toward Lamar. The shirt pocket. A flimsy black billfold, soaked through with blood. Reg took it and opened it with his fingertips. A few bills in the wallet. He took them. They were stuck together; he poured water from the jug onto the bills, the water turning pink as it ran off his hand. He peeled the bills apart: thirty-seven dollars. He stuffed the money in his pocket. There were photos, too, ruined from the blood, and what looked like a paper driver's license; Reg wiped his fingers on his jeans. If it hadn't been ruined, he could have brought the license home for Marigold to read, or the kid. The kid wouldn't ask questions.

Reg stuck the license back in the wallet and put the wallet in the shirt pocket; he dragged the body back and flipped it over to where it had been.

He stepped over to Lamar.

Lamar's eyes opened and stared past Reg. Reg poured water onto a rag and wiped Lamar's face. He straightened Lamar's collar. Picked up the pack of cigarets and put them in his own pocket.

He strapped on his duffel bag.

Lamar stared at the ceiling.

Reg wiped sweat from his eyes. He paced from one body to the next.

He took out the .45 and stepped over to Lamar.

He pointed it at Lamar's face.

The duffel weighed tremendously on his back.

He stared at Lamar.

He adjusted the duffel's straps and shifted its weight, but it remained just as heavy. Lamar closed his eyes.

Reg stared down the .45.

He thumbed the safety.

"I was never here," he said.

He remained over Lamar. Breathing. The pistol pointed at his cousin's face. Sweat stung his eyes, but he did not blink or wipe it away.

He pressed the barrel of the .45 to his cousin's forehead. The metal of the trigger was worn smooth. Lamar's eyes remained closed. Reg shut his own eyes. The gun kicked in his hand.

According to the radio, it was 12:15 in the morning.

Another day.

Reg sat in the dark Camino, pulled over in a picnic area near the Nullhegan County line, alongside the Connecticut River. New Hampshire lay out there in the darkness, across a hundred yards of rapids that Reg could hear but could not see. The needle of the temperature gauge had climbed and climbed, peaked in the red; he'd pulled over to let it cool. He'd wanted to make the last push home, but pulling over was better than breaking down.

Pages of torn newspaper blew from a trash can and swept across the gravel lot to stick to the trunk of a tree.

Reg chewed on a strip of jerky he'd found on the seat; his hands reeked of marijuana. He was exhausted, but when he thought of the weed and money his heart quickened. He'd made up his mind not to feel guilty about taking the bud and money. Lamar would want him to have it. Finding the money was an omen for him to get away. He'd set things straight with the Lavalettes, for Lamar. He'd have to choose the right time. But when he struck, they'd know it.

"Goddamn," he said. The mother lode.

He turned the key. The needle edged into the red. His eyes itched. He slouched against the door, yawning.

He awoke to a tapping sound, unsure, for a moment, of where, or who, he was.

Turning, he smacked his nose against cold glass. He recognized now where he was. But he did not recognize the bearded face that peered in at him. The man gripped a long metal flashlight in his hand, as if it were a club.

Reg coughed. The man outside stepped back from the Camino and gestured for Reg to crank down the window. Reg did, the cold outside air slapping him. He rubbed his face, glanced at the .45 next to him on the seat and rested a hand on it, tucked it under his thigh.

The man raised the flashlight, flooding the cab with light. Reg shielded his eyes, still barely able to make out the face in the darkness. The guy was in his late forties, maybe. It was hard to tell with the beard. His forehead gleamed. Reg could not see a vehicle.

"Everything all right?" the man said.

"Depends on who yah are and what yah plan on doin to me."

"Not a thing. Unless you're breaking some law."

Reg chewed what jerky remained in his mouth.

The man lowered the flashlight so it pointed at the Camino's door. He wore a black satin parka that rode up above a black belt. The jacket was zipped to his throat, its fake fur collar pulled tight at the sides of his face. His breath smoked and he kept blowing into his free hand. A black holster, polished to a shine, hung from the belt. The grip of a .357 stuck out from it.

"Sleepin ain't gainst the law, last I heard," Reg said.

"I'm Sergeant Janson," the man said, his voice suddenly deep and flat. He swept the flashlight over the back of the Camino, then back on the door again. "State Police."

Janson was probably the only cop within fifty miles. Reg didn't recognize him. Janson leaned in, rested a hand on the roof, "I'm off duty, heading home. Reason I stopped is . . . your parking lights are on. I didn't know if maybe whoever was in here had got tired and fallen asleep with the vehicle running. Every year or so someone dies that way. Same sad story. Kids mostly, carrying on. Had two last year."

Reg smacked his lips.

"You from around here?" Janson said.

"Ivers."

Janson leaned in closer. He smelled of spearmint. "Awfully close to home to be sleeping."

"Camino was overheatin," Reg said. "Thermostat. I was comin back from Caratunk and dint wanna push it." He'd tried to catch himself on the word, *Caratunk*, but was too late.

Janson crouched a bit, tucked the flashlight under his arm and rested his big palms on his knees. "Hunting?"

"What?"

"Were you hunting, in Caratunk?"

"Nothin's in season."

The officer nodded. "Been drinking tonight?"

"Nope."

"Sure now?"

"I'm sure."

Janson stood. "You want to give me your license and registration, please?"

"Not partic'ly."

Janson pulled a notepad and pen from the breast pocket of his jacket. "What's your name?"

"Reg."

"Short for Reginald?"

"How's that?"

"Your name. Short for Reginald?" He held the pen so the tip just touched the paper.

"Nope."

"Just Reg?"

"Yup."

"Got a last name?"

"Pretty strange, I dint."

"Mind telling me what that name might be." Janson grimaced and spat. He poked at his beard with the end of the pen.

"Yup."

"Maybe you better tell me anyway."

"Cumber."

"Well, Mr. Cumber. How about I ask you one more time, nicely, for your license and registration."

Reg took his wallet off the dash. He plucked out his license, handed it out the window without looking at Janson.

Janson said: "Registration?"

The cab was lit up again with the flashlight. Reg could feel the barrel of the .45 jabbing into his thigh. "It's in the glove box, somewhere," he said.

"I have time."

Reg leaned over slowly toward the glove box and sprung it open. Papers, loose shotgun shells and a map fell onto the floor. Janson swung the light to the far side of the cab. Reg fumbled around in the glove box, pulled out more junk, napkins, a glove, two old speeding tickets, a jackknife. He found the registration in a coffee-stained envelope. He took it and slapped the glove box closed without putting anything back. He passed the envelope over to Janson. Janson took the license and registration and lay them flat on the Camino's hood and studied them under the flashlight. Reg draped his hands over the steering wheel, tapped the dash with his ring. He began to hum.

Janson came back to the window, handed registration and license back to Reg.

"All right," he said. "You think your vehicle has cooled down enough for you to make it home?"

Reg shrugged. He set the license and registration down beside him on the seat.

Janson gave the roof a pat that made the metal burp. "Get home and get some sleep," he said. He backed away, flashlight loose at his side.

"That's my plan," Reg said. He cranked the engine. Hit the lights. He threw the Camino into gear. He was about to back out when Janson stepped closer to the Camino.

Reg looked up at him, raised an eyebrow. He rested his right hand on the .45.

"You know you got a headlight out?" Janson said.

"Do I?"

"The left one. You better get that fixed. I could write you up, if I wanted. I'll give you a break, this time; I won't the next."

"Sure," Reg said, and drove out of the lot.

Reg pulled the Camino in front of his cabin and shut off the engine and sat listening to it tick. No light shone from the surrounding cabins. No breeze disturbed the juniper and cedars. No waves slapped the shoreline of Unknown Pond. He was safe. For now.

He got out, climbed into the back of the Camino and unlocked the tool vault, the smell of marijuana rushing at him. He looked out into the surrounding darkness, then swung the duffel onto the ground and jumped down. A dog barked. Sounded like Harv's old beagle, Lucy. Reg lit a cigaret, picked up the duffel and carried it to the cabin.

The cabin was cold and smelled as if he'd been away for a long time. He pulled a string and stood in the stark light of a bare bulb; he rubbed his hands together and lit the oven. He took a handful of buds from the duffel and scattered them on a sheet of tin foil and stuck the foil in the oven. Throwing his cap on the table he ran his hands through his hair and took the wad of cash from his pocket. He undid the rubber band and fanned the bills out on the table. He grabbed a handful of fifties and smelled them, snapped the rubber band back around the rest of the cash. Tapping a finger to his lips, he looked around the room. An old painting of two duck hunters poling their boat through a vicious dawn hung behind the table. It had been there when Reg had first rented the place, five years ago. He found a hammer in the junk drawer, took the picture down, and pounded a hole in the wall. He stuffed in the money and rehung the picture. He looked at it from different angles, then scooped the bigger pieces of plaster up from the floor and tossed them outside, kicking the smaller pieces around with his boot.

He took a flashlight from atop the refrigerator and went outside.

The flashlight throbbed dimly in the dark shed; he removed a minnow seine from where it was draped over a lawn mower's handle, and shut the shed door.

Back in the cabin, doubled over in its cupboard of an attic, he stretched the minnow seine between eyehooks in the rafters. He dumped the buds from the duffel into the hammocked seine, spreading them out three or four deep. He sat on a crate and lit a cigaret. He sat, smoking, staring at the marijuana, wondering what he was going to do about Mack and Elis. They'd be at the Autumn 100 on Saturday, in two days. Afterward, he could count on them being at Broken Leg Lake, partying. They'd be plenty drunk, and it would be plenty dark.

Anna's kitchen was warm, small and clean. From her chair she watched a fly spin on its back in a finger of morning sun that inched across the floor. Tired of watching the fly slowly die, she bent from her chair and smacked it with a magazine, threw both fly and magazine out in the trash can, and washed her hands.

"Jess!" she called up the stairs, leaning into the stairway. "Breakfast."

She sat down at the table and speared a spoon into a half grapefruit. She looked around the kitchen. She was content living here. She worked with good people, made money enough to provide and save. She was fortunate, she knew. Opportunities were scarce. A lot of people looked down on contentment, likened it to boredom, monotony, a life gone static. But to her, contentment was sublime. A lot of folks fought their whole lives seeking, but never finding it. Or found it, but were so uncomfortable with simpler ways that they threw themselves back into chaos.

She finished her hot chocolate. With the spoon she stirred the sludge at the bottom of the mug. Jessup's waffles sat on the plate. Cold.

Another fly ticked against the kitchen window, trapped behind the curtain. Where were they coming from? Every fall they invaded the house for its warmth. They knew what would happen if they didn't.

She had to be getting off to work.

She called up again.

He was awake, she knew. She pushed her grapefruit over to his plate of waffles. Her back was stiff. Her blood seemed thick and slow; she was tired from getting little sleep the last two nights, worrying about him, worrying about whoever it was that had dropped him off in the rain two nights before. She'd had to work late yesterday, and had not yet talked with him. He'd been sound asleep when she'd looked in on him the night before. He'd looked as if he hadn't moved since the morning, and, for a second, she'd panicked, thought the worst. Then he'd moaned and shifted and she'd gone off to bed.

She had a half-hour drive to work. She would need every minute. She stood and took her wool sweater off the back of the kitchen chair. She tugged it on over her head, pulled her hair out, letting it fall as it liked. She picked her keys off the counter, opened the front door to a damp cloudy morning.

They sat at Ma's kitchen table, coffee mugs steaming. On paper plates, fatty bacon strips lay beside eggs bleeding yolk. The kitchen woodstove warped the air about it with heat.

"I'm gonna go up there today." Reg tottered his chair on its back legs, rested his socked feet up on a corner of the table. He gouged the blade of a jackknife into a wart on the back of his hand.

"Why didn't Lamar come down?" Hal said.

Reg shrugged.

"You go all the way up there and help him and he can't get his sorry ass down here? What, he's so rich now, he can't stand to make a few extra bills?"

"Ask him. Went up there and he never showed. Tried to find the place, and got lost and spent the goddamned night in the woods." Reg ate a piece of bacon. Dragged a wedge of toast through yolk.

Hal studied him. "That right?" he said.

Reg pushed his plate away, wiped crumbs from his hands, and looked at Hal.

Hal held his gaze.

Reg lit a joint. "Had a little trouble up there."

"Trouble?"

"Lamar did."

"That right?"

Reg smoked.

"A little trouble?" Hal said.

"Happened before I got there."

"What did?"

Reg finished the joint, snubbed it on his jeans and dropped the roach in his shirt pocket.

"What did?" Hal repeated.

Reg set the chair's front legs on the floor and leaned forward.

"Well?" Hal said.

Reg told him everything. Almost. He didn't tell him how Lamar had been alive. Or about the money, or the weed. When he was done, he lit a cigaret. Hal lit one, too.

A bank of smoke grew between them.

Reg stuck his knife into the corner of the wooden table, then leaned the chair back again.

"Don't stick the table. This ain't a fishing shanty," Hal said.

Reg yanked the knife out of the table.

Hal wheeled over to the woodstove. He put on a leather glove and opened the stove door. Embers snapped out onto the floor with a blast of hot air. "Hand me a couple logs there." Reg handed Hal two chunks of ash and Hal hucked the logs into the roar of the stove and closed the door; the cobwebs in the antlers of a deer mount above the stove fluttered in the rising heat. Hal hung the glove back on its hook and adjusted the stove's damper; the stovepipe pinged. Hal considered Reg.

"You do it?" he said.

Reg stuck his knife blade back into the table, twisted it, glanced up at Hal. "Fuck you."

"Touchy. Got any idea who it was?"

"Nothin left of his face, or ID. But I don't need any ID. Lavalettes've been foamin at the mouth to get hold of me and Lamar. Bidin their time, since they got Bump."

"You're paranoid as Lamar."

"As Lamar *was*."

"I saw Mack and Elis in town yesterday," Hal said.

"Well. It was one of them. Claude, maybe, or a cousin. Someone they put up to it."

Hal took a brass pipe from his pocket and unscrewed the bowl. "It doesn't matter to you if it's them or not, does it?" he said.

Reg extracted the knife from the table and tapped the blade on his leg. "Nope," he said.

"You've been looking for a reason."

"I didn't need *this* reason."

"If it is one of them, you better get yourself lost. Get that weed off the gap and get gone. I'd a been gone last night, I was you."

"Well, yah ain't me."

"Anyone know you went on up ta Caratunk? You tell anyone?"

"No," he said, remembering he'd told Edsel. "I dint have nothin to do with it, anyway."

"Course not."

"What the fuck's that mean?"

"I know how it is in Fairland. No one ever had nothing to do with anything. You've been wronged all your life. Lavalettes won't take blame, either, you fuck with em and *force* em to fuck back."

Reg dug the blade tip under a grime-packed thumbnail. "I ain't hangin around. But I'm gettin square first. Yah unload the weed we got here, and I get the stuff off the gap and I'm packin my shit and headin south. Gone."

"It's gonna take some doing getting that weed off a the gap." Hal removed the coffeepot from the stove and freshened his mug. He draped his face over the mug and inhaled.

Reg opened the refrigerator and looked inside it. "It's Pap's birthday today," he said, quietly.

"Is it?"

"Think about him all the time this time of year. Can't shake em for the life a me."

"I can't remember the last time I thought of him," Hal said. "Years."

Reg shut the refrigerator door. "Bet I could get that kid to help me," he said.

Hal lit a cigaret and pulled his plate of bacon and eggs to himself. He ashed his cigaret in his cereal bowl. "Bad idea," he said. He folded up a wedge of toast and sopped up yolks; he stuffed the toast, yolk dripping in strings on his fingers, into his mouth. He licked each thumb. A piece of yolk stuck to the corner of his mouth.

Reg reached out for the coffeepot. The hair on the back of his hand singed and the wool tufts of his shirt curled. He poured himself a mug of coffee. "Marigold said the kid was a lunatic, throwin logs offa the truck so hard and fast he nearly killed himself. He'd make a good pack mule."

"That's a mistake. You use him, don't let him know I got anything to do with it." Hal finished his bacon and flipped his paper plate aside. "Hear what I said?"

Jessup sat in his boxers, hunched over on the front porch steps, rubbing his legs: a snake shedding bad skin. His throat felt rasped raw and the morning chill did little to clear his swampy head. His lungs were two cinder blocks grating together. He spat. Was not hungry. He looked across the puddled lawn. He'd awakened, on and off, the previous day, but had felt ill, his body heavy, ponderously heavy, too heavy to lift.

He looked up. The Santa Fe had fallen over on her side. Abandoned over on the muddy ground. A good bike, sturdy and dependable, up until a couple of days ago. He couldn't blame the derailed chain on her. Not with the rough riding he'd forced on her this summer.

Yawning, he stood and rolled his shoulders. He walked over to the Santa Fe. "Hey there," he said; he grabbed the handlebars and stood the bike up and set the kickstand. He patted her seat. She was caked with mud. Mud on the sprocket, on the imitation leather seat, on the side of the frame on which she'd spent the past two nights. He wiped at the muck and slick clay, then wiped his hands on his bare legs.

"Sorry," he said, wiping the seat.

He needed a rag. He stood again, dizzy.

A red squirrel scurried down a nearby pine, facedown. It splayed its legs and chattered, neck stretched as it eyed him. Jessup leapt at it, gave a hoarse scream and it scuttled into the upper limbs.

He walked to the side of the toolshed where the Vega sat. All of its tires were flat, their rims settled into the ground. The sun snuck through lingering clouds, its warmth spreading over his bare back; he shuddered. The Vega was dappled with black drops of sap. Its door sagged on exhausted hinges when he opened it. He found some rags in the backseat, grabbed them, getting a whiff of mildewed plastic from the Vega's sun-cracked seats. A squirrel had hoarded a cache of beechnuts in the doorskin where once had been a speaker.

At the side of the house, Jessup cranked the spigot and uncoiled the hose, dragged it to the bike. He knelt, his stomach gurgling. He felt feverish in the humid morning air and lay back on the grass in the steaming dew, his eyelids falling shut. The hose running and running.

When he opened his eyes again, the sun was high. He sat up, his back itchy, his face embossed with the pattern of grass. He took a rag and knelt at the bike. He was wiping the Santa Fe down, washing and buffing between its spokes, when he heard a rumbling and looked up to see the El Camino pull into the yard.

"Why'd you let him go?" Marigold asked Hal. She sat in Pap's old recliner, its Naugahyde arms squeaking beneath her fingers. Hal lay on the couch, head buttressed on a stack of throw pillows, allowing his back a rest from forever sitting in the chair. An afghan covered the lump of his motionless legs.

"I didn't let anyone go anywheres. He won't listen to me."

"That boy. That wild kid. You two nearly killed him the other night. Why are you so spiteful?"

He rubbed his stubbled face. "We were just having fun."

"Fun," Marigold said and looked at her brother. He was home, finally, but his presence hadn't made her feel any better, perhaps worse: he would only leave again. His traveling life still seemed false to her. Only when he was here, near those who knew and loved him, those grounded by the same mountains, the same town and life, did he fully exist. In the few days he'd been home, Marigold realized, they'd managed to convey to each other only brief, sketchy summaries of the lives that now owned them. She tried to recognize in the man before her, the brother, the boy, with whom she'd grown up. Had she ever *had* a childhood? Sometimes she felt as if she'd suddenly been placed here, on this strange mountain, with no history, just a past life of false memories that dissolved like morning fog on a river when she thought on them too hard.

She shivered, despite the warmth radiating from the woodstove. "Now Reg's gonna drag that boy around up there. He's a good kid."

"He's a wingnut. And if anyone gets anyone in trouble it'll be that boy suckin Reg into it by runnin at the mouth."

"Reg gets his own self into trouble. He doesn't need any kid. I could've helped Reg myself."

"No." Hal tapped his cigaret into a beer bottle that rested on the floor beside him.

"I can use the money," she said.

"That ain't the point."

She sighed.

"Hess and I aren't getting along," she said. "He hasn't worked for months. Doesn't hardly talk."

"He fucking around?"

"No."

"You?"

"Funny."

"Course not," he said.

"It's just. The other morning he comes pressing into me from behind, rubbing against me. Hasn't so much as looked at me since March. Now suddenly he's just going to dog me there in the kitchen. It's because of that boy. No other reason. Hess saw me with him and suddenly he's got a hard-on again. I pulled a knife on him. I would've stuck him too, if he hadn't of backed off."

"I wouldn't mess with you with a knife."

"I'd like to tell Reg about it."

"Reg doesn't need anything more to get worked up about."

"What's he got to be worked up about now?"

"Nothing."

"It's always nothing with you two. You act like you're in a damn boys club, hiding in your tree fort."

"Cute."

"You do. Reg mostly. I could help him. He could pay me, if he's going to make enough to get a car and move south."

"Shit. Reg's a fucking big mouth. How long has he been spouting that line? Or one like it? Last ten years he's gonna make it big. *NASCAR.* Come on. Three years ago he was goingta be a big game guide in Montana. Before that, a bush pilot. Next he'll be running for president. Shit, that Galaxie hasn't run since March, and he won't get it running neither. He thinks driving that Camino fast on dirt roads is some sorta time trial. And that's worlds away from fucking NASCAR."

"He still stands to make good money."

"Good money? I stopped thinkin this was goin to do anymore

than pay my bills *five* years ago. I run a scam booth at county fairs. Look around you. Shit. Look around."

"I am. I do. I've needed to get something going since I got let go from the Lucky Spot. New place off the highway is ruining them."

"Everybody wants everything easy."

"Nothing wrong with easy, but you don't just start firing people. Even if I was part-time. I was thinking of moving to Montgomery, if I got a job there, at Mitel."

"You outta. Be good for you."

"Or maybe Burlington."

"Burlington's a sewer. Buncha people from somewhere's else, is all it is. Everybody's got big fish little pond disease. Fuck em. You don't wanta live there. Why not live here, at Ma's, for the time being?"

"I wouldn't feel right about it."

Hal rubbed both hands over his thighs, asked if she could throw some more wood in the fireplace. The sun splintered through the window. "God, I'm tired," he said.

Marigold went to the fireplace and jammed the poker into the burning logs. Sparks swarmed up the chimney like crazy, bright-orange bees. The smell of woodsmoke filled the room. She sat back down, her legs tucked beneath her.

"You want, I can talk to Hess," Hal offered.

"It might help. I don't know. What would you say?"

"Tell him how hard it was on me, at first. Tell him to quit being such a martyr."

"He lost one of . . . he cut one off, Hal."

"So fucking what?"

"Hey kid," Turnip said and jutted his elbow out the Camino window. He shut off the engine and stepped out. Mud squished under his boots and the sun shone in his sunglasses. He took the glasses off and pinched his nose and put the glasses in his shirt pocket. A smell of decaying dogwood and rancid bog carried on a breeze from the swamp.

Jessup pressed his hands on his knees and stood beside the bike.

"Thought yah fixed that thing." Turnip walked over, adjusted his cap.

He looked at Jessup's boxers and the drying clay on his arms and legs.

"She's fixed," Jessup said. "Your sister rigged her. I'm just oiling her, cleaning her. She's got to last me." He didn't know what to say next. Turnip seemed bigger than he had a couple days before. Older, too. Lines crinkled around his eyes and mouth when he dragged on his cigaret. Jessup fiddled with the rag in his hand.

"Nice house." Turnip looked at the place. "Folks in?"

"My mom's working."

"Uh-huh. In town?"

Jessup nodded.

"Listen," Turnip said. He squatted, took up a stick and carved a sharp point with his knife. "Where's that Vega a yurs?"

"Over there. Other side of the shed."

"How bout I take a look at her?"

Jessup stood, eager. But Turnip stayed put. He stabbed the branch into the ground. "Yah gotta do somethin for me first. Give me a hand. I'll pay yah good. Fifty bucks. If yah got the time?"

"Fifty?"

"Right."

"I got the time."

"Yah'll need clothes." He raised an eyebrow.

"I'll go get some on."

"You do that."

Inside, Jessup raced up the stairs, three at a time. In his room he found a T-shirt and jeans. Dressing, he heard Turnip shouting from outside. He hurried down, shirt in hand, pants unbuttoned. He came out onto the porch.

"Got any camouflage?" Turnip said.

"We going into the woods?"

"Yah got any?"

"Sure. All kinds. Army. Marine. Cold weather. . . ."

"Get a jacket."

Jessup ran back in and pulled his camouflage out of a wooden trunk. Dressed, he slid a shoebox out from under his bed and seized a new blue toothbrush from it.

"Hey!" Turnip called up from below the gable window. "Yah comin?!"

Jessup hustled downstairs to the bathroom and brushed his teeth, twice, then ran out into the yard where Turnip sat in the idling Camino.

The kid moved in the woods like some kind of jungle cat. Reg had warned him to move quietly and carefully, and he did, but he did it with remarkable deftness; he would appear and disappear, then fall in behind Reg just as Reg began to grow worried he'd lost him. Back along the road there had been no sign that a car or truck had been parked recently. But that didn't mean someone hadn't been up in the woods. Hadn't been dropped off, and was up in the woods at that moment.

Coming into the clearing, the slope of cut timber falling away under a sun low and bronze and cool, Turnip sat on a downed tree. Jessup sat nearby, on a stump. He twitched in place, scratching at his cheeks. He breathed easily, admired the landscape. He'd never been up this far before. They'd crossed Smuggler's Creek over an hour ago; he hadn't known the mountains ranged as far and high as this, and with each of the last several false peaks, he'd kept expecting finally to come to a summit. He shook from the excitement and exertion of the hike, wondering why they had come this far. Turnip hadn't said, and Jessup hadn't asked. You didn't ask when you were getting paid so much. They'd smoked in the car, Jessup breaking his promise to himself, his eyes tired now, his body caught in a long sigh.

Far away, a mountain rose above the foothills, and Jessup thought of how islands formed, grew from the ocean floor where before there had been nothing.

"Okay," Turnip said. "Let's get a move on."

They beat through briars that grew so tangled the two of them were forced to stoop, and finally crawl along narrow deer trails, knees padded by moss and mud, hands scraped by thorns and twigs. Jessup bowed his head and followed the huffing sound ahead of him, careful to remain far enough behind so he wouldn't be kicked by Turnip's deep lugged boots, so close he could smell rubber, and the rich silicate packed in their soles. He and Turnip burrowed onward, the sun blocked out by the canopy of vegetation, until Jessup felt the trickling coolness of sun on his neck, and they were in a small clearing in the thickets.

Jessup stood. Before him was a fence, woven with ferns and branches. If not for Turnip pointing it out, he would never have noticed it. An expert camouflage job. Jessup looked ahead. Inside the fencing grew enormous plants of a kind Jessup had never seen. Crammed together, the plants grew tall and lush and their giant leaves sagged from their own weight. A garden. The mountain air smelled of skunk.

i am Paul Bunyan

Hack. Jessup's machete whacked through fibrous stalks, the splintering sound sweet in his ears. Down they came like sugarcane, easing over on each other, branch tips springing like Christmas tree bows. Effortless work. He was glad to do it, and thought of the Vega purring down the road toward Massachusetts. Fifty bucks' worth of gas. An unfair deal, it seemed. He licked sweat from his upper lip. He could swing all day, forever, with the beautiful heft of the machete, its blade so fiercely honed he couldn't help but reflect on its brutal possibilities.

Turnip was winded, wiping his face and the back of his grimy neck with a bandanna. Jessup wheeled around to find another stalk. None remained standing.

"All right," Turnip said. "Okay. Let's take a breather and I'll learn yah the next step."

They sat astride a mossy, decomposing log, its wetness soaking through Jessup's jeans, making his butt itch. Turnip reached for his pack, which he'd hung from a tomato stake. He lit a cigaret, slumping his shoulders. He rested his arms on his knees and spat up phlegm.

Jessup blew at the mosquitoes hovering in front of his face.

Turnip picked up a small stalk and pointed at one of its branches. "This's a leader. Not a branch, a leader," he said, his voice curt.

It looked like a branch.

"What yur gonna do is take that knife I gave yah and cut all the leaders off the stalk. Give a quick slice and pull at the same time. Like this." He grabbed hold of the stalk and took out another knife from his jacket and brought the blade down where stalk met leader and cut and pulled. "Like that."

Jessup tried. It was easy.

"There yah go," Turnip said. "A natural."

They settled into a wordless pace of work, Jessup cutting leaders from the stalks, the knife slicing through with an effortless snap of the wrist. He piled the leaders between himself and Turnip, while Turnip stuffed buds into plastic garbage bags, and tossed the leaders behind him.

"Want any leaf?" he asked Jessup.

"Leaf?"

"Makes vicious brownies. I ain't got time to fuck with em. They're yurs, yah want em."

Jessup shook his head. "No," he said.

Turnip shrugged, picked the buds expertly, a quick, deceptive movement of thumb and finger, like picking burdock from a wool sweater. The tiniest of buds grew in the nooks where leaders branched from stalks or from larger leaders.

Jessup slapped a mosquito on his hand, smearing blood. *"Vampire,"* he shouted.

"Keep it down."

"Mosquito," Jessup whispered.

"Keep yur trap shut. That's one thing yah gotta learn."

Jessup fell quiet and looked at all the leaves and buds and leaders about them.

"Seems this would take a while to smoke," he said.

Turnip didn't say anything.

Jessup stopped and peered at him. "You sell it," he said. The idea had not occurred to him until he spoke the words.

"It's good money."

"So?"

"Listen to me. People that tell yah money don't make yah any happier than yah already are. Don't make life any easier. They're fulla fuckin shit. That's those with money talkin. Money's *everythin*. It's better to have money and problems than not have money and still have problems. Quicker yah learn that, better off yah'll be."

Jessup watched a wren hop up the side of a beech tree. It looked like a nervous winged mouse.

"I hope yah know that this stays between us," Turnip said.

Jessup nodded absently. His stomach grumbled. He could hear a flock of migrating Canada geese above him, but when he looked up, he could not see beyond the dome of autumn-emblazoned leaves.

Reg cleared his throat. "I'm really a race car driver," he said. "I jus do this because I have to. For now." The kid did not respond. He was gaping up at the treetops. "Did you hear me?" Reg said. "I said I'm really a race-car driver. That's what I really am. That's what I really do. Race cars."

The kid did not seem to hear; he was staring up toward the tree-tops and seemed to be listening to something far away, something only he could hear, seeing something visible to him alone.

Stan, proud owner of the Bee Hive, was saying something, but to Hess it was the sound of distant baying dogs, so absorbed was he in watching his image in the back of the soup spoon he held before him. His cup of chowder was skimmed cold, the oyster crackers globs of floating paste.

That fucking boy. Hess couldn't stop dwelling on him. And Marigold. How stupid did she think he was? He'd come into the kitchen and found dishes on the table and in the sink. She'd cooked the kid dinner. *Dinner*. He couldn't remember the last time she'd done that for him. He had no idea what the boy looked like. No way to recognize him. He wondered if the kid was from around here. He wondered where he lived.

"Hey," Stan said. He clapped shut a napkin dispenser and set it on the counter. Hess looked away from his reflection in the spoon, and into the ridiculous face of Stan's mopey eyes and flabby cheeks.

"What?" Hess asked.

"I said, 'are you feeling all right?' You stare into your chowder for an hour, and now you're gawking at your mug like some kind of movie star. You want me to get you something else? Aspirin? Or a beer? You don't even like chowder."

Hess spun around slowly on the chrome stool, its stem squeaking as he took in the diner's collection of stuffed squirrels, the bee and hornet nests that adorned windowsills and ceiling corners. He took in the red vinyl booths, the flicker of chrome-edged tables, the utensils that awaited the rush of dinner regulars. He could see his vague image in the shine of black-and-white-checked tile, and in the gold-flecked mirrors, which reminded him of old-time dance halls.

"Just not hungry," Hess said and slapped his hand down on the counter to stop his motion.

"You want coffee or milk? Something stronger?"

"Just wanna sit."

Stan grated the grill with a porous black brick that bore a charcoal silicate dust and the stink of sulfur. He poured cider vinegar from a plastic beer pitcher; the cider bubbled and danced and steamed as he scoured the grill with the brick, bearing down so it screeched like fingernails on a chalkboard. He turned back to Hess, sipped from his always-present bottle of Moxie. His soft cheeks ran with sweat, which he wiped periodically with the back of his hand.

"Is it your injury?" Stan asked.

Hess revolved again, this time swiftly, pushing off from the counter, the room a blur and his stomach having to catch up with the rest of him when he stopped.

"Fit as a fiddle, for a one-balled tomcat," he said, smirking and grabbing at his crotch.

"If you say so."

"I do," Hess said. Then, "Y'think I'm losing my looks?" He turned, offering Stan a profile.

"What looks," Stan said.

Hess picked up the spoon again, trying to catch his image in a favorable light.

"I used to be pretty handsome. In a rough-cut sorta way. Rugged," he said, stroking his chin. "Maybe if I shaved more often," he said idly, his smile gone.

"Listen," Stan said, turning away and making to go out back. "I got to cut up some chicken. Holler if someone comes in."

Hess nodded. "Say," he said, calling after Stan; he clasped his hands together and rested his chin on his extended index fingers. "What would y'do if Sheila stepped out?"

Stan turned around, came back toward the counter and ran his hands under the faucet by the milkshake blender. He splashed water on his face. "She wouldn't," he said.

"No. I mean, really. On the level. What if she did? What would y'do?"

"She wouldn't."

"I'm sayin . . . what if?"

"There isn't a *what if.*"

"Just for the sake of argument."

"You don't know when to stop, do you? When to quit."

Hess grinned. "No," he said. "I don't."

Driving back through Smuggler's Gap, the sun down but daylight still loitering in the trees, Reg piloted the Camino, the road tricky as it rose abruptly before him, greasy with the wet clay hardening in the quick cold of the oncoming night. The heater blasted rivers of hot air that wrapped around him and the kid, turned the inside of the cab into a warm cocoon. Trapped in the defroster, behind the dash, torn leaves and candy wrappers ticked like winged insects. The Camino was drenched in the smell of earth and sweat and fresh marijuana.

"*Woo,*" Turnip huffed, startling Jessup so he nearly spilled the beer wedged between his thighs.

Turnip pounded the steering wheel with his fists. "Fuck *me.*"

"What?" Jessup rubbed his eyes, "What?"

"*What?* Look at that."

Turnip raised a hand off the wheel and held it out flat for Jessup. "I'm shakin." The Camino already shook so badly, it was hard to discern anything. "Shakin like a bastard. This is a major *haul.*"

Alongside the Camino, tree branches reached like the arms of ghosts.

"I'm outta here," Turnip said.

Jessup hoped not before the Vega was fixed.

Turnip flicked on the lone headlight, but it did little in the half-light of dusk. They followed the road down into the Lamoille basin. As they came down out of the gap, the trees opened to flat forgotten farmland growing up into alder and crab apple and poplar, where ruffed grouse strutted and drummed and held fast before erupting into flight. A mist hung over the fields, hazy and luminous. Turnip lit a cigaret.

"Want one?" he asked.

"Uh-uh."

"Don't want for much, d'yah?"

"Not much, I guess."

"Yah gotta relax more. Live. Yah seem to've taken to reefer and beer."

"I paid for it." He grinned, recalling his wretched state, and his promise to himself *never* to touch either again.

"Pay for everythin, eventually. Might's well make the best of now."

Jessup stared out the window. This was the time of day for scouting deer, the hour when whitetails skulked out from wooded edges, roamed along barbed-wire fences and edges of fields, skeletal silhouettes in the last ruin of day as they rose from the goldenrod and swale grass where they'd bedded all afternoon. Jessup scanned the fields. "You see a piece of deer first," he'd told Emily. "A twitching ear, a white swish of tail, the crooked bend of a back leg. Then you adjust your eyes, put the whole deer together. They can remain still forever. Deer. Especially bucks. Frozen. A human can't stay that still, for that long. Our survival doesn't depend on it." He'd feared he was boring her, but she'd prompted him, squeezed his hand.

Turnip gunned the Camino along the straightaway and the back end slid. Jessup was impressed with how easily he countered each slide. He listened to mud slop against his door, liking the sound of it.

"Good time of night for deer," Jessup said.

Turnip looked from the road at Jessup, a slight smirk at the corners of his mouth, his eyes glinting. "Yah hunt?"

"No. Well. With a slingshot. Not a gun. My mom gave all my dad's guns away."

"Gave em away. Shit. If my wife ever gave my guns away, I'd—"

"You have a wife?"

"No. No. But if I did. What in hell'd yur old man let her do that for? Throw out his guns? Jesus."

Jessup looked out his window. "He's dead. My dad. My mom gave the guns away because my dad's dead."

Turnip snubbed his cigaret out in the ashtray. He blew out a thread of smoke and made a sound from the back of his throat. He looked straight ahead, wiped the inside of the sweating windshield.

"Mine, too," he said.

"Your dad?"

"Mine, too." His face looked translucent in the dashboard lights. He rolled down his window. "Sixteen years," he said. "Been alive longer without em than with em. Sometimes I wonder how difrent I'd be if he'd lived. Or if it'd been my ma. She and I can't be round each other more than five minutes without goin at it. Normal, I guess. How old were yah?" he asked.

"I wasn't born yet."

"Not even born. Don't know if that's better or worse. Not bein able to remember nothin."

"I imagine him."

"I mean not bein able to remember em, miss em."

"I do," Jessup said. "I miss him all the time. It feels like I have a hole in me. Like I have this tiny hole in me I'm always leaking from, but I can't seem to find exactly where the hole is, so I can stop from leaking."

Turnip looked at his cigaret and tossed it out the window. "I was fourteen," he said.

The headlight illuminated the fog so it looked like a bank of brilliant, fresh snow. It was becoming difficult to see what was right in front of them.

"My old man and me used to hunt birds round here." Turnip flipped his hand at the landscape. "We used to own most of this land. My famly. My grandparents, anyway. And their grandparents. Down the line. It was mostly sold off by the time I was born. Guess I miss the land the same way yah miss yur old man. I never did know what it was to have it, but I know what it is not to have it. My cousin, Lamar, and me, we used to hunt it, too. Together. All the time." He sighed. "Hungry?" He barked a laugh. "Course yah're. Worked yah like a goddamned dog." He patted Jessup on the knee. "Yur a hard worker." He brought his hand back to the wheel.

Jessup sat up straight, trying to shake his sleepiness; he rolled down his window and stuck his head out. "Yes," he said, bringing his head back inside. "I'm hungry."

"Been to Sarah's Sawmill?"

"I can't say I have."

"Can't say, huh?"

"No." It was one of a few places in town that Jessup's mother forbade him to enter.

The Camino came to Sawmill Bridge. On the other side of the Lamoille River was Ivers. If not for the mist, they'd have been able to see the few lights of town, flickering like tiny flames in the distant windows.

"Well. We'll go," Turnip said. "My treat."

Because her front door was ajar, Anna expected her son to answer when she came in and called his name. Instead her voice fell on an empty house. Jessup's bike was outside. He couldn't be too far. In the living room, alone, Anna sat on the couch, took off her shoes and rubbed her feet. Removing the bobby pins from her bun, she gave her head a quick shake and let her hair cascade down her back. She picked up the cache of mail from the past several days. There was a letter for Jessup, from that girl. She set it aside and went through the rest of the mail, junk mostly. She picked up the *Ivers Daily Press* and leafed through it. Not much going on, a game warden was missing up in Caratunk. He'd gone off into the woods up there last weekend, off duty, and had not come back. A lot of land to cover up there. There was another story about some poor kid over in Nullhegan who'd fallen off the cliff at a quarry and was lucky to have suffered only a broken leg. The town of Nullhegan was talking, again, about dynamiting the quarry. They wouldn't. Anna wondered where Jessup was. It was growing dark. She flicked on the lamp beside her and settled uncomfortably as the next night of her life came on.

Sarah's Sawmill Tavern lay in cigaret smoke and the amber cast of faux coal lanterns suspended from rustic posts and beams. The chipped-shellac tabletops shimmered with the reflection of candles burning in mason jars. From all about the tavern came the chink of forks and knives on ceramic plates. At every seat and booth men sat, their jeans and wool pants mud-slaked, elbows planted aside their plates, shirtsleeves bunched to the elbows to expose red union suits, faces hunkered over steaming plates of bloodied rib eye and T-bone, heaped greens and mashed potatoes. Loggers. Frenchmen. Their fleshy ears shot with sprigs of hair, noses resembling rotting pears. Heads of hair, purpleblack or shocked-white, burst like underbrush. Every third hand was missing fingers. The men gnawed their steaks, teeth working with chainsaw fury. Generations of men, a likeness in all their faces; traces of the callow, who still possessed most of their fingers, revealed in those of the older men, faces dark and cragged. They cut and forked and fingered meat and peas and potatoes, guzzled whole milk poured from frosted pewter pitchers and beer poured from cobalt ewers. Hunks of bread were torn from hot loaves and dredged through gravy and broth and pooling blood, the lulling din of the men's lowered voices, broken now and again by bursts of laughter or barked exclamations that fell off again as sharply as they had risen.

"Eat up," Turnip urged, waggling a finger off the stem of his spoon. He slurped chowder broth from the spoon, leaving potato wedges, the slick quiver of clam. He tilted the spoon, and tipped potato and clam alike into his mouth. "I dint buy that for yah to watch go cold. What's the matter?" He poked his chin down at Jessup's pile of potato skins gunked with melted cheese, sour cream and guacamole. "We got dinner comin soon."

Jessup scooped up a potato skin, greasy warm in his fingers. He was not hungry. He hadn't thought of Emily much for days, and felt that by not thinking of her he'd wronged her in some way. Now he made every effort to imagine her, but it was difficult to envision her face through the beer and marijuana and fatigue. He bit into the potato; grease dripped on the paper place mat that displayed a mural of the state and all its historic landmarks and state symbols in the margins.

A waitress struggled from the bar on the far side of the restaurant, weaving between tables, knocking the backs of chairs with her milkmaid's hips, a tray of food expertly balanced on an open palm she kept raised above her head. She worked her way along the edge of the booths and strode over to them. Her nametag announced: HELLO, I'M SARAH!

"How's everything?" she asked. Her red apron was cinched tight at her waist so her stomach bulged and sagged against it like a sandbag. Her bare arms were covered with swirls of black hair that did not match the stringy red tresses that fell limply on her wide shoulders. She held a folded stand in one hand, kicked its legs so it swung open, and set the tray down on its canvas straps.

"Where's our other waitress, darlin?" Turnip said.

"She was the hostess. Filling in for me while I took care of a big table."

Turnip sniffed. "What's that yah got on? Smells nice."

"Perfume. You all set?"

"Darlin, we'll take us another pitcher a beer," he said loudly and stacked his empty soup bowl and salad plate at the end of the table.

Jessup finished his beer, then dabbed his mouth with a napkin. He set the napkin back in his lap, smoothing it.

The waitress nodded; up close her age showed in the candlelight. Her furrowed skin was caked with a pinkish makeup that looked like frosting, and cracked like drying clay around her eyes and mouth when she smiled. Her eyelids shone purple, like some exotic moth's wings, and her eyebrows were slight, black, penned-in strokes.

She took their dirty dishes and empty pitcher and put them on the tray.

"Go head and put them potato skins in a doggie bag," Turnip said, pointing at Jessup's plate.

The waitress gave Jessup a scornful look. "Didn't you like them?" she asked.

"I wanted to save room." He patted his stomach.

"I see." She picked up a plate with a steak and a tinfoil-wrapped baked potato. "Porterhouse? Rare?"

"Right here, darlin."

"That," she said, pointing a finger at Jessup, "leaves you with the clam strips, 'extra, extra, tartar. On the side.'" She set Jessup's plate in front of him, and tucked her pad back in her apron pocket.

Jessup imagined seagulls, lighthouses, a pier from which hanged a dead man.

"Where'd these clams come from?" he asked.

Sarah lifted the tray and folded the stand, leaning on it. "The ocean," she said.

"Massachusetts? Cape Cod?"

"Maine, I think."

"Oh."

"Are you two all set?"

"Jus that beer, darlin," Turnip said winking, and jabbed his steak knife into the potato; he sliced the potato, pinched its ends until steaming chunks of spud blossomed. He drew his fingers away quickly, licked them.

"I'll be back with that," she said.

"Thanks," Jessup said.

She nodded and wormed her way back toward the kitchen door beside the bar.

Turnip grabbed five pats of butter from a tiny glass plate and thumbed them into his potato. He sprinkled pepper on his steak and potato until they looked as if they'd been dropped on a beach of black sand.

"Good-lookin bitch," he said.

"So *that* was Sarah." Jessup pinched a clam strip by its tip, and dipped it in the bowl of tartar; he tipped his head back and dropped the clam in his mouth.

Turnip stared at him. "*Who* was Sarah?" He sawed into his porterhouse.

"That waitress. Her tag said, 'Hello, I'm Sarah.'"

"Guess she's Sarah then."

"*The* Sarah. The owner."

"No. What're yah, a goddamned ostrich, head in the sand. Where yah been?"

"Nowhere really. I got my heart set on Cape Cod, though. And Montana and Kentucky. The coal mines. The bayou, too."

"Why all them places?"

"I got a . . . friend. In Massachusetts. We're going to travel the country together. After she gets up here."

"*She*, huh? Where's a crazy kid like yurself get off havin a piece of trim?"

"A what?"

"A piece of trim. Of ass. A *girl*."

"Oh. I met her here. In town one day. Her father's got a summer camp—"

"Rich one, huh? Summer girl. Careful with them kind."

"We're friends."

"Sure. Sure."

"We *are*."

"I ain't sayin difrent. That's good. Yah got a friend that's a girl. Good. Ain't nothin else worth grovlin over, and makin a mess outta yur life, than a woman. Jus be careful."

"You got a girlfriend?"

"Me?" Turnip set his fork on his plate and took up his napkin and wiped his mouth. "Not right now I don't."

"How come?"

Turnip picked up his steakbone and sucked at its marrow, then wiped his fingers on his napkin. "I been busy, gettin ready to head south and tryin not to get in trouble. Takes energy for me to stay outta trouble. I ain't got the time, the spare energy, for women."

"I see."

"Yah do huh? I ain't much good with em. Outta bed, anyway." He winked. "I jus ain't figured out how to make it stick, yet. Yah treat that girl good, hear?"

"She's a queen," Jessup said.

"Ain't they all?" Turnip picked at his back teeth with a finger. "Yah never heard the story bout Sarah? The owner's daughter? How she died in sixty-five? In the flood. She and the Smalley twins, Leroy and

Jacob. How the only one saved was Marigold. Even the guy doin the savin drowned."

"Flood?"

"Of *sixty-five*."

"I know about it," Jessup leaned across the table. "My dad drowned in it. Saving a girl."

"How's that?"

"He drowned, saving a girl. I wonder if it was her. Fl—Marigold. My mother wouldn't ever say who it was. Wouldn't give details. She told me the story once. Said, after that, she wouldn't tell me anymore. It was too hard for her. Made me swear not to talk about it, either. Not to ask any questions, either, because the town had suffered enough. Towns don't need to be reliving tragedies any more than a person."

"Yur *mother* told yah that?"

The boy nodded. Leaned in close as if Reg was going to reveal to him some secret truth. Reg scratched his temple then sat back with his arms spread out over the back of the booth. "Well. Yur old man dint save Marigold. Skinny Lavigne's old man saved her."

"Skinny who?"

"Lavigne, an old friend a mine."

"Who else drowned?"

"No one. Far's I know. Just Sarah and the Smalley boys, and old man Lavigne. A miracle. Worst flood on record."

"That can't be *right*."

"Right or wrong, that's how it was."

"That can't be. My dad drowned in that flood."

"Maybe yur mother got the year mixed up or somethin. Town's had a lot of floods."

"How could she do *that*? You think she doesn't know the year I was *born*?"

Reg lifted his hands off the back of the booth in surrender and studied the kid, whose attention was fixed on him, his hands busy with his napkin. Reg set his hands back on the back of the booth. "Maybe," he said. "Maybe I got it wrong. Probly do. I'm no history expert. If yur mother says so, it must be so. I jus never heard of it. Yah want to hear bout Sarah?"

"Sure." His voice low, defeated. "Sure."

Reg leaned forward and set his elbows on the table, clasped his hands before his chin. "I was twelve. Hal was sixteen. He knew her. Sarah. She was maybe a year older than him. He was fuckin her. I'm pretty sure. Never could get that outta him. But. Sometimes yah jus know."

The kid nodded.

"It rained all that March and April. All of it. Like a bastard. Rained and rained and rained. Farmers didn't get their crops planted till late June. Some till July. A few never did get nothin in the ground. I say the flood only claimed the four that I know of. Plus. I guess. Yur old man. But there was plenty suicides the next few years cus a that flood. Had a ton a snow that winter. Twenty feet up to the gap, and over on Ivers Mountain. Then on the first weekend of March, the weather suddenly got real warm, balmy. Like it sometimes does for a day or two in the spring. But it *stayed* warm, and all that snow started meltin. Then the rain came. Oceans of it. Rivers carved new courses, swolled up over banks and flooded towns, became goddamned lakes. Washed away bridges. Know that bridge in Cambridge? Backwards Bridge?"

"No."

"Well, it's called Backwards Bridge cus the original one got wiped out. A covered bridge. And they put in a steel bridge. It curves the wrong way, against the lay of the road, which they never fixed. Army corps of engineers lowered the bridge down backwards. Can't see for shit comin off the bridge from the south."

"I think I saw pictures of those bridges, before and after the flood, at the library."

"I don't know bout any library. Probly. There's pictures all round town."

"They're at the library. Library's got the best ones. The library—"

"Yah want me to finish or do yah wanna gab bout the goddamned library?"

The kid was quiet.

"All right then. Buildings started washin away. Terrible sound, nails screechin and tearin loose as yur house collapses into the water. Folks got together and started sandbaggin. Sandbagged day and night. Tryin to save the town. Their lives. My memé always said it

looked like Europe, durin the first war. All them sandbags. All that
mud. Ever'one runnin round. Ever'one helpin but the youngest and
oldest. The youngest kids, includin me, were put up in the haylofts of
barns that set above the flood plain. We were watched over by our
older brothers and sisters, who took turns sandbaggin, and we, the
ones between ten and twelve, was in charge a babysittin all the
youngest kids, cept the babies.

"Well, how can yah expect kids to watch over other kids? I remember watchin from the Dubuques's haymow, the four of em,
Sarah, and the twins, and Marigold. I dint know it was them, at first.
Couldn't see much, for the rain, cept it was some kids and a raft
they'd made out of inner tubes and pallets. They'd brought it down
to a flooded field; water looked still as a pond. They'd pushed the raft
out and drifted toward the middle before any grown-up caught em. I
knew there was trouble when I seen over a dozen men runnin out to
that lake of brown water, callin after the kids. I couldn't hear em, but
they had their hands cupped at their mouths and were stretchin their
necks out. The edges of the field was lined with people callin. Seemed
I was the only one not down there. The kids were tryin to get back.
They had a couple boards for paddles and they were workin up a
froth, but not goin anywhere and it was clear they were stuck in the
draw of the river. The river itself was still a good few hundred feet
away, but yah could see it, slowly suckin them toward it. Well, the
men run out, but the water got deep, fast, and they dint get a hundred
feet out before they were chest high and that water was too cold to
swim in. That raft was spinnin round and the kids were bawlin and
screamin and lookin round for some tree or rock to grab hold of. And
I was so worked up, so scared for Marigold, I bit a chunk out of my
palm. Dint feel a thing, till after. Still got the scar. Marigold was the
only one to get hold of a branch. An old elm. She grabbed onto it and
pulled herself up in the nook of its lower branches and hung on. The
others weren't so lucky. My memé said the most important things
come down to luck. I don't believe in shit like that, but that time I did.
Wasn't nothin for them others to hold onto once they got past that
tree, and the river got em. Some men got a little johnboat with a motor out there, finally. Marigold was clingin to that tree limb. And she

wasn't lettin go for nothin. Old man Lavigne had to get out onto the branch and hand her down to the boat. He got her in there safe, but slipped himself and fell in. Never did find em."

"You *sure* it was Mr. Lavigne that drowned?"

"I went to the funeral."

"But they didn't find the body."

"Don't need a body. Whole town saw him drown. He's probly at the bottom of Bloomfield Reservoir."

The kid squinted at the candle.

He mumbled, and poured a beer. "Jesus," he said.

Sarah came back and placed a pitcher of beer in the center of the table. Reg poured himself a glass, slurped at the beer, horselipped it.

"Anything else," Sarah said.

Reg peered at her over his glass. "Jus keep an eye on this pitcher. We're thirsty men here."

"Will do."

With one hand wrapped around his third beer, Jessup dangled his last clam strip, pecked at it, swallowed. He washed it down with the last of his beer. The candle flames doubled. About the tavern, a soft halo glowed around every object. His head felt filled with wet cement.

Reg sat with his back slumped against the wall, an elbow propped on the table, the other arm over the back of the booth, his legs stretched out so his boots hung over the end of the seat. His cigaret burned in a tinfoil ashtray. He took it between his fingers and smoked it, blew wreaths of smoke that drifted up and became part of a cloud of smoke in the rafters. He looked at Jessup, and took a fifty dollar bill from his shirt pocket and slid it across the table. "For today. Got some more work. If yur willin."

The kid picked it up and folded it, zipped the bill in a side pocket of his backpack. "I don't know. I got my friend coming up soon, and I'm busy getting ready."

"Too busy to make a quick seventy-five? I could give yah more. A hundred. Yah could take yur lady friend out to a nice place. Taker to Montreal."

"She doesn't like fancy restaurants."

"Sure she does."

"No, she doesn't, she—"

"She says she don't, but she *does*. Take my word. Not a woman born don't like to be takin to a fancy place. I could give yah a hundred. Yah can go a long ways on that with the gas mileage that Vega'll get once we getter runnin."

"Would we go into the woods again?"

"Nope. Yah gotta be my driver. Won't be but an hour or so. Tomorrow night."

"I get to drive your car?"

"El Camino."

"And you're still going to fix my Vega?"

"Sure."

The kid dipped the fingertips of one hand into the candle, then his thumb. He lifted his hand out in a claw and held it before his face. He blew on each fingertip then touched them to his cheeks, lightly stroked his jawline and lips. He sniffed the candle wax.

"All right," he said. "I'll do it."

Reg pushed off the table to try to sit upright. He waved his hand above his head, and snapped his fingers as Sarah glided by with a tray of ice cream sundaes. He lurched for her trailing apron string. She whirled around, then corraled the sliding dishes.

"Yes?" she said.

"Another, when yah get round to it." Turnip held up the empty pitcher.

She grabbed it and stalked off.

"Fiesty."

The kid peeled the wax from his fingertips.

He set each wax mold on the table, then picked each one up and held it over the flame, letting the wax drip. The waitress returned, set a pitcher of beer down, without slowing her gait.

Reg poured himself a beer, the foam spilling down the sides to pool at the base of the glass; he dipped his head to the beer like a bird at a puddle, grasping the glass, keeping it steady. Foam clung to his lips. He filled the kid's beer glass.

"Drink up," he said. "This is our last."

The kid rested an open palm on the mouth of the mason jar and the flame sputtered until it seemed to extinguish, the wick an ember. He lifted his hand and the flame struggled, a tremorous flame that intensified to glow brightly again.

He tipped the jar over, poured a thin stream of wax into his cupped palm and placed the candle back down.

Reg emptied the rest of the pitcher into his glass.

"Yah some sorta firebug?" he asked.

The kid drank his beer.

"Take a match," he said. "Rub two sticks, click two rocks. *Fire.* Light those curtains in the window." He lit a match, held it near the curtains, then blew it out. "Light Sarah's apron. Her hair. *Woosh.* Up in flames. Everyone likes it. Didn't you ever have fires on Christmas? Tell stories around campfires?"

"Yur drunk. Yah drunkard," Reg said. "My pap used to build crazy bonfires in the backyard of the place. Tell stories. Ghost stories. Mostly. He dint talk bout himself. Said he'd leave the talkin about himself to others. To us. The kids. Said that the story about yurself should always be told by yur children. Guess that'll leave mine untold. He'd build these humongous bonfires with fence posts, and clapboard left over from the old barn. That wood lasted for years. Heated the house for four, five winters with that old barn. Ishams dint have use for an old barn, told us we could have what was left of it, if we wanted to raze and haul it off ourselves. I think my ma'd rather've frozen to death than heat her house with what little was left of her childhood. Might as well have been burnin the bodies of her family."

Reg dug his wallet out of his back pocket, stuck a few bills under the pitcher.

"How'd yah turn out so good without an old man around?"

The boy shrugged. "My mother. I guess."

"My old man was a hard worker. He taught me a lot. Lookit me now. Nothin."

"What about racing?"

"Yeah. Well. There's that." He waved his hand in front of him, then made to stand, but fell, whacking his chin on the table.

"Who's *drunk*?" the boy said drunkenly.

Sitting back up, Reg rubbed his jaw and spat into his napkin. He gripped the back of the booth with one hand, planted the other on the table and eased himself up to stand. "*There,*" he said, straightening the collar of his jean jacket. "God*damn* it, *there.*"

The restaurant had quieted and emptied almost entirely. A few loggers remained at a scattering of tables and barstools; mostly silent, they gazed bleary-eyed into whisky tumblers and beer glasses, dug pinkies into ears, or leaned back and smoked their hand-rolled cigarets. A few had found the company of women who seemed to have appeared from nowhere and now sat close to their men, legs spread wide apart in their tight jeans, palms rubbing the insides of their men's thighs, long white cigarets wedged between their own thick-knuckled fingers.

"It's his birthday today. My old man's," Reg said. "Same day he died." He rubbed his face.

The kid blew out the candle.

"Oughtta try it," Turnip said. He was ranting about fly fishing and drinking from a bottle of scotch he'd ordered just as they were leaving Sarah's. Single malt. "Best kind there is." He'd slapped the money down on the bar and bellowed: "I won't drink blended shit again." Sarah had eyed him warily.

The windshield wipers thumped, clearing the fogged windshield as Turnip sucked from a brass bowl. The Camino swerved all over the road. They'd been on the wrong side for a while now. "I'm *tellin* yah. I used to be into garden hackle, too. I could take yah *fishin*. With *minnows*. Yah'll never go back. All them places I'm sure Marigold blabbed about, she did *dint* she?" He jabbed Jessup's thigh. "Who yah think showed her them spots? They're good. But not the best. I ain't ever told a soul where those're at."

The Camino sped into a bank of ground-level clouds.

Jessup lit the bowl and inhaled. *i am an astronaut on the moon, i don't know gravity*

"I have to stop by, drop this mother lode off," Turnip said. "Then I can get yah home. Shit. I'd still be up there without yur help. Yah got good work ethics. I tell yah that?"

"You did," Jessup said and rested his head against the window. It would be good to have the Vega fixed. Get down to see Emily.

Columbus Day seemed so far off. Traveling the country and staying in hotels. That would take money. Turnip had a point. Jessup could use more cash. As he grew sleepy, he thought about the marijuana they'd taken off the mountain. He could grow it himself, he'd bet. Up at the Barker place. No one went up there. He could get books. There were books about everything. Except maybe what had happened to his father. He suppressed that thought. He didn't want to think about it now, why his mother would have told him what she had. One afternoon, in first or second grade, a couple of girls had told him they'd heard his father had just got up and left one day. At the time, on the playground, Jessup hadn't bothered to refute their story, it held so little merit. He'd ignored the girls and they'd never again teased him about it. He'd never disbelieved his mother. Never doubted her. At least not there, at recess, in the bright sunshine. But that night, under the dark eaves of his bedroom roof, he'd not slept well. Now, an anxiety spread through his chest as a taut breathlessness. He lit the pipe and took a hit. He set the pipe on the dash and felt his body drifting, flooding with warm waves. He dreamt of plants as tall as maple trees; huge marijuana trees; his arms were chain saws and all the leaves on the trees were million dollar bills.

He awoke, flinching, frightened to see someone next to him in the dark: Turnip. He rubbed his eyes, his vision suspect with sleep. The Camino was quiet, the engine off. Smoking a cigaret, Turnip sat tapping a finger on the steering wheel. He was humming. A low sorrowful tune. He didn't look at Jessup. It was as if Jessup wasn't there. The Camino was parked on a dirt road that was dark save for a lone light that filtered through the trees from a house. Turnip was looking at the light, watching the house. Jessup rubbed his eyes again and squinted. It was one of those Swiss houses. A chalet. An A-frame. Turnip revved the engine. When a set of headlights appeared behind the Camino, Turnip drove away, slowly, looking back over his shoulder at the house, as if to put it to memory.

The night hid the fog, but Hess, soused from the beers he'd put down at the Bee Hive, before Stan had kicked him out, could feel a mist on his face; it reminded him of the ocean.

He'd been to the ocean, once. On his honeymoon.

He and Marigold had escaped the woods for a week at Hampton Beach, a seaside town in New Hampshire. On the ride down, in the wood-paneled Hornet, its roofrack loaded down, its snow tires clacking on the pavement, Hess had had Marigold laughing so hard it seemed to have become her way of breathing. Early on, when they'd first met, he hadn't even had to try to make Marigold laugh; he'd been himself, telling embarrassing stories, knowing before he even started them that they would make her hysterical.

They'd stayed at the Ocean Breeze Motel, a mom-and-pop place run by an elderly couple from some foreign country, who'd seemed genuinely happy for his and Marigold's marriage.

In the afternoons they'd sunned on the beach, swam and rubbed lotion on each other; he'd made fun of his own farmer's tan, and she'd ribbed him about the flip-flops and sunglasses he'd bought at a gift shop. All week they'd lain in the sun, from late morning until late afternoon; then they'd strolled the boardwalk, holding hands, wandered in and out of gift shops, watching glass blowers and taffy pullers, making dirty jokes about the foot-long hot dogs they'd eaten. The air had smelled of salt and the sea, coconut oil and taffy. One afternoon they'd sat in front of the band shell and caught a local talent show, which a five-year-old ballerina had won. They'd talked about children. They'd walked into dim arcades, where tanned kids had escaped from the heat and sun, where budding girls, and boys in their dripping swim trunks and bare feet leaned their hips into the machines, and ground against each other in dark corners and behind the curtains of photo booths, their giggles and entangled feet giving them away.

Later, at dusk, Hess and Marigold had carried their blanket and a picnic basket to the beach, so they could watch the nightly fireworks. They'd spread their blanket out among the crowd, which stretched along the shore, and watched the night sky explode.

Hess kicked a stone in the road.

He walked along until he came upon Sawmill Bridge. He walked halfway onto it and stopped to rest and look out the side. The night was too dark and foggy to make anything out, but the surrounding countryside carried to him the smell of pine pitch. He threw a stone out into the Lamoille; here the river's surface was tranquil, but its current strong. As a boy, he'd jumped off this bridge countless summer days. He wondered if the rope swing still hung from the limb of an oak that leaned out over the river around the bend. He wondered if the tree still stood. Its roots had been exposed, even then, the bank crumbling.

He thought of the boy. "Nobody," Marigold had said of the boy. If he was nobody, why'd she hesitate when Hess had asked about him? "Who?" she'd said, as if she'd not had a boy in the truck. The fucking boy. Hess had asked Marigold about him without giving it any thought. "He was just giving me a hand."

Hess could give her a hand.

She'd better believe it.

He walked across the rest of the bridge. The whisky was running through him. He stepped to the side of the road, near the first row of a cornfield and pissed. Dried milkpods rattled and a warm mist rose around him. He was zipping up when he heard the sound of dual straight pipes. His piss steamed, weaving around his calves. A lone bright light cut through the fog like a lighthouse beam, and filled the covered bridge from the other side of the river. The vehicle clattered slowly over the bridge and Hess ducked as it appeared slowly out of its maw. An El Camino.

As it passed, it seemed quieter than it had from a distance, as if its roar was only an idle threat. Hess was sweating; frogs leaped to safety out of the headlight's reach. The passenger window was down and Hess could see a boy in the passenger's seat; if Reg and the boy could see him, standing alone and drunk in the bank of fog, they didn't show it.

Killing the headlight and engine, Reg drank the last of the scotch and rubbed his face. Marigold was here, her truck parked up next to the porch. The glow from the fireplace inside lit the two front room windows in an autumnal orange. The house a big jack o' lantern. The kid was snoring like a drunk in a hammock, face mashed against the door as he hugged himself.

"Hey," Reg croaked. "Get up. Wake up." He tapped the kid on the shoulder. The kid moaned. Reg grasped his shoulder and shook him. The kid lifted his head.

"We're here," Reg said.

"I've got to get home."

"Yah gotta give me a hand first."

Had anyone seen him, they might have thought that Hess, cowered in the grass next to the Camino, was searching the ground for a lost set of keys.

Silhouettes shifted in the house windows.

His feet itched in his wet leather boots. He watched the house from behind the Camino, then crept closer. Dew clung to his eyelashes. His thirst was immense.

He leaned on the side of the truck.

It occurred to him that he could go inside the house, if he chose. Walk up the steps and onto the porch. No knock. Just step in from the cold. "Hey. How're yah? Hal, good to see yah. How's things? Work? Well . . ." Hess kicked at a tire. "Have a beer? Sure. Why not? Already had a few." Maybe he'd get some looks. At first. He could haul in an armful of firewood. Toss a log or two on the fire. Apologize for getting out of hand the other afternoon. *Me? Just out walking. Cold night? Yeah. Eerie. Yeah. Yeah. All the way out from there. Hmmm? Oh, thinking. Thinking.*

That was his wife in there. Marigold Albertine Please. He coughed, covered his mouth. He dropped to his knees; his hands smelled of the diner. Of booze.

A shriek rose from inside the house. It came again. Like a bark. Marigold. Her laugh.

At the creak of the screen door, Hess slipped behind the truck, and watched through the cab's windows.

Reg stepped out onto the porch, smoking a cigaret.

He held something in his hand as he paced on the porch, looking out around the dark side of the house. Squatting, he faced the corner of the porch. It was hard to tell what he was doing; he was opening a burlap bag, taking something from it. Traps. Leg holds. He went about setting them next to the trash cans. Finishing, he clapped his hands; he tossed his cigaret into the grass, then stepped off the porch. Hess was caught between the urge to crawl under the truck and hide, or saunter out into the open. He didn't want to be discovered like this, spying through the truck windows.

Reg walked toward the truck, stopping about halfway and unzipping his pants. Done, he zipped and looked up at the sky. He turned and went back inside, the screen door clapping.

Hess waited to make certain Reg was not returning, then stood, watching the house. In a while, a sound, a low quiet sound, came from within, as if someone were moaning. He ran to the side of the porch, an ache working from his wound through his bowels.

He was about to peer into a side window when someone stepped in front of it; he moved away quickly. He looked around, snapped a branch from a fir and held it in front of his face; setting the branch aside, he began to claw at the ground. The grass was dead, but underneath, the soil was rich and wet. He raked handfuls of earth, then smeared it on his face and neck. The cold mud tightened his skin.

Hess picked up the branch and edged to the window.

He saw Reg first, stretched out on a couch across the room, his head on one arm of the couch, feet hanging over the other; in his lap he held a beer bottle. His cap was off, his black hair molded to his skull and cheeks. His eyes were shut but his mouth was moving. Hess realized the moaning he had heard wasn't moaning, but singing. Reg crooned, the words distorted by the window. Marigold had always bragged of Reg's voice, but Hess had never heard it. He listened and watched Reg mouth words he could not understand. Reg's Adam's apple bobbed, the sound he created lonesome and tortured. Unexplainably, Hess felt a deep loss, imagined famine, plagues. Floods. The voice stopped, but Reg's mouth remained open as he lifted his head from the arm of the couch. Hess froze. Reg brought his beer to his lips.

The entire room came into focus; the floor, varnished and as deeply grained as an old boat hull; the bear rug, its coarse hair having long ago lost its luster, its shellaced tongue sticking out, the bear's killer as forgotten and dead now as the bear itself.

On the fireplace mantle sat photos of members of the many-limbed family tree. In a duct-taped recliner sat Hal, a joint between his fingers, a corkscrew of smoke rising from it. Hess had the urge to put the joint out on his forehead.

Just below the window, so at first he had looked right over her, lay Marigold. She lay on her side, chin resting in the palm of one hand, fingers of the other hand weaving in the ratty hair of the boy who lay curled up, sleeping like the innocent.

At the sight of Marigold and the boy, Hess felt something give, as if he'd broken through the ice of a frozen pond and plunged into a numbing world that paralyzed him with panic. He tried to gain a single coherent thought or feeling. He stared at the two of them. His fingernails dug into the windowsill. *So.* He looked at Reg and Hal. He inched away from the window, trying to keep from screaming, tripped over a root and fell, his side and groin splitting with a hot pain. Gaining his feet, he turned and ran, mustering all his energy to carry him away from the house, the mud that had coated his face slithering down his cheeks. The scream finally came, a rising wail, as if he were falling from a cliff, below him nothing but rock.

When Reg heard a scream he tipped his beer over and kicked the ashtray across the floor as he swung his feet off the couch.

"What the fuck?" he said.

Hal wheeled his chair to the window, cupped his hands to his face trying to see out into the dark.

"A dog?" Marigold untangled her fingers from the boy's hair. The boy's breathing remained deep and rhythmic, warming the bare skin of her belly. "Was it an animal?" She went to the window with Reg.

"I don't see anything," she said, shielding her eyes.

"Coydog," Hal said, rubbing his palms on the wheels.

"That wasn't any coydog," Reg said.

Hal maneuvered his chair and looked at the boy.

Reg put his jacket on, put the .45 in its pocket. "Fuckers better hope they can run."

Outside, Reg crouched on the porch and regarded the dark yard; he tapped the pistol against the living room window. Marigold's face appeared, rippled behind the glass. He pointed to the dark porchlight. She disappeared and the porch light came on. It was still difficult to make out much. Reg stepped to the far end of the porch and looked around the side of the house by the chimney. It was darker there, with just the light from the single window. Carefully, he stepped off the porch. The ground was half frozen, and when he knelt to look, eyes adjusting to the darkness, he saw where someone had slipped and fallen in the mud.

He followed the tracks to the driveway, but lost them among tire tracks and stones. At the road he stopped and listened. A branch broke. He fought the urge to rush into the trees and fire blindly. The noise did not come again. Quietly, he backed away to the Camino and opened the door and felt around on the passenger floor. Finding a flashlight, he shut the Camino door. The flashlight wouldn't go on; he tapped it. The bulb flickered. He tightened the lens cover. The light shone steadily. He turned it off.

He looked back at the house, recalling nights of hide and go seek in this yard and woods; he'd played with an extreme competitiveness, the others had always accused him of cheating. He'd never cheated, back then.

He stepped quickly toward the trees. He peered into them, then entered the woods.

Somewhere before him water trickled over rock, the spring that he'd gigged frogs in as a boy. He heard a scurrying to his left and turned the flashlight toward the sound and flicked it on, its beam lighting the woods, catching a movement; he swung toward it. A flurry of leaves and a glimpse of movement, and Reg was firing.

Reg pushed past Marigold where she stood in the doorway holding open the screen door. He stalked into the living room and collapsed on the couch.

"Who shot?" she asked. She looked him up and down.

Hal considered Reg from his chair. "Well?" he said.

"Somebody was fuckin out there," said Reg. "Lookin in the window. I waited in the woods and when I heard em, I shot. Whoever's out there's gone now."

"You missed?" said Hal.

"Don't know. Flashlight died. If they were in there, they woulda shot back."

"Not if you hit them." Hal glanced at the boy. "We gotta get this shit outta here."

"I ain't bringin it to my place," Reg said. "Not now."

The boy stood up, pulling down a pant leg that had ridden up. "What's going on?" he said in a sleepy voice, hopping on the other leg as he yanked up his jeans.

"Get him outta here," Hal said, nodding at the boy.

"Right," Reg said. "But right now, I gotta figure where to stash it." He glanced at Marigold. "What bout yur place?"

"No," she said.

"How much?" he asked.

"I don't want it there if someone's looking for it," she said.

"How much?" He reached for his wallet.

"Quit that," Hal said. "I don't want it up to her place either."

"If you're planning on hiding something, I know a good place," the boy said.

The lone headlight lit the trees.

For miles Turnip had remained silent. Jessup had mentioned the Barker place and they'd liked his idea. But Turnip wasn't headed in that direction now, and Jessup didn't recognize the lake outside his window, flashing minnowlike under a brassy moon. He'd slept through a shooting; it was unclear exactly what had happened; they wouldn't say. But he was sorry he'd missed it. He needed to keep alert.

The smell of sour beer rose from the cans at his feet. In the moonlight, cabins and cottages hid among the trees. No windows shone. It felt very late. The road branched off again and again, growing darker, disintegrating to a narrow, treacherous lane of frostheaves; the lake appeared and disappeared through the trees. Frogs sat still in the road, then leapt in a frenzy as the Camino crept upon them. A snowshoe hare streaked out from the cedars along the roadside, zigzagged, then disappeared under the Camino. Jessup lifted off his seat in expectation of the thump, but it did not come. They came upon a place where several roads converged, crossroads marked with driftwood plaques carved and woodburned, roughshod signs made of birch and cedar branches, crooked arrows pointing the way to Birch Glen, The LaBlanc Fortress, The Ducloses, Lake Vista, The Shovers, The LaBerges.

A little farther along, Turnip pulled into a yard and a cabin lit up in front of the Camino. The cabin appeared uninhabited. Uninhabitable. The cedar shake siding was warped and without paint, black with fungus. The two windows, dull and scratched, did not reflect the headlight. Plexiglas. A tree had fallen on the cabin roof of mossy shingles, from which grew small whips of saplings. An old four-door car sat on blocks, its hood open.

Turnip cut the lights and motor and got out of the Camino and slapped his hand on the hood and jerked his thumb for Jessup to follow.

Jessup got out; a brisk wind billowed the shirt that Flower had given him two days earlier. He buttoned it to the top. This cold wind, more than had the snow that had fallen at the end of August, threatened winter.

Turnip had disappeared.

The wind sang and dead leaves cycloned about Jessup's feet.

A light lit the depths of the cabin; Turnip stood in the doorway, behind the screen door.

"Might's well come in. I'm gonna be a few."

Jessup nodded. Where were they? He walked over to the parked car. It was a green Ford. *Galaxie 500* read the insignia.

"Come on," Turnip said, holding open the door, his face concealed by the cabin's dimness.

Stepping inside, Jessup caught his shirttail on a rusty eyehook and turned to free himself. When he turned back around, he saw he was in a kitchen. Turnip was nowhere to be seen.

The kitchen was small and cramped, its ceiling low and slanting slightly toward the back. The floor was dirt, the cupboards without doors. The counter was hidden beneath old newspapers and car parts, beer bottles and dirty dishes and girlie magazines. With three steps, Jessup was at the other side of the room and at a two-burner gas stove.

One burner was lit, a coffeepot sat atop a weak blue flame; the pot didn't have a lid and the boiling coffee bubbled over, full of grounds, to hiss on the burner.

Where were all the dishes? Despite the few glasses and bowls that sat on a card table and in the sink, the cupboards were empty. There was no food. There were more dishes out at the Barker place than there were here. Jessup thought he'd offer Turnip the dishes from the Barker farm. It was difficult to imagine anyone living here. Didn't Turnip ever expect company? Was all his time in this place spent alone? Jessup couldn't envision that the neighboring cottages were in such ruin. Emily's cabin was bright and spacious and decorated with old furniture. An airy screen porch overlooked Sunset Lake. Jessup could picture Turnip's neighbors scornful and speaking badly of him, cursing the Camino's loud exhaust as they peeked from behind curtains and watched Turnip come and go at all hours. He imagined neighbors slipping nasty scribbled notes under windshield wipers, warning Turnip that he better clean up his place. But they would not leave many notes, they would back off because of something Turnip said or did in response that let them know he was not to be pushed.

A bare bulb hung from the ceiling. The stove was filthy with what looked like burned sauces and gravy. A sap bucket serving as a trash can in the corner, overflowing with coffee grounds, candy and jerky wrappers, spray-paint cans, beer bottles, greasy rags and more girlie mags, pages curled up on themselves. It looked as if there were a smaller room off the kitchen, through a low doorway, but it was too dark to make out anything.

This was a lonely place. A place where you lived when it was too late for anything else.

"Hey."

Turnip appeared from the dark room, lowering his head as he came into the kitchen, two duffel bags over his slumped shoulders, his eyes dark and furious and distracted.

He handed a duffel to Jessup, took a flashlight from atop the refrigerator; he moved aside a picture on the wall and reached into a hole behind it, pulled out something and stuffed it in his jeanjacket pocket.

"Whatsay we get outta this fuckin dump," he said.
"I'd say that was a good fuckin idea."
"Me fuckin too."

Reg's flashlight lit the floor of the Barker place. It had been decades since he'd beat around up here with Rick and Bernadette Barker; they'd had a sister who had died at the age of five, from a disease that troubled her breathing, clogged her lungs with phlegm and snot. Abigail. The family had moved, fled, the day after she'd died. Never sold the place. No one seemed to know why, or where they had moved to; some said Canada. Most didn't go near the place; the story, at least as Reg had heard it, was that the family had left Abigail's corpse behind, sitting on the porch swing.

Reg could feel the bigness of the place in the blackness about him.

"Sure yah ain't seen nobody up here?" Though he whispered, his voice exploded in the room.

"No."

"No yah ain't sure, or No yah ain't seen nobody?"

"No I haven't seen anybody, or signs of anybody."

"Hope not."

"That's it. That's the piano," the kid said, pointing.

The room smelled of ash.

"Whatsay we get these packs off?"

They took off their packs and faced each other, the kid coming only to Reg's chest, the flashlight glowing between them, their faces garish with shadows.

"Get up there," Reg whispered, motioning to the piano. "Weed's gonna mold some, but there ain't nothin to do bout it. One day can't hurt."

The kid stood on the bench, its casters crying.

He lifted the top of the piano in a cloud of dust.

"Forgot to dust up here," he said.

"Here." Reg handed a duffel up to him. The kid pushed it into the piano with difficulty, the piano sounding a muted chord. Losing his footing on the bench, he slipped, and his knee crashed on the keys.

"Jesus Christ," Reg said. He took hold of the other duffel bag and loosened up its drawstring and reached in and pulled out what looked to be another duffel.

"What's that?"

"Sleepin bag." Reg tucked the flashlight between his knees so it pointed downward. He untied a rawhide string from around the bag and it spread it out on the floor, dark and wrinkled and larval.

"Why a sleeping bag?"

"So I don't get cold. Yah don't think I'm gonna jus leave this stuff here."

"No one comes up here."

"We're here."

"I can't stay. I haven't been home since this . . . since yesterday morning."

"So?"

"I can't just sleep here."

"Scared?"

"My mom'll worry. If I don't come home . . ."

"Yur mom?"

Jessup shifted his weight on the piano bench. His mother would worry, that was true, but he didn't care. His concern for her was gone, replaced with a hollowness in his chest. But he wanted to stay here, without Em, even less than he wanted to go home.

Turnip patted two fingers against his lips. "Yah might as well stay and pay the price of the old lady yellin at yah."

"I can hoof it."

"That'll take yah till dawn. Yah won't be complishin nothin."

"She'll be less mad if I make an effort. Effort goes a long way with her."

Turnip looked down at Jessup; his brow pinched. He made a thin sucking noise with his tongue against his teeth. "Stay here." He turned and disappeared into the dark parlor hallway.

Jessup sat on the bench. He could just make out the pale glow of the Camino's domelight through the open foyer door. He wished he hadn't told any of them about the house. He had said it before in the excitement of the moment, without being fully awake or aware, but his enthusiasm had waned. He'd never been up here at night, or with anyone but Emily, and now he'd brought in an outsider.

He felt tired and sore and wanted to get home and write a letter to Emily. But what would he say? What would he tell her? What *could* he tell her? Not everything. Would *not* telling her everything be lying, he wondered. Yes, he decided. It would.

The Camino's door shut, boots on the porch. No flashlight shone. All was dark, until the orange trace of a cigaret ember arced upward. Turnip's face grew visible. An animal, a raccoon, or a squirrel, *something*, was scurrying in the room above them. Turnip flicked his cigaret to the floor. Sparks danced.

Jessup stamped the cigaret out.

Turnip reached toward Jessup and Jessup saw a metallic flash in Turnip's hand, felt cold metal against his cheek.

"Listen to me," Turnip said.

The jangle of keys.

"Take the Camino."

Jessup looked at the keys hanging from Turnip's pinkie.

"Take it. Yah ain't the only one tired round here. Quicker yah scram, the quicker I sleep."

"I guess."

"Might's well get used to drivin it. Jus make sure yur back here by ten. No later."

Jessup nodded.

"Yah got an alarm clock?"

"Yes."

"Set it. And bring up some donuts or somethin. Some coffee, too. Plenty of coffee." He stuck a hand in his front pocket and came out with a wad of crumpled bills. He separated one from the others and held it out for Jessup. A twenty. "Here. On me." He stuffed the other bills back in his pocket.

Jessup looked down at the crumpled twenty. "I got a lot of stuff to do tomorrow."

"Yah goin back on yur word?"

"No."

"Yah don't seem to want that Vega fixed."

"I do."

"Well I'm gonna fix it. Soon's were done. I'm payin yah and fixin yur car. That's a good deal. Ain't it? Am I right?"

Jessup nodded.

"Go on. Take the Camino."

Turnip put a hand on Jessup's; Jessup's own fingers were clenched; Turnip pried them open and placed the keys in his palm.

"Go on," Turnip said.

Jessup walked toward the porch, his hands out before him. Turnip did not turn the flashlight in his direction. From behind Jessup, a voice echoed: "Ten. No later. And don't forget them donuts and coffee."

In the Camino, Jessup fought to bring the seat forward among cans and bottles crammed beneath it. He turned the key. Nothing happened. He tried again. Nothing. He pumped the gas pedal and tried again. Nothing. He licked his lips and tried once more. He rested his forehead on the steering wheel and closed his eyes. When he opened them again he was right where he had been. He tried the key. Nothing. He threw the keys on the dash and stormed out of the Camino, slammed the door shut and kicked it. He looked down the drive toward the outline of dark trees lit in the headlight.

"Problem?" Turnip had come out onto the porch.

"She won't start."

"Flood her?"

"I don't know."

"Well. What's it doin?"

"Nothing."

"She turnin over?"

"Nothing. It's doing *nothing*."

"Testy."

"Well. I don't know a *damn* thing about cars."

"Don't take it out on me." Turnip came over to the Camino. "Get in and jiggle the steerin wheel."

Jessup glared at the Camino.

"Go on. Give it an effort."

Jessup threw open the door and sat down heavily; he grabbed the keys from the dash, fumbled with them until one jammed home into the ignition; he jiggled the wheel and turned the key.

"See," he said, exasperated. *"Nothing."*

Turnip came up to the opened door and leaned on it. "You're engaging the clutch, right?"

Jessup looked down at his feet. "Of course," he said. He shook the wheel hard, pushed his foot down on the clutch and turned the key.

The Camino fired up.

"All it needs is a good jiggle sometimes," Turnip said. "Get her in gear. Yah ever drive a standard before?"

"Not really."

"Not really, huh? Well. Put yur hand on the gear shift, there." He motioned with his chin. "Keep yur foot down on the clutch."

Jessup grabbed the gear shift.

"She's in first now," Turnip said. "Upper left."

"Upper left," Jessup mumbled.

"Second is straight down from that. Pull the shift down and keep yur foot on the clutch."

Jessup pulled the shift toward him and felt it fall into gear.

"Good. Now third is up and over to the right. It's a little tricky."

Jessup pushed up and over. The gears gnashed.

"Try it again."

Jessup pushed the gear up and over. The gears ground again, but the shift slid up and over. "There," Jessup said.

"Take it down to second and do it again."

Jessup did, finding third easier this time.

"Do it a few times. I don't need yah ruinin my transmission. I coulda driven yah halfways home by now."

Jessup worked the shift. Second to third to second, up to first, down to second, up and over to third.

"All right. There's a fourth gear. But yah won't need it. She'll go plenty fast nough in third. Reverse is way over, and I ain't gonna show yah now. It'll take too long."

"I can learn it."

"Tomorrow. Till then jus park where yah can turn round good."

Jessup eased off the clutch; it wanted to spring up under his foot.

He let off it slowly, gave the Camino a little gas—the clutch sprang and the Camino pitched forward, but did not stall. Jessup cranked the wheel and took the Camino out onto the dirt drive and steered it so it faced downhill toward Gamble. He gave it a little more gas and heard the crunching of stones and felt the Camino surge ahead. Advancing on the trees, he tapped the horn and waved out the window, but he could not tell if Turnip was on the porch anymore, he could not see anything in the rearview for the darkness.

Soon he was going much faster than he thought possible in such a short distance. He looked at the speedometer. Thirty, through the trees. He did not need to shift into second. A mist unfurled from the low banks of cedar and he had the idea that he was driving through clouds, that he was manning an airship.

The Camino passed the trailer; Flower's truck was parked out front, but the trailer lights were off, the place so still, so overgrown, it seemed abandoned, lifeless.

Pulling onto Gamble Hill he put the gas pedal down hard, gaining speed and shifting into second.

When he arrived home, he turned off the headlight before he swung into the yard; remembering that he didn't know reverse, he made a wide circle and parked in front of the shed, facing out toward the road. He turned off the engine and got out, shutting the door quietly. He could hear the engine ticking and pinging and smelled burned oil. The woods and swamp behind the house were soundless save for the hoot of an owl, unseen in the firs behind the shed. The house stood in the darkness, its windows darker still.

Keys cupped in his hand, he walked to the porch steps and took them warily. He eased the porch door open partway, sucking in his breath. He opened the door a bit more and squeezed between it and the main door. He took a breath and tried the knob; it was unlocked. It turned with a *clack* as bolt receded from frame. He drew another breath and looked back over his shoulder at the yard; the moon shone down on the mist-shrouded lawn. The Camino looked alien, lurking in the darkness by the shed. He put his shoulder into the door and swung it open in one swift motion and stepped inside.

The house was completely dark.

From the kitchen, a few feet away, he could hear the refrigerator hum, then shudder into silence. The grandfather clock in the living room ticked away each passing second.

Listening to the house, he thought of the story of the flood that Turnip had told him, of the screech of nails as homes wrenched apart, and he felt like a prowler, as if he'd entered a house that was not his, and in whose bedrooms he would discover a family he did not belong to and did not know.

I am a marauder, he whispered.

He thought of the story.

He could hear the scurrying of a mouse behind the stove, feeding on crumbs.

The floor creaked as he tiptoed to the foot of the stairs.

"Jessup."

He didn't move.

"Jessup." Her voice was deep with worry.

She was there, framed in her bedroom doorway. Her tericloth robe was inside out, pocket liners hanging like dog ears. Her hair was limp, her arms folded across her chest. Her feet were bare.

"Let me look at you."

He looked away. Through the window beside the door, he could see the hood of the Camino shining under the moon.

"I can't see you, Jessup. Come here. Let me see you."

He dug a thumbnail into the newel post.

"I'm tired." His voice was scratchy and raw from smoking and not having anything to drink since . . . yesterday afternoon.

"*You're* tired. Come *here*."

His thumbnail dug and dug.

"Jessup."

He shuffled toward her, aware now of his clothes reeking of cigarets and pot and spilled beer. He came to stand a few feet away from her. She reached a hand out and rested it on his shoulder.

He could not bring his eyes to meet hers.

"I had no one to call," she said. "You were missing and I had no one to call. I realized this. No one. Not a soul."

He felt like an impostor, as alien here as the Camino looked in the yard, and he felt that any gesture, any sound he made, would expose him, reveal him as something he wasn't, or for what he really was, but had not yet revealed to anyone, including himself.

"Do you know what that's like?" she said.

He did not move.

"Do you? You don't. You don't have any idea what it's like. I had no one to call. No one."

Her eyes were glistening, but he could not tell, and did not care, if it was from tears or fatigue.

"I hope you never do," she said. "I hope you never know."

"I was all right," he said, his voice an escape of air.

"I'm supposed to know this? I can read minds?"

Jessup scratched his temple.

"You stink of smoke," she said.

"I had dinner. At Sarah's Sawmill."

"Sarah's? What were you *doing* at that place?"

"I helped . . . I gave someone a hand. This race-car driver. I helped him. He gave me fifty dollars."

"Who? Who'd you help that gave you *fifty* dollars?"

"Turnip."

"Who?"

"This guy. Reg. He's going to fix the Vega. He's going to take me backcountry fishing. He's—"

"No he's not."

"He—"

"He's the one that dropped you off. The other night."

Jessup nodded.

"Trash. An idiot. What's a man running around with a boy for anyway?"

"He hired me."

"I can't imagine what for, and I don't want to know. It doesn't matter now anyway. I know men like that. In and out of jail."

"He wasn't ever, I don't think—"

"No. No, you don't think."

"I . . ."

"I don't want you near him again."

"But, the Vega?"

"You got along fine without it this long."

"He *owes* me."

"Have him pay you instead. Outright. Or I'll give you the money. Whatever he was going to."

"I want the Vega fixed." Jessup stepped away from Anna and her hand fell from his shoulder. "I'm working for him tomorrow. You're the one who wanted me to work."

"Jessup, I forbid you."

"Go ahead. Forbid me."

"*Look* at you. I found your bike toppled over in the grass. Abandoned. Rusting. Would you like that? To be abandoned like that? To be ruined?"

"I was. I am."

"What?"

"You heard me."

"I don't know—"

"You *do* know. *Drowned.* You liar. You lying bitch." He turned and ran to the stairs; with a hand on the newel post he turned to shoot her an injured look intended to wound, to change her heart.

But she was not there; she was gone and her bedroom door was shut and no light came from underneath it.

Upstairs, he threw himself on his mattress, screaming until his voice grew hoarse and the back of his throat tasted of blood.

PART IV

Jessup's bedroom door squeaked.

"Jessup."

His mattress sunk beside him as she sat down, a hand on his forehead. He opened his eyes, but did not look at her; he looked toward his window. Morning. A piece of down stuck to his bottom lip.

"Jessup, I'm not mad. I'm . . . concerned. Whose car is that out front?"

Mad? What did she have to be mad about? He sat upright, pulling the blanket to his chin, suddenly wide awake. "Jesus," he said.

"Don't use that word."

"What time is it?" he said. "What time is it?"

"It's almost noon. I took a long lunch so we—"

"Shit," he said. He pushed back the covers. "He's going to *kill* me. *Noon.*"

"Who? What are you talking about?"

He was up and standing, still dressed from the night before, and thankful for it.

He found the Camino's keys on the floor.

"Jessup, I'm not done. I took the afternoon off so we could talk. So I could . . ."

He laced a shoe and hurried past his mother and out of the attic, down the stairs.

"Jessup."

Hess was in the Bee Hive, sitting at the far end of the counter, downing a handful of aspirins with coffee when the El Camino pulled in.

He braced himself. The night before he'd felt sure he'd been shot. The woods had lit up and his ears had rung. He'd dropped to the ground, anticipating the pain, hoping it would be brief.

But he hadn't been shot. He'd heard leaves underfoot, a grumbling as the light bobbed in the trees. He'd not lifted his head to see who it was, knowing it had to be Reg. He'd lain fast until the light had diminished and the screen door had shut.

Then he'd taken off, walked until he'd fallen asleep in a field. If sleep was what you'd call it. He'd awakened at first light.

He shifted on his stool now and snapped up a section of newspaper someone had left behind.

Cowbells clacked as the diner door opened.

Hess peeked over the top of the paper.

The kid.

Hess looked around for Reg. He wasn't out at the Camino, or in the parking lot, and he hadn't come into the Bee Hive. The kid stood alone at the other end of the counter, waiting behind Mack and Elis Lavalette, at the cash register. Stan was busy flipping hotcakes and French toast.

Hess looked back at the kid. Did he think he had to wait to be seated? His hair was a mess. His jeans wrinkled, his shirt untucked. Hess set the paper down and studied the kid's shirt; it was too big for him; he was lost in it. The shirt. It wasn't the kid's. It was his, Hess's. Wasn't that sweet? She'd given him his shirt.

The kid eased himself between Mack and Elis and took the cover off a glass pedestal to get at some donuts. He grabbed a few donuts, held them to his chest and replaced the cover. Stan handed his wife three plates of eggs and bacon and hotcakes to bring over to a booth by the door, then he came over to help the kid. From under the counter he brought out a bag with a honeybee on it and opened it with a snap of the wrist and held it out for the kid to dump in the donuts. Elis Lavalette looked the kid over and asked him something. The kid looked out at the Camino and shook his head. Elis grasped the kid's shoulder and pointed a finger at the kid's face and said something and laughed; Mack didn't laugh. Stan folded the top of the bag a couple of times and set it on the counter. The kid raised two fingers.

Stan nodded.

Elis said something to Stan, handing him money. Stan nodded, made change, and counted it into Elis's palm; and Elis and Mack turned to leave. Elis clapped the kid on the back again and pointed once more at the kid's face, wagging a finger, glancing at the Camino.

Stan washed his hands at the sink behind the counter, poured coffee into two Styrofoam cups and secured plastic lids on each with the heel of his palm.

Finishing his own coffee, Hess rose with a spin of his stool and dug a couple bills from his pants pocket and tossed them down, forgetting he owed for the drinks from the night before. He walked toward the door, between the stools and the booths along the front window, and squeezed by the kid who was waiting while Stan seated the coffees in a cardboard holder.

Hess went outside.

The kid came out, wincing in the sun, coffee holder held out before him, bag of donuts tucked under an arm. He tried to balance the coffees in one hand and fish for his keys with the other.

Hess leaned against the Camino. He folded his arms across his chest and nodded. "Got a handful there," he said.

The kid nodded and set the coffee and bag down on the hood and reached in his pants for his keys. The shirt was buttoned wrong and its sleeves, despite being rolled up, came down to his fingertips. The collar stuck up on one side and was tucked under on the other. The kid got his keys out and looked up at Hess.

"Good night, last night?" Hess faced the kid, planting his palms on the Camino's hood.

"Excuse me?"

"I said y'look like y'had yourself a good night. Last night."

The kid looked down at his keys.

"Well?" Hess said.

The kid looked at him; his eyes were very dark, as if the pupils had swallowed the irises.

"Y'have a good night last night or not?"

The kid nodded.

"Looks it." Hess swept a hand up and down to indicate the kid's wrinkled clothes.

The kid looked down at his unlaced sneakers. "I didn't hardly sleep," he offered.

"Makes two of us."

The kid tossed the bag of donuts in the Camino's open window. "Well. Nice talking to you."

"What's the hurry?" Hess said, hands still planted on the hood. "Don't like my company?"

"No. I mean. Yes. I like it fine. I just got to get this car back. I'm real late already." He opened the door and picked the coffee carton up and set it down carefully on the seat.

"Car ain't yours?"

"No, sir."

"*Sir* and *every*thing? Whose is it?"

"What?"

"The car."

"A friend's."

"Hell of a friend. Sharin his car. Mighty big of him."

"I guess."

"Share a lot, does he?"

The kid glanced into the Camino as if to check that the coffee hadn't spilled. He looked at the Bee Hive.

"Share a lot of other stuff?" Hess repeated.

"I guess."

"Man who shares his car's liable to share about anything."

"He doesn't have much else to share, I don't think."

"I bet. Which way y'headed?"

"Gamble Hill."

"What do y'say to givin an old man a ride? A helpin hand?"

The kid picked a piece of dried dragonfly wing from the Camino's antennae. "I don't know."

"Y'can drop me off wherever y'like, wherever y'turn off."

"I don't know."

"Got a bum leg." Hess lifted his shirt to reveal the beginning of his scar.

The kid winced.

"Okay," he said.

"Thatta boy."

"So y'work for him?" the man asked.

Jessup nodded. "Sort of."

"Either y'do or y'don't."

"I do."

"Doing what?"

"I help him out with whatever he needs help with."

"Like?"

"I don't know. Hauling stuff."

"Stuff?"

"Firewood."

"In this?"

"His sister's got a truck."

"That so?"

"Yes, sir."

"Sir *again*. Ain't that nice. *Sir*. What's she like, his sister?"

"Nice."

"Mmm I bet."

Jessup let off the gas and downshifted as he drove around a blind curve and nearly ran into the back of a logging truck that struggled up Gamble Hill. He downshifted again, the Camino close to stalling. The logs on the truck were debarked, their slick orange meat exposed. Skunk Hollow was coming up soon and Jessup was glad for it. He wanted to get rid of this man; he smelled tangy, like rotten fruit. His questions were odd. So curious. The two grubby men in the Bee Hive, too. All three interested in the Camino in a way that didn't make sense.

"Bet she's pretty," the man said.

"Who?"

"Y'boss's sister. Y'friend's sister."

"Marigold?"

"*Marigold*. Pretty name."

"Like the flower."

"She smell like a flower?"

"No. Not much. I guess."

The logging truck slowed. Jessup tried to shift to first and the Camino stalled and slowed to a stop. It began to slide backward. Jessup pushed down on the clutch and turned the key. Nothing. The Camino was rolling backward faster now, dust rising. He looked over his shoulder to see where he was going, trying to crank the wheel in the right direction. But it locked and the Camino headed toward the trees. He stood on the brake and the Camino bucked to a stop.

He swiped a hand over his face and took a deep breath and started the Camino, tiny tremors running through his body. The Camino slowly gained speed. The truck was out of sight over the next rise.

"Close," he said.

"No it wasn't." The man's voice startled Jessup; he'd forgotten about him.

"So what's she smell like?" the man said.

"What?"

"This Marigold. What's she smell like if she don't smell like flowers? Between us two men."

"Cinnamon."

"Sugar and spice and everything nice."

Jessup concentrated on the road, hands fastened at three and nine o'clock, his back erect.

The man shifted so his back was against the door, and he faced Jessup. "Smell her? Her pussy?"

Jessup stared straight ahead.

"Bet y'got a good whiff of that sweet twat, huh? Mmm-mmm." He sniffed his fingers.

Jessup reached for the radio knob, but the man slapped his hand and Jessup pulled it away. What was the man talking about? He seemed outraged. Jessup wanted to stop and ask the man to get out.

"Stick your tongue right in her, I bet." He licked the air. "Right in that ripe snatch."

Jessup checked the sideview. Sweat gathered at the sides of his nose.

"*Answer* me," the man said, rapping his knuckles on the dash.

"I didn't *do* anything," Jessup said, but his creaking voice seemed to confess rather than deny.

"Didn't slip her the old fingers? Stick that little boy's pecker in her? Slip a thumb in her ass? She like that? A stiff cock in that ass of hers? I'd *bet* on it."

Jessup checked the speedometer; he'd slowed to twenty. He was trapped. A single cloud blocked the noontime sun, the sun lighting it from behind in a way that made its center glow, and its edges dark.

"I guess y'probly didn't stick her," the man said. "I guess y'probly wouldn't know what to do with cunt if it sat on your face."

Jessup blinked and gave the Camino a little gas. The man was digging around in his coat pocket. He took out a jackknife and levered out a blade with his thumbnail. It locked with a click. He scraped the blade on his thumbnail, the nail's surface curling like ice shavings. He lifted his thumb to his mouth and licked the shavings off with the tip of his tongue.

"What in hell *did* y'do with her?" He wagged the knife at Jessup. "*Nothing.*"

"The truth now. God's watchin."

"I kissed her. Well. She kissed me. I mean. We kissed. Each other. That's all."

"That's how it starts."

The man whittled fiercely at his nail.

"You know her?" Jessup stammered.

The man glared at Jessup. He pointed the knife at him and Jessup drew himself closer to his own door. "No, I guess not, I don't," the man said. "I guess maybe nobody ever knows nobody, do they?" He inched the knife closer to Jessup. It looked very sharp. The tip of the blade was against Jessup's thigh. He was sweating, trying not to shake. He'd read that you should never show your fear to a wild animal, they could smell it on you, see it in your eyes. He tried to breathe regularly, but couldn't.

"Do *they?*"

"Do they what?" Jessup said, his voice rising. He couldn't remember what the man had asked. All he could think about was the knife. The Camino had slowed considerably, but he didn't dare look at the speedometer. Didn't dare give it gas.

"I said, 'I guess nobody ever knows nobody, do they?'"

"I guess not."

"Guess y'don't know her then."

Jessup could feel the tip of the knife pricking his thigh. The steering wheel was gummy.

"Guess y'don't know me neither," the man said.

Flower's mailbox came into view. As the Camino closed in on it, and the trailer came into sight through the roadside scrub, the man casually removed the knife from Jessup's leg. Jessup's heart loosened. He relaxed his grip on the wheel. He could see the truck in the yard.

The man stared up at the trailer; he touched the knife blade to the window and drew the tip down the glass, scratching it. Blood seeped from a slice that ran from his thumb's cuticle to its first knuckle.

Jessup hit the turn signal and was about to pull onto Skunk Hollow to the trailer, when the man punched his arm. *"Stop."*

Jessup stopped the Camino and the man opened the door and got out and shut the door and looked up through the roadside trees at the trailer. He patted the Camino's roof and stepped away. He waved the knife at Jessup and winked.

Jessup, trembling horribly, eased the Camino by the man, fearful that if he pulled away too quickly the man right run after the Camino, throw open Jessup's door, and pull him out and pummel him, or worse.

Turning onto Skunk Hollow, Jessup looked in the rearview and noticed the man had begun to walk away, toward where they had come; he wondered why the man would ride all the way out here for nothing. The man's walk was odd. He limped, and it seemed to Jessup that he'd seen him before. He tried to picture where he'd seen him, that limp, but no recollection surfaced.

He drove up to the trailer.

Turnip was leaning on the truck. Flower stood beside him. Wheelchair was nowhere to be seen. Jessup parked and got out.

Turnip crossed his arms over his chest. Flower put a hand on her brother's shoulder. "Where in fuck yah been?" Turnip said.

Flower turned her head slowly, as if working out a crick in her neck.

"It's after one. Yur *goddamned* lucky I slept till noon," Turnip said.

Jessup shut the Camino's door. "I got held up down at the Bee Hive." He handed Turnip the coffees and donuts.

"For three fuckin hours?" Turnip unstuck himself from the truck and set the coffees and bag of donuts on the hood. He ate a powdered donut, licked the dusting from his fingertips, sipped his coffee.

Jessup didn't want to admit that he'd slept late and had broken his promise to set the alarm. But there was no getting around it completely. "My alarm didn't work. But these men held me up, too. At the diner."

"Men?"

"Friends of yours. I guess."

Turnip bit the lip of his Styrofoam cup. "What'd they look like?"

"They had on camouflage pants and shirts. Had big beards. They were real dirty. Grubby."

"What'd they want?"

"They were ribbing me about the Camino. Wanted to know if you'd sold it. Asked if you'd fallen on such hard times you had to sell your Camino. They were laughing though, so I knew they were kidding. I told them you were doing all right. That I was working for you."

Turnip picked at the edge of his cup, breaking small pieces off so they flit to the ground. He seemed to be waiting for Jessup to say more, but there wasn't much more to say.

"They laughed at me working for you," Jessup said.

"Did they?"

"They wanted to know how you rated so much that you could afford a little helper, and what was it I did for you exactly, anyway?"

Turnip finished his coffee and tore the rest of the cup up and let the pieces fall from his hand. "Whadya tell em?"

"Said I helped you."

Flower nibbled at a donut. She looked at Jessup for the first time and winked. Jessup looked back at Turnip. Lightness coming to his chest.

"I told them I helped you haul stuff and that I was your driver."

Jessup was about to say more, tell him about the limping man, how he'd punched Jessup, and held the knife to him; how Jessup was certain the man was going to hurt him, use the knife on him. But Turnip said through his teeth, "Yah always go round tellin fuckin strangers everbody's fuckin business? Ain't yah got any fuckin sense? Are yah as stupid as yah fuckin look?"

"I thought they were your friends," Jessup said, disappointed with himself for being unable to accomplish the simplest of things. He wondered why his mistakes became so evident only *after* he'd made them.

"I ain't got friends," Turnip said.

Flower straightened up from leaning on the truck. "It's no wonder," she said and stepped toward Jessup and whisked a piece of his hair from his face and patted his shoulder and brushed her lips against his ear. "I'll see you later," she whispered, squeezing his hand. She went inside.

Jessup felt as if he'd been filled with helium. He looked down at his feet, certain he was hovering. He was standing on his tiptoes, as if about to reach for something shelved just beyond reach. He settled his heels back in the grass and turned and thought he saw, for a moment, ducking into the woods, a man. The man. The one with the limp.

"Let's go," Turnip said. He grabbed the two duffel bags from behind him. "Was gonna put these in the Camino's vault. But they might be better left up there." He threw them in the Camino, brushed by Jessup.

"Let's go," he said.

Hess crouched just inside the woods above the trailer, watching Reg and Marigold and the boy, wondering why he'd let the kid off so easily. Perhaps because Marigold was the guilty one; she'd gone looking for it. Seduced the boy. The boy was a pussy. He didn't even know Marigold was married. She hadn't told him.

Hess's thumb ached where he'd sliced it. He hadn't meant to cut so deeply in trying to keep himself from using the knife on the kid. As innocent as the boy might be, Hess had struggled against forcing him to pull over so he could drag him into the woods and leave him for the crows to pick apart. It would have made him feel better. He had the right. He should have done it. Done something. Like now. How good it would feel to run out from the woods to the trailer and see their faces as he pulled the knife and stuck it into one of them.

A car door slammed. Another. The kid and Reg were getting in the Camino. Leaving. Leaving Marigold alone. Unless her crippled brother was in there. But what could he do? Hess didn't want to bring Hal into this, but he could go down and take a peek. And if Hal wasn't around.

The Camino backed out of the yard. Hess could smell exhaust. He made to sneak along the stone fence, to the back of the trailer, but stopped when the Camino did not go down Skunk Hollow to Gamble, but backed out so it faced up toward the old Barker place. What would they want up there? The Camino pulled away from the trailer. Marigold came out on the steps and waved to the kid. The kid waved back. How sweet. The Camino disappeared through the trees toward the old farm. Hess took off, working his way over a knoll. On the other side he stopped at the edge of the woods.

Reg had parked in front of the old house, and was getting out, looking around nervously. He ran onto the porch with two duffel bags and ducked into the house. What the hell was he doing? The boy remained in the car. Hess crept closer, keeping low, eyes on the boy. He could easily sneak up to the Camino and grab the kid. The screen door slapped and Reg ran out, without the duffels. He got in the Camino, turned it around and drove off.

With the Camino gone, Hess stepped from the woods. A raven cawed from atop the peak of the hay barn. Hess approached the Barker place; he'd see to Marigold later.

The Camino ate the road as Jessup held fast to the door handle. Turnip clenched and unclenched the steering wheel. He did not speak, but snuck quick glances at Jessup.

Jessup rubbed a fingertip where Flower's lips had brushed his cheek.

"So," Turnip said loudly, "laughing, were they? Mack and Elis?"

They hadn't laughed that hard. Jessup had embellished, not realizing how it would upset Turnip. But he couldn't say otherwise now, break Turnip's trust in him.

"We'll give em somethin to laugh about."

"They were just having fun."

"We should have some fun. We're due a little fun." Turnip punched Jessup's shoulder and jammed the lighter into the dash. He lit a joint, held it out for Jessup.

Jessup shook him off.

They passed a small cow pond, skinned with luminescent green algae. A lone teal, a hen, slept on a log in the middle of the pond, bill tucked under a wing.

"Let's get one thing straight," Turnip said. "Keep that little motor mouth of yurs shut. Zipped. Got that? *Fermez la bouche.*" He took a drag.

Jessup nodded.

"Let's hear it."

"Zipped." Jessup made a gesture to zip his mouth, shut and throw away the key.

Turnip admired himself in the sideview. "Good. We understand each other."

They pulled into the Bee Hive parking lot, the Camino's image distorted in the diner's plate-glass window. Turnip turned off the engine and squinted at Jessup.

"What say we have us some lunch? Them donuts dint do much for me."

Inside, two men, who looked a little like the ones who had talked to Jessup earlier, bearded, grimy, and talking loudly, sat in a booth at the window. It was just after two o'clock, between lunch and dinnertime, and the only other customers were an old man and a girl a few years younger than Jessup. The old man sat on a stool bent over a mug, breathing in steam, his eyes closed as he wheezed and mumbled. His overalls swallowed his scarecrow frame, his face ghastly with moles. The girl sat a few stools down, engaged in eating her hamburger, grease squeezing out the back of its bun with each bite.

She bit and patted her fingertips on a napkin beside the plate. As she lifted a tall glass of milk to drink, she flipped a long pigtail back over each shoulder.

Jessup followed Turnip between the booths and the counter, to the far end of the diner, where they took the last booth in the corner.

Turnip snatched a menu from its wire holder. He studied it for a moment, then slapped it down. He leaned in toward Jessup. "Yah'll earn yur money today." His voice was low. He took off his cap and smoothed back his hair, pulled the cap back on and peered from beneath its brim. "Yah'll earn it."

"How?" Jessup leaned in.

"Tonight. Don't yah worry."

Turnip was acting mysteriously, as if he was trying to get back at Jessup for running his mouth earlier, for being late, by making him nervous. He wanted to ask Turnip more about what they were going to do, but the pinched look on Turnip's face stopped him.

A waitress sauntered over to their booth. Jessup had seen her before, but had never been waited on by her: he didn't come in too often, and always ate at the counter. The waitress was old, over sixty. She wore Band-Aids on both her ankles, just above her pristinely white canvas shoes. She winked at Turnip, which surprised Jessup. "Look what the cat dragged in," she said.

Turnip introduced the woman, Ruth, to Jessup. She scribbled their order then sat beside Turnip. She slung her arm around his shoulder, and they shared a cigaret.

"Why aren't you racing right now?" she asked.

"Car's all fucked up. The Carburetor."

"That's a poor excuse. Who am I supposed to cheer for?"

"Cheer for the youngest guy. I'm gettin too old for yah, anyhow, darlin."

She smiled and they laughed over jokes that were beyond Jessup. Then she stood, tying her change apron tighter around her waist. "Stay out of trouble." She swiped a thumb under Reg's chin. "Hear me?"

Jessup had not realized his own hunger, but when his lunch, a breakfast really, *The Whole Damn Mess #2*, finally arrived, he hardly knew where to begin. The bacon or sausage? Eggs or French toast? Hash browns or pancakes? He drenched it all with maple syrup and dove in. The secrecy that surrounded the upcoming night made him nervous, and hungry. The food didn't lessen his hunger, instead it only stretched his stomach, made it impossible to fill. Turnip smoked and ate, licking his fingers and working at his back teeth with a toothpick. Stan drifted to and from their booth with more coffee, asking Turnip why he wasn't at the Autumn 100, and whether or not he'd put up a tree stand for bow season yet.

When they were finally finished, Turnip tossed his napkin on his plate. Jessup did likewise, resting an arm on the back of the booth and taking a toothpick himself from the dispenser.

It seemed to have taken only minutes to gorge themselves, but when Jessup looked over Turnip's shoulder to the clock, which a stuffed squirrel held to his belly, he saw it was after three. The diner had begun to fill with clamoring customers. People were coming in on their way back from the track. Jessup saw, in the opposite far corner, seated in a booth under a magnificent hornet nest, the two men.

"That's them," Jessup said, pointing.

"What?" Turnip said.

Jessup pointed at the two men who had talked to him earlier. Turnip told him to quit pointing and threw down some bills and got to his feet, taking a quick final sip of his coffee. He hitched up his belt. "Follow me," he said. "And don't say nothin."

Turnip strode to the booth at the other side of the diner, pushing off a woman's hip as he eased by the register.

He came to stand at the end of the table where the men sat wolfing burgers and steak and gravy. He leaned over, resting his palms flat on the end of their table. He looked from one to the other, as if trying to tell them apart. He adjusted his weight, and Jessup saw a pistol, tucked in the back of his pants. He wondered why he had it, and if he'd carried it all along. Neither the two men, nor Turnip seemed to notice Jessup standing there. It was as if he'd vanished, or was the ghost of some murdered boy. The two men continued to eat. But something in their behavior, the way they absolutely refused to acknowledge Turnip, betrayed their composure. They could not see the gun from where they sat, and Turnip seemed so relaxed and comfortable, it was if he were unaware himself of having a gun stuck in the back of his pants. The gun worried Jessup. There didn't seem a reason for it.

Turnip stood up straight and rested a hand on one of the men's shoulders. The other man licked gravy from his thumb with a childlike enthusiasm. Jessup hadn't noticed before, when the men had harassed him, but now he saw they each had the worst teeth he'd ever seen. Worse than his own. What was left of them. The color of tobacco, rotten and loose, gums so pale and receding, it was a wonder the teeth stayed in their mouths.

Turnip squeezed the man's shoulder.

The man turned slowly and looked him up and down. "Problem, Cumber?" the man said.

"That's up to you." Turnip squeezed the man's shoulder harder. His voice was low and deliberate, and Jessup had the image of a molester pretending to be a police officer on the playground, someone who wasn't what he appeared to be.

The thumb-sucker took his thumb out of his decayed mouth. His hand scavenged in his beard and Jessup half-expected fleas to spring from it.

"Now. Now," Thumb said, his voice tainted with sweetness.

Turnip pointed at Thumb with his free hand, and Jessup thought the man might bite it. "Careful," Turnip said, tightening his grip.

"We were just razzin the kid," Thumb said.

"Think this is bout the kid?"

He picked up a fork. The tendons in his wrists stretched taut.

Thumb cocked his head the slightest. "*Relax*. We were just fuckin with em." He waved a backhand at Turnip's pointing finger. In one quick move, Turnip grabbed the man by the throat and pressed his thumb deep into his Adam's apple. Thumb's eyes bulged. With the hand that had rested on the first man's shoulder, Turnip reached behind his back and brought out the pistol and pressed it tight against the first man's ribs. Jessup felt his breath catch and stomach tighten; he looked around the room.

Customers were beginning to look. Ruth stopped in the middle of pouring a cup of coffee.

"Keep it up," Turnip spat under his breath. He had a lock on

Thumb's throat. His finger was on the trigger. The man did not budge, seemed not even to breathe. "Say one more fuckin word, yah'll end up like Lamar."

He let go of Thumb, who grasped at his throat. "Cocksucker," Thumb said. "What's Lamar got . . ."

Stan pushed through the customers, but Reg glared at him and he halted. Everyone in the place was standing, gawking and chattering; Jessup could hear their feet scuffing the floor. "Get out to the car," Turnip ordered, backing away as he pulled the gun from the man's side.

Jessup moved quickly to the door, thinking he would be stopped and accused of something. His temples throbbed.

Turnip was behind him, pushing him along. Stan was standing at the door now, the muscles of his face rigid. "Don't bring that crap in here again," Stan said. His face seemed to collapse oddly, as if he might cry. Ruth stood beside him, a cigaret in her mouth, the ash so long it seemed impossible that it hadn't fallen.

Turnip shoved Jessup out into the late afternoon.

In the center of town they stopped at the gas station. Turnip hopped out and took a gas can from the back of the Camino, barked at the attendant to fill it, and the Camino, too, and strolled into the station. He returned with a six-pack and two candy bars, one of which he tossed through the window, into Jessup's lap. He paid the attendant, wished him a good evening, toasting him with an already opened beer as he got in the Camino. They tore out onto the road.

"There," he said.

Jessup could make no sense of Turnip's behavior. It was as if what had happened at the diner had been a joke that Jessup had not understood. Turnip didn't seem at all worried.

Three blocks down, they pulled up in front of the liquor store and Turnip told Jessup to keep an eye on the Camino. In a few minutes he came out with a bottle in hand, already out of its bag. He jumped in and turned on the radio.

"Where to?" He asked.

Jessup figured Turnip knew where they were going. Jessup was the one following.

"Well?" Turnip said. "I got some things I need to take care of. Yah wanna go home, or go to the trailer? To Marigold's."

"I don't want to go home."

When Turnip dropped him off at the trailer, Marigold wasn't there, and the truck was gone.

"Go on in and make yourself at home." Turnip said. "She can't be gone too far."

Dusk had settled on Unknown Pond by the time Reg pulled up to his cabin. The trees and surrounding cabins were dissolving into blackness. Dew clouded the cabin windows. He wasted no time.

Inside he grabbed the twelve gauge, a hunting knife, a lantern, and a camping stove he hadn't used in years, and likely didn't work any longer. He loaded these into the Camino's vault and hurried back inside. He found a garbage bag and took it into his bedroom, where he stuffed his clothes into it and tied it tight. He folded his army cot, dank and musty, the legs strung with cobwebs. When he picked his blanket up from the floor, a mouse fled between his feet.

He grabbed the pie safe from the counter.

He cleaned out the shed. Hauled three toolboxes to the Camino. A minnow seine. An ax. A dozen leghold traps. A spare tire. And four decoys that he and Lamar hadn't been able to carry that day.

Done, he stood at the back of the Camino. The sky was dark. He lit a cigaret, and picked up one of the decoys. A dense, rugged block of cork and wood. The paint had held to the cork, but the head was beat up.

He dropped the decoy in with the others.

That was it.

It wasn't much.

Half an hour later he pulled into the fishing access at Broken Leg Lake, headlight illuminating muscle cars and jacked-up four-by-fours. Drunk partyers appeared briefly in the headlight, then fell off into blackness again. He drove to the far end, away from the masses. Car stereos detonated music that echoed across the broad calm black lake.

He leaned back in the seat, dragged on a joint, and looked out the windshield into the darkness. Far off, along the shore, a bonfire glowed. Down by the boat launch, dark silhouettes, lit by a Jeep's halogens, scurried toward the shore, a shuffling horde of caterwauling drunks on pilgrimage to the fire. Fools. Suckers. Old high school scums and chums fixed as stone to the landscape and as predictable and trustworthy as hounds left alone with steaks thawing on a kitchen counter.

Mack and Elis's trucks were parked beside a trash dumpster.

Reaching next to him, Reg found the bottle, knocking the .45 to the floor. He picked up the gun and tossed it on the seat. He took a long drink. The whisky stirred his belly into a fire.

He rolled down his window. Bullfrogs groaned. An engine revved, girls shrieked, and a car raced out of the access with a scattering of stones. He swung his door open, sipping whisky. Crushed limestone crunched beneath his boots as he walked to the front of the Camino, unzipped, and pissed in the lake. At the back of the Camino he stood the bottle on a rock, tugged on the tailgate. It was stuck and he yanked furiously until it dropped down on his knees.

"Mother Christ," he said and sat down on the tailgate, rubbing his knee.

Gravel crunched behind him.

"What'szup?" a voice slurred, a form evolved out of the pitch.

"Edsel," Reg said. "Makin a fuckin career outta scarin me?"

"Quite the scene, eh?" Edsel said, his arms sweeping at his surroundings. He rested an unsteady hand on the tailgate and sat down drunkenly. He raised an eyebrow at the bottle.

"Whisky?" Reg said, feeding him the bottle.

"Don't mind I do." Edsel finished his beer, crushed the can and tossed it into the lake. He took the whisky bottle by the neck and raised it, crossing his legs. "To a good party." He nodded and smiled. "Back from Maine early. Couldn't resist, huh?"

"Never made it up."

"I didn't see you at the Hundred today."

"Dint wanna be there if I wasn't racin."

"I can 'preciate that. LePage won. You would've made a race of it though. It would've been a real race, for once." Edsel drank, shook his head and whinnied. "Good whisky."

"Play hard. Work hard. Right?"

"You bet." Edsel raised the bottle. "You bet." He drank, handed the bottle back to Reg.

Reg pulled from the fifth. He slapped Edsel on the back.

Edsel fell off the tailgate, onto the ground, where he stared up at Reg, mouth twitching.

"What say yah follow the rest a them lemins." Reg looked off toward the drunken group working its way to the far beach, to the bonfire.

"Lemins?" Edsel peered up at him. Reg lent him a hand and pulled him to his feet; he was a pitful sight. He brushed himself off. "You coming?" Edsel asked.

"I'm all right where I am."

Edsel staggered off toward the fire.

Reg looked at his belongings in the back of the Camino. Junk, mostly. A few good tools. He looked at the gas can.

Out in the water a group of skinny-dippers splashed and laughed, their bared bodies luminous as fresh snow under a full moon. Crazy shits. He rolled up his jeans and wrestled off his boots and sat them on a log, peeled off his socks and stuffed them into the tops of the boots. The icy water soaked the cuffs of his jeans as he stepped into the lake. Greenie Bishop and Carl Baks reeled out of the darkness and stood on the shore, facing him. Baks's hair hung like overcooked spaghetti in his eyes, clung to cheeks pitted and scarred from a boyhood of ravaging acne. They'd been friends in high school. Reg pushed his shirtsleeves up to bunch at the elbows. A pair of loons cried back and forth to each other, across the lake.

"What's up?" Greenie said.

"My cock," said Reg.

Baks lit a joint and passed it to Greenie.

"My old man's going to try to get you on full-time next summer," Greenie said to Reg. Greenie was the only full-timer left at Bishop's Auto, his old man being the proprietor.

Greenie was shirtless, and his shaved, iron-pumped chest, slick with baby oil, seemed to reduce his already-short legs to mutant stumps. He shifted his midget feet, his workboots digging into the shore. Tattoos covered his chiseled arms. His movements were muscle-bound. He hit the joint, held it out to Reg.

"Best weed I've had all summer." Greenie wheezed, tiny hands fluttering like birds.

"Elis spotted me it," Baks said.

"Elis?" Greenie said.

"My sister's seeing him."

"I thought Tracey was married?"

"Separated. They're just fucking. She spends too much time over to their place, though. Hope they haven't turned her onto coke."

That's who she was, Reg thought, the fat girl who'd been tanning herself out on the rock behind their A-frame. She'd sure packed on the weight.

Baks picked up a handful of stones and threw one out into the darkness.

The skinny-dippers yelled at him to watch where he threw rocks. He told them to fuck themselves. Reg imagined the rings from the rock spreading out; he recalled himself and Hal, as boys, competing with Pap to see how far they could throw rocks out into Unknown Pond. Pap, and then later, Hal, had never let Reg win. It wouldn't do to have Reg get a swelled head over a fixed game. That wasn't reality.

Reg clacked stones together. He rolled them in his palms.

He threw a stone and the skinny-dippers moved down the shore. He thought again of himself and Hal at Unknown Pond. He stared over toward the bonfire, toward the hollering of Elis and Mack.

He tilted the whisky bottle to his lips. The night had grown cold.

"I bes be headin," he said, and clapped Baks on the shoulder. He gave Greenie a nod.

"It's early," Greenie said.

"Y'boys enjoy yourselves." He walked away without looking back.

He drove the back roads for a good long while, drinking.

He drove out to the flats, to the old orchard, the piece of land that had been prime farming a generation ago. He pulled the Camino down an overgrown orchard road, among the trees, and parked. He sat on the hood. It was warm. The radiator gurgled. He was glad for the cold night. It kept him awake. He and Lamar had haunted these acres. Their whole damned youth spent here and at Broken Leg, and the many roads in between. He thought of Marigold. He hoped she'd land herself a job. What did he care if she worked at some computer plant, or who owned it, if it paid her bills and kept her busy? Made her happy. He hadn't seen her smile in a long time. He was a son of a bitch. He wondered if Greenie was serious, about his old man giving him more work next summer. Likely he was talking out his ass. He thought how Hal would be leaving soon. They hadn't done much but argue his whole visit. Same as the last few visits. He felt bad about it, but it seemed it couldn't be helped.

He sat for a long time thinking of nothing at all.

He began to shiver.

He finished the bottle and drove out of the orchard.

Back at the fishing access, only a few cars remained, among them Mack and Elis's trucks. He could hear the brothers' drunken hoots, down along the shore. Reg, drunk, waited for a car to leave the lot. Gripping a knife, he stumbled from truck to truck, and jabbed the walls of each tire, the tires sighing and collapsing as if in long-overdue relief. From the back of the Camino he grabbed the gas can and poured fuel onto the hoods and front fenders of both Chevys, splashing gas on the gravel between them. He lit a cigaret and stood and smoked and listened to the mindless cries of Elis and Mack and the rest of them. He dragged on the cigaret. He stooped and touched the ember to the doused gravel, then stepped to the Camino and got in it and cranked it over and eased it out of the lot, the flames behind him, their images mirrored in the rearview, blazing greatly, raging brighter, as he crested the hill and was again immersed in darkness.

Jessup sat on the love seat, aware of the warmth radiating from her as she sat down beside him and offered him a beer.

She'd bustled in, announcing she'd found a job, exclaiming how it was a miracle that he was here. "Damned appropriate," she said, giddily. She had a six-pack, of which two cans were already empty. She'd bought crackers and cheese. She'd been prepared to celebrate alone. "It's not much," she'd said of the job. "I mean a monkey could do it. But it pays. It's something." Her modesty touched him. She'd left him to shower.

Now, she plucked at a thread on the love seat.

The trailer was lit with candles; Jessup drank his beer quickly.

"Slow down," she said and took the empty bottle from him and rested it on the coffee table. She wore a haltertop and he could see her tan line and the side of her pale breast when she sat back.

She sidled closer. He had an itch behind his knee.

Her hand brushed his thigh as she reached for her own beer on the coffee table. She smelled of a warm bubble bath. She brought the beer to her lips and sipped, her throat undulating as she swallowed.

She placed her beer down and situated herself to face him, sitting on one foot, the other on the floor, both of them bare.

She looked at him. Her hair was just in her eyes and she tucked it back over her ears and touched his arm. "You're quiet."

He could think of nothing to say. He was nervous, but beneath the nervousness there was slackness in his lower abdomen. He cleared his throat. He was about to explain to her how tired he was, how unbelievably long the last four days had been, or seemed, the longest he'd known; how he'd found out things about his mother, about his father, about himself, that he would never have guessed at; how he felt foolish for not realizing those things earlier; he'd been about to tell her what had happened at the diner, how he'd been afraid, but keyed up, too, impressed; how he had a girlfriend whom he missed, though her name escaped him just at that moment. But he was unable to tell her any of this for she was pressing her hands flat against his chest, her palms warm, her lips too, warm on his neck, on his ear, and his lips.

His eyes were closed, but he heard her zipper, felt on his cheek, the air displaced by her clothes as she let them fall; he felt the colder air of the trailer touch his chest and stomach as she lifted his shirt over his head, felt it on his legs as he lifted his hips and she helped him from his jeans, his shorts. He was trembling. He opened his eyes the slightest. Her skin was brown and slick, except for the places that had not seen the sun.

He held his arms out and closed his eyes again. Her lips brushed his thigh.

He kept his eyes closed throughout, but he could smell her, her hair, her breath, smell her sweat, and taste it; he heard her moan, heard himself moan, as she grabbed hold of his shoulders, her lips grazing his stomach on their way to his mouth, her fingernails digging, her knees squeezing at either side of his legs as she straddled him and lowered herself and eased him inside.

"Marigold," he said.

She began to move.

After, he dressed in the bathroom. Glancing at himself in the mirror, he smiled, a wide grin that looked as awkward as it felt, a wry smile he did not recognize as his own. His muscles, some he'd never known he had, felt fatigued and lame as never before; but they were oddly relaxed, too. There was a looseness about him. He felt light-headed and weak, yet invulnerable. Immortal. He splashed cold water on his face.

In the living room, she was adjusting her halter, her back to him. She turned, tying her halter as she faced him, and kissed his cheek and told him he was sweet and beautiful; she did not seem aware of the tears that ran down to the corners of her mouth; did not wipe them. And then a headlight lit up the trailer and Reg was calling out, and Marigold was telling Jessup he had to go, hustling him outside, into the cold.

Jessup drove along Avers Gore Road, just as Reg had instructed. The road up to the gore was dark and steep and full of sharp curves, the trees closed in tight. He hit the wipers now and again, against a thickening mist.

It felt strange to drive the Camino while Reg rode beside him, sitting quietly, humming and smoking and stroking his beard. His silence made Jessup uneasy, made him want to speak, say something, *any*thing, but each time he'd been about to utter a word, he'd known it was the wrong thing to do.

They passed by a house, the only one he'd seen. An A-frame.

They climbed farther and Jessup downshifted; the gears ground. He cringed, gripping the wheel. He glanced at Reg, but if Reg cared or had even noticed, he gave no indication. He sat in silence. He turned on the radio. Reg shut it off.

Jessup's thoughts turned to Marigold, her hands working his zipper, tugging down his pants, helping him out of them. Her breathing so shallow, she'd been nearly panting. Her toes had curled and pushed into the tops of his own bare feet. She'd clung to him, desperately, as if to keep from drowning. It dawned on him then that he could smell her now, on himself. Had been smelling her for some time. The scent of her seemed to rise from under his shirt, from his chest. Or from his hands. Or lips. It was difficult to locate the source. A fleeting scent, ripe and arousing one moment, then fading, growing so soft and modest it was nearly undetectable. He was worried Reg would smell it, smell his own sister. He thought about the man with the limp. About what he'd said about smelling Marigold.

"Right here," Reg shouted. A wave of heat crawled over Jessup's skull. He stopped the Camino. "This is good," Reg said.

They were nowhere. Absolutely nowhere. The only house, the A-frame, was over a half-mile back.

"Turn off the headlight," Reg said.

Jessup looked at him.

"Go on."

Jessup killed the headlight.

The only light in the cab was the tip of Reg's cigaret. It grew bright and Jessup could hear tobacco crackling, hear Reg draw smoke deep into his lungs.

"Plank Road's bout another mile up the gore." Reg's voice was without inflection. Without emotion. "After I get out, I want yah to drive up to where Plank Road crosses this one. Wait a bit. Half hour, or so. Then turn round and come back down through here. Go slow. If yah see a branch in the road, stop and wait. I'll be nearby. Close. When I hop in, take off. Not fast. Slow. *Normal.* Got that?" He put his cigaret out in the ashtray and the cab fell dark. Jessup could hear himself blink. Reg lit another cigaret, the matchglow painful to Jessup's eyes.

"If yah don't see a branch, drive down to where this road comes out to Town Road and turn round and come back. Jus keep drivin back and forth. Till yah see that branch. *Don't* hit the horn, and *don't* leave, even if I'm not there right away."

Jessup was about to ask why Reg might not be there right away, but the Camino door opened, the domelight blinding, and the door shut again. Reg was no longer beside him.

Jessup's blood rushed in his ears. He couldn't see anything in the dark. Couldn't see Reg.

He took a deep breath, trying to see out into the night.

A tapping came at his window. He flinched. Reg. Jessup could just make him out. Reg leaned in so his face almost touched the window. Jessup opened his window a crack.

"Might wanna turn them headlights on," Reg said, grinning. Jessup hit the headlight. He could see Reg's breath as he stood there, out on the road, breathing. Reg grabbed a duffel bag from the back and turned toward the woods. He paused and came to the window again, a hand on the roof. Jessup cranked the window down farther. Reg looked at him. "Thanks," he said. Then he turned and vanished into the woods.

Jessup drove up the steepest part of the gore, thankful that he could not see the woods alongside the Camino, knowing how the roadsides fell off to sheer cliffs, along that stretch. There were no guardrails.

The road leveled and he came upon Plank Road. He pulled off to the side, near a state forest gate. The intersection was desolate. The mist had turned to fog. He kept the headlight on and the engine running. A cigaret pack sat on the dash. He turned on the radio, hoping to get a radio station, but none came in. He thought of Marigold, her arching back. How she'd cried. He smelled the back of his hand. Moths bombarded the headlights, made flicking sounds as they fluttered into the windshield.

When he thought enough time had passed he turned the Camino around in the deserted crossroads and drove back down through the gore. He idled the Camino along, safely, in the middle of the narrow road, looking for the branch. There was no sign of it. No sign of Reg. Or anyone. Not a car or truck. Nobody walking. The only light was that of the A-frame as he passed by, picking up speed slightly as he did, something telling him not to attract attention to himself from anybody who might be in the house.

The A-frame's light faded behind him, and he was again in the dark, save the glowing fog before him. He made it down to Town Road without seeing a branch. He sat there, the Camino idling; he toyed with the radio, then decided to head back up the gore.

At the Bee Hive, when Reg had behaved so mysteriously about the night's prospects, Jessup had felt a sense of danger in the enterprise, and had liked that Reg entrusted him to execute his part of a mission. His adrenaline had surged. But now, out here, alone in the gore, black trees hanging over the road, slapping the windshield, the secrecy created a suspicion that frightened him. He imagined at any moment someone, or something, might run out in front of the Camino. A lunatic waving him down.

He reached Plank Road and stopped, unsure how long to wait, and not wanting to. He looked at the pack of cigarets on the dash, then turned the Camino around and made his way back down through the gore.

He was steering around a severe corner when something swept down in front of the windshield. A bird. It flew straight away from him, a spectacular white phantom that made not a single flap with its wings as it coasted ahead. A snowy owl; nearly around the next bend, following the road, it flew up sharply and into the trees. Jessup had seen only one other snowy owl in his life. He'd encountered its body in the pines along Broken Leg Lake. Someone had shot it. Looking down on the dead owl he'd decided to take its wings. He'd sawed at the wings with his pocketknife, but the tendons had proved stubborn, his knife dull. He'd planted a foot on the bird's chest, twisted and hacked at the wings to get the joints to break and the tendons to rip, the wings finally tearing free of the body. He'd fanned the wings out in front of him. Splendid, ghostly. They would look good pinned to his bedroom wall. He'd looked down at the owl again, and had been seized with dismay and shame at the sight of the poor bird's desecrated body. He'd dropped the wings and run into the woods, and never returned to the lake.

He drove by the lone A-frame.

He wondered where Reg was. How long he was supposed to drive the road. He didn't have much gas left. What was he supposed to do about that? He chewed the inside of his cheek. His anxiety from being alone, this far out in the woods, this late at night, without knowing why, began to evolve into resentment.

A small, isolated area on his shoulder blade ached. He wondered if Marigold had left a bite mark.

He stared at the pack of cigarets. Wiping his mouth he grabbed the pack and dropped it in his lap. Fiddling with the cardboard flip-top, he glanced from his lap to the road and back again. He tipped the opened box with one hand and a last cigaret fell out. He picked it up, and palmed the steering wheel. He brought the cigaret to his lips and flipped the pack beside him on the seat. The cigaret was filterless and bits of tobacco, bitter and tangy, burned the tip of his tongue. He cranked down the window, the outside cold biting his earlobes. He spat and picked tobacco bits from his lips. When he swallowed, the tobacco left a sweet coolness on the back of his tongue.

As the Camino prowled along, Jessup noticed a branch, off to the side. He slowed. Perhaps he'd already seen the branch, but had been so stuck on the idea that it had to be in the *middle* of the road that he'd passed it by without consideration. He brought the Camino alongside the road's shoulder. He tucked the cigaret behind his ear and tapped the steering wheel. The engine wanted to stall; he gave it gas, racing it. He grew aware of a tick in the engine, loud and inconsistent, a rattle. It was annoying and he wondered how he had not heard it before.

The branch lay just ahead of the Camino in the cast of the lone headlight; leafless, it looked like a severed arm, its shriveled bark dead skin gripping tight to the bone.

The engine ticked.

Jessup tapped the dash.

Where was Reg?

A car drove up fast and passed him, nearly running into him, causing his heart to beat hard.

Reg hurried across the yard to the house. Putting his face to a window, he could see the kitchen, and a light from another room.

He tucked his hair under his cap and pushed in the screen. He heaved the sash open. Listened. No sound came from inside. He tossed the duffel through, then hoisted himself up. He sucked in his breath and crammed his way in, falling on the counter with a racket of silverware.

He stood in the kitchen, a hand on his .45.

The reek of cat piss was sharp, but did not overwhelm the odor of bacon grease, and cigaret and pot smoke.

Ignoring the strewn silverware and fallen cereal boxes, he stepped to the refrigerator and opened it. A butterfly magnet fell and a crayon drawing floated to the floor. In the fridge a pitcher of lemonade sat among cartons of milk, two packs marked VENNISON, a twelve-pack of beer and the remains of a chocolate cake.

He drank from the pitcher of lemonade, picked up the duffel and went toward the dining room. A cat dish skidded at his feet. On a table sat cereal boxes and bowls, glasses slimed with orange juice. Utensils lay about like stainless steel fingerbones. He took a breath.

A shag rug gave beneath his feet.

A cat slept, stretched out before a console TV.

He heard *squeaksqueaksqueak*, but couldn't locate the source.

A door was open at the near end of the hall. He went to it and found stairs descending into darkness.

Down in the cellar, a windowless darkness, the smell of damp concrete and laundry soap. He lit a match. Mason jars and coffee cans stuffed with nails and screws and bolts sat shelved on a rickety aluminum rack. Seatless bikes. A torn armchair, its material faded and blooming mildew. Bags and boxes stuffed with board games and puzzles. No plants. There was a door to the outside, the front of the house, under the front balcony deck.

Upstairs he went through the living room and down the hall. A bedroom to the right, its door open. He threw on the light. A bed, heaped with clothes, jackets and coats and boots. Most of it camouflage, or wool. A card table under the window, stacked with magazines and model airplane parts, glue and paint. Two planes suspended from the ceiling by fishline, caught in an endless dog fight. A gun cabinet in the corner. Shotguns. What looked like a .22 rifle.

At the end of the hall was a closed door. He eased it open, seeing by the light from the other room. He jerked at a movement and drew the .45, tripping its safety. His image in a mirror, returning a surprised gaze. Unshaven. Unkempt. Black hair leaking from beneath his cap, the cap's chain-saw patch and the embroidered word, ꙅnɿɒʌbꙅuH. The .45 pointed at his chest.

A stuffed chair. A bureau. A jewelry box atop it. He opened the box and sifted his hands through jewelry, scooped necklaces and bracelets and bandless watches and earrings. He dropped the jewelry into the duffel and opened the bureau drawers. The first three revealed only clothes, T-shirts, socks and panties, threadbare and comical in their hugeness.

In the bottom drawer he found candlesticks, road maps, rolled pennies. Rope. Porn and fetish magazines of lactating women. Handcuffs. A set of keys on a purple rabbit's foot chain. Scarves. Insect repellent. Band-Aids.

He dumped the pennies into the duffel and opened a closet door. The smell of mothballs was heavy. No plants, but an attic hatch was recessed in the ceiling, a string dangling from it. Light spilled from around its casing. He shook his head, smiling. He pulled on the string but the hatch would not relent. He adjusted the duffel on his back, set the .45 on the nightstand and pulled on the string with both hands; the string broke. "Fuck," he whispered and dragged the stuffed chair over, struggling to get it into the closet. He stood on it and took hold of the eyehook and pulled. The attic stairs unfolded with a creak and the ringing of heavy-duty springs. He shoved the chair out of his way, grabbed the lowest step and pulled down the stairs. From the hole above came a fluorescent glow. The smell of marijuana. He picked up his duffel and climbed the stairs.

Lights and plants emerged with each step. He stood in the attic among them, awash in phosphorescence.

He cupped his eyes. The window at the gable end was covered with black garbage bags stapled to the frame. The lights' timer ticked and ticked; he dug in his pockets for a pair of pruning shears. There were over twenty plants, buds as big as pinecones. He went to work.

Marigold came in from a drive to town, to clear her head and pick up another six-pack, in order to continue celebrating on her own. She couldn't wait to tell Hal.

She sat on the love seat, propping her feet up on the coffee table, and took a sip of beer. Its cold yeastiness slipped down her throat, a taste she normally didn't care for, but satisfied her tonight.

She drank, thinking about the boy, his smile and fine muscles. Guilt spasmed in her chest; not for what she'd done to Hess, but for the guilt she *didn't* feel. It frightened her a little. At *no* time, while with the boy, had Hess crossed her mind. She cradled the cold can of beer on her chest.

She couldn't help but feel that she'd slighted the boy. As much as she'd wanted him, as good as he'd felt against her, *in* her, it would not happen again. Could not. She'd known it all along. He would be hurt. She imagined it was his first time. Though he'd certainly caught on. She thought of her own lost virginity, at fourteen, to Danny Meyer, in his parents' basement closet, a closet that smelled of plastic rain gear and turpentine. He'd been eighteen, slipped the bottom piece of her bikini to the side, and in less than one painful minute, had finished. She'd clung to him. Kissed him. Remembered him; even though, from the moment they'd stepped from the closet, he'd never spoken to her again. Had she expected more? Yes. Not the world, but a few kind words. Perhaps to be taken out a time or two. He'd been eighteen, still a boy, which was as good a reason as any for his ignoring her. But she'd not seen it then; he'd been a man to her, the more worldly of the two, and she'd cried for days. Not because she'd felt used; despite his coarseness, she hadn't. She'd wanted to discover what it felt like as much as he had, and it just happened to be him to show her. Her crying had grown out of a loneliness more profound than she'd ever known. A loneliness she imagined was surpassed only by what Reg seemed to have gone through after Pap's death. He'd taken it worse than anyone. Not outwardly. She and Ma had cried enough for ten generations of Cumbers. But Pap's death had altered Reg irreversibly. He'd withdrawn. His boyish brass and natural sarcasm had been replaced with caustic bitterness, a showmanship that merely mocked his previous youthful rambunctiousness and rebellion, and buried his truest feelings in regard to Pap. She'd never understood it.

She hoped the boy wouldn't be hurt too deeply.

She sipped her beer, feeling, in spite of her guilt, and the uncertain meaning of her actions, at peace. Glad for what had happened. Glad about her job. The *relief* of knowing she had a job, an employer who was taken with her *forthright attitude*, as the manager had put it. He'd been courteous, professional, younger than she'd expected. He'd explained to her the lack of romance in the manufacturing of *pieces*, but explained there was always room to move up. Grow with the company. She bought into it only so far: the *team* aspect. Nevertheless, it would be good to have a paycheck.

She closed her eyes. She could still feel the boy, his skin hot from a day of sun.

When she heard the click of the bedroom door from down the hall, she stiffened. But she did not open her eyes. Not even when she heard his voice. She did not need vision to know whom had spoken. She thought of running, but to where? He must have been waiting, hiding. She kept her eyes shut with the remote hope that, if she could not see him, he was not actually there.

She kept her eyes shut when she felt the cushions sink beside her on the love seat, felt his breath, smelled the stink of booze and sweat. She kept her eyes shut when his voice raised and he squeezed her jaw and demanded she look at him. She kept her eyes shut tight when the first blow came, and the ones that were to follow. Better not to see.

Reg had picked and bagged most of the buds when he heard a car pull in the yard. Damn that restless kid.

But the kid didn't *know* he was in the house.

A car door slammed. Reg hurried to the gable window and peeled back a corner of the black plastic to peek out. He could not see anything. Looking straight down, he saw the chrome bumper of a car, concealed by the deck below him. A few seconds later, from down the hall, a door shut, and he remembered the kitchen, its open window, the strewn silverware and cereal boxes. He'd left the cellar door wide open. He looked out the window; the drop to the deck was at least fifteen feet, another fifteen from the deck to the ground; the window was the kind that cranked, one through which he wouldn't fit. He looked at the plants. A few still had buds, another half-pound. He heard voices downstairs.

Forgetting the remaining plants, he made for the hatch door. In the closet he left the attic hatch open, using the attic light by which to navigate the dim room. He put the duffel on his back and was squeezing between the chair and the closet door when the bedroom door swung open and a light was flipped on. He couldn't see for a moment. Then, slowly, he recognized who was at the door. Tracey; she was shrieking, her hand at her mouth. And he saw too, who it was behind her; Elis pushing her out of the way, lunging toward Reg, his eyes bloodshot and savage. Reg reached for the .45 in his pants. It wasn't there, and he remembered, as Elis bore down on him, that he'd placed it on the nightstand. He turned to reach for it as Elis tackled his knees, his legs twisting underneath him as he fell. Elis jammed a knee into his lower spine, and was trying to rake his eyes, to turn him over to get at his face. He bit Reg's cheek. The girl was screaming and flailing her arms and kicking Reg's legs and stomach. Someone, Mack, was yelling from down the hall. Reg pushed with as much force as he could and got Elis off balance enough to reach up for the .45 on the bedside table. Elis was trying to get it too, having seen now what Reg was after. But Reg hung on and got the pistol turned toward the girl and pulled the trigger. The room detonated. The girl fell. And in the instant Elis turned to watch her fall, Reg bucked himself free of Elis's weight and turned the gun on him and fired just as Mack ran into the room, a revolver in his own hand.

The Camino had grown cold. Jessup rolled the window up and turned on the heat.

What was he, Jessup, doing, waiting out on this dark road? What did Reg want in the woods at night? Perhaps Reg was lost. Jessup considered hitting the horn. Reg might hear it and orient himself, find his way to the road. Perhaps he'd been calling out, but Jessup hadn't been able to hear him. Jessup rested his palm on the horn. He could imagine Reg running out of the woods, ranting at him for drawing attention, for not having any common sense. But he couldn't keep driving back and forth, and he couldn't remain parked beside the branch.

He worked the Camino into gear and pulled away. He would drive to the trailer and ask Marigold what to do. She'd help. Let him in. He needed to do *something*.

He drove by the house. The gable window emitted an odd bluish light from a lower corner. A floodlight lit up the front yard; the wet grass glistened and the limestone driveway glowed an ominous green. A car sat in the driveway, nearly hidden in the balcony's shadow. Jessup slowed and backed up to the bottom of the driveway. He stared up at the A-frame. Squeezed the wheel. He took the cigaret from behind his ear. He palmed the lighter into the dash. He pinched the cigaret as he had with the joints, but it proved awkward, so he set it in the fork of two fingers.

The lighter sprang. He lit the cigaret and took the smoke into his lungs. He didn't cough, but a burning sensation flared in his lungs and he was left with a heady sensation. He sat up and smoked.

When the cigaret was reduced to a nub, he flipped it out the window. The tip of his nose was cold. His fingertips, too. Cold. Numb.

He looked at the house. Another window was lit, downstairs.

For an instant he thought he saw a shadow pass by. He rolled his window down. The downstairs window filled with movement. A second figure appeared above the first. Then both fell from sight and the window went black.

The floodlight did not go out. Nothing moved. He thought of going up and knocking on the door. He had a suspicion that Reg was inside the house. Or that whoever was inside would know where Reg was. He thought about leaving. Not to get help. Just drive the Camino to the trailer and see if Marigold was home, if he could spend the night there.

He was thinking about Marigold's warmth when something began to emerge from the blackness beneath the deck; low to the ground, it scrabbled clumsily, like a huge insect, dragging itself from the shadows, as if to escape a pit of tar. When it stumbled into the floodlight, it mutated from insect to human, a man, doubled over as he fell toward the Camino and collapsed against its passenger door and slid to the ground.

Jessup locked the Camino door. He sat perfectly still. The man could crawl under the Camino to come up on the other side of the car, appear at his window. His lungs felt raw from the cigaret. He hadn't been able to tell if the man was Reg, or not. Whoever it was looked hurt. No sound or movement came from outside. Jessup unlocked the door. He opened it a bit at a time, listening. The night was very cold, the stars bright and clear, clusters of them so ablaze in the black sky they seemed to be pulsing, alive. A wind hushed through the upper reaches of the spruce.

He stepped out of the Camino.

He came around the other side.

The man on the ground was not Reg; it was one of the men from the diner. Thumb. He was lying on his side, against the Camino's front tire, his eyes open. He wasn't moving. Jessup leaned against the Camino, his legs feeble. He looked at the man on the ground, at the house. Reg was inside. He knew. He looked at the keys in the Camino's ignition.

He left the Camino to idle, and started up the drive, compelled by both curiosity and the need to help. Exposed in the floodlight, he crept into the trees and snuck along the hem of the woods. His shirt was soaked. He made his way across the lawn and under the deck. He pressed his back to the house, the siding rough, splintered. He smelled pine sap. He reached for the doorknob.

Inside, the cellar stunk like the bottom of an old well. He waited for his eyes to work, but the darkness was immediate and complete, save the barest slice of orange light hovering ahead and above him. He searched with his hands in the dark. His foot barked against something. A staircase. The slice of light floated closer, a rip in the blackness. The top stair was dimly visible. He latched onto a handrail. At the top of the stairs he put his cheek to the door and listened. The tide of his blood.

squeak squeaksqueak

He wished he had a gun. He had no idea how to use one, but it seemed having one would calm him.

He cracked the door and peered inside.

squeaksqueak

A lamp sat on a rustic end table, its shade yellowed and pleated. He opened the door further. The back of a couch appeared, blue and torn at the corners, its insides leaking spongy foam. He stepped uncertainly onto the rug. It yielded beneath his weight. It smelled of urine. A path, like an animal trail worn in the carpet, ran from the couch and out of sight, down a hallway.

Another smell reached him, above the smell of urine. He stepped further into the room, but did not let go of the doorknob, afraid to surrender his means of retreat.

squeaksqueak

He searched what he could see of the room with his eyes. Reluctantly, he let go of the doorknob and took two steps. The stench worsened. A gerbil trod on its mill, atop the TV, gaining nothing for all its effort.

squeaksqueak

Jessup looked around at a dining room table, the kitchen entrance; a phone lay on the floor, ripped from the wall. He felt a voice inside him urging him to leave. He craned his neck. "I looked," he murmured. He turned to leave and heard a sound.

It came from down the hall. Faint but familiar.

A woodstove sat in the living room, beside it was propped a fire poker. He looked down the hall, then at the poker. He looked at the stairway leading out of the house.

He crept over and took the poker in his hand and sat on the couch, shaking. But sitting unnerved him even more than standing, so he got up and walked down the hall toward the sound.

Just before a doorway, he stopped and gripped the poker. He took a deep breath, his back to the wall, then stepped into the bathroom.

Running water. He'd been right about the sound. Water ran in the tub and poured over the edge of the sink, turning the floor pink around where Reg sat slumped against the toilet, his shirt dark with blood. He tried to stand and slipped, cracking his head against the toilet.

"*Fuck,*" he said, hoarsely.

Jessup looked away, gagging. Wiping his mouth, he turned back. Reg was trying to pick up a pack of cigarets from the floor beside him. He fell on his side, his fingers working stupidly. "Fuck." He looked up at Jessup. His nose was broken, his face lacerated, *clawed.* His pants were around his knees. He wasn't wearing underwear.

"Help me," he said.

Jessup stared at him.

"*Help* me."

It was a battle for Jessup to lift Reg, the floor slimy and Reg, moaning and swearing, very heavy. It seemed Jessup would never hoist Reg to his feet. But he did, somehow, throwing up on himself, his clothes bloodied.

He helped Reg lean against the wall, and pulled up his pants and zipped them. Reg swooned and wrapped his arms around himself. He spit blood. His hands fell to his sides. Blood dripped from his dangling fingers. "Lot a fuckin blood in me." He wiped a hand on his jeans. "Or *was.*"

Jessup gave him the fire poker for balance. It was all Reg could do to hold onto it.

"What happened?" Jessup said. "Who . . ."

"My bag." Blood ran from Reg's nose and mouth, garbling his speech. "Get it."

He began to inch along the wall, out of the bathroom.

Jessup turned off the water.

In the hall, Reg lifted his chin toward the room at the end, then lurched toward the living room, leaning heavily on the poker. He fell and Jessup hurried to him. But Reg waved a hand weakly. "My *bag.*" He looked toward the door at the end of the hall.

Jessup went down the hall and into a bedroom.

He stopped just inside the doorway, his breath arrested. A body lay faceup, near a closet on the other side of the bed; a blue fluorescent light emanated from an attic hatch, lending a green hue to his skin, and causing the blood all over the walls and furniture and body to appear black. There was no danger of the man being alive, but this did not comfort Jessup.

The bedspread and sheets had been flung across the floor, a lamp was knocked over and broken, the bureau mirror shattered, bureau drawers tipped over and emptied. Blood. Everywhere, blood. Jessup made an effort to breathe through his mouth, to swallow. His throat seemed blocked, constricted.

He couldn't see the bag from where he stood. He looked over his shoulder, down the hall; Reg was trying to sit up against the back of the couch, but fell over to lie on the floor. Jessup stepped closer to the other side of the bed. The duffel.

And a hand, just poking out from underneath the far end of the bed. Pale and chubby. But delicate. Speckled with blood. The duffel's straps were entwined in its fingers. He took a cautious step. An arm came into view. It moved, the slightest. Twitched. Or seemed to. He heard a moan. He felt himself moving toward the bed, as if floating, more and more of the girl appearing, the room itself dissolving. The bedside table was tipped on its side, two of its legs broken.

He knelt at the edge of the bed and the girl's arm pulled away, her legs kicking at him as she pulled herself under the bed, hissing. He peered under the bed but she had her back turned to him; he could hear her, she was whispering, something he couldn't quite make out. He feared there was someone else under the bed with her. She was sobbing now, her voice hitching, just audible, a strained hush. "He's in the *room*." Her voice a fading whimper. She was on the phone. Jessup stood quickly, sweating. Afraid, even, to blink. The girl was silent. He looked down the hall. Reg was gone.

Jessup ran. Reg wasn't out in the living room. A trail of blood on the rug led to the open cellar door. Jessup tramped down the stairs.

Reg was lying in the driveway.

Jessup knelt beside him. He was breathing. "There's a *girl* in there," Jessup said, relieved to speak aloud, "on the *phone*."

"*Phone?* Where's . . . the bag?"

Jessup looked back at the house.

Reg brought the pistol out from his jacket. "*Stop* her."

"What'd you do?" Jessup said.

"*Go.*"

"What'd you *do* to that *girl?*"

"*Stop* her."

Jessup wanted to flee. He envisioned himself running through the woods, hoping that, if he put enough distance behind him, the last several days might peel backward in time and all of what had led up to now would disappear. But, looking at Reg, he understood this would not happen. In reaching home, he would find no relief. Reg needed his help. Jessup *did* want to give it to him. But he worried too, what Reg might do to him if he didn't go back inside.

He looked at the gun. He felt weightless. Without his senses. He took the gun and turned and rushed into the house.

Upstairs he stood at the bedroom doorway. Nothing stirred. His head pounded as if his skull might crack along its fused seams. The gun, heavy and lifeless, lent him no security.

He crept to the bed and knelt. His lungs filled and unfilled with air. She was still there. Her back was to him. He heard nothing but his thundering head. She lay perfectly motionless. He went around to the other side of the bed. He looked down at the gun in his hands. He couldn't tell if the safety was on or off. He looked under the bed. His vision fogged. His heart worked as if it would give out on him.

The girl was on her side, fetal. Her white shirt was drenched red, and torn open. The phone's receiver lay off the hook, on the rug. Her eyes were closed and she wore a serene look on her face. Her baby-blue sweatpants were ripped, and pulled down to her ankles. She was bloody down there. It was unclear if the blood was from the wounds in her chest and stomach, or from between her legs, too. Jessup looked away, unable to latch onto any one clear thought.

He pointed the gun at her. His stomach churned. He jabbed the gun against her. She didn't move. He poked her again. "Hey," he said. "Hey." He felt exhausted, as if he'd just finished sobbing. He poked her again. He checked the gun over for its safety. He found what he thought was it. It appeared to be off. He fumbled, his fingers disobeying his brain's signal, then flicked the safety back on with a *click*. He stuffed the gun in his jeans. His skin was damp and hot. "Hey," he said. "Hey. Come *on.*" He shook her by the shoulder. She seemed stuck under there, wedged, her cheek flattened in the carpet. "Hey. Come *on. Please.*" Her skin was cool, and he realized how hard he was shaking her. He heard a voice. The phone. He lay his cheek on the carpet, his ear next to the receiver. "Is someone there?" a sober voice inquired. "Hello? You hold on. Can you do that? Can you hold on for me? Hello? Tracey?"

Scared now for other reasons, Jessup stood quickly, the room reeling, and floundered to the other side of the bed. He reached for the duffel, feeling as if he would never be able to bend over far enough— but his fingers seized the bag and he ran down the hall, down the stairs and out of the house.

He ran down the driveway, falling, tearing his palms. He got up and scrambled to Reg, who was lying beside the Camino, near the other man, who hadn't budged. Jessup helped Reg into the Camino. He threw the duffel in the back. He closed his eyes and pushed the body away from the front tire and got in.

Reg was slouched forward, his head against the dash as he gasped and sobbed. He was trying madly to strip off his jean jacket. Jessup helped him out of it, and let it fall to the floor. Reg slammed his head against the dash repeatedly. He sputtered and kicked. He fell back against the door, his eyes not quite meeting Jessup's, as if he'd betrayed Jessup in some way, and could not face him.

Jessup pulled into the driveway and backed out. The headlight cast harsh light across the A-frame, and, for an instant, Jessup thought he saw a figure in a window.

Jessup had the Camino up to sixty miles an hour, but it felt as if they were crawling. "*What* happened?" he begged, but Reg, his eyes squeezed tight, only kicked the dash in reply.

Gaining the turn-off for Gamble Hill, Jessup downshifted, but couldn't negotiate the turn. He rode the brake, and the Camino pulled hard toward the trees, stammered along the shoulder. It slid to a stop, nose dipping to touch the road, then springing back up to settle with a protest of springs.

Reg flailed his hands before his face, spattering the dash. Jessup clasped Reg's hands in his own until they grew calm.

"Be still," he said.

He put the Camino in gear and turned up Gamble Hill.

At Marigold's mailbox he slowed and drove up the road and straight onto the trailer's lawn, the Camino sliding on the grass and stopping just shy of the steps.

The trailer was dark.

Jessup hurried from the Camino.

A light came on in the trailer; Jessup was about to knock on the screen when a woman opened the inside door, wearing nothing but a white T-shirt. Her hair stuck out as if she'd been electrocuted. In the headlight her face was a contour map of dark depressions, eyes lost in black pockets, the skin lit in places so it looked porous and orange as old brick. When Jessup moved between the headlight and the woman, the woman's face changed, her features altered. *Marigold.* She looked old. Destroyed. Her eyes and lips were bruised and swollen. Jessup stood aside and pointed at Reg in the Camino.

Marigold emitted a sound like a hiccup and pushed by Jessup; she opened the Camino's door so hard she fell back onto the ground. Reg toppled out onto her.

When they were finally able to get Reg into the trailer, they laid him on his back on the kitchen floor, where he remained motionless, his arms out from his sides. His head was turned on a cheek so, although his eyes were closed, he appeared to be looking for something beneath the stove. He was bloodslaked, his skin the hue of the drowned. Jessup sat on the floor, against a cupboard. Marigold knelt at Reg's side, as if about to pray or perform a ritual. But she was only attempting to unbotton his shirt. She pushed each button through its hole with delicate care, chewing her lip before going on to the next. When she had unbuttoned the last, she whimpered and began to open the shirt. Sobbing, she peeled away the shirt with great pains, as if flaying his skin and concerned it might tear. With the shirt open, she covered her eyes and made a choking sound. Jessup glanced at Reg's bared torso and fell back against the cupboard door and covered his eyes. He looked from between his fingers and said: "We need a doctor."

Marigold reached for the counter and pulled herself upright. She turned on the faucet and soaked a hand towel. "Nearest doctor's in Hancock. *New Hampshire.* Hour and a half's drive."

"We can call someone. A vet," Jessup said. The vision of the room was still broken up by his fingers, cutting Marigold into sections.

"A vet." She said. "We need a *surgeon*."

"We'll call ahead to Hancock."

"Can't."

"We have to."

"Hess tore the phone out the wall."

"Who?"

"Hess."

"Who's Hess?"

"My husband."

"Your . . . what?"

"Never *mind*."

"You didn't—"

"Shut up," she said. "Just shut up."

She stooped at her brother's side and dabbed uncertainly at his chest and stomach.

Reg stirred and turned his head toward Jessup. A sound like that of a wooden chair being dragged across a floor escaped Marigold's throat. She crouched and her shirt rode up, exposed a dark mound between her thighs; Jessup stared until she tugged the shirt over her knees.

"I'll take him to the hospital, myself," she said.

"I could go."

She shifted her weight, her bruised eyes changing colors, like a grackle's plumage, beautiful with shiny purples and greens and blues. Then they were bruises again. Black and ugly. Her mouth moved, but made no sound.

Reg turned over on his side. "Go up to the house," he whispered.

Marigold stared at him. Jessup wiped drool from his chin.

Reg tried to push upright, but Marigold laid her palms on his chest and settled him back.

"Careful," she said.

"The *piano*," he said.

Marigold looked at Jessup, her eyes wandering from his shoulders to his chin, elbow and crotch, as if to piece him together. "Don't," she said.

Reg, in trying to sit upright, had done something to himself. Around him on the linoleum, a lake of dark blood spread.

Jessup told Marigold what had happened. It was decided that Marigold would take the truck; slower perhaps, but they could not be certain the Camino hadn't been seen out on Avers Gore. Jessup would park the Camino at the Barker place, and hide the duffel in the piano with the others. He told her he would wait up there for her to return. But he wouldn't.

Marigold fetched blankets from her bedroom and they helped Reg to the truck and covered him; he was convulsing and cold, and his ashen color had drained from his face. His eyes kept rolling.

Marigold drove away.

When the truck was out of sight, Jessup drove the Camino up to the Barker place.

He could sense the frogs and crickets about him, huddled under stones and fallen trees, hiding. The silence seemed more complete than the darkness, the darkness softened by the moon. He looked at the house. It was not his. It was not a found shipwreck. It was an old house that had once been some family's home, and was now crumbling with disrepair, like any of the other abandoned houses throughout the county.

The night had become cold. Jessup took Reg's jean jacket from the Camino and put it on. He took the duffel and went in the house, where he found his way to the piano bench. He sat down with the gravity of an old man who has journeyed to a place to rest and reflect on the brevity of life. He yawned and rested his forehead on the piano, a clash of keys echoing. The notes signaled him to act, and he rose and stood on the bench, balancing himself; but he was stopped by a sound. It came from the darkest corner of the house, by the kitchen entryway. It had not been the wind. And it had not been an animal. It had been a cough. Jessup tried to call out, but his voice was reedy, his heart a hummingbird. An animal scurried upstairs. "Hello?" he whispered. A scuffing sound came from the darkness. And a smell. Booze. "Hello?" A breeze brushed like a spiderweb against his cheek and footfalls advanced on him from the dark as a figure lunged at him. His breath left him in a singular rush as he was slammed from the bench. He heard the flat crack of his skull on the floor; his vision erupted with a silver flash, then imploded back into darkness as he was struck again, and again, his head roaring, a voice bellowing—*cocksucker*, fuckin little son of *bitch*—and then another extravagance of brilliant light from inside his head, and a thought of Emily, and how far away she was, how impossibly far, and then darkness again. And then not even that.

Hess stood above the boy, sniffled and wiped his hands on his jeans. His breathing was regular and the sweat that broke on his face was not from exertion, but from whisky and exhilaration. He kicked the boy again. Spat.

Earlier, before he'd gone to the trailer, and smelled Marigold's sex, he'd searched the Barker house for hours, looking for Reg's duffels: the cupboards, the attic and cellar, closets, even the chimney, but had found nothing. He'd not thought of the piano. He stood on the bench and opened the top of the piano. The smell told him everything.

He clapped his hands and pulled the duffels out. He lifted the whisky bottle to his lips, the whisky flowing down his throat without him tasting it. He stood spread legged, his head back. He patted the bottom of the bottle, then threw it across the parlor. It hit the wall and clattered to the floor, unbroken. He hefted the duffels and, weaving across the room, fell out onto the porch. Though he couldn't feel it on his numb face, he sensed by the mist that the night was cold.

He saw the Camino and wondered soberly if Reg was in it. He leaned on the porch rail, watching.

Certain Reg was not there, he went to the Camino and tossed the duffels into the back, trying to hide them among a bunch of junk.

The keys were in the ignition. He started the Camino and pulled out. He noticed a pistol on the dash.

"Lookie here," he said.

He stroked the gun with one hand and steered with the other. Not having smoked since high school, he didn't know how much weed sold for, or how much he had, but he knew it was a lot, and he knew who to see about taking it off his hands. And even if they screwed him some, he'd still make out all right.

He'd have to thank the kid. *If* the kid ever woke up.

He found himself farther along the road without having memory of steering. He wondered, as the haze of booze retreated briefly, if he wasn't asleep, dreaming.

He headed toward Avers Gore. Pulling off Gamble onto Plank Road, he accelerated past the town gravel pit, the Camino's back end going loose on him. He hadn't driven a car in ages, hadn't known how much he'd missed it. He'd have to get himself a car, or a pickup. All those nights of hangdogging, what a goddamned waste.

He'd just gotten the Camino's slide in control when blue and white lights appeared on his skin, kaleidoscoped about the cab; and until he heard the howl of the siren, he thought he might be witnessing a miracle, or was being visited by a wraith.

The cruiser accelerated from behind and he thought for a moment that it would pull alongside him, then continue on to its rightful destination.

It didn't.

"Sonofa *bitch*," he said.

The cruiser pulled up close; its halogens swarmed the inside of the Camino. Hess squinted against their harshness.

A voice squawked over a megaphone. Hess couldn't understand what it said. Didn't care. He stood on the gas and the Camino shot along the road. The cruiser stayed right on his ass. He shifted up, and the Camino stalled. The cruiser bumped him from behind and he pulled over, spitting motherfuckers. He wiped at his face and tried to gain a semblance of composure, an erect posture of confidence and sobriety. The .45 still sat on the dash; he snatched it quickly, but had no time to stick it under the seat as the patrolman was now out of his vehicle and moving briskly. Hess wedged the gun between his thighs, hoping it wasn't visible.

The trooper tapped the window with a flashlight. Hess struggled with the window's crank.

The flashlight lit the side of his face.

"Trying to get away from me?" the trooper said.

"Just tryin to find a place to pull off."

The trooper seemed to give this little thought. The heel of his right hand rested on the butt of his revolver. The holster was unsnapped.

Hess focused his gaze out the windshield. Mist rolled in the headlights.

"In a hurry somewhere? *From* somewhere?"

Hess squeezed the steering wheel.

"*Well?*" the trooper asked. He seemed nervous, fidgety, as if he had someplace else he needed to be.

"No. I ain't," Hess said.

"Ain't what?"

"In no hurry."

"Been drinking?"

"No."

"You were swerving back there."

"Raccoon. Ran across in front me."

"Goin up to Avers Gore are you?"

"Nope," Hess said, though he didn't know why. Something in the way the trooper had mentioned the Gore made him nervous. What was he doing this far off the highway anyway?

"How about showing me your license and registration?"

Hess made a slow movement to rub the back of his neck.

The trooper stood on the tips of his boots, relaxed back on his heels. "Deaf?" he said.

"How's that?" Hess put one hand over the other on the wheel.

The trooper massaged his holster. With his flashlight he pushed his hat up from off his brow. "I asked if you were fucking deaf. You going to give me your license and registration or no?"

"No."

"I'm going to have to ask you to get out of the car. *Slowly. And keep your hands where I can see them.*"

"I ain't got neither on me's the problem," Hess stammered.

The trooper considered him. He swung the flashlight over the junk in the Camino's bed. Hess glanced in the rearview, sucked in a breath. The trooper moved close to the door again and shined the light on Hess. The trooper's belt creaked as he leaned in close. He smelled of spearmint. He sniffed the air; he sniffed again and Hess thought his eyes registered some kind of recognition or realization. It was difficult to tell; he didn't want to look the trooper full in the face.

"You got a name?"

"Course." Hess nodded. "Cumber. Reg Cumber."

"Cumber?" The trooper squinted. "Cumber," he said again.

Hess nodded.

The trooper murmured to himself, then shined the flashlight on Hess's face, so close that Hess could feel the heat of it. "Is that short for Reginald, your first name, Mr. Cumber?" His voice was flat with confidence.

Hess scratched an earlobe. "Course," he said. "Course it is."

"I see." The trooper pulled the flashlight from Hess's face and stood erect. He looked down at Hess. "Mr. *Cumber*, I'm going to ask you *once* to hand me over your keys, slowly, and then to sit tight. And if you don't do just *exactly* as I say, I'm going to ask you to step out of the car."

Hess bowed his head and took the keys from the ignition and deposited them in the trooper's open palm.

The trooper nodded and backed away from the Camino without taking his eyes off Hess, his hand perched on his revolver. Then he returned to the cruiser with a hurried, stiff gait.

Hess exhaled loudly, feeling as if he'd held his breath since the trooper had come to the window. His crotch was steaming; he glanced in the sideview and then in his lap. The gun was visible and the muzzle pointed up at him. He loosened his thighs from around it and took hold of it, keeping it in his lap. He worked the action to see the brassy glint of a cartridge, then allowed the action to slide back. He checked the rearview; the trooper was still in the cruiser. Hess blew his nose on his sleeve and wiped it with the back of his hand and spat out the window. And then he smelled it. Smelled it all around him; it filled the cab. He raised the back of his hand to his nose and sniffled. He wiped the seat beside him. Wet and sticky. It was everywhere. The passenger's side was smeared with it, as if someone had been gutted.

"*Christ,*" he said.

He didn't hear the cruiser door shut because the trooper hadn't shut it when he'd stepped out, and now when Hess glanced in the sideview he saw the trooper was halfway to the Camino, advancing with a swift commanding motion, his hand gripping the revolver as he screamed at Hess. But Hess paid no mind, knowing by the tone of the shout what was being demanded of him; he wasn't getting out of the goddamned car, not as drunk as he was, not with the gun and marijuana on him, and a stolen vehicle, *not* after what he'd done to the kid and Marigold, no way was he sprawling out on the road for anybody. The trooper was almost at the door, his voice detonating. Hess shifted in an attempt to hide the .45 under the seat, but the trooper was already standing outside the door and had noticed the gun. Hess fumbled for the pistol's safety. The door kept his left arm pinned from a full range of motion, but he thought he could still get a line on the trooper. He brought the .45 up clumsily, struck it against the steering wheel. The trooper's hand flashed from his holster with a practiced sweep of the arm, revolver in hand, and Hess, in his re-tarded effort, realized how utterly drunk he still was, and laughed at this realization, even as he turned and faced the trooper and the trooper's revolver, even as he knew that the .45 had already been brought out too far now to stop. *So,* he thought. But the thought ended there.

Marigold had to resist driving too fast, worried the bouncing of the truck was harming her brother, ripping apart his wounds. She could not bring herself to look at him.

He'd spoken at first, when they'd started out, and had seemed to be coming around. "Should've replaced the springs in this death trap, while I was at it," he'd said, hacking. But, he'd not made a sound for miles. They'd be coming to Route 28 soon, a better road, the inter-state after that. No so far, really.

She peered over at him. He was crumpled against his door, his cheek stuck to the window. She hit a bump, jarring the truck. "Marigold," Reg called out, as if he were lost in the woods and trying to find his way to her. He pressed his face to the window, as if he might find her in the dark outside the truck. He flattened one palm against the glass: "*Marigold.*"

Jessup awakened, cold and stiff, pain shooting from the base of his skull to his tailbone; he thought of himself as a frog; a frog just stirring from a grave of muck in which it had lain dormant an entire winter. Only one eye would open, and that only to a slit, the lid lazy and twitching. An attempt to move, to roll over on his side, brought convulsions of pain that made him sob. The sobbing worsened the pain, so he went rigid and grew giddy and euphoric with it. The pain ebbed and his body relaxed and he drifted in and out of sleep, though it was not possible to tell which state was which.

Lying there, he grew afraid that whoever had beaten him would return, so he began to creep along the floor, groping blindly, a mole whose back had been stepped on by a cruel farm boy. He inched forward, resting every few feet, fighting to remain conscious. The porch stairs were brutal on his ribs as he slid down them and into the yard, the grass and weeds cold and relieving on his face. He rolled over, sprawling on his back to ease the pain, arms and legs in an X. The moon sat low in the tree limbs, among the branches, just yards away, a blur of milky light as unaware of Jessup as it was of itself.

Groaning, he rolled over and pulled himself along, the hill growing steeper.

He was resting on his back when a light poured upon him and lit him so intensely he thought he might catch fire, might be turned to ashes and borne up by the light.

A sound came from beyond the light, and he knew he would not be reduced to ashes, just yet. A voice. Garbled. Two voices? One distant? *More* distant. But familiar. The other moving toward him. Growing louder. Still not seeming to talk to him, but to the other, distant voice. The stationary voice. The voice was next to his ear. The light blocked by the body that carried it. The voice termitic in his ear. Through his slit eye he saw . . . a dark movement. . . .

Still. Be still, he thought.

His body was being lifted and he cried out, feeling as if his arms were being rent loose from the sockets. But he was lifted regardless. Feet dragging. The light so bright now it seemed that one might be able to see through his clothes. Through his flesh to his organs.

Through him entirely. He could hear his heels scraping along the dirt road. Sleep overtook him. Then something more than sleep.

Cold. Wet. Against his face. A cloth. His eye sifted light in an attempt to make sense of his bearings. A couch. Purple. A TV. Broken on the floor. Beside it a cracked snowdome in a puddle of water. Movement before the light. A face in his. Hal.

"Howww yooo feeel???"

He tried to clear his throat.

"Drinnnk thisss." A glass to his lips and he drank as best he could, slobbering as a thirst built up inside him. He reached for the cup and drank and drank until nothing more came. His tongue cold and wet, his thirst roaring.

Hal peered down at him.

"Who did this?"

Jessup rolled his head slowly from side to side. His lips and tongue so swollen he didn't know if he could speak.

"Blindsided, huh?" Hal looked around. "What happened here?"

Jessup blinked.

"Don't know much do you?" Hal rocked his chair back and forth, his face coming in and out of view. "What about Marigold?"

Jessup lifted his head the slightest off the couch arm. He cleared his throat. "Oss-piddle."

"What's that?" He leaned in closer, his ear to Jessup's mouth.

"Oss-piddle."

"Hospital? What do you mean hospital? Someone do something to her, too?"

"Reg . . . Reg."

"Reg did this?"

Jessup held up a finger. "Jus im."

"Just him what?"

"Urt."

"Reg's hurt?"

"Mmm."

"She take Reg to the hospital?"

Jessup nodded.

"Why're both vehicles gone?"

"Stole."

"What?"

"Stole."

"What stole?"

"Camino."

"Who took it?"

Jessup moaned.

"I wish someone could tell me what in fuck is going on," Hal shouted.

A voice from the kitchen told Hal to calm down and think.

Hal turned away and Jessup closed his eye. He listened as the chair wheeled over to the kitchen, heard Hal murmur and the other man's voice respond. He heard footsteps come to beside the couch but he was too tired to open his eyes again. A warm hand caressed his forehead and a reassuring voice said: "I'm Lucian. A friend. I'm going to get you on over to the hospital. We're going to stop over at Hal's ma's place first, to use the phone and call ahead. Then we'll get you to Hancock, lickity split. You're like to lose the one eye you got left, we don't."

The car came to a stop and Jessup nearly fell off the backseat, where, apparently, he'd been lain; he was covered with a blanket, and had his head propped on a pillow: *Lucian*, he thought. He could hear Lucian getting out of the car, the jingle of keys, the trunk unlatch and spring free. The wheelchair banged against the trunk. Jessup could hear whistling. The trunk closed and Lucian swung open Hal's door. Hal peered over the seat at Jessup. "Hanging in there?" he said. Jessup's jaw muscles were too tight for him to open his mouth. He'd wet himself.

"Back in a jiff." Hal slapped the seat.

Jessup shut his eyes and listened as Hal huffed and shifted from the car to the wheelchair.

He heard Lucian sit where Hal had been. Heard the pop of a match and smelled sulfur. Cigaret smoke. His stomach turned.

"Dint expect this," Lucian said. Jessup opened his eye with a gri-

mace. Several of his teeth were missing. He hadn't noticed. The upper front ones were missing. Three or four, at least. He groaned.

"I know you're in a worlda hurt, but it'll be all right," Lucian said.
"I seen worse. Can't see nothing coming. Things work funny sometimes."

Jessup watched the back of Lucian's head, the shag of greasy
brown hair.

"You're a tough kid," Lucian declared. He turned around and
looked over the seat. "Cig?" he offered, and Jessup recognized him:
THE MUTILATOR!

The screen door banged shut and Jessup looked out his window to
see Hal, palming frantically, as he pumped the wheelchair down to
the car.

"He's gone," Hal shouted.

"They heading back already?" Lucian said.

Hal looked back over his shoulder at the house and stared at it, as
if waiting for someone to come out onto the porch. "He's gone," he
said. *"Gone."*

PART V

He could hear the clanging of a faraway churchbell drifting up through the hollow, clanging clanging clanging as he dreamt of a meager procession of cars, lead by a jalopy truck, the cars crawling past the Bee Hive and Rosie's, past Harv's Barber and Tobacco, their headlights on in the middle of the afternoon, in the middle of the afternoon, the church bell clanging clanging clanging.

Her boy lay on his sister's bed as he had since returning from the hospital two weeks before. She sat beside him on a chair. Thunder shook the window. Rain lashed the late-autumn leaves from their branches.

Jessup stirred, whimpered in his sleep. She placed the paper she'd been reading down on the bedside table: the state police had discovered the missing game warden's body. He'd come upon the wrong cabin in Caratunk.

Jessup moaned and scratched his eyepatch.

"Leave it be," she whispered and clasped his hand in hers and laid it on his chest. The unpatched eye winked open, a bloodied egg. But it saw her. He sat up on his elbows as she adjusted his pillow behind him. She touched two fingertips to his forehead.

She smiled at him.

He ran his tongue over the toothless space in his gums.

"My boy," she said and touched her fingers to his forehead again. He flinched.

She was silent for some time, looking at him, looking out the window. He closed his eye again, but he was awake.

"I talked to Gwenn," she offered.

His eye opened.

"Is she coming home?" he said.

"She can't."

He scratched at his patch.

She removed his hand from his face.

"She gives her love," she said.

He stretched his lips tight.

She glanced out the window; the trees rocked in the wind. The shingles on the shed were tearing loose in the strengthening storm; they rose and fell, flapped in unison, like feathers on a wing bent on lifting the shed from the ground. She looked at Jessup and patted his leg.

"Tell me," he said.

Her chest heaved. Somehow he'd found out about Caldwell. He'd been asking of him all week, since coming off his painkillers. She'd been stunned the first time he'd asked, if only because he'd gone so long without questioning that she'd fooled herself into believing he never *would* ask. She'd lived with the story, her lie, so long it had come to be the truth. He'd asked every day since for her to tell him. She'd denied him, faulting his poor health and physical pain as enough to bear. She'd told him that when he recovered fully she would tell him. In time. Now he was not asking her to tell him. He was demanding it.

She went to the window and looked out at the shed. How the wind tormented it. But it had suffered worse. As lilted and plumbless as it was, it would withstand. She drew the curtain shut and sat down again, this time on the edge of the bed.

His lone eye glowered.

"Jessup," she said.

He folded his arms across his chest.

"The truth," he said.

She stared down in her lap as if in it lay the courage and will for her to tell what needed to be told, and all she had to do was take it in her hands.

"Okay," she said. "Okay."

He closed his eye.

"He was good to me. Kind." He *had* been. At first. "But young. Both of us. We didn't *know* how young. He was eager and brash . . . impetuous . . ." She folded her hands in her lap. "He was faulted though. He was the first to admit that he was distracted, too wayward and fanciful and indecisive to be a fit husband. A father. He needed to venture into the world, to see things and make a go of another life. He said. To survive." She remembered how Caldwell had told her this, as if his admitting it aloud was the most noble of confessions ever spoken. He'd tried to twist his irresponsibility into the anguish of a lost soul. "It was supposed to be a trial separation. And after he'd struck out and made something of himself he would return, a better man, a better father. But, there was an accident. A car accident."

She rubbed the back of her neck.

"You see?" she said.

Jessup stared at her.

"He did love you."

She could not find it within herself to tell Jessup that what had caused Caldwell's distraction was other women, that his *indecision* was actually a lack of commitment brought on by self-doubt and loathing, and pertained less to whether he might be able to make a go at life than whether or not he would get out of bed in the morning. There'd been no *trial separation*. Gwenn had been a mistake, according to Caldwell, enough to handle, to keep him from his grand aspirations. Never mind a second child. He'd left without ever knowing his second child was a son. She'd never heard from him again. She had no way, to this day, of knowing if he were alive or not, and did not care. They were better off without him. She never thought of him.

Jessup turned away from her. She'd have no other opportunity to tell him the truth. But what she'd told him held more truth than the story of Caldwell drowning. She wanted to laugh at that story, realizing it had turned Caldwell into the martyr he'd always wanted to be. In a way, maybe Jessup needed his father to be that. She'd told as much of the truth as she could afford.

Jessup was shaking his head back and forth, almost imperceptibly. "Get out," he said.

Days passed and he moved back into the attic. His physical pain had drained slowly, leaving him with the dull ache of cracked ribs, as if he'd spent several nights sleeping in a cold rain; the ache would remain with him through the holidays. If not longer. His room felt cramped now, claustrophobic, dark and musty. Lifeless. He boxed up his outdoor magazines and his candles and his letters from Emily, and he had her, Anna, against her will, bring the boxes down to the cellar. He seldom spoke to her, and despite its dreariness, he seldom ventured from the attic. He came downstairs only to relieve himself or to take his plate of food from where she'd left it for him on the top shelf of the refrigerator. He ignored the notes she left with his food. Imagining what they might say was enough. Many nights he lay awake, the house, the world, so quiet that he could hear the churchbell, barely discernible, even in the dreadful silence, clang and clang and clang from down in town, and he thought of a line of cars, as if from some lost dream, but he did not know why, and did not know what it meant. He would lie awake counting off the seconds between the tolling of each hour. Three thousand six hundred seconds. Then start again. He looked in a mirror once, and not again, his face puffy and marbled with yellow and green bruises. He thought of his father and wondered why he had left. What had caused him to wander. To leave. Jessup did not go outside. He did not care to be out in the fickle elements of October, to be scorched by the sun or stung by the cold. He felt if he stepped into the wind he would be carried away like a seed, a germ.

One morning he awoke to what he at first mistook, in his fugue state of awakening, for the shrill cry of a jay. But even before he stood at the window, he remembered and knew its source.

He rose slowly from bed, dragging his sheets behind him, a mad, aged king dragging his ragged robe, and stood at the window, wiping with his palm a clean circle in it.

The tow truck backed up to the Vega and a man jumped out, his jeans and tank top smirched with grease, his face twisted and filthy. He was frighteningly thin, except for a gut that hung over his pants. Jessup wondered if he suffered from a tapeworm, or a tumor. He wondered if the man wasn't Skinny, proprietor of the salvage yard advertised by the sign on the truck door. Jessup had asked Anna to put the car in the classifieds. But he'd had no takers, and so he'd told her to find someone who would pay him for scraps, get it out of sight from the window. She'd protested. He didn't know, or care, why. She'd looked into it and found a salvage yard that would pay for junk; fifty dollars. Jessup had forgotten.

The man outside fetched over to the Vega with a hook and chain and lay down in front of the car and scuttled beneath it. In a moment he came back from under it and stood with a clap of his hands; he tugged at the hip of his jeans. He worked a lever at the back of the tow truck and the Vega lurched forward and her flat tires came up off the ground. Her springs shrieked as she settled behind the truck. The man peered around the dooryard and scratched his chin. He took something from his pocket, a piece of paper or an envelope, and looked at the house with suspicion, then walked out of sight onto the porch. Jessup heard the screen door open and then slam and saw the man step back out into the yard. He leaned against the truck fender and produced something from his jeans. A small pipe. He brought out a pack of matches and struck one and held it to the pipe and leaned his head back and blew out a cloud that hovered around his head. He smoked, tapped the pipe in his palm and stuck it back in his pocket. He looked around again and turned from the house and relieved himself at the corner of the shed, a dark stain spreading on its barn-board siding. He shivered and got in the truck and slammed the door. He sat there a moment staring up at the house, as if he'd seen someone in a window. But he was not looking at Jessup's window, and no one else was home.

Later that afternoon Jessup again heard a vehicle pull into the yard, and thinking it was Skinny, he crossed to the window, prepared to throw up the sash and yell down at him that he'd changed his mind, and to leave the Vega and take the fifty dollars from where he'd left it between the doors, and get his pissing, pot-smoking ass off his property.

But it wasn't Skinny.

It was a car he didn't recognize, the sun blinding as it mirrored off the windshield. The passenger door opened.

She stepped out of the car and into the afternoon sunlight and stood gazing up at the house, as if unsure she had the right place. Her hair, darker now, summer gone from it, and longer, spilled to her shoulders and shimmered in the sun like drawn copper. Her face was radiant, beaming, a hint of a tan remaining; but the corners of her mouth were turned down slightly. Her white blouse glowed, more an aura about her than clothing. Her faded jeans looked soft as chamois. She brought a hand up to touch her throat with her fingertips; the sun winked from her pendant which rested in the hollow above her breastbone.

She leaned into the window of the car and said something to the driver and Jessup recognized the car now: her father's.

She walked toward the house, her hair shining, and disappeared beneath the porch roof; Jessup slumped down on the floor, back to the wall, beneath the window, tapping a fist against his lips until his gums bled. A knocking came at the front door. Silence. More knocking. It grew persistent, as if she were knocking not to be let inside but to break down the door. Abruptly, the knocking ceased. It did not come again. Jessup clawed at the burning itch beneath his eyepatch. A voice sounded from below the window, the words muddy through the glass, but the tone and lilt of birdsong. He pictured her coming closer to the house, her face upturned to the window, the autumn sky. Her voice grew louder, became urgent and angry and pained; and in the up and down of it, he knew the word she was repeating: Jes-sup. *Jes-sup!* He imagined her stamping her foot, the one that kicked out at an odd angle when she'd run ahead of him. She cried his name. A ticking came at the window; pebbles against glass. He hung his head in his hands and covered his mouth. His palms were wet and salty. His heart galloped and he almost stood and smashed out the window and called to her, but a horn beeped and the stones and her own calling-out stopped. A car door shut and an engine started. He stood and spied from the corner of the window and watched as the car backed out, windshield glinting in the sun so he was forced to look away, and when he looked back again the car was gone, the only sign that it had been there a mote of dust wheeling in the dooryard where she had once stood.

The Indian summer continued, cool and clear, the mornings and afternoon sun relenting to clouds each evening, and he began to think again about going outside. Each day the temptation grew, and he thought about his rod and reel forgotten in the shed, thought about how comforting the cold clear water of a stream would feel on his legs. Thought about the sun, or a breeze, on his face. He thought of the heft of a large brook trout on his line, measured by the pound. And he thought about Marigold.

After a few days, the thinking became a longing.

One afternoon, while Anna was at work, he slipped downstairs.

In the kitchen he made peanut butter and jelly sandwiches and stuffed them in his backpack with a couple of cans of soda, a blanket and jean jacket. Then he went outside onto the porch.

He stood in the shade of the porch, staring at the patch of grassless earth where the Vega had sat beside the shed, as if the car had inexplicably left behind its shadow.

He stepped from the porch, into the cool afternoon. His shadow lengthened before him to climb the shed wall. The afternoon held the stillness and clean scent that follows a hard rain, though no rain had fallen for days. He crossed the yard. At the shed he leaned his shoulder to the door, and with the heel of his palm levered the piece of wood that kept shut the door. It fell open with a cry and dust spiralled and a spider quaked in its disrupted web and wedged itself protectively in the corner of the doorjamb.

The bike lay fallen on its side, its tires slightly deflated. He took hold of it by the seat and righted it and wheeled it out of the shed and onto the lawn in a play of sunlight and shadow. Another spider had woven its home in the rear spokes, which had rusted. The bike's seat was coated with dust, but he made no effort to clean it. He propped the bike against the shed wall and went back inside and took up his creel and fishing rod and adjusted his backpack. He unleaned his bike from the shed and sat on it and kicked off and pedaled out of the yard, advancing down Turkey Lane in the direction of town.

Inside Rosie's, he set a pack of splitshot and hooks on the counter.

"Pinkeye is it?" the clerk said. He had a new nametag that read: EDSEL, PROPRIETOR. "Pinkeye is intolerable. It will make you crazy. My father had pinkeye once. Gave it to the whole family. All of us had pinkeye. Highly contagious, pinkeye."

"I lost it. My eye. The use of it, anyway."

"Oh." Edsel nodded respectfully. "My apologies."

"It's temporary."

"Well. Good. Good. Is that all you got there? Hooks and sinkers? Or is there something else I can help you with?"

"I have an account I'd like to clear up."

"Account?"

"Yessir."

Edsel pressed his thumbs to his temples. He snapped his fingers. "I'm sorry. I didn't recognize you. I'm embarrassed. A man should know his valued customers."

"It's been a while."

"You have your slip?"

Jessup shook his head. "I lost it some time ago. It might've gone through the wash or something. Jessup. I'm Jessup Burke."

Edsel brought out from underneath the counter a tin recipe box. He flipped open its top and riffled through slips and produced two: one white, one yellow.

"Here we are. Someone found it and brought it in a while ago. Back in August." He looked from Jessup to the slip and back. "Charged a lot of fishing tackle on here," he said.

Jessup nodded.

Edsel relinquished the slip to Jessup and Jessup took it and tucked it into his chamois shirt pocket without so much as a glance.

Edsel figured on a calculator, his fingers nimble on the keypads. He looked up at Jessup, turned the calculator around to him, slapped down the white copy of the receipt and unsat a pen from behind his ear. He placed the pen between the calculator and slip. "Twenty-two dollars and seventeen cents," he said. "Just put the old John Hancock on her."

Jessup glanced out the window, then lightened his jeans pocket of his wallet and fished out the fifty dollar bill. He handed it over to Edsel who held it for a moment to the light of the plate-glass window, then rang the sale up on the register. He made change and counted it back, after Jessup signed the bill.

"This copy's yours now, too." He snapped shut the recipe box, stashed it under the counter.

"Anything else."

"Just the splitshot and hooks."

"Charge?"

"Cash." Jessup kept a five and tucked the rest of his change in his pocket.

"All right then. We can do that, too. I've never been one to turn down cash."

Jessup gave him the five.

Edsel rang him up and made change.

"You have any applications?" Jessup said.

"Applications?"

"For a job."

"Got some right here," Edsel said, and reached under the counter again and handed an application to Jessup. "Might need someone come Christmas time. Stock shelves. Sweep. To start. Maybe work the register a few days, with some training."

Jessup nodded and folded the application up and stuck it in his back pocket. He looked over Edsel's shoulder at his bike again. Edsel turned and looked out the window. "Good day for it. Fishing." He made like he was reeling in a fish, as if the gesture would prove him correct.

"It's the last day," Jessup said.

By the time he biked down to Gamble Hill, Jessup's jeans were stuck with sweat to his legs.

Skunk Hollow proved too difficult to climb, his legs weak and sore, and he had to unmount and push the bike up the hill, huffing, the tip of his rod trembling as he put his head down and pushed up and on toward the trailer.

Just down from where the trailer sat, he stopped to catch his breath and looked up. The trailer was not there. He stared and blinked and held his hand to his brow to cut the late afternoon sunlight.

A blue car and a truck were parked in the empty lot.

Jessup looked back down the road toward Gamble Hill. He felt lost, as if he were on the wrong road. He pushed the bike up the final few yards to the lawn, which had been mowed and raked and tended. Hay was scattered where the trailer had sat.

Two men, and a woman, the woman standing between the men, were all occupied with staring down at a large unscrolled piece of paper, spread out on the hood of the blue car. None of them looked up. The woman smoked a long brown cigaret. Jessup let the bike fall. The two men peered up.

The larger of the two men, who wore blue jeans, a denim shirt and a jean jacket, considered Jessup with a jocund look on his deeply lined face. An unlit cigar was in the corner of his mouth.

"Help you, son?" he said.

The man on the other side of the woman, a stout short man with an oddly thin beard echoed, "Yes what is it we can help you for?"

Jessup looked on, as if the three of them and their vehicles and the emptiness where the trailer had stood were a mirage, and if he were to stand there with enough patience the illusion would dissolve and be replaced again by what it was that should have been.

"Can we help you?" the denimed man said again.

Jessup clenched the cork handle of his rod tighter and looked down at the ground. At his feet was a circle of grass, black and greasy and dead where oil had dripped.

He looked back up at the strangers.

"I came for Marigold."

The soft man gave a perplexed look. "She has moved," he said.

"I came to see if she wanted to go fishing."

"She has gone."

Jessup switched the rod from one hand to the other. "Fishing?"

"No. No," the man said and laughed. "*Gone.*"

"What? Where? *Where's* she gone?"

"South."

"South? Where? Montgomery?"

"Where is Montgomery?"

"South. Downstate."

"No. No. *Florida*. She has moved last month with her mother. When her mother came up for to go to the funeral."

"Fune . . . ," Jessup began to ask, and then understood. He'd forgotten, somehow, impossibly.

"Who are you?" Jessup said.

"I am Roberge."

"No. No. Who are you? Why are you here? Where's Marigold's *home*?"

The woman glanced up from what held her attention and eyed Jessup with disquiet. She stood absurdly erect, reminding Jessup of a praying mantis. Her finger jabbed at what Jessup now saw was a map. Her eyes were bulbous, lizard eyes. She puffed on her cigaret.

"We tore that hellish eyesore down," she said. "Not before paying too much for it. She was one tough nut." She returned to her map. The denim man looked down with her, and she mumbled and the denim man shrugged.

Jessup swallowed.

Roberge looked at him with solace and said softly, "Is there anything else we can do for you?"

Jessup looked at the man, then around at the empty lot again. A collapsed stack of cinder blocks sat in the tall grass at the yard's edge.

"No," Jessup said.

The man looked back down with the other two and Jessup backed slowly away from them and felt for his bike in the grass, his hands tingling with numbness. He stood the bike and sat on it. Adjusting his creel and pack, he made certain of his grip on the rod and pushed off down the hill away from them.

At the top of Hardscrabble Hill he gazed down upon the town, out of breath.

The afternoon was cold. He removed the jean jacket from his pack and put it on. It was big on him. He slipped his hands in its pockets. Something was in one of them. He took it out, disbelieving what he saw. He held his discovery close to his chest, checking the road for vehicles. The bills were wrapped in rubber bands. Most of them were stained black. He thumbed through them and some, but not all, of the blackness flaked away. He counted each bill, holding his breath. There was more here than he'd ever seen. He stuffed the wad deep in his pants pocket. His backpack was tight and uncomfortable over the jacket. He took it off and threw it in the bushes. He could buy lunch. He took off his creel and set it, and his fishing rod, in the trees. It was time for new ones. He threw the application from Rosie's in the grass. He looked down on the town, then turned his bike away from it and pushed off down the hill. His legs pumped and pumped, pedals cranking so it seemed they might fly off; his legs were aching and weak. As furiously as he pedaled, the bike would not go fast enough.

Coming down into the floodplain, the road lengthening out before him he noticed the sun was just descending beyond the end of the road. He shook his head at the foolish notion of catching up to it.

Farther up the road he dismounted his bike and walked into the woods along the river. In a tangle of grapevines he knelt and dug into the earth. The pocketwatch was still there. Right where he'd left it. No one had found it. No one had cared to even look. He worked his way out of the woods and crouched at the riverside, and dipped the watch in the water and rubbed it, washed it as best as he could. He sat on the riverbank, clasping the watch, its brass cold in his hand. He wondered what to do; he could go anywhere, do anything, he imagined. He thought about his father, why he might have left, so long ago, why he might not have returned; if it made any difference. It didn't seem so unreasonable, just then, what his father had done.

He tucked the watch in his jacket and rose. The day had given itself completely to night. He ventured back into the woods, checking his pocket one more time, to make certain the money was still there.

ACKNOWLEDGMENTS

Thanks to my friends, relatives and teachers who supported me, in particular: George Garrett, Deborah Eisenberg, Lisa Williams, David Huddle, Brian Stephany, Mark Saunders, Lailee Mendelson, Sam Cleaver, Doug Day, Janet Peery, Alan DeNiro, Johnnie, Rob, Tom, and Basil.

Special thanks to Paul Slovak and Sloan Harris for their guidance and expertise.